350

W9-AHM-464

THE NEXT VICTIM

Jolene woke in darkness.

She was cold, shivering spasmodically, and her ears hurt. Somewhere there was the slosh and drip of water. With great effort, she formed a ques-tion through her chattering teeth.

"Am I dead?" she asked.

But even she didn't recognize the sound that came out of her mouth. Then there was a click, and she was bathed in the harsh glow of a hand-held light.

Jolene was nude, except for the gold cross that hung around her neck. Instinctively, she hugged her knees to her chest, trying to hide as much of her body as possible.

Ultraviolet lights buzzed to life, allowing her to see the confines of her prison. It was a domed chamber, and the walls fluoresced with other-worldly colors.

In the surreal glow, she could see a man sitting on top of a rock, his hand holding a remote for the lights. Behind him was a lake. Against a wall were some industrial-looking quart bottles that appeared to hold food and water. There were some blankets, and some machinery that Jolene didn't recognize.

"Where am I?" Jolene asked.

"The Moon Pool. . . ."

THE MOON POOL

MAX McCOY

LEISURE BOOKS   NEW YORK CITY

In memory of my dive buddy, Doc B.

A LEISURE BOOK®

June 2004

Published by

Dorchester Publishing Co., Inc.
200 Madison Avenue
New York, NY 10016

If you purchased this book without a cover you should be aware that this book is stolen property. It was reported as "unsold and destroyed" to the publisher and neither the author nor the publisher has received any payment for this "stripped book."

Copyright © 2004 by Max McCoy

All rights reserved. No part of this book may be reproduced or transmitted in any form or by any electronic or mechanical means, including photocopying, recording or by any information storage and retrieval system, without the written permission of the publisher, except where permitted by law.

ISBN 0-8439-5366-7

The name "Leisure Books" and the stylized "L" with design are trademarks of Dorchester Publishing Co., Inc.

Printed in the United States of America.

Visit us on the web at www.dorchesterpub.com.

AUTHOR'S NOTE

So many people were kind enough to share their time and expertise with me during the making of this book that space doesn't permit me to list them all. A few, however, were so generous that I am obligated to acknowledge their considerable contributions.

Chief among them are the officers, scientists, and staff of the Navy Experimental Diving Unit at Panama City, Florida, who spent one long Friday helping a novelist find a believable solution to the sometimes cold equations that govern survival at depth. Dr. John Clarke, the NEDU's scientific direction, deserves special thanks for his enthusiasm, patience, and guidance.

Arthur W. Hebrank, administrator of Missouri Mines State Historic Site, spent several hours after the park closed giving an impromptu lesson in Lead Belt history. Robert Lewis, a naturalist at St. Francois State Park, was good enough to share his intimate knowledge of the Pike Run Hills and his collected stories of unreconstructed Confederate guerilla Sam Hildebrand. Many city officials and residents of Bonne Terre, Missouri, shared their stories, including Earl Faircloth, who literally turned out the lights when the St. Joe lead mine closed there in 1961. Readers should not confuse the fictional St. Joan mine of *The Moon Pool*, however, with any of the area's historic mines once operated by the St. Joseph Lead Company.

Finally, a considerable debt is owed to various members of the Cave Diving Section of the National Speleological Society who related their experiences personally or, in some cases, posthumously through their publications.

Warning: Although *The Moon Pool* is a work of fiction, the hazards it describes in cave diving and other overhead environments are very real. More than 300 divers, including open water scuba instructors, have died in caves since organizations such as the Cave Diving Section of the National Speleological Society (CDS-NSS) began keeping count. To prevent your own death, never enter a cave without the proper training and equipment. To do so is to invite disaster. And there is nothing in any cave worth dying for.

THE MOON POOL

In Xanadu did Kubla Khan
A stately pleasure-dome decree:
Where Alph, the sacred river, ran
Through caverns measureless to man
Down to a sunless sea.

> —Samuel Taylor Coleridge

On ne pai qu'en sortant.

> —Pioneering diving psychologist
> J. S. Haldane, who borrowed the
> phrase from the wall of a French
> brothel. Translation: "You only pay
> on the way out."

Prologue:
Beneath the
Stone

So this is what it's like to die.

Dahlgren looked into Taylor's wide eyes behind her mask and knew it was what she was thinking, too.

They were a half-mile beneath the surface of the tiny village of San Augustín Zaragoza in south central Mexico, in two hundred and seventy-six feet of black water at the bottom of a sump that led to nowhere. Exhausted by the physical and emotional toll of having spent a week underground, of eating freeze-dried food and defecating in plastic bags, of sleeping in damp nylon hammocks slung over bone-chilling pools and hauling dozens of heavy scuba cylinders over rocks with angles like razor blades, they had made a series of mistakes that would collectively result in their deaths.

They had hoped to crack the sump with a fast no-decompression dive, to walk out on the other side into a passage that human eyes had never seen, and connect this particular cave, *cueva del hueso*, with the rest of the massive Huatla system. It had seemed likely a few hours ago, when the last push had advanced the line twenty meters past what seemed the bottom of the sump, with the depth steadily decreasing. But it turned out only to be an anomaly, and the sump plummeted downward again, and finally terminated against a wall where breakdown from the low ceiling had collected. There might be a passage behind the pile of rocks, but it would take a bulldozer to move it.

The goal had seemed so close that instead of sticking with the planned solo serial diving, in which a single diver advances the line a safe distance then belays it to be taken up shortly by another, Dahlgren had allowed Taylor to talk him into a buddy dive.

She wanted them to crack the sump together.

Dahlgren had been seduced by the image. He agreed, even though the other members of the team told him it was a bad idea.

After spending too many minutes trying to find a way around or through the sump's dead end, they had swum halfway back to the sump's false bottom when Taylor's primary dive light imploded.

She had two more backups, of course, but the concussive *pop!* had shaken her, and in the few moments it took Dahlgren to make sure she was okay, he had lost contact with the guideline they had placed going in.

Orange silt that had gone undisturbed for eons was now drizzling from the ceiling, loosened by the passage of their tanks and fins, and visibility in the sump had diminished to a few inches.

Despite incurring disappointment and a serious decompression penalty, they were not yet in trouble. At that point they still had two-thirds of their gas left in the twin sixties on their backs, which were the largest cylinders that could be hauled down by their caving sherpas (although Dahlgren now wished, impractically, that he had insisted on at least eighties). The bottom gas in the cylinders was trimix 15/50, a blend of 15 percent oxygen, 50 percent helium, and the remainder nitrogen. At this depth, the amount of nitrogen in regular air would send them tripping, and the oxygen would render them unconscious and, eventually, dead from drowning. The choices were trimix, in which some of the nitrogen was replaced by adding helium, or heliox, in which there was no nitrogen at all.

They had tried heliox on their last series of deep dives, but the lack of any nitrogen had made Taylor jittery and Dahlgren paranoid. A little nitrogen at that depth, they discovered, was useful to calm the nerves. Also, helium was expensive. Trimix used less of it.

Taylor smiled through her mask as she tied off a jump line and started a sweeping search for the guideline. After searching for a few minutes she found the nylon guideline, and soon she and Dahlgren were swimming together on either side of the line through the orange muck, headed for the constriction that Dahlgren had jokingly christened the Ballbuster after his first trip through. After pushing their tanks ahead and squeezing through, it would be a short swim but a one-hour decompression using tables that had been cobbled together from a set borrowed from an offshore oil company and their own experience during the previous season at San Augustín. They would make their last deco stop at ten feet breathing pure oxygen, supplied by a separate regulator attached to the pony bottle of O_2 mounted between the steel cylinders of trimix. They had opted to carry the O_2 with them because they thought they might be climbing out of the sump on the other side, where no bottles could be staged. Also, they routinely made a safety stop on O_2, even when there was no decompression penalty, to accelerate off-gassing and reduce the risk of decompression illness.

At the end of their deco hour they would climb out of the sump to Camp Six, where the sherpas and other Hell Divers would be waiting with warm tea and freeze-dried stew.

Except the line didn't lead to the Ballbuster.

It terminated around a piece of breakdown where they had tied it off and turned back the first time. They had swum in the wrong direction, and although the needles on their depth gauges were plunging again, they thought they were headed for the false bottom. But in the silt and confusion, they had missed the little plastic arrows they had clipped to the guideline, pointing to the way out.

That's when Dahlgren had looked into Taylor's mask and they both knew they were dead. They had less than a third of their gas left, and it wasn't enough to make it back. The others wouldn't know they were in trouble until it was too late. Nobody would arrive to save them.

Dahlgren cursed himself silently.

There were no rescues in cave diving, only body recoveries.

And he had helped kill the person he loved most in the world.

Taylor, however, was calm.

Dahlgren grabbed her by the harness and attempted to drag her back down the line, but she knocked his hand away. She made a V of the fingers of her right hand and pointed fiercely at her mask, giving him the signal for *look, dammit*.

She held up two fingers and shook her head.

Two can't make it.

She held up her index finger and nodded.

But one can.

Then she pointed at Dahlgren.

Dahlgren shook his head violently. Taylor was the logical choice. Her lungs were smaller, she would use less gas than Dahlgren, and it would be quicker for her to squeeze through the Ballbuster. And, of course, she was younger. Taylor was twenty-four, and Dahlgren had gotten four more years of life.

Dahlgren reached for the buckle of his tank harness. He would give her his gas and she would make it. But Taylor grabbed his hand. Behind her mask, tears were welling in her clear blue eyes. She scribbled something on her wrist-mounted slate and showed it to him.

Only choice, it said. *My choice.*

It was part of an ongoing conversation they had shared about cave diving and risk during the past three years. These conversations had moved them not only because cave diving was arguably the most dangerous sport in the world, but because they felt it was a metaphor for life and personal responsibility. To live without risk was not really living.

They had met, appropriately enough, while assisting with a body recovery from Amistad Lake near Del Rio in South Texas. An open-water scuba instructor had decided it would be fun to investigate the old powerhouse that had once dammed the Devil's River. The structure was in a hundred feet of water, and while his buddy waited outside, the instructor had drowned after becoming hopelessly lost in a silt-out without a guideline. After the dumbass had been pried from the guts of the powerhouse, Taylor had asked Dahlgren if he wanted to grab some real Mexican food. She knew this place just across the border, she said, in Ciudad Acuña.

The year before, Dahlgren had seen *Taylor Chastain, Austin, USA*, in the ledger book at the Café Sin Nombre in Tehuacán, where cavers bound for the Huatla left their unofficial mark, and he had wondered whether the signature belonged to a man or a woman. His caving buddies didn't know, but a writer who was gathering research for a book that he would never write took another shot of Black Death tequila and said, "Just another pit hippy from Austin."

When Dahlgren met Taylor she was married to someone else, a reliable man ten years older who sold insurance and kept the bills paid while Taylor worked on a doctorate in ethnobiology at UT. She became fascinated by the science fiction–like possibilities of extremophiles, microbes that had adapted to caves and other extreme conditions. Not only had their discovery contradicted the conventional scientific dogma that life required sunlight, but the organisms might hold the cure to cancer and other human plagues. Consequently, she fell in with a crowd that sought the deep and wet places of the earth. Taylor was already an advanced open-water scuba diver, and soon she added cave diving to her certifications.

A week after Acuña, she and Dahlgren moved in together and listened to bands on Sixth Street, and she filed for what she hoped would be an amicable divorce.

She had been to the Huautla cave system before, with another team that had been using experimental rebreathers, but now she switched and joined the Hell Divers. At the time, everyone believed the Huautla might be the deepest cave in the world, although it would eventually settle for being the fifth deepest—and probably the most dangerous.

When she wasn't caving, Taylor was busy collecting field notes from the local Mazatec Indians for her dissertation, and after interviewing a *curendera* she had accepted a gift of a teardropped piece of jade. It would, the healer said, offer protection from Chi Con Gui-Jao, "He Who Knows What Lies Beneath the Stone."

Unlike the other earth spirits of the Mazatecs, Taylor later explained to Dahlgren, the cave spirit was a trickster and the gatekeeper to the Gui-Jao, the underworld labyrinth where we go after death, and where our ancestors have gone before. A black dog waits by the river that runs through the Gui-Jao. If you've been good, Taylor said, he picks you up by the scruff of your neck and carries you to the other side so you can continue your journey.

"Do you know that's how they describe us?" Taylor had asked. "Chi Con Gui-Jao is the lord of the cave, but they also use that phrase for us, because we also know what lies beneath the stone."

Even more interesting, Taylor said, was that cave divers weren't the only Americans who had sought extreme experiences at San Augustín. In 1958, a Mazatec healer named María Sabina had shared magic mushrooms with a curious New Yorker, R. Gordon Wasson. Wasson had described the trip in *Life* magazine, and a steady stream of questing Anglos— including the Beatles, who were inspired to write "The Long and Winding Road" after—had made the pilgrimage to San Augustín for the peyote hunt ever since.

What were the odds, Taylor asked, that the goal of two so different but undeniably spiritual obsessions would come together in a remote village in the Huautla Plateau, in the narrow waist of Mexico, a mile and a half above the coastal plain?

Dahlgren had thought Taylor's interest in folklore was quaint but forgivable, and he never gave Gui-Jao another thought until he found himself fighting Taylor as she tried to give him her tanks.

Would the black dog take both of them, or just one?

There was only one thing that separated them from the dumbass that had died in the old powerhouse at Amistad, and it wasn't the training, the experience, or all the talk about risk and personal responsibility. It was the fact that there was a choice to be made, that one of them could live, and that both wanted it to be the other.

Ultimately, it was love.

And love defied logic.

Dahlgren knew that he couldn't force himself to drown and reached instead for the dive knife mounted on his forearm. Could he slice his own throat? Ironically, or perhaps fittingly, their grappling had reminded him of their lovemaking. But Taylor was out of her harness now, and she spit out the trimix regulator and grabbed the white hose that led to the pure-oxygen pony bottle.

Their thrashing had created a silt storm, and visibility was next to nothing, but when Dahlgren saw the flash of the white hose, he knew immediately what Taylor was doing. She had inhaled only twice from the oxygen regulator before Dahlgren could snatch it away, but at 9.4 atmospheres, it was several times what was needed to kill her.

Taylor doubled over, as if somebody had hit her with a sledgehammer in the stomach, then began to convulse. Her face twitched and her eyes rolled in the back of her head, then she was unconscious and swallowing water.

Dahlgren jammed his own trimix regulator into her mouth and hit the purge button, but the gas simply puffed out her cheeks, like a trumpet player's. The oxygen had hit her so hard that it had extinguished the survival reflex, and there was nothing Dahlgren could do to make her breathe. He had known you could cough and even vomit through a regulator, but now he discovered you could also sob with a second stage in your mouth.

Dahlgren was, literally and emotionally, lost.

Where was the line?

The silt was so bad it felt like being in the middle of an orange sandstorm. It was difficult to tell up from down, and he had no idea in which direction the line might be. That's when he saw the curious green glow flitting beyond the silt, and he thought he was experiencing the visual disturbances that accompany a host of maladies at depth.

The hardest part was going back through the Ballbuster.

He had to push through both sets of tanks, and then after he had squeezed through himself, reach back and pulled her gently through by the collar of her suit. The rest of the dive was just a physics problem, and because of Taylor, he had enough gas to solve it. Dahlgren shut off his emotions and forced himself to focus on the dive tables instead.

It was the logical thing to do.

The others knew that one of them was dead when they saw

only one set of bubbles coming up from the sump during the time both of them should have been decompressing. Two Hell Divers hastily kitted up and jumped into the water with stage bottles, but of course they lost their haste when they encountered Dahlgren holding Taylor's body at the twenty-foot stop.

Dahlgren wouldn't hand her off.

He completed the decompression, then climbed out of the sump, the body of just another pit hippy from Austin in his arms. Finally, he released her. Before they wrapped her in her sleeping bag and a blue plastic tarp and tied her to a backboard, they took the jade necklace from around her neck and gave it to Dahlgren.

Then they began the three-day climb out of the cave.

The trek through the cave included plunges through five of the other twelve sumps, seven drops of ten to fifteen meters, a pendulum traverse across a bone-chilling waterfall aptly named "Shock and Awe," and a harrowing seventy-meter ascent.

One of the sherpas got her hair caught in her Jumar while walking the rope during the ascent and had to be cut out; another broke his ankle when a Prusik slipped and melted during the traverse and he was thrown against the wall and lost the line on the backboard.

After a thirty-minute discussion and a close vote on whether Taylor's body should be recovered at all, it took five hours to abseil down and retrieve the corpse from the base of the waterfall, where it had fallen between the rocks.

By the time they arrived on the surface, the villagers were lining the path through the cornfield that led from the entrance to *cueva del heuso* to the white stucco Catholic church. Some of the cavers were waiting as well, and in a final defeat the Hell Divers learned that the rebreather team had succeeded in connecting the biggest cave systems during one spectacular push of several kilometers.

The villagers took Taylor's body and reverently placed it

before the altar in the church, even though it was leaking a prodigious amount of body fluid through the sleeping bag and plastic tarp.

A spontaneous and impassioned sermon was delivered by a village elder in a language that none of the cavers understood, with the exception of the occasional *Cristo Rey*, which did not translate well into Mazatec.

Frederic Bean, the novelist who had stayed on the surface smoking Atlas cigarettes and drinking *aguardiente* while the Hell Divers were below, was a polymath who had quickly picked up a smattering of Mazatec. He understood enough to know that only a fool would attempt to fictionalize the events of that week. To do so poorly would insult the memory of the dead, while doing so well would only risk the amusement of Gui-Jao.

Nine years later

One

She was sitting on the cracked sidewalk in front of the Soul's Harvest Rescue Mission, denim knees drawn up to her chest, back resting against the base of a high-pressure mercury vapor streetlamp. Hair the color of rust tumbled down the back of her neck and lay in tangled coils over the shoulders of her gray sweatshirt. It was the middle of October, and even though it was unseasonably warm, every so often a shiver would ripple down her back. As she turned to stare defiantly into the glare of an occasional passing car, her eyes became red-rimmed methamphetamine slits.

Geiger spun her into focus.

Although the sodium vapor overhead provided plenty of illumination, it was a broken-spectrum yellowish orange of about 2,000 degrees Kelvin that painted her skin sallow and skewed the true color of her hair. But when a black GMC pickup with Xenon lamps passed, she swiveled her head to glare at the driver and her features were revealed as if by the clear cold light of a winter's afternoon. Eyes the color of sea foam were framed by copper-colored tresses.

As the drunken farm boy leaned on the horn and shouted something unintelligible and crude, she responded with an ancient and unmistakable gesture, a bony middle finger thrust into the night. Then the headlights swept past, and as she turned her head back with a jerk, her hair swung from the side of her neck and the dirty sweatshirt fell a few inches below her shoulder.

Geiger had been scanning the mission's sidewalk through a pair of armored Zeiss binoculars with bug-eyed 60mm objectives. He had been sitting in an official-looking black sedan on the other side of the street, nearly a block away, in a vacant lot that butted up against the Union Pacific tracks that bisected downtown Joplin, Missouri.

This was the old, dangerous part of town, the haunt of the homeless and the hopeless, the driven and deranged, and one of the few areas of the city that had remained architecturally unchanged since the 1930s. But what time had left, entropy had taken. Citizens shopped elsewhere, at the ubiquitous Wal-Marts, the antiseptic strip malls, or the familiar and obligatory indoor mall at the edge of town. Most who lived here would never venture into any of the businesses that now lined what was once the heart of Main Street, for these few blocks had become a shadow city that catered to the disaffected and disposed: pawnshops and bail bondsmen, used furniture and appliances, a blade-sharpening service, used guitars and used guns, apartments that rented for ten dollars a night.

But at Soul's Harvest you could get a bed and a meal for free, if you promised to look for work and attend a twelve-step program and to read aloud with the others the obligatory Bible chapter. There was even a modest fenced playground for women with children in tow, and wired to the chain-link fence was a metal sign with the five commandments for use, each with a red check mark as if endorsed by Jesus himself: NO DRINKING, NO DRUGS, NO COOKING OUT, KEEP

NOISE DOWN, and PROPERLY DISPOSE OF YOUR BUTTS.

Even though it was past midnight, a lone child, a girl of three with Titian-red hair, wrapped in a bright pink winter coat, sat on the ground, scooping sand with a paper cup out of one of the five-gallon coffee cans provided for the proper disposal of cigarette butts. Every few minutes, the little girl would glance reassuringly at the young woman leaning against the lamppost.

A two-story mural on the side of the building, done in a primitive colorful style, depicted a harvest scene—a disproportionately large farmer with scythe was in the middle of a hand-holding circle of men, women, and children.

The mural amused Geiger.

Some buildings, long closed but not exactly vacant, were filled with the detritus of decades: Behind a peeling green door with no knob was a heap of shoes, waist deep, mostly for women but with a work boot here and there for good measure, all from the 1950s or earlier, and faded by the sun and powdered with dust to the same desert brown. Beneath the grime-streaked display window, in neat but faded block script, was the legend *Hamburgers 5 & 10 cents*.

Other storefronts along this dark canyon were more forbidding.

Broken windows were patched with plywood on which the street numbers had been scrawled in fluorescent spray paint—908, 917, 920—to comply with the city ordinance about clearly displaying addresses for emergency personnel. Somewhere on the rough panels was always tacked a store-bought KEEP OUT sign, or perhaps a red-and-black NO TRESPASSING, and the adjacent doors were not only locked but secured with a heavy chain as well. Condoms, syringes, and empty liquor bottles in exquisitely crumpled paper sacks littered the thresholds of the doorways.

There was sometimes a bullet hole in the storefronts as

well. Many were crusted with age, but there were a few crisp strays from a forty-three-round gunfight between the city police and a parole violator with a stolen .44-caliber Magnum Ruger Super Blackhawk. It ended when an officer with a Colt AR-15 assault rifle put a .223 round diagonally through the parole violator's chest from a block and a half away. He fell facedown on a side street, firing his last round from the Blackhawk into the asphalt.

The parolee's name was Paul E. Cox, the local paper reported, he was thirty-seven and recently divorced, nobody knew why he decided to shoot it out instead of surrender, he apparently hit nothing he aimed at except the rear tire of a departing truck he had attempted to commandeer, and he was dead shortly after he hit the ground.

Although Joplin was a midsized town tucked into the corner of otherwise bucolic southwest Missouri, this three-block strip from Seventh to Tenth resembled the typical inner city. And that is why, every few years, Geiger came here to hunt.

Paul Cox would be remembered because he had been killed in a desperate and stunningly stupid shoot-out that had since been diagrammed by police with the precision of an engineering blueprint. But others had drifted toward death along this street, had frozen in winter or disappeared in the heat of a summer's night, had been lured into dark corners of no return, both literally and metaphorically, and their names were now as forgotten as if they had been written in the dust on the storefront windows.

But the sidewalk traffic had been unusually sparse this Friday night, and Geiger had been ready to move elsewhere when the cold Xenons pierced her and the sweatshirt fell. With an elbow braced against a door panel to steady the 15x image, Geiger studied the girl in the gray sweatshirt.

The tendons on the back of her neck were in sharp relief, and where he could see her naked left shoulder, the tendons ramped down to an unexpectedly graceful and sculpted trapez-

18

ius and well-shaped rhomboid. She was now making chatter with a filthy young man, standing, who had given her a cigarette, but he was excluded in Geiger's vignetted field of vision.

She was seventeen or perhaps eighteen, of medium height, and thin, but not painfully so. She was certainly a drug addict, and the back of her hand went to her nose constantly, but she had not been using long enough to destroy her youth. Her concentration now was mostly devoted to the filter cigarette she was smoking; when it wasn't in her mouth, causing her to squint from the smoke, she was holding it delicately in her left hand or trimming the ash with a fingernail. When she wasn't doing some business with the cigarette, she was gathering her long red hair in her right hand and placing it over her opposite shoulder.

As Geiger watched, a black-and-white crept toward him along Tenth Street in the rearview mirror, and as it neared he lowered the binoculars. The patrol car slowed and then stopped in the street. The officer, a rookie female with a jarring buzz cut, glanced in the black sedan's direction, and Geiger waited a moment before briefly flashing the spotlight near the driver's wing mirror. The officer, believing she had encountered an unmarked car on stakeout, drove on.

Geiger noted several things as the squad car rolled past: the electronic display from a radar gun glowing in the cockpit, the muzzle of a shotgun peeking over the dash, the hockey puck–shaped GPS transceiver on the trunk lid. Like Geiger's black sedan, the squad car was a four-door Crown Victoria with police package.

The rookie glanced at Geiger's plates and idly wondered what federal agency they belonged to.

Geiger would certainly have to move now.

He started the Crown Vic and snapped on the lights, but before he placed it in gear he took one more look through the binoculars.

She had shifted position, and now he could see her face

without having to wait for her to look over her shoulder. Her companion had said something witty or, more likely, suggestive. She flicked the cigarette into the street and flashed a crooked smile, revealing a set of unexpectedly white and even teeth.

For a long moment Geiger was lost in the old familiar rush. The glowing green LED readout on the dashboard read 12:35, and he knew it would stay there for a long time, because time was suspended.

It would all happen easily now.

Her filthy companion took a last drag on his cigarette, flipped the butt into the street, and turned on the heels of a pair of well-worn cowboy boots to go back inside the mission.

The black Crown Vic floated out of the vacant lot, caught the four-way light at Main Street on the green, and drifted slowly toward the curb in front of Soul's Harvest Mission. She watched it approach, and fearing the authoritative demeanor of the car, turned her head away.

The passenger's window glided down.

"I know it's past curfew, but I'm twenty-one," the girl said defiantly in a thick Ozark accent.

"I'm not a cop," Geiger said in dulcet tones.

"You sure as shit look like one."

"Looks can be deceiving," Geiger said. "It's late. It's getting colder. Would you like some breakfast?"

"Breakfast?" The girl laughed.

"No? Then how about some crystal?"

"You ain't got no crank. You just want some pussy. But you ain't getting none. But I'll blow you for forty bucks. Around back."

Geiger sighed.

"I have to stay close enough to watch my kid."

"Not here."

"Twenty," she negotiated. "A blow job for Mr. Jackson."

"Get in the car."

It must be now, now, now. Time was beginning to move again. Another ten heartbeats and the game would be lost: Someone might get a good look through the open window, and the girl herself was becoming a liability if she didn't get in the car.

He put the car in gear.

"Stop."

The girl leaned in through the open window

"I'll fuck you if you really have crystal."

The passenger's door thumped as it unlocked.

"Get in."

"You really have it, right?"

"Get in."

She hesitated.

"Now."

The girl opened the door and slid into the passenger's seat.

"Nice fucking car," she said. "Where's the shit?"

"Backseat."

She turned to peer behind her.

"Wait until we find someplace safe. What's your name?"

The girl turned back forward, ran her knuckles beneath her raw nose, then lifted the sweatshirt to scratch at an imaginary bug on her abdomen.

"What's your name?" Geiger asked gently as he turned off Main Street.

"Sylvia," she said.

"Last name?"

"Sylvia Porter. I'm from West Plains originally."

"Well, you have the most beautiful eyes, Sylvia Porter from West Plains, Missouri. Has anyone ever told you that?"

"Yeah, my stepdad before he made me suck his dick. You don't have to bullshit me. Don't worry, you're going to get fucked."

"No, I mean it. You're special. And you're not going to have to have sex with me. I'll share what I have, I promise."

21

"Christ, are you some kind of Jesus freak? You're not a fucking Mormon out here to try to save me, are you?"

The Crown Vic swung around the block and pulled into a railway scrap yard on the northeast corner of Tenth and Main. The car slipped through a break in the fence and came to a stop behind a massive pile of tracks.

Sylvia pulled her sweatshirt off in one motion. She was wearing nothing beneath it, and her smallish breasts glowed green by the digital readout of the dashboard clock, which still read thirty-five minutes after midnight.

"Shoot me," Sylvia said, "and then I'll suck your dick like I'm sucking the chrome off a trailer hitch."

"Not original," Geiger said as he retrieved a black medical bag from the backseat. "That was used in that Willie Nelson and Kris Kristofferson movie. What was the name of it? *Songwriter?*"

Geiger held up a plastic syringe, flicked the needle with his forefinger, and pushed the plunger so just a few drops dewed on the tip.

Sylvia began to salivate, and drool leaked from the right side of her mouth. She had already taken the surgical tubing from the bag, held one end of it between her teeth, and pulled it tight around her upper left arm.

"*Electric Horseman,*" Sylvia said between the surgical tubing. "Starred Robert Redford, but Willie had a bit part. He's the one who said it."

"I stand corrected," Geiger said as he tested her veins by tapping her track-marked forearm. "But no chrome removal necessary." Finding a promising blue trace, he swabbed it with alcohol and then plunged the needle into it. Slowly, with his thumb, he eased down the plunger.

Sylvia's head rocked back against the headrest and her right hand slipped inside her jeans to touch her shaved and pierced genitals, as she prepared for the expected amphetamine rush. The rushes had become less intense during the last few weeks, but she still could count on a racing heart, a feeling of falling headlong through space, and a series of intense sexual spasms from just the touch of her own hand. As Geiger's drug entered her bloodstream, however, she felt her heartbeat slow and a weight crush her diaphragm.

"What the fuck?" she asked, jerking her arm away.

The plunger was only a third of the way down.

"Remain still," Geiger said.

"You're poisoning me," Sylvia croaked, and it was the last thing she managed to say, and it was true. The mixture Geiger had partially completed injecting was Rohypnol. It was fatal in large doses, but Geiger wasn't trying to kill her, at least not yet. He just needed her to be compliant.

But Sylvia's body had developed a tolerance for drugs, and the dose she had received wasn't enough.

Her hand shot out for the door handle, and she tumbled from the car onto the ground in a kind of anesthetic fog, but with her survival instinct intact.

Sylvia ran from the dark railway scrap yard toward the warm sodium vapor lights of Main Street.

Geiger hesitated, unsure of what to do, and for a moment the universe seemed to collapse inward into chaos. The dose wasn't enough to kill her. The dashboard clock read 12:43. If anybody believed her story after she came around, not only would she jeopardize him, but greater things were at stake. Perhaps it was part of the cosmological plan that had been revealing itself since he was a boy, or perhaps it was just a random act of chaos that required his full attention. He was the chosen, and the test would not be given unless he was ready for it.

Geiger gathered himself, willed time to a standstill, and grabbed the dive knife and a roll of duct tape hidden in the bottom of the black bag. The knife had a nine-inch black titanium blade with a line-cutting notch near the tip, a blood channel that ran all the way back to the hand guard, and a red composite handle.

23

Then he put the Crown Vic in gear, backed calmly out of the scrap yard, and took off after her. There wasn't another car on Main Street as Sylvia stumbled, topless, down the middle of the road, not another person to gape from the sidewalk. Nobody peered from windows, and the four-way lights on either end of the block didn't change. The only sound was the crying of a child in the playground.

When Sylvia became aware that the black sedan was moving slowly behind her, she ambled toward the east side of the street. In her anesthetic fog, she had already passed the Mission with its always-open door, which had been her intended refuge, and found herself in the row of vacant storefront between the Soul's Harvest and the Main Sreet Apartments.

Her legs were failing her, and she dropped to her knees as she came to the green door with the mountains of shoes behind. She pulled herself into the entryway and reached for the doorknob, but found the door had been padlocked and the knob removed from the plate.

The black Crown Vic pulled to the curb.

She banged on the door, but nobody heard.

Sylvia placed her back against the door with no knob and brought her knees up and covered her face with her forearms, trying to hide.

The man was out of the black sedan. He left the engine running and suddenly he was rushing toward her with a big knife in his left hand and a roll of silver duct tape in his right.

With one smooth motion, Geiger tore off a six-inch strip of tape and placed it over Sylvia's mouth, but left her nostrils free. Then he pressed the scalpel-sharp point of the dive knife against the side of her throat, above the carotid, not hard enough to do real harm but forcefully enough to draw blood.

Sylvia didn't feel the sting, but she did feel the odd sensation of warm water trickling down her neck and between her breasts. Her right hand reached out and up, still trying to find a doorknob. She could hear her little girl crying. She glanced in the direction of the playground but couldn't see from her position on the sidewalk.

Geiger held the knife steady for a few seconds, inspecting her shoulders. He looked again at the stomach and breasts he had seen in the car, then shoved her far forward to check the small of her back. He found a serpent peeking above her jeans, writhing its way down her spine toward her buttocks.

Sylvia's fingers were clawing at the door.

"Tattoos," Geiger said in disgust. "Why do you young people do this to yourselves?"

Her fingernails scratched furrows in the green paint.

He drove the knife upward, beneath her sternum, then twisted.

The clawing stopped.

Geiger looked around to make sure he was alone. Then he withdrew the knife and wiped the blade on her denim thighs. He walked back to the car, and when he opened the driver's door, the warning buzzer sounded briefly.

Sylvia was already dreaming.

She was back in West Plains, the summer before she quit high school, that last carefree summer before she became pregnant, working at the McDonald's on the highway. It was the only job she had ever held, the only honest money she had ever made.

"I used to hate this job," she mumbled through lips dappled with bloody froth.

Behind the counter were the three friends who had been killed in the car crash the summer before, the grandfather who had taken her fishing and then died when she was eight, the long-dead aunt who used to play tea party with her when her mother worked late at the poultry-processing plant.

Then she heard the buzzer, and she knew the fries were ready to come out of the vat.

Two

Geiger dreamed that night as well.

She was as beautiful as Sin.

Her skin shone like the reflection of the moon on black water, her red hair pillowed behind her head, and her eyes had rolled backward in their orbits, turning only crescents of white upon the darkness that engulfed her. A broad silk ribbon with a snakeskin pattern was draped across her shoulders and serpentined down each arm. Her breasts nestled invitingly between her python-clad shoulders, and the nipples had turned a shade of bluish pink that all but fluoresced.

But it was her mouth that fascinated him the most.

Her marbled lips were slightly parted, and behind them a bubble had formed, trapped in the corner of her mouth. Floating over her, he brought the head of the wrist-mounted light close to her face to examine the bubble, all the while filled with the realization that this grape-sized bubble clinging to the soft pink inside of her mouth represented her very last breath of air.

It had been coaxed from her lungs by a change in depth of a few meters while he made her ready to face eternity, and was now held in place only by surface tension and the angle of her repose. He smiled, thinking of Wallace Stegner. Gently, he turned her body toward heaven, and the bubble rolled from the corner of her mouth to the center, passing through the exquisitely marbled and gently parted lips, to race upward.

He followed the bubble with the wrist-mounted beam as it sped into the darkness, already growing in size, in perfect compliance with the unbreakable laws of physics. But as it sped away, he saw in the shimmering mercury sphere his own mirror image, as if recorded by God's own eye: a figure clad in red, breathing silently, looking upward through the tempered glass of a diving mask, pointing a hand that threw cold blue lightning, and with the embodiment of Sin stretched perfectly before him.

When he woke, he was surprised that he was safe in bed and not hundreds of feet underwater. What winter had he been dreaming of? Was it 1968 or 1978? Certainly, no later than 1980.

He had slept only a few hours, and the alarm had not yet gone off, but he reached up and turned it off, then swung his feet to the floor. As he had grown older, he had begun sleeping less and waking sooner. It was a normal part of aging. *Ars longa, vita brevis*, he thought. Life is short, but art endures.

Besides, he had an early flight to catch.

Three

Cathedral pillars and limestone arches supported a rock ceiling spanning a subterranean lake of achingly clear water. Passages radiated from the central cavern like spokes from a hub, and in the side of the lake was a newly built dock. It was laden with equipment: banks of scuba cylinders, a compressor, a mixed-gas manifold, lights, cable. A row of rebreathers, each in a black clamshell housing, awaited use. A chalkboard in the center of the dock read: OCT. 30. WATER TEMP: 16.6 C. VISIBILITY: 70 METERS. BE CAREFUL!

Six divers sat in a semicircle on wooden benches or leaned against equipment lockers, listening to a somewhat older divemaster. They wore wet suits in colors that matched the helmets of the waiting rebreathers; hanging in the equipment locker were dry suits and other gear that was also matched by color to each diver.

"Our objective is a group of mine shacks forty-three meters down," said Loren McAfee in his best high-school science teacher voice, and the slight reverb coming back from the rock walls added to his authority. His arms were folded across the chest of his silver wet suit.

"This is an easy dive, and a relatively short one, so let's not screw it up," he continued. "Don't forget to monitor your partial pressures on both your primary and secondary readouts, and keep an eye on your cap color and that of your buddy."

McAfee paused. He was used to people listening when he talked, and it annoyed him when they didn't. He had been talking now for five minutes, but Staci Johnson wasn't listening. Instead, she was doodling on her slate with a grease pencil while looking over at the edge of the dock where their mascot, a California sea lion named Nemo, waited anxiously.

McAfee smoothed the edges of his salt-and-pepper Vandyke.

"Staci, am I boring you?" he asked.

The twenty-three-year-old brushed a fall of strawberry-blond hair back from her neck, revealing a glimpse of a Celtic knot tattooed on her nape, and looked at him with sleepy green eyes.

"No," she said.

"Then do you mind telling me our maximum depth for this dive, and what kind of deco we're going to do on the way back up?" Loren asked evenly.

Potts and Addison, who were sitting together as usual, exchanged knowing glances. Potts was in his middle thirties, and his most distinguishing feature, besides the purple wet suit bottoms he now wore, was his shaved head. Addison was a year younger, his wet suit was royal blue, and he was black. His head was shaved as well. Potts was an ex-SEAL, Addison was a former Coast Guard rescue diver, and the lax discipline of civilian life amused them.

Staci looked blank for a moment, then recited:

"Forty-three meters, or about a hundred and forty feet. Air mixture. Deco at ten meters and safety stop at three with O_2, as usual. What do you think?"

She turned her oversized slate over and showed him a very good sketch of Nemo in red grease pencil.

Cal Bentham, who had been standing near Loren in order to hear the briefing better, covered his mouth with his hand and did a poor job of stifling a laugh. At sixty-eight, he was the oldest person on the dock, and the only one not in dive gear. Instead, he wore jeans and a leather biker vest, and a red bandanna against the chill. He was a former hardhat diver, and the only one allowed to poke fun at McAfee.

There was an uncomfortable pause as McAfee regained his composure. Finally, he said: "That's very good."

"Thanks," Staci said as she wiped the slate clean with the forearm of her turquoise wet suit.

"Hey," called Norman Baker. He was sitting with the other divers on one of the benches made from two-by-fours, and although it was chilly in the mine, he had the top of his orange wet suit pulled down to his waist. In his hands was a Nikonos V underwater camera. "That was good, baby. I could have taken a picture of it. Why'd you do that?"

Staci shrugged.

Claire Connelly, who was standing behind the others, knelt on one knee behind Staci. "Attitude," she whispered into the younger girl's ear.

Staci looked annoyed.

"Okay, any questions?" Loren asked. "Anybody?"

Staci raised her hand.

"Yes?"

"When are we going to explore something interesting?" Staci whined. "We've spent a month mapping the edges of the city. I'm tired of drawing shacks and mine equipment. When are we going to get to some of the bigger buildings, like the hospital or the barracks?"

The other divers laughed.

"What were you expecting?" Norman asked. "Atlantis?"

"I just thought it would be more exciting," Staci answered in a sulk.

"Don't worry," Claire said, placing a hand on Staci's shoulder. "You'll learn that boredom is good. Excitement is bad. You'll know that the first time you get bent or nearly drown. People die when things get exciting. Hope instead for rewarding."

"You want excitement, baby?" Norman asked, walking backward in his fins to the edge of the dock. "Watch out, because things are about to get freaking *phreatic*."

He fell backward into the water, forcing the others to cover their faces from the geyser of water that marked his entry.

Four

Holding a microphone in one hand and a reporter's notebook in the other, Dana Casteel looked into the lens below the red tally light and attempted to read from a page of notes that was bleeding away in the rain.

"Officials here at the scene say a Missouri Highway Patrol trooper was killed about three hours ago on the bridge behind me," she said, summoning most of it from memory. She turned slightly to indicate the background. "This location is just minutes away from Branson. The usual tourist traffic, combined with today's miserable weather, umm, is hampering investigators."

She brushed a tangle of wet brown hair from her face, then abandoned the notebook entirely.

"The trooper's name has not been released. Details are sketchy, but from what Color Three Springfield has been able to learn, the trooper was making what he thought was a routine traffic stop, at the far end of the bridge from us, when unknown suspects opened fire from the back of a black van. Although wounded, the trooper—*Jesus!*"

Dana jumped as a bolt of lightning split a tree not thirty yards behind, showering sparks and sending a branch into the windshield of a parked highway patrol car.

"Nice one, Dana," the camera operator said from beneath the bill of his baseball cap, his right eye still mated to the viewfinder as he regained the shot. "Another for your growing blooper reel,"

"Fuck you, Dave," Dana said. "You flinched, too."

A trooper walked past and shook his head. Rain poured down the brim of his Resistol-wrapped Smokey's hat. He paused.

"Miss, you and your partner better take cover," he said. "This is no place to be holding the end of a microphone cable."

Dave nodded his agreement.

Dana smiled.

"Yes," she said, "but I'll bet that looked pretty cool. Ready? Give me another countdown."

"Why is all talent crazy?" Dave asked. "All right. But if it gets any worse, you're going to be shooting yourself. From five. Four. Three."

Dave pointed at Dana.

"There you just saw how tough conditions here are at the moment," Dana said. "As I was saying before being interrupted by the storm, the trooper returned fire and briefly gave chase, until a fusillade from one or more fully automatic weapons forced his car over the bridge railing and into the water below."

The camera turned from Dana to zoom in on a Missouri Water Patrol boat riding the waves near the bridge. Smoothly, Dave pulled back to Dana and regained the frame.

"No word yet from officials on the identity of the suspect, or a more complete description of the vehicle," Dana said. Her

33

makeup was running now, streaking her checks with black rivulets. "The highway patrol is requesting all civilians to clear the roads surrounding the Highway 13 bridge here at Kimberling City. A spokesman told me earlier—"

The sound of a piston-driven aircraft threatened to mute her.

"—that a specialist in underwater crime and accident scenes has been called, and that he is expected to arrive at any moment by aircraft," Dana continued. "I find it incredible that anything is flying in such weather, but the airplane we're hearing in the background may indeed be that investigator."

A high-winged, single-engine aircraft on pontoons flew low over the bridge, waggled its wings, then banked in a wide turn into the wind, preparing to land. Just as the plane touched the lake, a finger of lightning traced its way across the dark sky over the bridge, followed by a gut-thumping peal of thunder.

"That's it," Dave said, unplugging the microphone cable from the XLR jack and unlocking the camera from the tripod. "I'm going to find someplace that is safe, warm, and dry—and stay there."

The plane was an old but well-maintained Helio. It taxied on the rough water toward a small marina tucked into a cove a few hundred yards from the bridge, where a lone officer in a yellow rain slicker waited on an uncovered section of dock.

The aircraft was predominantly white, but with a flat black engine cowling and tarnished aluminum pontoons. A faded red stripe ran the length of the fuselage from the air intake to the tail, and the same shade was used on the leading edges of the wings and the tip of the rudder. Behind the aft window, in black letters a foot high, was the registration number: N357XS.

On each side of the broad black cowl, just forward of the doors, was a stylized skull wearing a red-and-white diver down flag as a bandanna. The skull also had a knife in its teeth. Beneath, in red script that was cracked and fading, was *Hell*

Divers. On each door, in sedate block letters, was TRITON INVESTIGATIONS. Below that, in smaller script, was *Pittsburg, Kansas*, and a phone number. The area code, which had changed years before, was covered in duct tape and the new area code scrawled in black marker: 620.

The pilot cut the engine, allowing the momentum to carry the plane toward the marina, and the sound of the rain on the high, broad wing became suddenly apparent. The choppy water slapped at the plane's pontoons, and the rudders moved in tandem as the pilot guided the unpowered plane alongside the dock. The plane had just enough momentum left, despite the wind, to kiss the dock's rubber bumper.

Richard Dahlgren stepped out of the cockpit and onto the rain-slicked pontoon. He was wearing a hooded blue nylon paddle jacket over a pair of faded jeans. His cowboy boots slipped on the wet aluminum and he grabbed a strut to keep from falling. Then he flipped a line toward the dock, where it was caught by the rain-slickered cop.

"Think it'll rain?" Dahlgren asked.

On this day in late October, Dahlgren was approaching his thirty-seventh birthday, although a casual observer might have guessed he was older. He had spent too many years in the sun for his face to be considered handsome. He swept the nylon hood out of his way while he kneeled and made the aft line fast to a cleat, revealing a tangle of brown hair that had been bleached nearly blond by the summer sun.

A Missouri Water Patrol boat glided up to the dock on the opposite side, an outboard Merc idling roughly. A water patrol officer was at the wheel, while a highway patrol trooper stood near the passenger's seat, one hand gripping the wet windshield.

Dahlgren stopped unloading cargo.

He wiped the rain from his eyes.

"You wouldn't have a cigarette, would you?" he asked.

The driver of the boat shook a Marlboro out of a hard pack and tossed it up to Dahlgren, followed by a book of matches.

"You Dahlgren?" the trooper asked.

Dahlgren had the cigarette in his mouth, but by the time he managed to ignite a match, the cigarette was hopelessly soaked.

"You expecting somebody else?" Dahlgren asked.

The cigarette had fallen to pieces and was hanging limply from his mouth. Disgustedly, he threw it into the lake.

"You must be one crazy sonuvabitch to land a float plane in this weather," the boat driver said. "Do you know what you're doing?"

"Theoretically," Dahlgren said as he used both hands to pass down a pair of hundred-cubic-foot steel scuba cylinders linked by a twin-port DIN manifold. The valves were protected by a wire cage, and it was all mounted to a stainless-steel backplate and harness. Sandwiched between the plate and the tanks was a red U-shaped flotation bladder, commonly called "wings" because it expanded from the diver's back. The bladder was empty now and was kept from flapping by elastic cords every six inches around the perimeter of the backplate.

The driver gasped as he wrestled the tanks to the carpeted deck of the patrol boat.

"Man," he said, "that is heavy."

"You want to secure it?" Dahlgren asked.

"Hey, this is a different kind of tank valve than we're used to seeing," the driver said as he slipped a bungee cord around the tanks.

"It uses threads instead of being forced against the yoke by pressure," Dahlgren said. "DIN, for German Industry Standard. Common with technical divers."

"Technical divers?" the driver asked.

"Wreck divers," Dahlgren said. Then he added: "Cave divers."

"Oh, yeah."

"What's the situation?" Dahlgren asked.

36

"We thought you knew," the trooper said.

"Tell me again," Dahlgren said as he handed over a mesh bag of evidence-collection tubes made from plastic sewer pipe with screw-on ends. "I'm slow."

The boat driver looked suspiciously at the bag.

"Harry Combs made a car stop on the bridge this morning," the trooper said matter-of-factly. "He was in the middle of logging the tag when all hell broke loose. Dispatch said it sounded like the battle for Kabul. All we got before he went over the side was a partial vehicle description, a black Ford van with Arkansas plates. We also found a couple hundred shell casings from an AK-47 on the bridge."

"Who carries Kalashnikovs around here?"

"Take your pick," the driver said.

"What was Combs driving?"

"Chevy Impala, two years old," the trooper said.

Dahlgren handed over the last dive bag, the padded one containing his Poseidon regulator with the DIN first stage.

"You want the tape," Dahlgren said.

"We want the tape," the trooper echoed.

"Where's the VTR?"

"The camera was on the rearview mirror," the trooper said. "The cable ran to the recorder in the trunk, above the driver's wheel well."

"Terrific," Dahlgren said.

"Problem?" the trooper asked.

"Trunks are a bitch," Dahlgren said. "Sure the camera was on?"

"Hoping," the trooper said.

"Can't you just hook a line to the differential and use a wrecker on the bridge to winch the vehicle up?" the boat driver asked.

"The Chevy may have planed two hundred yards," Dahlgren said. "The weight of the cable would be too much

37

for any wrecker I know of, and that's not counting a full-sized car filled with water—several hundred gallons at eight pounds per."

The trooper nodded.

"Well, we'd like to have the body," he said.

"It's not like it would do him any good," Dahlgren said. "And it won't make any difference to him whether it's today or a week from today. No offense."

"Then what are you doing here if there's no rush?" the driver asked.

"You dumb shit," the trooper said suddenly. "Don't you think we need that fucking video just as soon as possible, even if it is in the middle of one of the worst October storms in ten years? Every minute that passes helps the sonuvabitch who killed Harry to get away."

The driver's mouth worked silently.

"Look," Dahlgren said. "I'll do what I can. But it may not help. Water immersion isn't exactly recommended for magnetic recording media."

"Just get us the tape," the trooper said.

"Tell me about the water."

"Like most of the lakes around here," the trooper said. "Green and murky. Looks like Harry went down right into the old river channel. The bluffs are pretty high on either side, and there are still plenty of trees."

"Depth?"

"Anywhere from sixty feet to a hundred and sixty."

Dahlgren had already slipped out of his boots and jeans and was struggling with the bottom half of his seven-millimeter wet suit. The boat was rocking so violently that he had to reach for the gunwale.

"Cast off," the trooper called.

The driver threw the bowline on the dock, then went to the wheel, cranked it around, and throttled up the Merc. The boat threw a rooster tail of water behind it as it sped toward the bridge, thumping heavily into the wind-driven waves.

By the time the boat slowed, as it neared the iridescent sheen of gas and oil, Dahlgren was nearly ready. The boat driver started to raise a mast with a dive flag.

"I'd rather take my chances with boat traffic than be hit by lightning," Dahlgren said. "Unless, of course, you're going to cite me for diving without a flag."

The driver shrugged and lowered the mast.

Dahlgren mounted the Poseidon's first stage on the dual manifold, connected the low-pressure inflator, and spun the valves to the fully open position. There was a hiss of compressed air and the hoses stiffened with pressure. The trooper then helped him into the tank harness, and Dahlgren sat on a boat seat while he assembled the rest of his gear. The excess bit of strap that protruded from the buckles of his mask and his fins were wrapped with duct tape. He slipped a spare mask over his head and turned it around, so the lens was facing the tanks and the strap was hanging below his chin.

When he was finished, Dahlgren was wearing 135 pounds of equipment, and he inched his way toward the bow. Because of the negative buoyancy of the twin 104s and the steel in his backpack, he didn't need a weight belt.

"Don't you guys usually dive in pairs?" the driver asked as Dahlgren reached down with his right hand, found his primary regulator, and jammed it between his teeth. "The buddy system and all that?"

Dahlgren took a breath of cool, dry air, checked his compass and gauges, then took the regulator out of his mouth.

"Those rules don't apply in my business," Dahlgren said. "Makes sense for recreational divers. But this kind of stuff? A buddy is just as likely to get you killed—or to die trying to save you."

39

Dahlgren paused for a moment, timing the swell of the water and the slap of the hull, then stepped outward and turned at the same time. He tucked his head forward, keeping one hand on his mask and the other on his web belt, as his tank broke the water and a froth of green water closed over his head. Table Rock Lake was just as he remembered it had been, while diving it twenty years ago with members of his scuba club.

His back-mounted buoyancy compensator "wings" were deflated, so Dahlgren glided quickly down into the green murk, his exhaust bubbles rushing past his ears with every exhalation. He pinched his nose closed through the silicone of his mask and gently blew, and his eardrums crinkled as the pressure in his Eustachian tubes and sinus cavities equalized. At twenty feet, he shot a little air from the low-pressure inflator into his wings to slow his descent.

At thirty feet, it got very cold.

He had passed the thermocline, where the cold water lay stratified beneath the warmer surface water, and it felt as if tiny nettles were stinging the exposed portion of his face. The water temperature had dipped into the upper sixties Fahrenheit, and while that would only be a bit chilly in air, in water—which is twelve times more thermally efficient—it was like running out in a snowstorm.

There had been little sunlight that afternoon, and by the time Dahlgren reached the tops of the trees, at eighty-five feet, he switched on a bucket-sized halogen dive light. He pumped more air into his wings to slow and finally arrest his descent, and he hovered for a moment in the trees, swinging the beam of light back and forth, searching.

The water was dirty from being churned all day by storm surge, and most of the light was reflected back into Dahlgren's eyes from backscatter. Dahlgren covered the head of the light with his hand for a few moments, allowing his eyes to adjust to the gloom. Waiting, he checked his old Seiko dive watch.

Seven minutes had already passed. The crystal was a cobweb of scratches and pits accumulated during twenty-three years of scuba diving, car repairs, and bar fights, but once under, these filled with water and the watch, like his gauges, looked new.

When he could just make out the trunks of the trees below him, he purged some air from his wings and sank lower.

Holding the halogen light at waist level, Dahlgren took his hand away and painted the trees around him. He had almost completed a circle when he saw the light reflected back from tempered glass. Lazily kicking his old black Rocket Fins, Dahlgren moved toward the reflection, and soon he could discern the outline of the patrol car. His light had been reflected from a rear side window. The car itself was nestled upside down in the fork of an oak tree.

"Crazy," Dahlgren said through a burst of exhaust bubbles.

When he was within five feet of the car, he could see that its tail lights were still glowing— dimly. Dahlgren glided down ten feet, forcing his maximum-depth needle on his gauge to 130 (and the part of his brain that kept track of time and depth automatically noted that he had exceeded the Navy table's ten-minute no-decompression bottom time). The headlights were glowing weakly as well. The hood and driver's side door were punctuated by bullet holes, the windshield was stitched but not shattered, and a black hand protruded from the narrow gap between the driver's window and the door frame.

Dahlgren floated back up, wary of disturbing the delicate balance of car and tree, and unclipped the Dive-Rite safety reel from his harness. He grasped the loop at the end of the eighth-inch nylon line, pulled out a few feet, and passed the line beneath the car's rear axle. Then he passed the reel back through the loop, backed off the lockdown screw so the spool would turn easily, and snapped the reel onto the bottom of a bright yellow lift bag that had been folded and stowed against one of the tanks with surgical tubing.

Dahlgren removed the Poseidon second stage from his mouth, positioned it beneath the throat of the lift bag, and thumbed the purge button. A geyser of air burbled upward and pooled at the top of the bag. Although the bag was less than a quarter full, Dahlgren released it. It grew in size as it rose, unspooling line below. There was 150 feet of line on the reel, a length that Dahlgren thought would be just about right. Later, when the storm passed, it would be easy enough to follow the line down to recover the patrol car.

Dahlgren put the regulator back in his mouth.

He swam over the gas tank and dropped below the bumper. He tried the trunk lid, hoping it had been sprung by the impact with the water. The latch, however, held.

"Shit," Dahlgren muttered.

He would have to go inside.

Dahlgren shone his light over the interior of the car, trying to reckon the best way in. Both rear doors were clear, but a wire cage separated the backseat from the front. The passenger's door was resting against a good-sized limb, so that was out. The only way in was through the driver's door.

Dahlgren swam over to where the black hand beckoned beyond the window, grabbed the rain gutter, and tried to rock the car. There wasn't much give. Satisfied but still apprehensive, Dahlgren grabbed the door handle and pulled. He was expecting the door to be jammed, but it opened easily.

A bloom of papers, blood, and gore followed the suction, and a swarm of panfish darted after scraps of flesh. The black hand waved in the turbulence, but the corpse remained belted into the driver's seat.

Dahlgren pulled himself into the interior of the car, trying not to look up at the ruined skull of the driver, but unable to keep from nudging the corpse.

"Sorry," he said.

He took off his gloves. The water stung his hands. Carefully, he gathered up all of the floating paper he could quickly grab and unzipped his wet suit jacket halfway. Shivering from the rushing cold, he stuffed the papers and the gloves inside the jacket, then zipped it back up.

Dahlgren paused and reminded himself that the car was upside down. Groping his way through the murk, he pulled himself deeper into the car, found the glove box, struggled with the latch, and finally opened it. With his mask and the halogen light just inches from the glove box, he found the orange trunk-release button and pushed it, but did not hear the click of the solenoid.

He backed out the way he came in, found the steering wheel, then searched for the key-release switch. Dammit. When was the last time he'd driven a car that had one? It was easy to find on his ten-year-old Jeep Wrangler. He hadn't driven a full-sized Ford since the night he blew the head gasket on the old man's 1972 Torino, let alone a late-model Chevrolet. He had lost most of the feeling in his hands. He fumbled and probed around the steering column while watching his exhaust bubbles pool in the floorboards. He shoved his right hand down into his wet suit jacket for a few moments, then, when the circulation began to return—and the hand began to burn—he tried once more and found the switch. He depressed it with one hand and turned and slid the key out of the ignition with the other.

The car's lights winked off.

He backed out of the car, checked his submersible pressure gauge, then looked at his watch. Twenty-three minutes had passed. He was accumulating a serious decompression penalty now, but he knew his forearm-mounted computer would guide him through the stops. And he still had more than two thousand pounds of air in each of the twin 104s. He could afford, he decided, five more minutes.

By the warm beam of the halogen dive light, Dahlgren inserted the key in the trunk lock and turned. The latch clicked and the lid fell open an inch or two, then stopped. It was jammed somehow. Dahlgren took a pry tool from his belt and jammed it into the trunk. He levered, the lid sprang open, and the trunk vomited jumper cables and tools and a red metal gas can that floated lazily in the opposite direction, toward the surface.

Dahlgren clipped the pry tool back on his belt and removed a pair of wire clippers. He eased himself into the trunk, looking for the recorder above the wheel well, but found nothing. Then he reminded himself that the car was upside down. The right wheel well would be on the left.

He found the lunchbox-sized video recorder tucked above the wheel well, just as the trooper had said it would be, and he struggled to pull the box forward in order to snip the wires. The wires were well secured, however, and the recorder just wouldn't budge. While Dahlgren struggled to get enough room, his exhaust bubbles were pooling in the bottom of the trunk and fenders. With every breath, he was changing the car's balance, but he was too absorbed in the task to notice. He had finally managed to get the recorder out far enough to snip it free, when the branch gave way.

Dahlgren *felt* the crack more than heard it.

It was percussive, like a rifle shot, and even before the car began its downward plunge, he knew he was in trouble. Most of his body was wedged in a car trunk that loomed over him like a basket, and when he tried to back out, his power inflator hose snagged on a trunk hinge.

The car dropped twenty feet through the branches and grazed a limestone bluff, dislodging a shower of rocks and muck, then yawed and came to rest, miraculously upright, on a narrow ledge.

Dahlgren's head bounced against the lip of the trunk when the car hit the bluff, peeling the scalp back and cracking the lens of his mask. Green ice water rushed in, and he ripped the mask off and let it sink away. He managed to disentangle his power inflator from the hinge mechanism by feel. Blind, he grabbed the spare mask from the nape of his neck, turned it around, tucked the edges of the seal beneath his hood, and began to purge it by blowing through his nose and holding the top of the mask against his forehead.

The lake water receded as the volume in the mask filled with air. He was breathing heavily, his exhaust thundering around his ears, and he detected the coppery taste of blood seeping in around the silicone mouthpiece of his second stage. He had lost his big dive light, so he retrieved a penlight-sized backup that was clipped to his harness. He pointed the light at his wrist-mounted computer. READY TO DIVE? The batteries had jarred loose, resetting the display.

He had dicked up.

Dahlgren concentrated on calming himself and not becoming just another corpse that some other diver would have to risk his life to retrieve. He shone the light on the console hanging from the high-pressure hoses. His depth gauge read just shy of the 150-foot mark. With every breath, the needle on the submersible pressure gauge jerked downward. His head hurt, although he didn't seem to be seriously injured, but that could just be the narcotic effect of the nitrogen. He didn't usually get narced this shallow, but he usually didn't take plunges in the trunks of submerged automobiles with dead men at the wheel.

After a moment of focus, he slowed his breathing.

He checked his watch. His bottom time was twenty-eight minutes. Then he unzipped a small nylon pouch that was clipped to his harness and removed a laminated set of U.S. Navy dive tables. He found the information he was looking for on the back of the fourth page. He rounded up to the next time and depth column, moved his finger across the table, and found that he required thirty-two minutes of decompression. His hang time would be eight minutes at twenty feet and twenty-four minutes at ten feet.

The last, given the weather, would be tough.

But the nylon line was still attached to the differential of the patrol car, pointing up to the lift bag on (or now, perhaps, just under) the surface. It was either follow the line and take his chances in the open water, or swim up the side of the old river channel, through the trees, and up the bluff, and find a spot to cling to and hope the storm surge didn't bash his brains out against the limestone.

There are no right or wrong choices, he heard a long-ago voice say in his head, *only choices with different consequences. It is a question of personal responsibility. We alone are responsible for the consequences of the decisions we make.*

For a moment, Dahlgren thought about simply staying on the bottom. That's what he'd been waiting for all these years for anyway, wasn't it?

Fucking nitrogen.

Dahlgren admitted to himself that he was slightly narced. He had been taught in his basic cert class, taken during the last century, that every fifty feet of depth is like having a stiff martini. He'd just had a three-martini lake lunch, and he'd become a maudlin drunk.

He'd have to handle the line gently, because it wasn't as tough as the quarter-inch sisal that wreck divers routinely carried as an emergency up-line. That the line hadn't snagged or been parted by a tree branch was the only bit of luck he'd had so far.

Dahlgren clipped the penlight to a D-ring high on the left side of his harness, so the beam pointed down. He tucked the VTR under his left arm while holding his inflator button and his gauge console in his left hand, in a position where he could read it in the beam of the penlight. Then he gently circled the line with his right thumb and forefinger, shot some air into his wings, and kicked upward.

* * *

"Think he's okay?" the trooper asked. "It's been nearly an hour since he sent the buoy up. I don't even see it now. Hasn't he been down kind of long?"

The driver, who was huddled beneath the boat's canvas top, flicked another Marlboro into the lake and shrugged.

"All he has to do is find the car and open the trunk," he said. "How dangerous could it be? Besides, the car's probably in sixty feet of water. He has unlimited bottom time."

The trooper rubbed his nose with the back of his right hand.

"I'm not so sure," he said.

"What'd they call this clown for, anyway?" the driver asked. "I thought the patrol had its own dive team trained for this kind of stuff."

"We do," the trooper said, then turned back to the water, squinting into the rain. "But you don't investigate a shooting involving one of your own. You call somebody from the outside. We've worked with Dahlgren before. And he was the only person who picked up the phone on a Saturday afternoon and said he'd be here in two hours."

The trooper glanced at Dahlgren's dive bag. A pager was clipped to an outside pocket and its red light was blinking.

"The storm is easing up," the driver said as he lifted the lid of a blue Coleman cooler and withdrew a can of Sam's Club cola. "Want one?"

"I don't know how you can drink that stuff when it's so cold and wet," said the trooper. "And this storm isn't letting up. We'll be lucky if we have dry weather by Monday."

Several yards off the stern, there was a scald of bubbles and Dahlgren broke the surface. He coughed, inflated his wings to get his mouth and nose out of the water, then jerked off his mask and washed his forehead with lake water to clear away the blood.

"Jesus," the trooper said.

47

Dahlgren rolled on his back and kicked his way over to the boat. The waves threw him against the stern three times before he could finally grasp the ladder. Instead of hauling himself up, however, he thrust the VTR upward.

"Take it," Dahlgren gasped. "Throw it in a bucket of water. I don't have an evidence tube big enough for it."

The trooper snatched up the recorder and handed it off.

"No bucket," the driver said, holding the unit uncertainly.

"Goddammit," the trooper muttered. He turned, grabbed the cooler by both handles, and turned it upside down, emptying the ice and soft drinks into the lake. Then he scooped it full of water, placed the recorder inside, and closed and latched the lid.

"Some help?" Dahlgren called. Exhausted, he was hanging on to the ladder with one hand, his Rocket Fins looped by the straps over his wrist.

The trooper returned, reached down for the fins, then grabbed the chrome valve of Dahlgren's tank and pulled him up the ladder and into the boat. Standing shakily, Dahlgren pulled the quick-release buckle and slid out of the harness and steel backpack with its attached tank, regulator, and wings.

Dahlgren looked ill. The front of his wet suit was torn, blood ran down his face from a scalp wound, and his hands were an alarming shade of blue.

"God, I hate storms," he said.

"That's a pretty nasty cut," the trooper said. "Sure you're okay?"

Dahlgren stared at him incredulously.

"Do I fucking *look* okay?"

"You look worse than you really are," the trooper said, indicating bits of brain and bone on the front of his wet suit. "At least, I'm assuming those are pieces of Harry and not of you."

Dahlgren picked at some of the pinkish gray matter, considered flicking it overboard, and finally placed it in an evidence bag.

Suddenly, his stomach seemed to turn inside out. He lurched toward the gunwale and vomited so violently over the side that it felt as if somebody had hit him in the nuts. He purged his stomach until there was nothing left to bring up. Finally, he turned and lay heavily against the boat cushions, helpless to the pain that radiated from his testicles.

"Decompression sickness?" the trooper asked.

"Seasick," Dahlgren managed to say. "I'm not bent." But the tinge in his gut said *maybe*. Not only did he push the limits, but the dive was cold and strenuous. The pain was starting to ease. How close had he come to rupturing himself as well? "I did my stops, hanging against the bluff. Just need somebody to close this damn cut on my forehead."

The trooper nodded and keyed the microphone that was clipped to the collar beneath his slicker. There was a squawk, then a dispatcher asked if he had traffic.

"Request EMTs meet us at the Kimberling City marina," he said. "Our diver has suffered what appears to be minor injuries, but I'd like him checked out. Also, please relay to Jefferson City that we have secured the package."

The rain had slacked off from a torrent to a steady drumming on the tin roof of the marina by the time the water patrol boat pulled into a slip. A pair of troopers were waiting, and they received the cooler with the video recorder and hustled it off the dock, toward a waiting car.

While Dahlgren waited for the others to tie up, he sprawled against the cushions and held a hand rightly against his forehead, trying to staunch the flow of blood. Somewhere on the dock a transistor radio was playing, and Dahlgren could just make out church bells in the distinctive jingle of the radio station.

"Christian radio for the Ozarks," the male announcer said smoothly. "Next up on KOBZ is *Lifeline* with Jolene Carter. Jolene has the answers you've been looking for, friends. Why not call in?"

Dahlgren closed his eyes as he listened to the jockey give the toll-free number. If his cell phone were handy, and if his head didn't hurt so badly, he would have been tempted to call in and ask where he could find a cigarette and get laid, in that order.

"You must be the diver," a female voice said.

Dahlgren opened his eyes.

The EMT was an athletic-looking woman in her late twenties with short blond hair and, despite the rain, a crisp uniform. She held a tackle box of medical supplies in one hand. Dahlgren got to his feet, then lurched against the gunwale.

"Hold it," she said. She put down the tackle box, stepped into the boat, and helped him up onto the dock. "Sit down, there on that bucket."

Dahlgren sat while she opened her kit.

"Got a cigarette?" Dahlgren asked.

"Sorry, I don't smoke," she said while she flicked a penlight in both eyes. "And neither should you."

"Been trying to quit," Dahlgren said.

"What's your name?"

"Richard Dahlgren. What's yours?"

"Hope," she said. "Have you been breathing compressed air, Mr. Dahlgren?"

"I'm not bent," Dahlgren said. "I've been bent in the past, badly, and I know what it feels like. I *am* bleeding, however, my head is killing me, and I'm cold."

"Not exactly the strong, silent type, are you?"

She pulled his hand away from his scalp, made a face, and caught a rivulet of blood in a square of gauze.

"You need stitches and a tetanus shot," she said.

"Okay, but only if you give it to me," Dahlgren said.

"Are you disoriented or just stupid?" she asked.

But she was smiling.

"Come on, we're taking you to the emergency department to get stitched up," she said. "Any other problems we ought to know about?"

"Yeah," Dahlgren said. "My clients are dead people."

Five

At 141 feet, in a subterranean lake of near-freezing water, Loren McAfee turned and pulled the doorknob of a machine shed.

And the door was stuck.

It was attached to a shack of corrugated metal, and although it had been submerged for decades, the water had done little except create a fine web of cracks in the industrial-gray paint of the door's surface.

McAfee payed out the yellow nylon safety line from the reel at his belt to have some room to work and gave one last tug on the handle, but the door remained closed. He had already marked the depth and location of the shack in grease pencil on his slate, and behind him hovered Claire and Staci, idly brushing the roof and sides of the mine shack with their dive lights.

McAfee considered leaving the door shut—after all, there were half a dozen shacks on this slope, and most of them contained nothing except rusting tools. It used to be exciting to find anything, and every helmet and dinner plate had seemed a treasure, but the novelty had soon worn thin.

McAfee unsheathed the dive knife that was cable-tied upside down to the harness of his rebreather, and drove the four-inch blade with the blunt tip between the door and the jamb. The door popped free, and McAfee grasped the knob with a gloved hand and tugged.

Propelled by the suction of the opening door, an angel floated out of the shack.

McAfee dropped the slate and grease pencil and stared at the figure that drifted above him.

Her arms were outstretched, as if in supplication, and her body was alabaster marbled with the faintest shades of blue. Her lips and nipples and bare genitals were darker. Her glossy red hair flowed about her like a wreath, her unseeing eyes were open, and the whites of her eyes had turned a pale shade of blue. She couldn't have been more than twenty, but her expression was one of unearthly wisdom and earthly longing.

Six

Inside the cramped control booth of KOBZ on the campus of Ozark Bible College in Springfield, Missouri, Jolene Carter adjusted her headphones, leaned forward on her elbows, and whispered into the microphone.

"It's 6:23 P.M. on a stormy Saturday night," she said, "and you're listening to KOBZ, noncommercial Christian radio for the Ozarks."

She paused, brushed her straight blond hair from her eyes, and continued. A small gold cross on a delicate chain swayed between her sweatered breasts.

"This is *Lifeline*, and tonight our call-in show is about storms," she said. "Christ calmed the waters of Galilee, and no matter what kind of storm you are experiencing in your personal life, He is the answer. Call in, please. Let Him help."

The multiline phone in front of her lit up.

Jolene selected the first blinking button and pushed it.

"You're on the air with *Lifeline*."

"Hello, Jolene?" a quavering young voice inquired. "My name is Beth. I'm twelve."

"Hi, Beth," Jolene said. "What's your problem?"

A pause.

"Beth?"

The phone line was on a five-second tape delay before it went over the air, and Jolene was reaching for the kill button when the girl answered.

"Our pastor said that Halloween is evil," she said. "Those kids that shot the others at that school in Colorado—our pastor says videos and role-playing games caused that. You know, pretending to be something you're not. Like Halloween."

"Beth," Jolene said. "I can certainly understand your pastor's concern. But I can also see the fix you're in. Halloween is tomorrow night."

"*Exactly*," Beth said, brightening. "My best friend is having a costume party."

Jolene paused and inched closer to the microphone.

"Listen carefully, Beth," Jolene said slowly. "The real question is not whether it's okay to have fun, but whether we unknowingly invite evil to come into our lives."

"Oh-*kay*," Beth said.

"This is a real problem for Christians, even when we have the best of intentions," Jolene said. "It's not just about whether to go to your best friend's Halloween party. It's about reading your horoscope in the morning newspaper, the urge to call the psychic hot line you saw on television, that Ouija board in the hall closet . . ."

"So that means I can't go?"

"You have free will, Beth. That's one of the marvelous gifts the Lord gave to us. But he also gave you brains, and I think you can figure this one out on your own."

"But I wanted to be Harry Potter."

"It's your choice, Beth," Jolene said. "Just promise me you'll think about our talk tonight, especially the part about inviting evil into your life. You wouldn't want that, would you?"

"Harry Potter *fights* evil," Beth protested.

Seven

The stewardess inched the beverage cart down the aisle, handing out drinks in plastic cups wrapped with paper napkins, asking for correct change. Only about half of the seats were filled, the cabin was dark, and most of the passengers were asleep.

"We'll be arriving in New York in less than an hour, gentlemen," the stewardess said softly with a British accent. "Is there anything I can get either of you?"

"I'll settle for another cocktail," the younger man in the aisle seat said. He was in his mid-thirties, had a short business haircut, and wore a tie loosened at the collar. The middle seat was empty, but in the window seat was an older man, perhaps in his late fifties, who was looking reflectively out the window at the full moon over the Atlantic.

"Seven and seven, right?" the stewardess asked.

"No obvious organic dysfunction," the man noted.

"Pardon?"

"Nothing," the man said. "You have a good memory."

"Thanks," the stewardess said. "I think."

He took the drink and placed it carefully on his tray table while the stewardess looked expectantly at the occupant of the window seat.

"Jake?" the younger man asked. "Hey, Jakob."

The older man shook his head, then stuttered: "No, thanks."

The stewardess unconsciously bit her lower lip in response to the older man's stuttering, then smiled brightly.

"Did you have a good trip?" she asked, wanting to linger.

"Christ," the younger man said. "English pathologists are even more boring than their American cousins."

"You gents work together?" she asked, attempting to prolong the conversation.

"Yes, we're colleagues. We practice at—"

"St. Louis," the stewardess said. "Oh, I know where Dr. Geiger is from, all right. It says right on the back of his book."

"Ah, there it is," the younger man said. "I'm Frank Smith, Dr. Geiger's assistant."

"Charmed," the stewardess said. She knelt and retrieved a book from the bottom of the beverage cart.

"Do you think he would mind awfully?" she asked.

"I'm sure it would be Jakob's distinct pleasure," the assistant said, taking the hardcover book. The title was emblazoned in red on a black background: *Silent Witness: The Story of Forensic Science*. Beneath, the subtitle was a come-hither whisper: *Join the hunt for history's worst serial killers*.

Geiger had been listening to the exchange. He already had donned his half-rim bifocals and uncapped a black Cross gel pen. As he took the book, he looked questioningly over the glasses at the stewardess.

"Who should he make it out to?" the assistant asked.

"Amber," the stewardess said. "Oh, my mother will be so jealous."

While Geiger turned his attention to writing another one

of the thousands of meaningless inscriptions he had penned in the two years since the book's release—*To Amber, with my sincere hope that you never cross my examining table, J. Geiger*—the assistant finished the drink and asked for another.

"Say, Amber. Do you lay over?"

"You're horrible," she said, and laughed.

"Let me guess," the assistant ventured. "You're named after *Forever Amber?*"

"How did you know?" the stewardess gushed.

"Just a feeling," Smith said.

"You know she was just sixteen when she wrote that book," Amber said.

"You don't say," Smith said, not bothering to correct her. Kathleen Winsor was twenty when she began the book that was the mother of all bodice rippers. "Tell me, what do women find attractive about serial killers? I've been with Jakob at a dozen book signings in the past couple of years, and while he has plenty of male readers, they don't seem to . . ."

"To what?" Amber asked.

"To get the same look in their eyes as the women," Smith said. "They look interested, yes, and they like the stories that Jakob writes about. But with the women, it's as if they're reading stories about *romance* instead of factual accounts of crimes that turned the stomachs of even the most hardened cops."

"I'm not sure I know what you're getting at."

"Never mind," Smith said. "Not important."

"I just like the stories," Amber said defensively. "And when Dr. Geiger writes, he is so smooth that it's like he's sitting across from you. And the introduction, when he described how he never saw his parents again—it took my breath away."

"Didn't know he stuttered?" Smith asked.

"No," Amber said.

"That's why he writes," Smith said. "Or at least, that's what he claims, because you don't stutter when you're writing. It's rather like singing. Also, it's one of the markers that profilers use to identify serial killers."

Amber's eyes widened.

"Not that every stutterer will become a killer, but it is somehow linked to that predisposition. Somewhat like the so-called serial killer triad of fire-starting, bed-wetting, and cruelty to animals."

"I just wanted an autograph," Amber said weakly.

Geiger gave Smith a sidelong glance. Then he smiled, closed the book, and handed it directly to the stewardess.

"Enjoy," Smith said.

It was a moment before Amber took the book. The cover was facing down, and Geiger found himself staring into the photograph on the back of the dust jacket: the author as a nine-year-old boy in short pants, standing with his thirty-something parents in a jungle setting. The parents are standing behind Jakob. The strong father is clutching a Bible; the handsome mother has her arms around both of them. The parents are smiling, but not Jakob.

"What does Geiger mean?" Amber asked as she tucked the book back into the cart.

"Pardon?" Smith asked.

"His name. What does it mean?"

Geiger mimed playing a violin.

"Fiddler," Smith said. "It's German for fiddler."

The beverage cart rattled as the stewardess proceeded.

Geiger returned to the window and the waxing moon beyond. Jet flight always felt somewhat surreal to him, and having signed the book in the dark and humming confines of the airline cabin amid Smith's libidinous, slightly drunk, and inane patter caused his mind to drift. With his body suspended between heaven and earth, Geiger allowed his consciousness to peel back the years, to the River of Doubt, in the Amazon Basin, during Christmas week of 1954. The colors in his mind were those of aged Kodachrome, particularly the blood, and the story that unwound in his memory was not one that was included in the introduction to his book.

The camp was in shambles.

The hut where they had been living for the past month was a smoldering pile of embers and ash. The shortwave transceiver had apparently been tossed through the doorway of the hut, then beaten with staves as it lay in the mud, beaten in the way you would beat an animal that deserved to be killed; the radio's gray metal cabinet was dented and dimpled, and the delicate vacuum tubes that his father had packed and unpacked so carefully during the journey down the river were now bits of glass and wire in the mud.

The twentieth century now seemed impossibly remote.

The heavy wooden picnic table had been overturned, the food looted, clothes were scattered across the clearing, and Bibles were flung everywhere. Their onionskin pages fluttered in the breeze, creating a sound that reminded Jakob of the wind in the trees back home in Missouri.

Amid pages from the dozens of "gift" Bibles were bigger and more substantial pages, immediately recognizable to Jakob, because they were from the only other books the family had taken: *Bulfinch's Mythology* and *Gray's Anatomy*. Homesick, Jakob had spent hours with each of the books. Both transported him out of the jungle to places that were safer and more familiar, in stories that were old before the birth of Christ, or in the anatomy he shared in common with every other human being.

Now the wind was mingling all of the pages together.

His father's body lay in the center of the camp. Jakob tried not to look at it, but he could not help himself. The blood seemed almost too red. A spear had been thrust with great force into his father's mouth, breaking his teeth and dislocating his jaw, and passing through the back of the neck to pin him to the earth. The wound, which had been delivered long before his death, was symbolic. The father had been telling lies.

Later, almost as an afterthought, the father's brains had been dashed out with one of the staves that had been used on the radio.

Jakob and his mother were kneeling in the center of the camp, their heads down, attempting to relieve the pressure on the cord that went around their necks to their hands, which were tucked beneath their knees. The cord was much too short to allow their hands to move up behind their backs or down under their feet. The only position, in fact, that the cord allowed at all was the hunched posture they both had assumed, and even then the cord bit deeply into the backs of their necks.

Jakob could see the blood running down his mother's bare back, and felt it run down his own.

Both of them were nude, although they were covered in so much mud and filth that it hardly seemed like nudity to Jakob. He had seen his mother's breasts before. She had not been a particularly modest woman, and Jakob—after reading of Oedipus in Bulfinch's—had sometimes wondered if she had meant at times for him to see her body.

"Are they going to martyr us as well?" Jakob asked.

His mother could not talk, however, because her mouth was gagged with her underwear, held in place by a bit of rough twine. Her eyes, however, were answer enough. They went wide with terror, and then she squeezed them tightly shut, tears spilling down her cheeks.

"I suppose they must," Jakob concluded. "Our Father, who art in heaven. Hallowed be Thy name. Give us this day our daily bread, and forgive us our trespasses, as we forgive those who—"

Jakob stopped.

"Those who . . ."

Strangely, he could not recall the rest.

Just before he lost consciousness, a strange calm settled over Jakob, and he left his body and hovered over the scene of carnage and destruction. Dispassionately, he could see himself alongside his mother in the mud, and the smoke curling from the remains of the hut, and his father's body. It was late in the afternoon, and he could see the setting sun perched on the rim of the jungle, and how it turned the river into a finger of molten gold tracing a path through the rain forest.

He remembered how his father had carefully explained to him that morning how the coming night would be the longest night of the year back home, that it was the winter solstice in Missouri and the rest of the Northern Hemisphere, and of course it was also Christmas week. Below the equator here in the Southern Hemisphere, his father had patiently explained, it was the shortest night of the year, and the beginning of summer. His father had laughed when Jakob asked why it was still Christmas in the rain forest, when it wasn't even winter.

When Jakob returned to his body, he was stumbling down a muddy path through the jungle. It was raining, and seconds after the lightning would flash, he could feel the thunder shaking the ground and coming up through the soles of his feet.

The cord had been removed from his neck, but his hands remained tightly bound behind his back. His mother was in front of him, her bare feet sliding in the clay. Mud was smeared across her thighs and buttocks, marking the times she had fallen, unable to use her hands to catch herself.

It was full night now, and to Jakob their captors were dark and threatening figures with spears and arrows. It was easy to imagine they had stepped out of the book of Hieronymous Bosch paintings that had so fascinated him in elementary school. Every day after school, he would go to the free library, select an oversized book from the arts section, and sit quietly near the heavy oak-and-marble hearth in the reading room. From his seat, he could hear time passing in the ticking of the grandfather clock that stood, sphinxlike, just inside the library entrance. The librarian had told him the clock was from England and was nearly three hundred years old. She had worried about his choice in picture books, but because Jakob was bright and well-mannered, she allowed him to choose for himself.

Bosch had frightened him, but others—especially the paintings by Rossetti and his Pre-Raphaelite brothers, and later works by Waterhouse and the others—induced a near-religious ecstasy. The works had a curious dreamlike quality, and the depictions of nude women in classical poses excited Jakob.

The architecture of the library itself contributed to the effect, and the Beaux Arts building of smooth Bedford limestone seemed to belong in the paintings he loved so much. He would not have been surprised, one afternoon when the October wind was chasing the fallen leaves, to find Persephone or Circe or the melancholy Lady of Shalott beckoning from between the cool limestone columns beneath the library's pediment.

Jakob was thinking about Bosch when lightning split the top of a nearby Jatoba tree, which projected beyond the canopy of the rain forest. The bolt sizzled down the branches right to the roots of the old tree and left the resin in the trunk sizzling and giving off the distinctive earthy aroma of copal.

The flash illuminated the faces of his tormentors, and they were more terrifying than anything he had perused in the reading room of the Bonne Terre Memorial Library. Their thick moplike hair was smeared with some reddish substance, their eyes were glassy in the way he had seen with some of the tribes that habitually chewed coca leaves, and their expressions were grim.

The lightning strike seemed to have unnerved them.

These Indians were unlike any of those that he and his parents had encountered on their journey down the River of

Doubt. They did not wear cast-off T-shirts and baseball caps, and they did not beg for cigarettes or whiskey. Instead, they had swept out of the jungle as the wind sweeps through the trees, and they had not said a word as they set about their task of bloodshed and destruction.

Jakob wondered if they were the Viejos, the old ones, the tribe that his parents whispered about late at night when they thought he was asleep. The Viejos were the ones that the Europeans could never reach, the tribe that went deeper into the jungle as white civilization advanced, the people that resisted all attempts at Christian conversion and, it was rumored, still worshiped the old gods with human sacrifice. His father had said it all was nonsense, but his mother had not seemed so sure.

The path led to a cave, and just inside the entrance his mother slipped again. She fell heavily in the mud, then got her feet beneath her and rose, and as she did the lightning flashed again, burning the image deep into Jakob's soul: his thirty-two-year-old mother standing defiant, long blond hair plastered against her breasts, her pale skin shining with rain in the places where it wasn't smeared with mud. Her blue eyes were clear and her face was calm. He had seen the expression before, in Draper's *The Gates of Dawn*. Then darkness engulfed them once more, and Jakob and his mother were jerked into the interior of the cave.

Torches blazed just inside the entrance, and the guards proceeded single-file into the cave, with Jakob and his mother in the middle. The first room was cavernous, and although the firelight failed to illuminate much of it, Jakob knew it was big from the time it took the echo of their bare feet slapping on the clay floor to return. A few dozen yards later and the passage began to narrow and lead downward, and the ceiling was smudged black. By torchlight Jakob could see petroglyphs on the walls, of snakes and spiders and clockwise spirals.

The passage became narrower as it went deeper into the

earth. They freed their hands. Jakob found himself turning sideways or sometimes crawling in order to follow. Rocks flailed at his palms and elbows, his knees and shins, and his blood mixed with mud and stones. When he thought he could go no farther, he heard the sound of distant chanting and his nose twitched at some acrid scent.

The passage gave way to a room that was nearly as big as the one at the cave entrance, and things glistened and flashed in his peripheral vision. Jakob could hear the sound of lapping water. The floor sloped downward and became sand instead of mud, and he and his mother were led to the edge of an underground lake. At the edge of the water was a jumble of stone slabs the size of automobiles, and covering the surface of these stones were row upon row of calcite-encrusted human skulls, minus the mandibles. Jakob knew something about caves from his reading, such as how slowly stalactites and stalagmites formed. How long must these skulls have been undisturbed to become so heavily encrusted with calcite from the slow drip of cave water from the ceiling? Jakob asked himself. A hundred years? A thousand? As they neared the edge of the gin-clear lake, Jakob looked down. The bottom was littered with hundreds of human jawbones.

Jakob had not noticed the red figure perched atop a half-submerged slab, and when it jumped down onto the water in front of his mother, it seemed to Jakob as if he had appeared from the darkness. This was obviously an important member of the Viejo tribe. Not a chief, Jakob knew, but some kind of priest or shaman. He was nude, except for a codpiece that hung by a leather thong around his waist. All of the hair had been shaved from his body. He was also completely covered in a pigment made from cinnabar, which gave him a shining red skin.

"What's that smell?" Jakob asked.

"Sulfur," his mother said.

The warriors behind them pushed them forward and they

fell into the shin-deep water. They allowed Jakob to stand, but they forced his mother back to her knees in the water before the shaman, who reached out and placed his hands on the mother's breasts, not in a groping fashion, but with palms flat and fingers splayed. When he withdrew, two red handprints were left.

Jakob felt an odd sensation in the bottom of his stomach. His face burned with shame when he realized his penis was stiffening.

He glanced away.

"Jakob, listen carefully," she said. "Whatever they do, it is done merely to our bodies. Not our souls."

Jakob nodded.

The shaman took a wooden bowl from one of the others, dabbed a cloth in it, and was painting her face blue. Years later, Jakob would learn that in the timeless world of the Viejos, blue was the color of sacrifice.

"You must forgive them," she said. "They know not what they do."

The shaman dabbed a cloth in another bowl and smeared the same red pigment he wore over Jakob's chest.

"We're in God's hands," she said.

The shaman took a gourd from one of the others and pressed it to her lips. She refused, turning her head. Two of the warriors stepped forward, forced her head back, and pried open her jaw with their fingers.

The others held Jakob back.

The shaman poured the liquid down her throat, then clamped a red hand over her nose and mouth. Her eyes widened, and she gasped and coughed, then finally swallowed. The shaman removed his hand, leaving a red print across her lower face.

The two holding her released her, and she slumped to the ground, savagely wiping her mouth with the back of her hand. The shaman sat on his haunches beside her, watching her closely. In his right hand was a flint knife, its faceted blade shining in the torchlight.

The handle was smeared with red.

The shaman leaned close to her, so close that his lips were nearly touching her ear, and he asked a question. Jakob didn't understand the language, but he knew it was a question from the expectant look and the tone of the shaman's voice.

His mother was silent.

The shaman draped his right arm around her shoulders and drew the edge of the dark stone knife across her throat. She did not flinch. Blood welled in the line drawn by the knife, then spilled down her throat and over her breasts and stomach.

"Doctor?"

Geiger flinched, feeling the knife on his shoulder.

"Sorry," Amber said.

She quickly withdrew her hand.

Geiger managed a smile.

Smith was asleep, and the stewardess was leaning over him, speaking softly.

"The captain has illuminated the seat belt sign," she said apologetically. "We're on final approach. Do you mind?"

Eight

Dahlgren sprawled carelessly on the rumpled polyester quilt covering the double bed in room 107 of the Mozarks Resort Motel, on Highway 76 just outside Branson. He was drinking Jack Daniel's from a quart Nalgene bottle filled with tiny motel ice cubes and mixed with Coca-Cola he had gotten from a vending machine next to the ice maker. The clear blue bottle with the black plastic lid was so scuffed that it looked as if it had been rolling around in the backs of Jeeps, aircraft, and kayaks for the past couple of years, which it had.

Dahlgren was stripped down to a black T-shirt and a pair of blue capilene boxers printed in a wave pattern. The cut on his scalp had been stitched up, and he was watching the local news on an ancient color television bolted to a wall covered with thirty-year-old wood paneling.

On television, a young dark-headed reporter was standing in the rain near the Highway 13 bridge. In the background, Dahlgren caught a glimpse of his Helio coming in low over the lake.

The sound of running water from the tub in the tile bathroom was competing with the audio from the television. Dahlgren searched for the remote before realizing there wasn't one. More than a little drunk, he crawled to the edge of the bed, stood unsteadily, and turned the volume knob a few degrees clockwise.

The scene changed, and the reporter was back at the desk in the studio, talking with the middle-aged male anchor.

"We understand a suspect has been taken into custody," she said, "after the Missouri Highway Patrol obtained an arrest warrant for this man: forty-three-year-old Benjamin Sharps, a self-proclaimed white supremacist with a long felony record of gun violations."

A mug shot of the feral-looking Sharps was flashed on the screen. The sound of water from the bathroom stopped with the squeak of a faucet and a throb of pipes.

"The recovery of the videotape from the trunk of the submerged patrol car has given authorities a graphic and chilling record of what happened earlier today on the bridge across Table Rock Lake at Kimberling City," the reporter said breathlessly.

The television cut to a view from the interior of the patrol car, with the date and the time in digital numbers beneath. The windshield was streaked with rain and the camera's focus seemed soft, but the back of a black Ford van was clearly visible—as was the Arkansas tag number.

"The Missouri Highway Patrol has released this portion of the video, taken from a camera mounted in the windshield of the car driven by Trooper Combs."

The back door of the van burst open and Sharps bounded out, the AK-47 at the ready. Then the tape went to snow.

"Dana, am I correct in assuming that there is more video?" the anchor asked. "It doesn't end there, does it?"

"No, it unfortunately does not end there," Dana said. "But that's all the highway patrol believed they could release, out of respect for the trooper's family. A patrol spokesman from Jefferson City told me just about an hour ago that the reason they released any of the video was because Sharps was still at large. As you can see from the video, he looked quite a bit different than his last mug shot."

"The beard," the anchor said, his head bobbing.

"The patrol spokesman said this video—which, if you've been tuned in to Color Three this evening, you know has been airing near continuously—was instrumental in apprehending the suspect, who was found trying to buy black hair dye at a convenience store in Gateway, Arkansas."

"Amazing," the anchor gushed.

The reporter faced the camera and began to read her summary from the TelePrompTer.

"Authorities are stopping short of calling this a hate crime, but they have identified the van as being registered to a right-wing 'Identity Christian' organization known as the Sword of God, which has a compound on the shore of Bull Shoals Lake in Arkansas," Dana said conversationally. "The organization has a history of spreading racist propaganda, and has long predicted—some say urged—the coming of a race war."

The television cut to a scene of Sharps, surrounded by a dozen state and federal lawmen, shuffling his way in shackles and an orange jumpsuit toward the inmate entrance to the Greene County Jail at Springfield. Sharps grimaced as he neared the camera's point of view.

"This is the end time of American society," Sharps ranted. "Parents will eat their children, Muslims will kill white Christians, witches and Satanic Jews will offer human sacrifices to their gods."

"Keep moving," a black man in a blue windbreaker with ATF on the back in yellow block letters said, pulling him away from the reporters.

"Blacks will rape white women," Sharps shouted over his shoulder. "Homosexuals will sodomize whomever they can. . . ."

71

Another cut, and this time it was a shot of the water patrol boat rocking on the waves, and the trooper reaching down to help Dahlgren into it.

"The crucial videotape was recovered from the submerged patrol car by expert diver Dick Dahlgren," the reporter said.

Dahlgren moaned.

"Authorities told Color Three News that Dahlgren may be the country's only private underwater accident and crime-scene investigator," the reporter said. "According to some Internet scuba sites, Dahlgren was also a pioneering cave diver, but dropped out of that extreme sport in the middle nineties. And ironic as it may seem, he is apparently based out of a small town in Kansas."

Unsteadily, Dahlgren stood again and twisted the volume knob until Dana Casteel's image vanished into a glowing white dot in the center of the screen.

"Don't call me Dick," he said.

The door of the bathroom swung open and Hope, the EMT from the dock, came out wrapped in a thin motel bath towel.

"Now, why would I call you that?" she asked.

"They did, on the news," Dahlgren complained.

Hope hovered over him.

"Congratulations," she said.

"For what?"

"You helped catch a cop killer," she said. She kissed him on the ear. "You're a hero."

"It's not like I save anybody," Dahlgren said. "My clients are beyond help. Hey, did I ask you if you had a cigarette?"

"I still don't smoke," she said. "And you quit today, remember? Also, you shouldn't be drinking on the Percocet they gave you at the emergency department."

"It's just to help me sleep."

"You'll end up in a coma."

"I spend my life in a coma."

Hope let the towel drop.

Dahlgren pulled her onto his lap and kissed her hard on the mouth. She grabbed his T-shirt and pulled it off over his head. Although the skin on his face and his arms was deeply tanned, the rest of his body was pale. Old scars covered his stomach and left side. There were also a couple of fresh blue-black bruises on his right arm and shoulder and upper arm.

"You're all beat up," Hope said.

"And that's just on the outside."

"Is your work that hazardous?"

"Not ordinarily," Dahlgren said, wincing as she touched the bruises on his arm. "Today was an exception. The scars are nine years old, from when I was young and stupid."

"You're wiser now?" Hope asked.

"No, just older."

"Nice underwear," she said, feeling his boxers. "I've never seen any like this."

"Expensive, but worth it," he said. "It's part of my personal style I call 'Expedition Modern.' The central piece of art in my living room back home is a sea kayak hanging from the ceiling, and my furniture consists of camp chairs."

"You're obviously not married," Hope said.

"Obviously."

"What's this?"

Hope touched a finger to a teardrop-shaped stone that Dahlgren wore from a black cord around his neck. The stone was green but streaked with brown and yellow, and it reminded Hope of looking into a human iris.

"It's incredibly beautiful," she said.

"A dive buddy gave me that a long time ago," Dahlgren said carefully. "It's Aztec jade. Supposed to protect you, like a meso-American St. Christopher's medal."

"Does it work?" Hope asked.

"I don't know," Dahlgren said. "Taylor gave it to me in Mexico."

"Where's your friend now?" Hope asked.

Dahlgren drained the Jack and Coke.

"Gone," he said.

"Gone?" Hope asked. "You mean as in away, or . . ."

"As in dead," Dahlgren said. "Look, you're a nice girl, and I appreciate your concern, but this is something I really don't want to talk about. In fact, the last thing I want to do right now is talk, so if you don't mind, I want to engage in a relatively common human activity that, given your considerable charms, will render me, for a time at least, speechless."

Nine

The black Crown Victoria glided between the semis and the RVs in the parking area in the westbound side of Interstate 44 near Conway, Missouri. It was dark, and raining. Beads of water shimmied on the Vic's freshly waxed hood.

The car slowed near a bronze marker with a square cement base that proclaimed this stretch of road a "Blue Star Memorial Highway." The marker had been erected decades before by a garden club in honor of World War II vets, but somebody still cared enough to keep the marker polished and the big five-pointed star on top painted a bright baby blue.

The teenaged girls who were sitting at the base of the monument, Geiger thought, probably could make no connection with the words on the plaque. Not only were they unlikely to know anyone who had fought in that long-ago war, they probably had only the dimmest notion of what the sides were, or who had won.

Geiger lowered the passenger's window to get a better look. They were dressed inappropriately for the season, their light jackets were unbuttoned, and their jeans rode low on their hips, revealing too much skin for their ages. One was tall and thin, with blond hair, and the other was shorter, but not fat, and dark. Their hair was matted with rain, but they seemed not to mind. They were passing a rubber Halloween mask between them, taking turns posing, and although the mask was obviously a caricature, at this distance Geiger could not place who was being satirized.

"DARE," the dark-haired girl said through the mask while jabbing a finger at the other, "to keep your president off Peruvian blue flake."

Both collapsed with laughter.

"Ah," Geiger said in recognition.

The NPR station Geiger had listened to for the last hour was breaking up badly, so he reached down and gently touched a fingertip to the scan button. The green digital display cycled through a handful of frequencies before finally locking on 97.7.

". . . a beautiful but rainy Halloween night here in the Ozarks," a young woman said. "This is *Lifeline*. You've found Jolene, or perhaps we've found each other."

Geiger was listening attentively.

The girls sitting at the base of the monument had noticed the big black car with the lowered passenger's window. They had stopped their play and were peering into the interior.

"For the next two hours we're going to field calls and ponder questions about life, love, death, and God's plan for us," Jolene Carter said soothingly. "The number is 1-417-FOR-KOBZ. That's a long-distance call for those of you outside of Springfield, Missouri, so if you're under eighteen, be sure to get permission first."

Geiger smiled.

"Hey, you freak," the short, dark-haired girl said as she removed the Halloween mask and glared. The other girl extended a middle finger while Geiger nudged the accelerator and the Crown Vic surged forward, toward the ramp leading back to the interstate. The headlights brushed a road sign that said SPRINGFIELD 35.

Ten

Behind the locked red door of Triton Investigations, in the north end of hangar A at Atkinson Municipal Airport at Pittsburg, Kansas, a phone was ringing. It was eight o'clock on Friday morning.

The sound of the unanswered phone echoed from the hangar's high ceiling and, to twenty-six-year-old Starla Dwyer, who waited with her shoulder blades pressed against the unyielding door while clutching a manila file folder, it was an appropriate score to the feeling of helplessness building in her chest.

Starla winced at the shrill whine of an air wrench. A mechanic was working on the engine of one of the light planes in the hangar. He was a large, bearded man with fists the size of mallets, wearing blue work coveralls with his name in script in an oval over his left breast, and he seemed particularly protective of the red door.

"Richard Dahlgren can be a hard man to catch, if that's who you're looking for," the mechanic said as he changed sockets on the air ratchet. "It would be best if you called ahead to make an appointment."

Starla smiled politely and thanked him, but told Bruno— *that is the name on the jacket, isn't it?*—that she would wait because she had driven a long way. That much at least was true. She had gotten up hours before dawn, showered and dried her long brown hair and squeezed into her best green dress, and hit the road to make Pittsburg, Kansas, by the start of the business day.

"You may be waiting all day," Bruno said, and he stared at her a long moment. She became suddenly aware of the green dress. Starla wasn't beautiful, but she knew she could fill out a dress, and she never wore a bra.

She smiled at the mechanic, and he looked away.

"Suit yourself," he said from beneath the engine cowl, and the scream of the air wrench continued.

The response frustrated her, but how could she explain to this stranger that she had worn this dress to make Dahlgren like her, to make him acknowledge her as a person, to make it harder for him to say no? It was easy to dismiss people over the telephone, to wash your hands and never think of them again, and that's why she had to have a face-to-face meeting, to make him look her in the eye—to look at the dress, perhaps— if he was going to turn her down.

No, she decided, she would not leave and make an appointment for later. She had already waited an hour, and she would wait all day if necessary.

But the ringing phone made the waiting worse, and it seemed to ring forever. She involuntarily found herself counting the rings, and on the seventh ring after she began counting she was surprised to hear the sharp beep of an answering machine.

"This is Triton Investigations," she heard the prerecorded message say. "Leave your name and I'll get back to you. If this is an emergency, you can reach me twenty-four hours a day by paging—"

Then the air ratchet started again and Starla had to press her ear to the red door to hear the number.

"—0700, star 357."

Starla repeated the last four digits of the number and the code to herself as she dug in her purse to find a couple of quarters. There was a pay phone on the wall between the detective agency and the aircraft repair service. A pager message was by its very nature brief—and one-way—and she could just ask him to meet her at the hangar. She hadn't caught the prefix for the number, but it was likely to be the same as the number painted on the sign over the door. She had dropped the quarters into the phone and begun to dial when she heard footsteps ringing on the hard concrete floor.

It was a man, in his late thirties, wearing sunglasses and carrying keys in one hand and a black flight bag in the other. As he approached the red door Starla noted his clean but faded denims and tan cowboy boots, although he wore a blue work shirt and navy tie, and for a moment she was unsure. She had expected another suit in what had become a quest amid a long procession of suits.

Starla banged down the receiver and the unused quarters dropped noisily into the coin-return box. She scooped up the coins, put on her best grin, and turned toward the man who was now unlocking the red door.

"I'm Starla Dwyer," she said, extending her hand. "You must be Mr. Dahlgren?"

"That was my father," he said as the door swung open.

"Oh. Will he be in later? I've been waiting here for more than an hour to see him."

"No, I meant that nobody calls me 'mister' around here," he explained. "I'm Richard Dahlgren, and I own the agency. I'm sorry you had to wait so long, but we don't get much walk-in traffic here. Most people call—"

The air wrench drowned out the words, and he motioned for her to step into the office so they could talk. Dahlgren flipped on the room light and swept a pile of newspapers, dive magazines, and *Penthouses* from one of the chairs facing the broad metal desk. A buoyancy compensator jacket and an octopus rig of regulators, gauges, and hoses were draped over the other chair. The surface of the desk was covered with books, papers, and styrofoam coffee cups.

The pager on his belt went off as Dahlgren took a seat behind the desk. A scratchy message asked him to contact Captain Walker with the Missouri Highway Patrol in Jefferson City ASAP.

"Forgive the mess, but I haven't been able to spend much time on cleanup lately," he said. "Excuse me while I make a phone call. This will only take a minute."

Dahlgren flipped through a well-thumbed Rolodex and turned only slightly to the side as he dialed.

Starla studied the rest of the office as she waited. It seemed more like a storeroom or equipment locker than anything else, despite the tacky paneling and the row of file cabinets along the east wall. Diving equipment was everywhere— bright yellow cylinders in the corner, wet suits hanging from plastic hangers, underwater camera equipment strewn about the work table. A heavy door to the west was marked "Compressor," and its window was covered with wire mesh. A hole the size of a softball had been punched through the door at waist level. The office had a single smudged window, behind the desk where Dahlgren sat, which offered a view of her battered 1977 Cougar in the parking lot and, beyond the chainlink fence, the runway. The sky was dark, the color of blue steel, and raindrops began to streak the window.

"What's the depth?" Dahlgren asked. Starla pulled a cigarette from her purse and lit it before she realized there were no ashtrays in the office. He jotted a figure down on his desk blotter and asked, "Bag or basket? How long has she been under?"

Dahlgren motioned for her to use one of the paper cups for the ashes as he tried to listen. "Give me a GPS location," he

Max McCoy

said. Her smoking annoyed him—he had thrown a carton of Marlboros and every ashtray in the place into the Dumpster three days before, and now he had an eye-popping headache and a sensation as if his skin were migrating across his body. "What's the nearest landing strip? No. Is there a road in front of this mine? Good. Can a trooper meet me there? Right. Fifteen hundred hours."

Dahlgren put the phone down and rubbed his eyes.

"All right, Miss Dwyer, I've got about fifteen minutes before I start packing. What can I do for you?"

"It's Mrs. Dwyer," Starla said, and handed him the file folder.

Her voice had a touch of hillbilly twang, Dahlgren decided—southern Missouri, perhaps, or Arkansas. Definitely not the flat, hard inflections of Kansas.

"What's this?"

"It's my husband's case file," Starla said, and began the plea she had been practicing in her head since leaving home. "His name is Duane Dwyer and he is sitting on death row at the Missouri State Penitentiary at Potosi. He's scheduled to be executed by lethal injection in a few weeks, but he's innocent. I can't prove it, but I think you can. They found her Camaro in Norfork Lake. There has to be something on the bottom of that lake they overlooked."

"Such as?"

"Her body, for one," Starla said.

She had taken an eight-by-ten color photograph out of the folder and handed it to Dahlgren. It was of a redheaded girl in her twenties with a band of freckles stretching across the bridge of her nose.

"So they were involved?"

"Yes," she said. "Duane was no saint. And of course they found his 'genetic material' inside his car. But Duane told her it was over, and I think she committed suicide by driving her

82

new car into the lake. You could tell that, right? Whether she drowned or was killed?"

"How long ago?"

" 'Ninety-seven."

"Justice is swift these days," Dahlgren said.

"It's not justice," Starla said. "It's murder."

"Look, I can't help you," Dahlgren said flatly, then handed the photograph back. "I'm sorry about your husband, but it's been too long. Even if I could find the body, there would be very little to go on after that long in the water. I'm sorry."

Starla Dwyer took a breath, squared her shoulders, and looked Dahlgren in the eye. She was plain but well-built, and when she was mad she was striking.

"Maybe you can get a private investigator," Dahlgren said. "Somebody else who—"

"There is nobody else," she said. "Damn you, look at me. You don't know what we've been through with this thing. Duane is innocent. You're the only underwater detective I could find on the Internet."

"I'm not the only diver," he said.

"This is not something I can get the local dive club to do," she said. "They wouldn't know what to look for, or what to do with it if they found it. But everything's in the file. There has got to be some kind of evidence in that car that will free my husband."

Her cheeks were flushed and she was breathing fast. It was raining harder, drumming on the hangar's metal roof. She couldn't see the runway now.

"You don't even know what you're looking for, do you, Mrs. Dwyer?" he asked.

"Hope," she said softly. "I'm looking for hope. Duane has been in that prison for the last seven years of his life. Now they're going to take away the very last thing he has, his life, and he's only twenty-eight. They might as well take my life, too."

She began to unbutton her dress.

"I'll do anything to help him," she said.

"Don't," Dahlgren said.

She slid the top of the dress down over her shoulders, revealing her perfect breasts. This time, she did not look up. "You can take me," she offered. "Right here, on the desk. All you have to do is help me. It's not wrong—not if you help me."

Dahlgren was ashamed for dwelling a moment too long before glancing away.

"Put your dress back on," he said.

He pushed the thick file toward her.

"I can't help you," he said.

She nodded as she tugged the dress back over her shoulders.

"I'm sorry. I mean—"

"No sympathy," she said as she brushed her brown hair from her collar. "If you have something to offer, then offer me help. Keep the file—I have lots of copies. My number is written inside. But don't bother after next month, because there will be no point."

Dahlgren sat facing the window, arms crossed over his chest, watching the storm. Rain whipped across the runway in sheets, as if someone were shaking the end of a rope, and the clouds had moved close to the ground. Starla Dwyer, without so much as a newspaper to protect her, kept her head up as she walked to the Cougar. Her dress looked in danger of running like watercolors down her legs.

Dahlgren felt sorry for her, even liked her more than he wanted to, but he had recovered too many bodies from too much water to believe the story of her husband's innocence. Duane Dwyer was probably a pathological liar—the prisons are full of them—and anything found at the bottom of that lake was likely to be further proof of his guilt.

There was a knock.

"Come."

It was Bruno.

"Thought I heard the pager," he said.

"Keeping your ear pressed to the door again?" Dahlgren asked.

"Just thought I'd ask if you need a hand."

"You can prep the Helio." Dahlgren turned to the desk, opened his black flight bag, and began stuffing items inside. "They have a sinker for me south of St. Louis. I need to run over to the terminal for a weather advisory and a sandwich from one of the machines."

"Want the floats?"

"No, this is a wheels landing. Flooded mine—all the water's underground."

"You look like hell," Bruno said.

"I feel like hell."

"What did the girl want? Figured her for a debt collector or a process server, the way she was stuck to this door. Thought somebody was trying to hit you with some more paper."

"That's all I would need," Dahlgren muttered. "No, the girl was just bad news. Her husband is sitting on death row. She believes he's innocent, of course, and she wanted to hire me to review the submerged evidence."

"Are you?"

"No," Dahlgren said. He found himself wishing for a cigarette again. "You know how it is—desperate, blinded by love."

"That young woman did not look the type to be blinded by anything," Bruno said.

Dahlgren closed the flight bag, took his blue paddle jacket from the tree next to the door, and flicked off the lights. He stood for a moment with his hand on the doorknob, then he returned to his desk, unzipped the flight bag, and tucked Starla Dwyer's manila folder into it.

Eleven

The Helio made a lazy turn and then lined up for a final approach on the flattopped expanse of dirt and tailings that had been described by the highway patrol dispatcher on the telephone earlier that day. It had been been just as she had described it: a couple of hundred barren acres northeast of the old business district and west of the four-lane asphalt strip cut by U.S. Highway 67.

It was one of the beautiful autumn days following a bad storm that often occur in the Midwest; at dawn, the ground had been shrouded in fog, but by noon it had all burned off, the barometer had been steadily rising, and the deep-blue sky was dotted with fluffy cumulus clouds.

As Dahlgren throttled back and the plane descended, he could see the tracks left by the Caterpillars and other heavy equipment that had been crawling over the tailings pile, and the big chain-link fence that surrounded the perimeter. Butted up against the fence to the east were a couple of big expanses of grass that marked an old cemetery and, incongruously, a golf course.

Dahlgren had Googled the town that morning and had found that the tailings pile was officially called "Bonne Terre Mines Remediation Site" and was the biggest of seven old mine sites designated for federal Superfund cleanup. The area had, until about forty years before, been where most of the city's mines and ore mills had been located, and the tailings that had been left behind were heavily contaminated by lead. The Environmental Protection Agency had decided the best way to deal with it was simply to cover the tailings with dirt. The project, which was nearly finished, cost $1.5 million, created twenty-three full-time jobs, according to a press release written by some EPA public relations hack, and nearly a million tons of contaminated soil had been covered.

The highway patrol trooper waiting on Dahlgren had watched as the Helio circled the tailings pile, then lined up for final approach, and he had deployed some road flares to indicate the smoothest place to land.

The Helio slowed to twenty-five knots, dropped to half of its forty-foot wingspan, and floated on ground effect for a moment before the soft rubber tires contacted the earth. The plane hopped once, almost imperceptibly, then settled on the forward gears, followed gently by the tail wheel. The sun glinted from the aluminum spinner over the three-bladed prop, and even though the 295-horsepower Lycoming engine was idling, it was kicking up clouds of dust.

The trooper indicated with a sweep of his arms that the aircraft should taxi to the edge of the flattopped remediation area, toward a concrete-block building painted bright blue.

The EPA had left this half-acre section of the project alone, and Dahlgren guessed it must have been the original entrance to the mine, but there didn't seem to be much left: the blockhouse, a couple of weathered tin outbuildings, some rock crushers and other equipment that blazed with orange rust, and an automobile and two trucks that were deteriorating down to their hubs. Not much grew in the rocky soil except some scrub and a few stunted trees.

The blockhouse was thirty feet wide and forty feet long, with an overhead door big enough to drive a delivery truck into. The diver down flag—a white diagonal on a red field—hung limply from a length of PVC pipe attached with hose clamps to the corner of the blockhouse near the overhead door. Beneath the diver down flag was its international equivalent, the blue-and-white pennant-shaped Alpha.

Parked around the blockhouse were a couple of police cars and a hearse from the funeral home in Bonne Terre. There was a Crown Victoria, the ubiquitous police car for the first decade of the new century, and an older Ford Explorer. Both were white, and both had the Bonne Terre police emblem on the front doors—standing black bears that flanked a seal that proclaimed, "United We Stand, Divided We Fall," and a bit of heraldry that included the American eagle, a crescent moon, and an animal that looked, for some inexplicable reason, like a polar bear. Beneath was the universal pledge "Service and Protection."

A couple of police officers in blue fatigue uniforms were standing near the vehicles, and one of them was smoking a cigarette and drinking thermos coffee.

When the plane was sufficiently away from the road, the trooper made a slashing motion across his throat with the flashlight. Dahlgren killed the engine, removed the headset, and unstrapped himself from the seat. Then he went aft and slid open the cargo door on the port side.

"Richard Dahlgren?" asked the trooper, standing outside. He had a wide jaw, short black hair streaked with gray, and steady blue eyes. "I'm Sergeant Bryce. If there's anything you want or need, just ask."

Dahlgren jumped down.

The trooper stuck his Smokey the Bear hat under his left arm as they shook hands. "That's one helluvan aircraft you have," he said. "Helio, right?"

"Courier 295."

"Haven't seen one like it since Vietnam."

"This was made in 1973," Dahlgren said. "After it came back to the States as Army surplus, some drug smugglers bought it and used it to fly cocaine out of Central America. The feds busted them, seized the plane, and I eventually bought it at auction."

Bryce nodded his approval.

"Did you fly?" Dahlgren asked.

"No, just sat in the jungle and wished I could."

"It was with the First Air Cav, as a forward observation plane," he said. "Didn't have the rockets mounted under the wings that the Stallions did, but it apparently was on the receiving end of some real combat. My mechanic is constantly finding bullet holes and slugs throughout the fuselage, and he's convinced some of them must have been fired from old French flintlocks."

"So it wasn't part of the Air America fleet?"

"Not that I know of, but I haven't traced its certification. Hard to pin down those CIA connections," Dahlgren said. "But anything is possible, I suppose. Hey, when I'm finished with this little job, would you like a ride, for old times' sake? There still should be a couple of hours of daylight left by then, and it will be a beautiful sunset."

"Yeah," Bryce said. "Know what they used to call me in 'Nam? Wild Bill. Haven't thought about that in a long time. Not good memories, mostly."

Bryce stared at the tips of his steel-toed shoes.

"I have some contacts over at Troop D," he said, "and they told me what you did to recover that tape. Harry Combs was a friend of mine. I'm not good at this sort of thing—you know, expressing thanks—but when I said if there's anything you need from me all you have to do is ask, I meant it."

Now Dahlgren looked at the tips of his scuffed cowboy boots.

"I didn't do anything," he said. "You guys caught the bastard. The mine entrance is near the blockhouse? I could use a hand hauling my gear up to there."

"No problem."

"Also, can someone who's been down there give me an orientation?"

"Yes, sir. The man who owns this property—the one who discovered the body—is waiting to brief you. Why don't you go on up and get started, and me and the city officers will haul the stuff up to you. Do you want everything out of the cargo hold?"

"Everything that's not bolted down."

"All the scuba bottles? There must be a dozen."

"Yeah, they contain different gas mixes—the 104s are nitrox and air mostly, but the smaller green ones are oxygen. The red pony bottles contain argon. It's all at three thousand pounds of pressure or more, so ask the boys to handle them gently, if you would."

"Don't drop them on the valves," Bryce said. "Got it."

Dahlgren grabbed his flight bag and started up the hill toward the building. The city cops watched his approach with the same vacant expressions they reserved for automobile fatalities. As Dahlgren neared the building, a glowing cigarette butt landed at his feet.

"You the frog man?" the one who had flicked the butt asked. He was forty pounds overweight, his belly hung over his belt, and his hair didn't look as if it had been washed in days. His right hand rested idly on the butt of his Glock.

Dahlgren ground out the cigarette with the heel of his cowboy boot, then carefully noted the name badge pinned to the blue fatigue uniform: BUNTZ.

"I'm the diver," he said quietly.

"Well, there's one thing we'd like to know," Buntz said, stepping suddenly close. "Are you a cop or what?"

"I would be the *or what*," Dahlgren said.

"Knock it off, Rudy," the other officer said. He was in his twenties, had close-cropped hair, and the name on his uniform said SCHWARTZ. "He's here to help."

"Shit," Buntz said, brushing the hair out of his eyes. "He ain't even a cop."

Dahlgren ignored the remark and entered the building. He had encountered morons like the deputy before, and experience had taught him that he couldn't afford the luxury of being angry until the job was over.

The building was painted the same shade of blue on the inside. A map of the mine covered the wall to the right. To the left there were shelves and cabinets in various states of assembly. A pair of double wooden doors set in the far wall. A long folding table in the middle of the room had a thirty-cup coffeemaker on one end and a telephone in the middle.

Two men were sitting at the table.

The younger man, the one with the Vandyke, was drinking from a plastic bottle of Evian. The other, the one with the gold badge pinned to his white shirt, stood.

"Clancy Brown," he said. "Chief of police. We appreciate you coming all this way on short notice."

"It's my job," Dahlgren said as he shook his hand. "Those your boys waiting down the hill?"

"That would be Michael Schwartz and Rudy Buntz," Brown said. "Don't pay Buntz any mind. He's all mouth. He was here when I hired on. But Michael is a good officer. A bit of a klutz, but honest."

Dahlgren nodded.

"So you're not from here?"

"No way," Brown said. "Came from Detroit. No offense to the locals, but this is Mayberry RFD compared to that. Oh, sorry. This is Loren McAfee," Brown said, indicating the other man. "Loren discovered the body, and he'll be diving with you to help bring it up."

Dahlgren took a quick inventory of McAfee: approximately forty-five, balding, beard. Dahlgren didn't trust men with Vandykes. But McAfee's brown eyes were clear, he appeared to be in good shape, and he was confident. The chief, in contrast, was retirement age, had white hair and a slight paunch. Life must be good in Bonne Terre, Dahlgren thought.

"Want some water?" McAfee asked.

"No, thanks," Dahlgren said.

"Most people don't drink enough," McAfee said as he placed the bottled water on the table and stood. "It's important to hydrate regularly. I think we know each other."

"Oh?" Dahlgren asked, shaking his hand.

"You're a caver, right?"

"I was," Dahlgren allowed.

"About ten years ago, in the Sierra Mazateca," McAfee said. "We were with different teams, trying to connect deep caves in the Sistema Huautla." McAfee pronounced the name in perfect Spanish, *wow-tla*. "We met at the church in San Augustín the day after—"

"I know why I was there," Dahlgren said quickly. "And it was nine years ago. I just don't remember *you*."

"Well, everybody knew who you were," McAfee said, then turned to Brown. "This guy was twenty-six, twenty-seven years old, and just had this huge article written about him in *Outside* magazine. The Huautla is to cave divers like the Himalayas are to mountain climbers, and Richard Dahlgren was king of the mountain. Then, in 1995—"

"That's history," Dahlgren said, cutting him off with a smile. "Here is what I do now."

Dahlgren gave them each a Triton Investigations business card. BODY RECOVERY—ACCIDENT INVESTIGATION—U/W CRIME SCENES. The card had the skull-and-crossbones Hell Divers logo, and beneath Dahlgren's name and contact information was a proverb: "Those who go to sea for pleasure would go to hell for pastime."

"Hell Divers," McAfee said.

"That's what we used to call ourselves," Dahlgren said. "Like Wes Skiles and the Moles in Florida. Only, we had a more exaggerated opinion of ourselves."

And you paid for it, Dahlgren imagined McAfee thinking.

Gingerly holding the card, Brown cleared his throat.

"Mr. Dahlgren, how much do you charge?"

"It depends on time, depth, and difficulty," Dahlgren said. "There's a flat thousand-dollar fee for every hour I'm under water, down to a hundred and fifty feet. Higher rates apply for depth, water temperature, environment, and degree of difficulty. And then there's travel expenses."

Dahlgren hated talking business. It always made him uncomfortable, which, he thought, was probably the reason he was quickly going broke. So he took a notebook from his flight bag, uncapped a pen, and turned his attention to McAfee.

"You own the mine or just dive it?"

"Own, for about six months now," McAfee said. "Plan to make a tourist attraction for technical divers."

"You rich?" Dahlgren asked.

"I'm a high-school science teacher," McAfee said. "So what do you think? But I have hopes of being rich someday, if Bio-Lume, my diving technology business, works out."

"What can you tell me about where you found the victim?" he asked.

"Well, quite a bit. How much do you know about Bonne Terre?"

"Very little," Dahlgren said. "My grandfather worked for National Lead at Fredericktown during the Depression, but he died long before I was born."

"Bonne Terre was the flagship mine of the St. Joan Mining Company," McAfee explained. "The company started operations here just after the Civil War, and some of the drifts in this mine probably date that far back. So, what we have is a mine that was continuously worked for a hundred years, until they literally turned the lights off in 1961."

"And what is Mineral City?'

"That's the interesting part," McAfee said. "By the fifties, most of the operation had moved underground—a virtual city beneath the earth. All of the mines around here had their shops underground, so they wouldn't have to bring their locomotives and drills and other machinery to the surface for repair, but the St. Joan mine did them one better. They located nearly *everything* underground except the mill and the powerhouse. The offices, barracks, even the infirmary, all at the bottom of the Number One Shaft. Part of the reason was that there just wasn't room on the surface in Bonne Terre for anything else—it had all been taken by the St. Joseph Lead Company, which incorporated the town in 1864, although there had been a community here since the late 1700s."

"Bonne Terre," Dahlgren said. "What's it mean? Good what?"

"The good land," McAfee said. "Or good earth, depending on which translation you like best. The history of mining is a lot like the history of diving, which means it was dominated by the French. If there's anything you can say in English about either, you can always say it better in French."

Dahlgren nodded.

"So the mine was worked out by 1961?"

"Well, not completely, but the price of ore made it economically unfeasible to continue. So they shut it down, locked the door, turned off the lights, and when the pumps stopped, the mine filled with water. And one of the things that makes Bonne Terre so unusual is the water table is very close to the surface, and the town is extensively undermined."

"Can you show me where the body was found?"

McAfee moved to the wall.

"This is a map of the big room beneath us, and Central City is at two hundred station, which means two hundred feet below the surface on Number One Shaft," he said. "Let me describe what you're looking at, then you can get some idea of where the body was in relation to the rest of the mine. Here's the structure."

"Structure?" Dahlgren asked.

"Yeah, the iron frame that capped the top of the Number One Shaft," McAfee said. "That's where the miners were hoisted in and out of the mine in mancages, and the ore was brought up in skips."

"Got it."

"The black perimeter line is the contour of the cavern at water level. The thing you have to remember is that this is the world's largest man-made cavern—there are eighty miles of interconnected passages here, all filled with water. Most of it has rock ceilings where you can't even get to the surface, and in other places there are shafts that are a hundred and twenty meters deep."

"About four hundred feet?" Dahlgren said.

McAfee nodded.

"You always talk in metric?"

"I think in metric," McAfee said.

"What's the average depth?"

"That depends on which end of the mine you're in. It starts out here, where we have our dock, at about ten meters, then steadily deepens as you go west. We found the girl here, at an equipment shed, at a depth of forty-three meters, at the edge of the Mineral City."

McAfee took a red marker and placed an X at the location.

"Show me where we are now."

"Right here, at this black dot," he said, and made a circle.

"This building will eventually be the entrance and dive shop. We'll be following the old mule trail down into the

95

mine. It circles around the main room, and the Number One Shaft. This black line, about the length of my index finger, is the old mule trail."

"Do we walk?"

"I have plans for golf carts eventually, but for right now, we walk. Get ready for a rather brisk hike. There are a hundred and sixty-eight steps leading down into the mine."

"Tell me about Mineral City."

"It's located here in this quadrant, and these squares represent the buildings we've mapped so far—here's the hospital, for example, and the business offices. There's the mule barns and, over here, the machine shop. Barracks for the miners. Lots of little outbuildings. But this section, to the west, is largely unexplored."

"Air shafts?"

"They're scattered around town—one goes to the funeral home basement, for instance—but they were all capped long ago. Anyway, we don't seem to need them. We get enough air exchange from the mule entrance. It's cold, by the way. The air temperature is a constant 16.6 degrees Celsius, and the water can run just a bit colder."

"In English, please," the chief asked.

"Sixty-two degrees," McAfee said.

"Dry suit time," Dahlgren said.

"We get by with seven mill wet suits for shorter dives," McAfee said. "There's no thermocline and no current. No indigenous aquatic life in the cave, either, because it's so cold and sunlight never reaches the water. No fish, no bugs, nothing."

"How about unnatural life-forms?" Dahlgren asked.

"Well, we do have a pet—a California sea lion named Nemo—but we have to bring his fish down to him. He's harmless but sometimes gets in your way. I'll put him up while you dive for the body."

Dahlgren thought the sea lion was odd, but kept silent. Wouldn't it be lonely? But Dahlgren would be out of there in a few hours, so he decided there was no point in questioning McAfee's eccentricities.

"Is the mine contaminated?" Dahlgren asked. "The federal government is spending an awful lot of money to hide the lead tailings around here. Is the water safe?"

"Perfectly," McAfee said. "In fact, the mines supply most of the drinking water for Bonne Terre. Lead doesn't leach into water like other minerals. You're fine, unless you find some lead and eat it."

"What's the visibility?"

"Superb. It averages seventy to a hundred meters."

"I find that hard to believe."

"Everyone does, until they've seen it for themselves," McAfee said. "We've strung underwater floods on some of the trails we've mapped—around the dock and the hospital building, for example—and it creates a terrific effect. They're also useful as visual references."

"What are the other places marked in blue?"

"Those are what I like to call our 'major attractions.' Here's Rainbow Bridge, a magnificent rock arch, and there is a row of ore carts. The calcium carbonate falls. And here's one of the air bells—"

"What's an air bell?" Brown asked.

"An air pocket," Dahlgren said. "Some are just big enough to stick your head out of the water, while others are big enough to get out and walk around in."

"It's sort of like a diving bell in the rock," McAfee said. "You can breathe in them if the air isn't polluted, but you have to remember that the air is at the same pressure as the ambient water, so it doesn't cut down your bottom time. Push a drinking glass upside down into a sink of water and you'll see the effect—the volume of the air shrinks."

Brown nodded.

"How much of the mine is unexplored?" Dahlgren asked.

"Seventy to eighty percent," McAfee said. "We've just covered the shallow, accessible places. And there are drifts and shafts that radiate out from the main chamber that seem to go on forever. There's an old story that you can take a boat from here to St. Louis underground, but it's a myth."

"How do you think she got down there?" Brown asked.

"She wasn't dropped down an air shaft, if that's what you're thinking," McAfee said. "They've all been capped. Besides, there wasn't a mark on the body, and she was inside the shed. Somebody had to place her there very carefully."

"Then it must be . . . ," Brown began.

"The murderer is a diver," McAfee said, "and apparently a very good one."

Dahlgren studied the expression on McAfee's face. Was he boasting? It wouldn't be the first time a murderer had "found" the victim and led police to the body.

"Tell me something," Dahlgren said. "You've done body recoveries before, right?"

"Like everybody else who has their Abe Davis."

Brown looked questioningly at Dahlgren.

"An award the Cave Diving Section of the National Speleological Society gives for a hundred logged cave dives," Dahlgren explained. "So, Loren, why didn't you just bring the girl up yourself?"

McAfee seemed amused.

"I didn't kill her, if that's what you're thinking," he said. "And I didn't bring her up because this wasn't a normal diving accident. It was obviously a crime scene. Also, I had six very shaken divers to take care of afterward, including an extremely talented twenty-three-year-old girl who swears she will never dive in an overhead environment again."

"Smart cookie," Dahlgren said.

There was the sound of a pickup truck on the gravel outside the building, then the boom of a tailgate falling. Sergeant Bryce came through the door carrying the underwater camera cases. Schwartz and Buntz followed, struggling with green-and-yellow steel cylinders labeled "EAN-32" in each hand.

"Oh, I wish I had known," McAfee said absentmindedly. "Still diving nitrox? You didn't have to lug those 104s here."

"Thanks, but I like to mix my own gas," Dahlgren said.

"You don't understand," McAfee said. "Cave diving has . . . well, *progressed* in the years you've been out of it. The technology we're using is cutting edge, you might say."

Dahlgren forced himself to break eye contact with McAfee. The guy was seriously getting on his nerves. His gaze settled on the far wall, where dozens of boxes of Sofnolime were stacked.

"Rebreathers?" Dahlgren asked, making no attempt to hide his contempt. "That technology is fifty years old."

"To be accurate, rebreather technology is over a hundred years old," McAfee said. "They used hemp and potash back then as a scrubber instead of soda lime, and it didn't work all that well, but it did work—sometimes. But go ahead with your objections."

"As I was saying," Dahlgren continued, smarting at having been given a history lesson, "rebreather technology is *old*, and only half the problem's been solved: You can monitor your oxygen content, but carbon dioxide buildup is a wild card. There's no carbon dioxide sensor that will work in the humid conditions of the breathing loop, at least none that you'd want to trust your life on. And if your scrubber material fails prematurely, you go hypercapnic."

"Hyper catnip?" Brown asked.

"Capnic," Dahlgren repeated.

"It means you will probably die from carbon dioxide poisoning," McAfee explained. "You'll drown, but only after the carbon dioxide buildup makes you pass out."

"Blame it on Dalton's Law," Dahlgren said. "Say you have a gas mixture that is two percent contaminated on the surface.

At a hundred and twenty-three feet, it's the equivalent of breathing a mixture that's ten percent contaminated, and you're dead."

"Absolutely," McAfee said.

Brown shook his head. He wasn't getting it.

"I'm a pilot, so let me use an aviation analogy," Dahlgren said. "Diving a rebreather is like getting on a commercial jet and having the captain tell you there's no fuel gauge on the aircraft. He says they've made the flight in the past with this amount of fuel, and he thinks it will be okay this time as well, but there's just no way to tell for sure."

McAfee folded his arms across his chest, but he couldn't supress a smile. "I built my own airplane," he said. "And it *has* a fuel gauge."

Twelve

The sea lion galumphed across the dock and nuzzled McAfee's hand in search of food. McAfee caressed the whiskered snout and explained apologetically that it was too early for dinner and led the sleek animal toward a chain-link pen next to the compressor shed.

"Nemo, don't look so sad," McAfee said as he threw a row of switches on the electrical panel. The sea lion barked at the sound of his own name, a hoarse and aching sound that echoed from the high rock walls. The water beneath the dock began to glow a crystalline blue, and Dahlgren glanced over the edge.

He could see pebbles on the bottom.

"That's fifteen meters beneath us," McAfee said. "Those little rocks you see are actually some good-sized boulders. The water is so clear it will play tricks on you."

Dahlgren was suddenly taken by the sensation that he wasn't looking into water at all but was peering over the top of

101

a very tall building at a very nasty drop. Instinctively, he jerked away from the edge.

"Spooky down here," Dahlgren said.

"It's not that bad," McAfee said, "once you get used to the Morlocks."

"I'll keep my matches handy," Dahlgren said.

"That shallow bottom you're seeing is part of the old mule trail we followed down," McAfee said. "A little farther out, it drops off to about fifty meters."

Dahlgren looked up. The rock ceiling was about fifty feet above. "So that would be two hundred station?" Dahlgren asked. "Mineral City?"

"The edge of it," McAfee said.

Dahlgren was sweating from the walk with his gear bag down the trail, and the chill air of the cavern stung his cheeks. He could already feel his sinuses start to block up.

Brown sat on one of the wooden benches and briskly rubbed his arms. "Three-oh-one," he said as he keyed his portable radio, "this is three hundred. If you're not ten-eight, bring my jacket from the trunk of my car."

"They can't hear you," McAfee said. "Too much rock between us and the surface. I haven't found a radio yet that will work down here."

McAfee opened an equipment locker and rummaged for a moment, then threw the chief a large gray hooded sweatshirt. "I keep some spares down here."

"Thanks," Brown said.

"Where are the rest of your divers?" Dahlgren asked.

"Gave them the day off," McAfee said.

"They work on Sunday?"

"Most of them have real jobs during the week," he said. "But I didn't want them hanging around when we brought the girl up. Once you start associating images like that with the place where you work, it's trouble."

"And you're immune?" Dahlgren asked.

"I don't have a choice," McAfee said. "I own the joint. So I might as well be helpful. Besides, this place is not very forgiving of first-timers. More than twenty open water divers drowned here in the seventies, before the Cave Diving Section placed the Grim Reaper signs and had the entrance padlocked."

Dahlgren nodded.

He had already assembled his Canon F1n SLR, vintage 1986, and 24mm FD lens in its Ikelight housing with dome port and strobe. He had also laid out his dive reel, his primary dive light, and two backups.

"Ready to meet the future?" McAfee asked, grinning.

"Lay it on me," Dahlgren said.

"Okay," McAfee said. "We're going to do this by the book. I know you have hundreds of hours in caves—"

"Thousands," Dahlgren said.

"Thousands of hours in caves, but this technology is much different. Open-circuit experience isn't much help. So we're going to do a thorough predive briefing before we get into the water. By the book—*my* book. That okay with you?"

"I don't think our victim is in any hurry."

McAfee nodded.

"You agree that you're diving at your own risk with experimental equipment, and that you will hold me harmless in the event of an accident caused by failure, misuse of the equipment, or your own failure to follow instructions?"

"What, you want me to sign a release?"

"No, we have a witness," McAfee said, inclining his head toward the chief. "Seriously, my rebreathers are prototypes. They are very advanced prototypes, and we've never had a failure, but they are not in production yet. In a year or two, maybe."

"I fucking accept the risk," Dahlgren said. "Get on with it."

McAfee nodded.

He picked up a rebreather and matching helmet from the end of the rack, walked it over, and placed it in front of

Dahlgren. The rebreather's shell was all black, with no trim color, and had "X07" stenciled in white.

"How'd you know seven was my lucky number?"

"This is the Bio-Lume *L'Étoile*," McAfee said. "I've sacrificed twelve years, most of the hundred grand my uncle left me, and two marriages to develop it."

McAfee removed the housing. Dahlgren recognized the oxygen and helium cylinders, the scrubber cannister, the counterlungs, the oxygen-injection valve, and the bailout regulator.

"It's a mixed-gas rebreather?" Dahlgren asked.

"Yes. Helium as a diluent, of course. The gas-blending unit is controlled by triple-redundancy microprocessors that monitor depth, partial pressures, and the diver's decompression commitment," McAfee said. His voice was both proud and enthusiastic, as if he were a parent. He handed Dahlgren the helmet.

A pair of LED lamps were mounted on each side, like headlights. The power had to be supplied from elsewhere, Dahlgren noted, because the bulges in the helmet were only big enough to accommodate the cluster of LEDs, the reflectors, and the dime-sized lenses.

He imagined being wedged in a narrow passage and trying to remove the helmet for more slack. Also, the helmet was attached to the rebreather housing by the double-hose regulator and an umbilical. The chances of removing your backpack and pushing it through ahead without removing the helmet were slim. You'd have to doff it all and use the bailout regulator and a backup mask.

"I'm not sure I like full masks, much less integrated helmets," he said.

"The silicone bottom half, where the mouthpiece comes in, detaches to allow use of an open-circuit regulator," McAfee said. "The helmets take a little getting used to, but in the long run most people like them. Besides, in cave diving you have to wear a helmet anyway. This one is light, it's made of aluminum, and it and the mask have been tested to make sure there's no CO_2 retention."

"Where's the data displayed?" Dahlgren asked.

"There's a heads-down display that reflects inside of the diver's faceplate. Also, all the data is automatically stored in a one-gig compact flashcard."

"A black box?"

"A black box, including audio."

Dahlgren whistled.

"That's handy," Dahlgren said. "No need to scratch farewells to loved ones on your tank with your dive knife anymore."

"The goal is to avoid farewells," McAfee said gently.

As much as Dahlgren wanted to dislike him, he was having a hard time working up any animosity toward McAfee. He turned the helmet over and peered inside.

"Just who are you talking to, then? Making field notes to yourself?" Dahlgren asked.

"Other divers, or the tender," McAfee said. "The helmet has an integrated VOX unit, with the transducer mounted inside the rebreather housing. Couldn't do that with a half-mask. Not enough air space for speech, and you have a regulator clenched between your teeth."

"It works with all this rock?"

"Line of sight," McAfee said. "As long as you can see your buddy, you can talk to him. It's voice-activated up to about thirty meters; beyond that, you have to use the push-to-talk, because of the gas density. Also, the deeper you go, the more clearly and slowly you have to talk to be understood. Around seventy-five meters, it becomes unintelligible. Not only because of the density, but because of the helium. The chipmunk effect, you know."

"I'm familiar with it," Dahlgren said, nodding.

"That's why there's a descrambler built into the helmet."

"You're kidding," Dahlgren said.

"I kid you not," McAfee said. "It's actually a pretty simple computer algorithm, and the size of microprocessors has shrunk so in the last few years, it seemed silly not to incorporate one."

"Just one?" Dahlgren asked, bemused.

"No need for triple redundancy on the descrambler," McAfee said. "It's not a life-support function. It corrects for the Alvin effect but doesn't work well deeper than a hundred and fifty meters, because the air density is too great, and your helmet is an air pocket. But it's good for the mine."

"Okay, I'm impressed," Dahlgren said. "You're up there with Bill Stone in my book. But where's the carbon dioxide sensor?"

McAfee flipped the unit over and held up the double-hose mouthpiece. "It's next to the mushroom valve on the inhalation side of the mouthpiece," he said.

"That's an odd place in the loop for it," Dahlgren said.

"Not when you consider how it works," McAfee said. "I was thinking about the CO_2 problem years ago, during a night dive off the beach at Cozumel. I was stumped by the same electronic problems that everyone else was having. It was incredibly beautiful at sea that night, with a big full moon over the island, and as we dove I noticed trails of bioluminescent organisms, probably plankton, swirling from the tips of our fins. That's when I realized the solution to the CO_2 sensor problem was biochemical and not electronic."

"Come again?" Dahlgren asked.

"It took me a decade to work out the details," McAfee said. "But the rush of air molecules in the air intake excites the organic luciferins in the sensor. Try it."

"The unit isn't even powered up."

"Take a breath."

Dahlgren gripped the silicone mouthpiece between his teeth and inhaled gently. A band of blue glowed near the intake valve. Dahlgren exhaled, then inhaled again, and the blue band grew brighter the harder he sucked.

"Crazy," Dahlgren said.

"Blue is best," McAfee said. "Red is dead."

"How'd you—"

"If I explained it all to you, then you'd be trying to get a patent for it," McAfee said. "It's not perfect, but it's reliable. I would have liked to make it go from green to yellow to red, but we're stuck with blue and red. But those are the colors nature dealt us."

"Any way to incorporate the capnic partial pressure in the data display?"

"Not yet," McAfee said. "But there are some advantages to the cap color indicator. You can see at a glance if your buddy is breathing, and if so, what his capnic level is. For your own level, you just have to glance down."

"How'd a high-school teacher come up with this stuff?"

"I observe nature," McAfee said. "Ninety percent of the sea creatures that live in the zone between two hundred and a thousand meters are bioluminescent, so I had a lot of possible chemical reactions to choose from."

"Still . . ."

"Also, I got some help along the way from friends at the Navy Experimental Dive Unit at Panama City. One of our team, Cal Bentham, was a Sealab diver for Papa Topside Bond. I gathered some pointers from the Navy's rebreather programs."

"Are they still using the Mark 16?"

"Yeah," McAfee said. "They shelved the EX-19 UBA, and lately they've been testing various commercial mixed-gas units, but they haven't found one that will stand up to military specs. I understand the Prism Topaz came close."

"And you're hoping Bio-Lume will cinch it?"

"Well, yes," McAfee said. "Frankly, the NEDU has completed unmanned testing with our unit, and the test pool is next. Then it's on to the Ocean Simulation Facility, and if we're lucky, offshore trials."

"How long will all that take?"

"Who knows?" McAfee shrugged. "It's the government. Besides, the Navy has made DOD stuff a priority, so we might have a long wait. *L'Étoile* is designed to make diving safer, longer, better. It doesn't kill people."

"You're going to have to change the name," Dahlgren said. "Speaking French has become un-American, since they wouldn't help us bomb the shit out of Iraq. Why don't you just call it the Bio-Star?"

"I probably should," McAfee said. "Except I read Jules Verne as a kid . . . in the original French."

Dahlgren was bemused.

"Most divers I know are smart," Dahlgren said, staring into McAfee's eyes to see if he flinched. "And all the technical divers are very smart, even if they are a tad crazy. But you're scaring me. If you're as smart as you appear to be, then you're a fucking genius."

McAfee shrugged but didn't flinch.

"Who's to say?" he asked.

Brown cleared his throat.

"I hate to break up this pissing match," Brown said, "but we're here for a reason. The body, remember?"

"Right," Dahlgren said.

"You feel fully briefed?" McAfee asked. "If so, we'll do a shallow-water check and then get on with it. The only things you'll need are your fins, your backup lights, and your wet suit. Buoyancy compensation is built into the unit. Take your pouch for whatever else you want to carry. Food tubes are good, if you have them. And, oh yeah, you'll want your camera, I suppose. Unless you want to try my digital."

"Thanks, but I'm used to my F-1," Dahlgren said. "Digital cameras still haven't been accepted in court, because they're so much easier to manipulate than a film negative. So I'll remain in the twentieth century for a spell longer, if you don't mind."

Dahlgren kicked off his cowboy boots, unbuckled his jeans, and slid them off. Then he stepped out of his socks and boxers and stood self-consciously, nude from the waist down, as he pulled on a pair of expedition-weight bottoms that looked like black hose.

"Son," Brown asked, "what in the world are you doing?"

"Keeps you warmer," Dahlgren explained as he stepped into the legs of his thick black wet suit. "Makes it easier to get into your neoprene."

"And the color so accents your legs," McAfee teased.

Dahlgren peeled off his shirt and pulled himself into the rest of the wet suit, tugging and wriggling, then finally reached around to the back and found the pull strap that was attached to the zipper. In one motion, he sealed himself in the suit, then reached for his hood and gloves.

"You mean there are some people that do this for fun?" Brown asked. "I'd be exhausted before I ever got wet."

"It's not as bad as it looks," McAfee said as he zipped up his silver neoprene jacket. "This stuff is unwieldy on the surface, but you don't feel any weight when you're in the water, because you're neutrally buoyant."

McAfee helped Dahlgren don the rebreather, attach the cables to the helmet, and power the rig up. Dahlgren checked the glowing display reflected in the lens of his mask—Depth 0, Time 0, ppO_2 1.0—and gave the thumbs-up.

"Remember, you can talk." McAfee laughed, then thumped the top of Dahlgren's helmet. "I'll lead you to the body, and you take as long as you need to do whatever it is that you do. When you give the signal, we'll head back up, and then just follow the decompression solution in the heads-up display."

"The set point is adjustable on the fly?" Dahlgren asked.

"Yes, but you won't have to," McAfee said. "The microprocessors automatically adjust for optimal results. Also, the decompression times are accelerated, because the unit adjusts the oxygen partial pressure incrementally—like having a different deco gas available not just at every stop, but with every breath. Above twenty feet, we're breathing pure O_2."

"And what if all three computers fail?" Dahlgren asked.

"Then you use the bail-out bottle and good old dive tables," McAfee said, and pointed to his feet. Neatly printed on the blades of each of his silver fins were rows of figures representing depths and times. "If we get separated, stick with the line. Follow the arrows, and they will lead you back to the platform beneath the dock."

McAfee put on his helmet.

"How long will you boys be under?" the chief asked. "I'd just like to know when to get worried."

McAfee put his helmet against Brown's head so he could understand him. "You won't have time to worry," McAfee said. "But if we *had* to, with the rebreathers we could stay under for at least twenty-four hours."

Brown nodded.

"Ready?" he asked, and Dahlgren was mildly surprised to hear McAfee's voice inside the helmet.

"You got the bag?" Dahlgren asked.

"I've got the body bag." McAfee took a giant stride off the dock. Dahlgren switched on his dive light, grasped the camera housing, and followed.

Thirteen

Dahlgren was flying.

There was no other way to describe it. The water was so clear that the sensation was not of swimming but of gliding through the air. He swallowed and did a closed-mouth yawn to relieve the pressure that was building up in his ears, and kept his hands by his sides, kicking lazily, as he followed McAfee's silver fins down to the staging platform.

McAfee paused, hovering over the platform, and looked Dahlgren over carefully. The twin LED beams from McAfee's helmet went slowly from Dahlgren's helmet to his feet. Dahlgren noticed that some of the light was channeled through the sides of the helmet lens, which softly illuminated McAfee's face, so it wasn't necessary to shine your dive light in your buddy's face to read his eyes or his expression.

Clever, Dahlgren thought. He had seen something similar used in *The Abyss*, his favorite movie. He had thought the helmets worn by Ed Harris and the others were just for cinematic effect, but now he realized the practical application.

Communication was more than just hand gestures or even speech. Also, whenever he heard divers describe HPNS to nondivers, they always used the vivid depiction of the psychotic SEAL in Cameron's movie, down to the paranoia and shaking hands. It occurred to Dahlgren that James Cameron was the modern counterpart to Jules Verne. The French (there it was again) novelist had more or less accurately described a modern sub, down to the nuclear power plant, nearly a century before the fact. Divers had always owed as much to dreamers as to engineers. A century from now, Dahlgren wondered, would divers be making contact with extraterrestrials in the deep ocean?

Dahlgren glanced down, looking for his console with its depth and submersible pressure gauges, then remembered to glance down at the glowing numbers.

Depth: 20 feet. Time: 55 seconds.

"I toggled your data to display English units, so you won't have to do a mental conversion for depth," McAfee said. "Are you doing okay?"

Fantastic, Dahlgren wanted to say. But that seemed disrespectful, considering the job ahead of them, so he simply said, "Fine."

"Good," McAfee said. His voice wasn't quite as clear as talking on a telephone, but it was close, and the absence of noise from a periodic torrent of exhaust bubbles helped. "Don't skip breathe. No need to conserve gas. That's one of the big differences between this and open circuit. Also, you might want to adjust your trim a bit for more of a head-down attitude. That's good. Do you like music?"

"Now, that's an odd question to ask," Dahlgren said as he joined him on the platform.

"Not really," McAfee said as he pushed a couple of buttons on his wrist display, then dropped off the edge of the platform and descended slowly headfirst, like a slow-motion skydiver.

As Dahlgren followed, an angelic voice filled his helmet—in stereo.

"*Au borde d'une fontaine je me suis reposée,*" the woman sang passionately over a simple accompaniment. "*Je me suis reposée au bord d'une fontaine.*"

The effect was so profound that Dahlgren felt he must be dreaming. The water could not possibly be this clear, there couldn't be an underwater city lit by halide floods below them, and you can't listen to ethereal music while diving.

"It's a French folk song," McAfee said, "and it's three hundred years old. Now it's on MP3 in my VOX unit. It's called 'La Fontaine,' and that's Connie Dover singing. She does mostly Celtic stuff, but this is my favorite."

Au bord d'une fontaine je me suis reposée, et l'eau était si claire que je me suis baignée.

"Connie's the best folksinger in the country, but hardly anybody knows about her outside the incestuous folk circuit," McAfee said. "The only reason I know about her is that I have a friend who lives close to her up in Weston, near Kansas City, who turned me on to her."

"Cool," was all Dahlgren could say.

"Enjoy it while you can," McAfee said. "It'll sound like crap once we hit thirty meters, because of distortion caused by the air density. But we'll go slow enough so you can hear the rest of the song before I shut her down."

Avec des feuilles de chêne je me suis essuyée.

"I always think of it as the soundtrack to the best movie I've never seen."

"I'm in love," Dahlgren said.

"And you haven't even see her picture on the CD yet. You'll really be a goner then," McAfee said. They had been hugging the wall of the cavern, following a trail of low-wattage lights around the shallow area, making a lazy semicircle. Now McAfee paused, hovering over a wall. Dahlgren reckoned they had to be about under the dock once again. He looked up and spotted the platform above them. Then, as Dahlgren neared the rim, he could see a cluster of tin-roofed buildings illuminated by the cold glare of four-hundred-watt halide floodlights stretching below them.

"Twenty meters," McAfee said. "This walls marks the division between the training area and the deep stuff. That's Mineral City, fifty meters below us. How do you feel?"

"Okay."

"Just okay, or are you good?" McAfee asked.

"I'm good," Dahlgren said emphatically.

McAfee nodded.

"Do you think anybody would pay for this?" he asked. "This experience, I mean. It's cold, it's dark—"

Dahlgren's heart swelled in his chest.

"It's a religious experience," Dahlgren said. "Who wouldn't pay to fly over a sunken city and listen to a beautiful woman sing French folk songs? Loren, I haven't felt like this since my first time, when I was sixteen years old."

"Your first dive or your first girl?"

"Both," Dahlgren said.

Then later, he thought, *when I took my first real cave dive with Taylor. Why couldn't I have come here under different circumstances, when I didn't have to recover somebody's daughter from the black places within the earth? When did I lose the joy in life?*

The answer came quickly: *Nine years ago.*

Dahlgren stifled an unexpected sob.

"What?" McAfee asked.

"Nothing," Dahlgren said. "Just equalizing."

They were passing sixty feet now, and the water pressure was collapsing the neoprene of their wet suits and reducing the volume of their lungs, causing them to descend faster. Dahlgren shot some gas into the rebreather's bladder to slow his descent, to stay just a little longer with the music and the sensation of flight.

"Loren," Dahlgren said, "if this wasn't a bag job, I'd be glad to pay you cash."

At the edge of Mineral City, McAfee found a yellow nylon guideline tied off to a big pneumatic drill that sat on a heavy tripod. They followed the guideline out of the comforting circle of light, into the darkness, with McAfee in the lead and Dahlgren keeping one gloved hand skimming the line.

It led over a barren expanse where their fins kicked up puffs of silt, and Dahlgren adjusted his buoyancy again to a more head-down attitude, trying to keep his fins as high as possible. The floor began to slope upward, and Dahlgren noticed that the depth numbers on his heads-up display were decreasing. The maximum depth, 203 feet, was displayed in red, while the actual depth flickered in green digital numbers. The numbers slowed as they neared 130. The farther they got from the lights, the more the more the darkness closed in and the smaller the mine seemed. It was not an unfamiliar sensation to Dahlgren, but it was one that stirred an old sensation in his gut telling him to be careful.

McAfee came to the terminus of the line, where it was tied off around a piece of pipe that jutted from the silty floor. He waited for Dahlgren to come abreast, then turned his head to the left. The LEDs on the sides of his helmet illuminated the side of the corrugated tin shack, swept over the open door, then found the slate and pencil attached with surgical tubing on the bottom. Just beyond was a pair of feet and toes, white against the blackness, marking where the body had glided after being sucked out of the shack.

Dahlgren held his palm toward McAfee, indicating he should wait while Dahlgren checked things out.

"You can talk," McAfee said. His voice was distorted now by the increased air density, and he had to repeat himself so that Dahlgren could understand.

"I know," Dahlgren said. "I just didn't feel like it."

115

"I understand," McAfee said. When Dahlgren looked puzzled, he repeated himself, then added: "It'll get easier with practice."

Dahlgren nodded.

He thumbed the switch on the underwater strobe to the on position. The orange ready light began to glow, and he could hear the capacitor rising in pitch as it charged. Then he checked his camera housing, looking for signs of water pooling in the bottom. It was dry. He used the big black lever on top to advance the film and cock the shutter, then set the aperture on the 24mm lens at f/5.6. The shutter was already synced at a ninetieth of a second.

Satisifed, he adjusted his buoyancy so he was floating three feet from the bottom, and advanced with small and slow kicks. He brought the housing to eye level, spun the focus ring, and composed a shot through the Canon's speedfinder, a big viewfinder that replaced the prism on top of the camera and gave a sharp image even when viewed from several inches away, such as through a scuba mask. He pressed the shutter button, and the strobe fired, then whined again as it recharged. He made two more photos, bracketing the exposures a stop on either side.

It was unusual to recover a body in water so clear, and Dahlgren was determined to make the most of it. These were evidence photos that, someday, would be published in a forensic textbook he planned to write. He had thirty-six frames of Ektachrome to document the scene, and he intended to use them all.

Then he moved in and shot the slate where it lay on the bottom, moved on to the victim's feet, and hovering carefully above her, worked his way to the top of her head. He paid particular attention to the translucent silk wrap around her midsection and the ribbons around her wrists.

She was lying prone in the silt, but her head was resting on her right cheek, and her red hair was swept back so that her left eye was looking up at Dahlgren.

Dahlgren marveled, because she was the most perfectly preserved body he had ever seen. At first, he had thought McAfee's description of her had been twisted by wishful thinking. Some people, when confronted by death, will describe the victim as beautiful or serene as an unconscious way of softening the horrific. But this girl *was* beautiful. McAfee had accurately described her, right down to the alabaster skin and those sightless blue-tinged eyes. She couldn't have been down very long, Dahlgren decided, because the living organisms in our guts tend to bloat corpses and then tear them apart rather quickly. This water was cold, but probably not cold enough to delay that process for very long. Also, when he touched the skin of her upper arm, it didn't have that loose, soapy feel that drowning victims quickly acquire.

Dahlgren moved in as near as he dared for the most important shots, a close-up of her face. He didn't see any ligature marks around her neck, or any bruising or teeth marks, but the photographs might reveal things that weren't apparent in the water. He took several frames, then took a yellow ruler with black numbers from his pouch, and placed it in slow motion on the bottom next to her nose. But as careful as he had tried to be, her red hair rippled and silt began to creep from the edges of the ruler.

He took three pictures in quick succession, opening the aperture a couple of stops and not waiting for the ready light to stop blinking between frames. By the time he had advanced the film for his fourth shot, the silt had obscured the frame.

Dahlgren retrieved the ruler, then took some clear plastic bags from his pouch. He placed them over her hands and her feet and secured them in place with rubber bands. The spot was pretty silted up by now. He rose a few feet and turned his attention to the door and interior of the shack.

What had the shack been for?

Some type of machine work, perhaps. There was a wooden workbench along one side, and an overturned chair, but otherwise the shack was bare—nothing except for a mining-supply calendar hanging on the wall, open to October 1961. The bottom half displayed the days of the month, while the top half was a picture of a topless girl caressing a pneumatic drill bit. The colors were still shockingly bright. He spent the last six frames of the roll of Ektachrome on the interior of the shack, including one of the calendar. Although he didn't yet know the identity of the girl in the silt outside, he now knew how he would unofficially refer to her: Miss October.

Before he motioned for McAfee to join him with the body bag, Dahlgren took some orange plastic stakes and placed them around the shack, measuring with line from a reel that was knotted at ten-foot intervals, marking off a perfect square twenty feet on each side. He then clipped several fluorescent orange plastic markers on the line that read "CRIME SCENE—DO NOT CROSS."

Dahlgren had a bad feeling in the pit of his stomach about this recovery. The killer might not have left anything behind except the girl in her silk and ribbons, but there was a possibility something could be buried in the silt. And this wasn't the type of murder that was likely to be solved by identifying the victim and matching her to an abusive husband or boyfriend. Although most murder victims are killed by people who profess to love them, those bodies are dumped in convenient and familiar locations—in a swimming hole or fishing spot, or perhaps in a creek beneath a bridge on the way to the murderer's place of employment. This, however, was bizarrely different. *Who hides his victim deep in a flooded mine, and carefully decorates her body with ribbon and silk?*

Dahlgren suspected the answer but was afraid to even think about it. *Maybe it was a one-time thing,* he optimistically told himself, *a night of passion that got out of control.* But that's not how these things worked.

If the murder couldn't be solved quickly, it would be necessary to go over every inch within the four hundred square feet he had marked off, using methods that had originally been developed for underwater archaeology, looking for a key to unlock the puzzle.

The advantage with this dump location was that it would remain undisturbed by weather, wildlife, or spectators until Dahlgren decided—or was compelled—to return.

He motioned for McAfee to join him with the body bag. The victim was short, five feet three or four, and they laid her easily into the bag and zipped it up.

Dahlgren glanced at the data display. He had spent more than forty minutes photographing the scene. He motioned thumbs-up, and he and McAfee swam upward, with the body bag between them. Then Dahlgren stopped, remembering that he had left McAfee's slate on the bottom.

"I forgot your slate," Dahlgren said.

"That's okay."

"No, I'll get it," Dahlgren said. They were only twenty feet above the shack. "It's a nice slate."

Dahlgren swam down headfirst and scooped the slate from the silt. As he raised his head to go back up, his helmet lights brushed the exterior of another shack, well away from the one where Miss October had been found. He hadn't noticed it the first time, because it was so dark at the edge of Mineral City and he hadn't looked in that direction.

"Did you search the other shack?" Dahlgren asked.

"Say again?" came the reply.

"There's another shack down here, about thirty yards due east of the one where you found the body," Dahlgren said slowly. "Did you look inside?"

"No," McAfee said. "I didn't even know it was there."

"Stand by," Dahlgren said.

"Understood," McAfee said.

He clipped the slate to a harness ring and kicked over, staying high above the shack to avoid the silt, then descended fins-first to the open door. When his helmet sank beneath the level of the header, it illuminated the interior of the shack.

There were three more girls inside, all nude, sitting on a high-backed wooden bench, arms locked in an embrace. Silk and ribbons floated around them.

Fear serpentined up Dahlgren's spine and poked into his rib cage, rummaged among his heart and lungs, and got a python-like grip on his throat. He suddenly felt sick and very cold. He closed his eyes, took a deep breath, and forced the beast back down.

When his heart had quit thumping and he no longer could hear the blood rushing in his hears, he opened his eyes again. The bodies were still there, sightless eyes aimed his way, blank expressions on dead faces.

"What do we do now?" McAfee asked an hour later, as he helped Dahlgren carry the body bag up the wooden steps. They had already removed their fins and thrown them onto the dock, and the lower parts of their masks were unsnapped.

"We contact the FBI," Dahlgren said.

They placed the bag on the deck and began to peel off the rest of their equipment, beginning with their helmets.

"I don't think there's any need to bring in the feds," Brown said as he took Dahlgren's camera housing and placed it on a bench. He had only the surface part of their conversation.

"You don't understand," McAfee told him.

"We found three more down there," Dahlgren said.

"Girls, like the first one."

"Somebody needs to jog up the mule trail and have Sergeant Bryce make the call pronto," Dahlgren said.

"Boys, I'm in no shape for jogging," Brown said calmly, then knelt beside the body bag. It was leaking, and a pool of reddish liquid was growing beneath it, and leaking between the planks to splatter in the water below. "You're sure of what you saw? Three more victims?"

"Absolutely," McAfee said.

"Sure they weren't drowning victims or—"

"Wearing only silk and ribbons?" Dahlgren asked.

"Where'd you find them?" Brown asked.

"Another shack," Dahlgren said. "They were posed in some sort of scene, like a painting."

"Did you get pictures?"

"I used all my film on the first one."

"I'm the fittest," McAfee said matter-of-factly. "I'll hike up and tell Bryce."

"No, I'm the youngest," Dahlgren said. "I'll do it."

"Quit your pissing match," the chief said. "Let's think about this for a minute before we get the federal government involved in our little problem."

The zipper growled as he opened the bag.

"Damn," the chief said, holding the body bag open and peering inside. "Did you boys bag the right one? There's nothing in here but bones."

Fourteen

"I'm not calling the feds," Brown said as he filled another Styrofoam cup with bad coffee from the big aluminum pot. "We have four victims, and there's no indication their bodies have been transported across state lines. They could have all been killed here, in which case it remains my jurisdiction."

"You think four girls could disappear from a town of four thousand without somebody noticing?" Dahlgren asked. "Got any missing-persons reports lately?"

"No," Brown said, returning to the folding table where Dahlgren and McAfee sat. "Not yet. But you said yourself the bodies looked fresh."

"Come on," Dahlgren said, stretching his legs and crossing his cowboy boots. "You just want to keep the hassle factor down by keeping the feds out, and I don't think you can. This is a federal reclamation project, isn't it? Doesn't it automatically make it FBI territory?"

"No," McAfee said. "Technically, the blockhouse and the

mine entrance are not part of the reclamation site. Mineral City is private property, and within the city limits."

Brown nodded.

They had taken the map down from the wall and placed it on the folding table. There were big red grease-pencil X's where McAfee had marked the location of the bodies.

"It's getting cold in here," Dahlgren said.

"That's because it's getting cold outside," Brown said. "Television says first frost tonight."

"I'll have to remind myself to drag an electric heater in here," McAfee said absentmindedly. "Didn't think I'd be spending much time up here. It's warmer down in the mine."

"Yeah, but my radio doesn't work down there," Brown said.

McAfee sighed heavily.

"Okay, we've got four bodies," Brown said. "And the flesh melted off the bones of the first one we tried to recover. You're the body-recovery expert, Mr. Dahlgren. Now what?"

"We recover them," Dahlgren said.

"Shouldn't you figure out why the first one melted?"

"Not my job," Dahlgren said. "I'll leave that to the patholo-gists. We know the bodies are stable in mine water, so we'll bring them up in mine water, like you do with a smaller piece of evidence to keep it from decaying when it hits the air."

"What do you use for the smaller stuff?"

"Evidence tubes," Dahlgren said. "Sounds important, but they're really just sections of PVC sewer pipe with screw-on caps that you get from the hardware store. Nalgene bottles and Ziploc bags for the really small stuff."

"Can't you use the body bags?" Brown asked.

"We need something that won't leak," Dahlgren said. "I don't know about you, but I don't want to carry anything that's seeping that pink stuff out of it."

"Okay," Brown said. "What about fifty-five-gallon drums?"

"Hard to get one clean enough to use," McAfee said. "You

123

don't want to contaminate your victim with whatever was inside the drum before."

"Also, I don't want to have to fold the victims to get them inside," Dahlgren said. "It's disrespectful. We need something full-length. And we need at least four of them."

"Aquariums," McAfee said. "They make aquariums that are two meters long and hold maybe a thousand liters of water. Problem is, when we get to the surface, the things will weigh more than a thousand kilograms."

"What's that in pounds?" Brown asked.

"A couple of thousand," Dahlgren said.

"More," McAfee corrected him. "We can bring them up in the bags, then transfer them to the tanks in shallow water. We can rig a hoist from the dock, or maybe an electric winch that goes to the head, and place them in the back of a trailer, or maybe Staci's old Scrambler, and take them up the mule trail."

"Who's Staci?"

"The smart cookie."

"What if you crack the glass?" Brown asked.

"We won't," McAfee, "because we'll do it very slowly, walking all the way beside the trailer. Once we get the aquariums up here, we put them in a box truck and send them to the morgue."

"We usually send our bodies to Farmington for autopsy," Brown said.

"How far?" Dahlgren asked.

"Twelve miles."

"That's too far," Dahlgren said. "You wouldn't risk transporting a two-hundred-gallon aquarium full of fish that far, at highway speeds, much less somebody's daughter. Where's the nearest hospital?"

"Parkland," Brown said. "Down the road about a half-mile."

"Call them," Dahlgren said. "Tell them we need a secure

The Moon Pool

room to use as a morgue until we can hand the bodies off to the pathologists. Is there a pet store in town?"

"Used to be," Brown said. "Still is, I think."

"Then call and ask if they have four aquariums at least six feet long," Dahlgren said.

"I wonder how much that will cost," Brown said.

"I guess you could ask to borrow them," Dahlgren suggested.

"That's tacky," McAfee said. "Can you imagine some jerk bragging: 'Come see my tropical fish, they're in one of the tanks they used to haul those dead girls out of the mine'?"

Brown nodded.

"I'll see what I can do," he said.

"I'll call Cal Bentham and we'll get a hoist rigged," McAfee said.

Dahlgren glanced at his Seiko.

"It's almost five o'clock," he said. "You'd better get hustling on those calls. Think we can have everything rigged by tomorrow morning?"

"We can try," McAfee said, standing.

"Don't forget the heater," Dahlgren said.

"What about you?" Brown asked. "What're your plans for tonight?"

"That depends," Dahlgren said. "Are you going to have somebody stationed here all night?"

"I can," Brown said. "Michael likes overtime."

"Then do it," Dahlgren said. "Otherwise, I'll sleep with the Helio. But more important for you is the chain of evidence. Make sure nobody goes back down in the mine."

"Nobody can get down there," McAfee said. "It's locked tight."

Dahlgren looked at him and smiled.

"Don't take this the wrong way," he said, "but at this point you're a suspect, as well as the rest of your team. The killer has to be a diver, and a good one. You and your people obviously

125

have access to the mine. Logic makes suspects of you all. Chief, it probably would be a good idea if nobody goes down in the mine without one of your officers being present."

"I guess Buntz could use some overtime as well," Brown said reluctantly.

"Sure you don't want to hand this off?" Dahlgren asked. "This is just the beginning. Do you even have a detective on the force?"

"Maternity leave," Brown said.

"Doesn't sound like you're prepared for a major case," Dahlgren said. "And what if you actually catch this guy? Think your officers can handle it?"

"I ran vice in Detroit, for Chrissake," Brown said. "I can handle it. Just get the girls out of there."

"Okay," Dahlgren said. "But you don't want to dick this up and have the feds come in to clean up the mess."

"There will be no mess," Brown said.

"Glad to hear it. I'm going to grab something to eat and get some rest," Dahlgren said. "I'm beat. You've got my cell number. Otherwise, I'll see you back here at eight in the morning. Any decent motels in town?"

Brown whistled.

"Well, there are a couple of bed-and-breakfasts."

"I hate those," Dahlgren said. "You're always on your best behavior, like you're staying in somebody's guest room. Anyway, I'm on a budget."

"I rather like bed-and-breakfasts," McAfee said.

"There's a Super Eight across the highway," Brown suggested.

"I've stayed there, but I wouldn't recommend it," McAfee said. "It's the worst Super Eight in the world. The rooms smell, and the carpet crinkles when you walk on it."

"No, I've stayed at the worst Super Eight in the world, and it's in West Memphis, Arkansas," Dahlgren said. "I can put up with carpet that crinkles. How about some place for dinner?"

"There's the usual fast-food joints near the highway,"

Brown said. "I would ordinarily recommend Vargo's on the hill, but I'm not sure they've reopened after the fire. Guess I'd recommend a local joint in the center of downtown, at the intersection of School and Division. It's walking distance."

At the Crossroads Bar and Restaurant, a blond waitress in a pair of tight jeans and work boots brought Dahlgren a bacon cheeseburger dripping with grease and a cold Budweiser in a long-necked bottle. He had asked for a Tecaté, but they didn't stock that brand of Mexican beer.

Dahlgren sat by himself at the bar, glad to be alone for a time. The waitress was attentive but not curious. She didn't ask him why he was in town, and Dahlgren was glad. For now he wanted to remain anonymous, just a stranger passing through town, which he was.

He planned to be gone by the next night.

After Dahlgren finished the burger, he called for the waitress to bring him another Budweiser, and he glanced idly around while he drank it. It was a nice joint; it had a good feel. The crowd was beginning to pick up, and people were enjoying themselves. There was a game going on at the pool table, a jukebox was playing an old Bryan Adams tune from the eighties he liked, and a college football game was playing on the big-screen television. Dahlgren didn't know who was playing and didn't care. Except for a little baseball as a kid, he had never followed team sports.

Fifteen minutes later, the waitress asked if he wanted another beer.

"Just the check."

She placed it on the table, faceup, and he handed her a ten.

"Keep the change," he said. "I'll need a receipt."

She nodded, penciled in the amount at the bottom of the ticket, and tore it off for him. Dahlgren stuffed it into his billfold, along with the month's worth of other receipts he hadn't filed yet and would probably lose.

"What is today?" Dahlgren asked suddenly.

127

"It's Halloween."

Dahlgren laughed.

The waitress was confused.

"Is that funny?"

"Not really," Dahlgren said.

It wasn't funny. It was *pathetic*, he thought. It was his birthday, and he had eaten dinner alone.

He got up to leave.

The football game had ended. Somebody had won and somebody had lost. One of the bar's drunken patrons was unsteadily clutching the remote, flipping through the channels, trying to find another game, when he accidentally stumbled on the end of the six-o'clock news from St. Louis.

"Finally, a macabre story from tiny Bonne Terre tonight," the handsome anchor said, and a locator map of St. Francois County against the outline of Missouri was flashed on the blue screen behind him. "The Associated Press is reporting that the bodies of four women have been found by scuba divers in a flooded lead mine beneath the city."

"Holy shit," the drunk said.

"The AP first suspected this story was a Halloween prank, because it was called in by the owners of a pet store who reported that local law-enforcement officials were trying to locate four aquariums large enough to place the bodies of the women in," the anchor said. "The pet store owners said the police offered no reason why aquariums would be needed. But when the AP called Clancy Brown, the town's chief of police, he confirmed that bodies had been found. He declined comment on whether aquariums had actually been requested, however."

The bar had gotten very quiet.

"The chief said the last of the bodies had been found this afternoon," the anchor said, "but declined to give details, citing an active investigation. He did say, however, that a press conference would be held sometime tomorrow. Action News will be there." The anchor dropped his voice a notch, indicating the end of the story. "Bonne Terre is about sixty miles southwest of St. Louis."

Dahlgren hadn't reached the door by the time his cell phone began to chime.

"That was quick," Dahlgren said as he stepped onto the sidewalk.

"Less than two hours after we talked about it?"

"Big news from the Styx."

"Guess we should have thought about how it would sound, asking for aquariums," Brown said. "I had Michael call the pet shop, and it scared the hell out of them."

"He didn't ask them to keep it quiet?"

"The pet shop folks thought it was a prank, then called the newspaper at the Cape to see if they'd heard anything about it."

"The Cape?" Dahlgren asked.

"Cape Girardeau."

It was a beautiful evening. The sky was Parrish blue, stars were beginning to twinkle, and a light wind chased brown and red leaves down Division Street.

"We should have thought of the timing," Dahlgren said. "*War of the Worlds* and all that. So when are you having this press conference?"

"I don't know," Brown said. "What am I going to tell them?"

"Well, you're going to have to tell them something," Dahlgren said. "Stick to the truth. McAfee found one body yesterday. I found three bodies today. We don't know who they are."

"Right," Brown said.

"Did you find the fish tanks?"

"Yeah, in St. Louis. I sent Michael after them."

"Who's at the mine?"

"Buntz."

"Did McAfee have any luck?"

129

Max McCoy

"Don't know. Haven't asked yet."

"Give him a call," Dahlgren said.

"I will, first thing tomorrow."

Dahlgren paused.

"Think," he urged. "This town is going to be crawling with reporters in the morning. Do you want them shooting video of dead girls in aquariums being loaded on a truck?"

"We're not going to sleep tonight, are we?"

"No," Dahlgren said. "See you at the blockhouse in thirty minutes. I need the walk. You'd better start calling your people and working out around-the-clock shifts."

Dahlgren thumbed off.

A gaggle of ghosts and goblins swept past. None of them was older than ten, and the youngest had legs so short that she had trouble keeping up. They were laughing behind their masks and swinging plastic jack-o'-lanterns full of candy, unaware of the evil beneath them.

Fifteen

Geiger was dreaming again.

He was nine years old and his mother was kneeling in the subterranean lake before the shaman. His red handprints smeared her breasts and face, he was kneeling close to her, and blood was streaming from a shallow cut across her throat. The shaman had asked her a question, and he was waiting expectantly, peering intensely into her unfocused eyes.

"I don't know," she said. "I'm sick."

She swayed and began to fall into the water, but the shaman caught her. Her head lolled against his chest, and she suddenly spewed vomit over him.

He didn't seem to mind.

"Patterns," his mother said weakly. "Shapes. Dizzy."

The shaman wiped the vomit from her mouth.

"Someone's here," she said. "A woman. It's . . . my grandmother. She says not to be afraid. Behind is her mother, and her mother before that, until I can't recognize them anymore."

The shaman made a low, comforting noise.

"There are others here, too. Some aren't human."

Several minutes passed as his mother mumbled and whispered about things that only she could see. The shaman listened carefully to it all, and although he gave no indication that he spoke English, it was clear he understood her tone. Finally, when his mother's eyelids fluttered and her eyes rolled upward, showing only the whites, he slipped his other hand beneath her and picked her up.

He carried her as if she weighed nothing. Cradling her in his arms, as one would carry a sleeping child to bed, he waded slowly into the lake.

The others held Jakob back. When he tried to fight, to run to her, a bone-crushing grip on his neck drove him to his knees in the water. Jakob tried to cry out, to speak, to call to his mother, but could find no voice.

The shaman asked the question.

Jakob began to sob.

His mother opened her eyes at the sound of Jakob's voice.

The shaman asked the question again.

"Yes," his mother said.

The shaman regarded her compassionately.

They were in chest-deep water now, his mother as much floating as being held. Her hands were looped around his neck, and with great difficulty she managed to lift her head from the water. He bent low over her, bringing his left ear close to her mouth, and his mouth spoke in a language Jakob didn't understand.

The shaman smiled, then released her.

Her fingers lost their grip on his neck, coming away smeared in red, and her eyes were focused now and staring at Jakob. As she floated away she began to sink into the dark water, and the last thing to disappear was a wisp of blond hair.

Jakob thought his chest would burst. The sound finally came, ripped from his lungs in one long spasmodic exhalation: "M-M-M-M-M-Mother!"

The Moon Pool

* * *

Geiger woke.

He was wearing a red robe, sitting in a leather chair in his loft apartment in a "rehabilitated" 1850s tobacco warehouse on the northeastern corner of Morgan and North First Streets in the old riverfront district. The room was dark, save for a warm cone of light cast by a reading lamp, and a biography of Robert Graves lay open on his lap. Above him there was a framed print of Waterhouse's *The Lady of Shalott*, her face forever frozen in erotic longing. She drifted toward Camelot, a tapestry draped in the water, three candles and a crucifix on the prow of her boat.

Beyond the south-facing window he could see the apex of the illuminated 630-foot stainless-steel arch that had been the city's signature landmark since 1965. A decade later, work began to rip up the asphalt that hid the original nineteenth-century granite paving bricks that had carried the iron-rimmed and iron-shod traffic to the levee, two short blocks to the west. This had created an emotional bond in Geiger with the riverfront district, since the tough "pavers" that had replaced the limestone blocks that crushed to a choking dust under the heavy riverfront traffic had come from near his boyhood home in the St. Francois Mountains, eighty miles to the south. Millions of these pavers had been cut from inferior blocks of the range's 1.5-billion-year-old granite, by hand, with hammer and chisel, and had brought a price of nine cents apiece. More than a century later they were still in use, serving as the street surface for the Midwest's most historic riverfront.

Geiger carefully closed the Graves biography and placed it on the table next to the lamp. The television was on, but the sound was muted. It was the ten-o'clock news from one of the local stations, and Geiger recognized the outline of St. Francois County on the Missouri map behind the anchor.

Superimposed across the map was a cartoonish image of a

Max McCoy

body outlined in chalk, and Geiger could lip-read the words "Bonne Terre" and "mine."

By the time he had found the remote in the cushion of the chair and unmuted the set, the story was over and the anchor was reminding viewers to set their clocks back one hour, because it was not only Halloween but the last Sunday in October and the end of daylight saving time.

Geiger switched off the set.

So it had begun. He knew that eventually some of his sacrifices would be found, but he had never dreamed it would take forty years. And yet there was comfort in the number. It was sacrosanct in Scripture and important in English common law. Moses was forty days on the mount, the flood lasted forty days and forty nights, and for forty days Jesus fasted. Alchemists believed forty days was the charmed period when the philosopher's stone would appear. Sanctuary lasted forty days, a widow was allowed to remain in her dead husband's house for forty days, a stranger offered hospitality for forty days.

But forty *years*.

When he began, having attained manhood but not yet given the right to vote, the sporting-goods salesman who had sold him the U.S. Divers double-hose regulator and the steel 72 had told him that it was impossible to get the bends on a single tank of air. The Beatles were about to arrive in America, the country was grieving the death of John F. Kennedy, the St. Louis arch had not yet been completed, and the bathyscaphe *Trieste* had located the remains of the submarine *Thresher* in 8,500 feet of water but could not determine the cause of her sinking.

The press of history tightened his chest.

Forty years.

Not quite, he reminded himself. There had been only thirty-nine sacrifices so far. Jolene Carter would complete the cycle. The days were short and there was much left to do. But Geiger knew that if he was careful, there was still time to complete his task.

* * *

The dawn was clear and cold and reminded Dahlgren of those mornings he had spent shivering in duck blinds, his waders heavy and cold against his legs, a shotgun covered with frost across his lap. In a neat bit of synchronicity, Dahlgren heard the whistle of wings and looked up in time to see a flight of mallards silhouetted against the cobalt sky. Their wings were set and they were apparently headed for some pond beyond the remediation area.

"Hunter?" McAfee asked.

"Used to be," Dahlgren said.

They watched as Michael Schwartz put the yellow Ryder truck in gear and pulled slowly away from the blockhouse. Brown was leading the way in his white Ford Explorer, the light bar silently pulsating red and blue, the tires crunching lazily on the gravel. There was no hurry to get the last victim to the basement of Parkland Hospital and the locked room where the thermostat had been turned down to sixty-two degrees.

"Why'd you quit?" McAfee asked.

"Decided I didn't like killing things," Dahlgren said. "Haven't picked up a gun since."

McAfee nodded.

"Ever get your room at the Super Eight?"

"Nope," Dahlgren said.

"Then come stay at my place," McAfee said. "I've got to be at school in a couple of hours, and you'll have the run of the place. Sleep as long as you want. Eat what you can find."

Dahlgren hesitated.

"Or would it be too much like a bed-and-breakfast?"

"It's not that," Dahlgren said. "Do you have *cable?*"

"Get in the friggin' truck," McAfee said, walking suddenly toward his old blue Ford. "At least you'll be warm. You've been complaining about being cold all night."

Dahlgren smiled.

Friggin'? he thought. *That's the best McAfee can do?*

Dahlgren turned and looked at Buntz, who was sitting in a folding chair just inside the door of the blockhouse. His feet were propped up on the folding table and a cigarette hung from the corner of his mouth.

"It's all yours, buckaroo."

Dahlgren shoved his hands into his jeans pockets and followed McAfee.

Sixteen

Geiger had waited for two hours that Monday morning in the parking lot across the street from Jolene Carter's apartment complex for her cordless phone to ring.

He didn't know, of course, that Jolene had a cordless phone, but the odds were in his favor. If a college student had a phone at all other than a cell phone, it was likely to be a cordless model. And a working-class Bible college student on a tight budget was likely to have an older model, one that had been passed down through family or friends, and more important, one that operated in the 46-megahertz band, that could still be picked up by a handheld scanner.

Geiger had programmed the twenty most common pairs of base and handset frequencies into the scanner, and had replaced the stubby antenna with a BNC connector and coax that led to a quarter-wave antenna on the trunk lid. He had started picking up signals immediately, as there were several dozen cordless within range, and at least a couple in use at any given time. As he eavesdropped, he locked out those channels that were obvious misses, the ones that were baby or room monitors, or in which the participants were both male or elderly.

The black Crown Vic had pulled into the grocery store parking lot while Jolene slept. He didn't know where her apartment was located in the complex, and he couldn't even see her building from the lot. He had gotten her address from the Bible college's student directory, but he took care to stay far enough away so that a casual observer would not realize he was stalking her. Besides, anyone bold enough to peer through the Crown Vic's tinted windows would conclude that the gentleman in the suit and tie listening to a handheld radio was probably an undercover police officer.

Although unaware of her activities, Geiger waited patiently while she showered and dressed, while she ate cereal out of a plastic bowl, and while she gathered her books and placed them in the backpack on her kitchen table.

She had slung the backpack over her shoulder and was headed for the door when the phone rang. She paused, her hand on the latch, fighting the middle-class urge in her gut to respond when summoned by a telephone or a knock on the door. At the fifth ring, she sighed heavily, crossed the room, and picked up the white handset from the kitchen table and pressed the talk button.

"—lo?" Geiger heard Jolene's voice over the scanner.

"Are you feeling well?" an older woman asked.

"Yes, Aunt Connie," Jolene said.

Geiger locked in the frequencies.

"I didn't think I would catch you at home this late."

"I didn't run this morning," Jolene said.

"I had a feeling you were ill."

"I'm not ill," Jolene said. "I just overslept."

Geiger glanced at his watch—9:12—and wondered *where* she ran. There didn't seem to be any convenient location in this section of Springfield, which was filled with strip malls and busy streets.

"Sure you're okay?"

"I'm fine," Jolene said. "I just had a really long shift at the radio station last night. Look, Aunt Connie, I'm in kind of a hurry right now. I've got to be in my Spanish class in twenty minutes."

"What are you taking that for?" the aunt asked. "I've had it with all the Mexicans in the stores around here, yammering away in a language you can't understand. They should make a law that when you move here, you speak English."

"You know I volunteered for Bolivia after graduation," Jolene said. "None of the children at the free clinic at Madre de Dios will be speaking English, so I've got to have some way to communicate with them."

"I suppose that's different," the older woman grudgingly allowed.

"Got to run," Jolene said. "Call you later, okay? Love you. 'Bye."

The line went dead.

Geiger stroked his jaw. He didn't know where she ran, but he knew approximately when—probably an hour earlier. Did she run alone or with a partner? Alone, he guessed, because a partner wouldn't have let her oversleep.

He also guessed that Jolene wouldn't be frightened of isolated running trails. She was headed for Bolivia, after all. She would seek a natural setting, in a city park or perhaps a trail at the edge of town. Was there a public trail nearby that opened about eight A.M.? That meant she would have to drive to get there, but Geiger had no idea of what make or model of car she would use. No car was registered to her, at least not when he checked with the Missouri Division of Motor Vehicles.

A plan was forming, but Geiger lacked information.

And it was already November 1, All Saints' Day. Subtracting the requisite twenty-eight days in the underworld, that left him less than three weeks to research, to plan, to act. The universe ran according to immutable laws, and time was something he could not afford to waste. He was ashamed of having wasted time with that little methamphetamine whore in Joplin.

But Jolene Carter would more than make up for that misadventure. Jolene Carter, Bible college student, aspiring missionary, and radio morality adviser to the Ozarks' fundamentalist children, could be the most delicious of all.

She was *Persephone*.

But there was no room for mistakes. Geiger was fifty-nine years old. Sixty next August. Sixty! Who would take his place when he was gone? Smith? He showed little promise. Geiger couldn't think about it now. There were more pressing matters at hand.

Geiger knew he must use every opportunity to its best advantage. A *little help*, he thought. Was the universe listening? Was Great Pan truly dead or just sleeping?

Just then, the putter of an old Volkswagen beetle brought him out of his musings. It was faded yellow, with cankers of rust on the rear fenders, and an engine that apparently lacked a working muffler.

It pulled into a parking space nearest the entrance of the grocery store.

Jolene Carter stepped out.

She was running late for her Spanish class, but routine dictated that she stop for a diet Dr Pepper and a tin of Altoids on her way to school.

Loren McAfee's house was a modest ranch-style on Plum Street, a couple of blocks north of the tiny business district and not far from where McAfee taught at North County High School. McAfee showered, dressed, hung a tie around his neck, and left Dahlgren alone.

After Dahlgren showered, he rifled the refrigerator and found some peanut butter, which he spread on a single piece of bread and devoured in three bites. Then he filled a tall glass of water and drank it while standing at the kitchen sink.

He crashed on the couch in the living room and tried to sleep, but couldn't shut off his mind. He worried about the film he had exposed of the victims and had yet to develop, he worried whether the Helio was still tied down properly at the remediation site, and he wondered if there was anything else in the mine they should worry about. Then he started worrying about how they were going to identify the victims.

After half an hour, he rose and pulled on his boots and jeans and blue workshirt, borrowed a canvas jacket from McAfee's closet, and locked the door behind him. He first walked to the mine site, where he reassured himself the Courier was safely staked to the earth, and learned from Michael Schwartz that Brown had scheduled the press conference for two P.M.

Then he asked Michael if there was a one-hour photo shop in town, and for the telephone number of the artist who had loaned them the Scrambler to get the bodies out of the mine.

"Ready?" Brown asked.

"Just a sec," Dana Casteel said.

"Give me a white balance," Dave, the camera operator, said as he peered through the viewfinder. Dana held a page of her notebook in front of the chief's face.

"Got it," Dave said.

Brown was sitting behind a long table in the high-windowed meeting room just inside the entrance of Bonne Terre Memorial Library. Just across the hall was the reading room with the oak-and-marble fireplace mantel where young Jakob Geiger had been introduced to the erotic art of the Pre-Raphaelite Brotherhood, and where nearby the three-hundred-year-old clock still mocked the duration of a single human lifetime.

But Brown could not appreciate the irony.

He had chosen the location because the library meeting room was where the city council met at seven P.M. on the second Tuesday of every month, and it was the only room the chief could think of to hold a press conference that might draw more than a handful of people. For the last six years, city hall had been located in "temporary" quarters around the corner from a Subway sandwich shop in a strip mall on the other side of Highway 67. It was cramped and hard to find, unless you were a regular Subway patron, and Brown was afraid it would make the wrong impression on out-of-town reporters.

The municipal offices had been formerly located downtown, in Heritage Hall (originally the St. Joseph Lead Company's Department Store, and built for some now-obscure reason to resemble Shakespeare's home on Stratford-on-Avon), but had moved to the shopping mall to await repairs. The police and fire departments had relocated to the north end of Division Street, in equally smallish quarters, and Brown was afraid of having the fire department's garage doors blocked by news crews. But the library had recently been remodeled, was easy to find, and was already in use as the meeting place of the city council.

None of this last-minute strategy, however, had prepared Brown for the packed room he faced that afternoon.

A bouquet of microphones had been placed on the table in front of him, and a dozen video cameras on tripods were aimed his way. A couple of newspaper photographers loitered in the back as well, carrying their motor-driven cameras and fast lenses with the same studied bravado he had seen displayed by wiseguys carrying guns in Detroit. The sunlight streaming in through the windows had been deemed insufficient by the television corps and was now supplemented by a brace of high-wattage video lights. The lights and the heat generated by the number of bodies in the room had driven up the room temperature, and Brown could feel the sweat beginning to collect on his upper lip. Also, he was dead tired. His eyeballs felt as if they had been rolled in sand.

Dahlgren slipped into the room with a thick file folder under his arm and leaned against a wall in the back. All of the chairs were taken.

"Everybody ready?" Brown asked. "I've got a prepared statement."

He cleared his throat.

"At approximately seven hundred hours today, the remains of four individuals were removed from the old St. Joan Lead Mine within the Bonne Terre city limits and transported to Parkland Hospital," he read stiffly from a page on the table in front of him. "All of the remains were recovered by scuba divers in about a hundred and forty feet of water. None of the individuals have been identified, and the case remains under investigation."

He stopped.

"That's it?" Dana asked.

"That's it," the chief said.

He started to rise, but the room erupted as thirty reporters tried to ask questions at once.

"One at a time," the chief said.

"Chief, are the victims women?" a reporter from St. Louis asked.

"Yes," Brown said.

"Were they murdered?"

"We're not sure," Brown said. "We're awaiting autopsy results."

"What about reports that your department was requesting aquariums to transport the victims in?" a woman from the Cape Girardeau newspaper asked.

"I can't comment on that," the chief asked.

"Why not?" the woman asked. "Is it true?"

"It involves the investigation," Brown said. "No comment."

"*Chief,*" Dana Casteel said, louder than the others, then

143

asked her question before she was recognized. "I talked to some employees at Parkland Hospital this morning, and they told me that the bodies in the aquariums there seemed to be in a remarkable state of preservation."

"Which employee did you talk to?" the chief asked.

"He asked that I not use his name," Dana said.

"Sorry," the chief said. "I don't comment on rumors that come from unnamed sources."

"He also said that the victims were exsanguinated, and that there was some substance in their veins other than blood. I believe he said it was bluish."

"Exsanguinated?" the chief asked.

"Drained of blood," Dana said. "And what about the way in which these girls died?"

"No comment."

"Come on, chief," Dana said. "They didn't take off all their clothes, pump the blood out of their own veins and replace it with God knows what, and then drown themselves so their bodies could be arranged in what one of the divers called . . ."

She glanced at her notes.

". . . *tableaux mordants?*"

"What's that mean?"

"I had to look it up," Dana said. "Fortunately, we're in a library. A *tableau vivant* is a scene presented by living actors in which the performers freeze in position. A *tableau mordant*, then, would be a frozen scene in which the subjects are dead."

"And this information came from this unnamed employee?"

"He said he's friends with a scuba diver named Staci Johnson who was with the group that discovered the first body," Dana said. "He said she was really quite shaken. This is pretty chilling stuff, Chief."

"What are you getting at?"

Dana looked him in the eye.

"Do we have a serial killer working in rural Missouri?"

Brown coughed.

"Miss," he said, "if you put that on television, you're going to scare everybody to death."

"Maybe they should be scared."

Brown had had more than enough. He hated journalists, the press conference had become a disaster, and rumors that he hadn't even heard yet were being aired in public.

"No more questions, please," Brown said, exasperated. "This press conference is over."

"Please, just a little background on the mine," the Cape Girardeau reporter asked. "And I'm not sure I understand how and where these bodies were discovered. What were the scuba divers doing in the mine in the first place, and where did they find them?"

Brown hesitated.

In the back, Dahlgren waved and caught Brown's attention. Relieved, Brown nodded.

"I'm not a diver, but the gentleman who supervised the recovery is here," Brown said. "I'm going to defer questions to him. I think he can answer your questions in a general way that won't compromise our investigation."

Dahlgren squeezed past Dana as he made his way to the front of the room with a manila folder under his arm.

"Dick Dahlgren," Dana said.

"Richard," he said. "Do we know one another?"

"I covered the body recovery of the trooper a few days ago at Table Rock," she said. "I'm with Color Three, Springfield. I've been calling your office in Kansas because I'd like to do an interview, but all I get is an answering machine."

"That's because I'm not there," Dahlgren said, and walked around the table. He leaned over and conferred quietly with the chief, then showed him the contents of the folder. The chief paused for a moment, then nodded.

Brown introduced Dahlgren, then gave him his seat.

"I'm happy to answer your questions about diving, body recovery, and what I've learned recently about the history of the St. Joan Lead Mine," Dahlgren said. "But first I would like to ask for your help in identifying the victims. As you apparently have learned, the victims lacked clothing or anything else on their persons that might help identify them."

Brown had dragged a bulletin board from the corner of the room to within Dahlgren's reach, and Dahlgren turned and began to tack up pencil sketches.

"We took photographs of the victims before we recovered them from the water," Dahlgren said. "The photographs are excellent forensic tools, but they are a little too graphic for public consumption. So we asked the talented artist who is a member of the St. Joan survey team—the one you've already heard about—to attempt life sketches from the photos, and I think you'll agree that she did an excellent job on such short notice."

Dahlgren tacked up the last of the drawings.

In addition to front and side views of the faces, there were a couple that showed the bodies as they were found in the shacks.

"We're asking anyone who recognizes these women to call the Bonne Terre Police Department," Dahlgren said. "Chief Brown is prepared to track down any promising lead in identifying these women. What's that number, Chief?"

Brown coughed, then gave the direct line to his office.

"We're only a ten-officer department, so if your call isn't answered immediately, please leave a message and we'll contact you as soon as possible," he said. "Please don't call nine-one-one, because those calls are routed through central dispatch in Desloge, and it's for emergency traffic only."

"Making a positive identification may be the first step in catching the killer," Dahlgren continued, "so we'd like to ask that you keep these faces on the air—and in your newspapers, for you print folks—until we know who these girls are."

"How were they killed?" the St. Louis reporter asked.

146

"I don't know," Dahlgren said. "It wasn't apparent from my field examination. They could have drowned, but I can't say that's a fact."

"What department are you with?" he asked.

"I'm a private consultant," Dahlgren said, then spelled his name for them. "And I go by Richard only, so please don't call me Dick."

The room laughed.

"That sketch of the three women together with their arms on each other's shoulders," the Cape Girardeau reporter said. "It looks vaguely familiar, like something I saw when studying art in college."

"The Three Graces," someone called.

"Yes, our artist thought so too," Dahlgren said. "I'm not familiar with it, but she was quite sure. It might be just a coincidence, however."

Two hours later, Dahlgren was shaking hands with the reporters and photographers as they filed out of the meeting room. He managed to avoid Dana Casteel, however.

When the room was finally empty, Brown placed a hand on Dahlgren's shoulder and thanked him.

Dahlgren shrugged.

"I'm used to talking in public," he said. "I used to give lots of lectures and magazine interviews. Not so much now. Really hadn't intended on taking over, but I got to thinking about how to identify the victims, and figured putting their faces on television was the fastest way."

"Can't hurt," Brown said. "At least, I hope not."

"The killer will already know we found them," Dahlgren said.

"I'm sure he's already getting the hell out of Dodge."

"Can't say," Dahlgren said. "The only thing I know about serial killers is what I've seen in movies, but I can't imagine they're that charming in real life. Listen, I'm going to take off.

You've got the evidence photos in the envelope, and I'll send you my reports within the week. Wish I could say it was my pleasure, but I can't."

As they shook, Dahlgren's cell phone chimed.

"Aren't you going to answer it?" Brown asked.

"If this were a movie," Dahlgren said, "I'd know better."

But he took the phone from his belt, listened intently for about a minute, grunted a couple of times, then hung up.

"That was Loren," he said. "He and a couple of his divers went back down for a look-see, just to make sure the area where they recovered the bodies was clear."

"And?" Brown asked.

"They found two more in the barracks."

Seventeen

Grace Matheson parked her government sedan a hundred yards from the bright blue blockhouse, tucked the morning's edition of the Cape Girardeau newspaper beneath her arm, and started off across the muddy expanse.

Her eyes were shaded from the bright autumn sun by a pair of old Foster Grants, and she was dressed in a conservative blue business suit. Her black overcoat was unbuttoned and flapped in the breeze as she walked.

A twenty-year-old camper towing a gas-powered generator and a brace of high-intensity lights passed her on the way to the mine entrance, splashing rust-colored mud on her slacks and overcoat. On the RV's side was ST. FRANCOIS COUNTY CIVIL DEFENSE MOBILE COMMAND POST. A television news van with a satellite dish on top nosed in behind the camper, and an annoyed police officer in blue fatigues waved the van to a stop.

"Didn't you see the sign?" Michael Schwartz asked. "We've

got to keep this area clear. You're going to have to pull back to the road and park in the designated area."

"But we need to do a live feed for six o'clock," the driver protested.

"I'm sorry, sir, but if you need the van for that, you'll just have to do it from the parking area," Schwartz said. Then he added: "Thanks."

The van began to back up but was stopped by the bleat of a horn from a telephone company truck. A news helicopter from a competing St. Louis station swooped overhead.

"Pardon me," Matheson said, approaching Schwartz. "Can you tell me where I can find Chief Brown?"

At the end of the mule trail, the dock was the focus of activity. The main board had been enclosed by a boxlike structure of two-by-fours and heavy plastic, and the makeshift office was heated by a pair of oil-filled electric heaters. Bigger and more detailed maps of the mine than the one up in the blockhouse were tacked to the board, along with Dahlgren's evidence photos of the six victims.

Inside the plastic tent, a cable employee unreeled coax from a spool, then began crimping a connector to the end. A twenty-three-inch television was strapped to a wheeled cart beside a large metal desk, and on top of the desk was a multi-line telephone.

Dahlgren and the chief were sitting at the desk, and Dahlgren picked up the telephone, then slammed it back down in disgust.

"Why does the cable guy always beat the phone company?" he asked. "And can you tell me why cops are dressing like soldiers now? You know, the military look."

"Nine-eleven," Brown said.

"It started before," Dahlgren said.

"That bothers you?" Brown asked.

"Well, yeah," Dahlgren said. "That's one of the things my dad—USS *Pennsylvania*, Pearl Harbor, thank you very much—said made us different from other countries, that our cops weren't the military and that we didn't have to have papers to go from one state to the next."

"Got to have security," Brown said.

"At what price?" Dahlgren asked, warming to the fight. "I'll bet the average German felt *secure* under the fucking Nazis, at least until they came and kicked down his front door."

"Did you kiss your mother with that mouth?" Brown asked. "I think I liked you better with no sleep. You were a helluva lot quieter."

"You want HBO or Showtime?" the cable guy said, interrupting. "How about the Playboy Channel?"

"Just basic," Brown said. "As long as we get the St. Louis stations and CNN."

The chief picked up the remote and hit the power button. The snow on the television screen was suddenly replaced by a soap opera—*like sand through the hourglass.*

"Let's not be hasty," Dahlgren said. "Loren is paying for this, and I think he would *want* the Playboy Channel."

The cable guy grinned.

"Excuse me," Matheson said, somewhere between apologetic and indignant. She absently brushed her short brown hair from her forehead. She had been standing at the edge of the dock for more than a minute. "Chief Brown? Hate to interrupt your male bonding, but—"

"How did you get down here?" Brown asked. "They're not supposed to let anybody past the blockhouse."

"Well, I showed them this," Matheson said, taking her FBI credentials from her pocket. She opened the wallet and allowed the chief to examine her creds, but not to hold them.

"I apologize," Brown said.

"Do you prefer Grace, or do you have a nickname?" Dahlgren asked.

"Agent," she said. "I'm the resident over at the Cape."

"How far is that?" Dahlgren asked.

"About an hour away," Brown said. "Look, I don't mean to be rude, Agent Matheson, but we hadn't requested any help from the Bureau."

"That's what I understand," she said. "The St. Louis field office has been following the case in the press and asked if I would pay your department a courtesy call."

"So this is an unofficial visit?" Brown asked.

"You can call it that," she said. "Of course, you can deal directly with St. Louis, if you like."

"That won't be necessary," Brown said. "Why don't you grab one of those folding chairs and let's chat."

"Sorry," Dahlgren said, bringing her the chair.

"You must be Richard Dahlgren. I saw your picture in this morning's paper. Do you go by Dick?"

"Not if I can help it."

"Mr. Dahlgren, then," Matheson said. "Let's drop the sparring, shall we? Frankly, for the last year all I've done is track down foreign nationals whose names end in vowels and give free advice to the locals on their Social Security problems while desperately waiting for something to happen. Mind if I smoke?"

"Well, yes," Dahlgren said. "There's a shitload of compressed oxygen behind us. And I quit last week."

"Congratulations. How's that working for you?"

"If you lit one in front of me," Dahlgren said, "I'd have to kill you for it."

"Great," Matheson said. "As I was saying, the good thing about the kind of assignment I have is that resident agents have a good deal of latitude in helping with cases that aren't strictly under the Bureau's jurisdiction."

"Like this one," Brown said.

"Yes," Matheson said. "But I have the feeling that once some of the victims are identified, this might become a Bureau matter. State lines and all that."

"Forgive me," Dahlgren said, "but are you new to this area? You seem out of place."

"You do catch on," Matheson said. "From what I've read this morning, I'd say you need some help. What you're dealing with is not just a serial killer but a different kind of killer, one that is drawn to the hidden corners of the earth and the human mind. A subtern, if you will."

"Did you practice that?" Dahlgren asked.

"Yes," she said. "In the car, this morning. How'd it sound?"

"Not bad," Brown said. "Go on."

"Thanks."

"What do you mean by subtern?" Dahlgren asked.

"It's a term I use to describe a subterranean subject—not just an unknown subject, which is an unsub in Bureau jargon, but one that is deep underground. In this case, literally. This is not your typical thirty-three-year-old loser with a history of bed-wetting, torturing animals, and fire-starting."

"The homicidal triad," Brown said.

"Exactly. That is what the Bureau has traditionally used to profile serial killers," Matheson said. "But your guy, I'd say, *unofficially*, is a professional male in his fifties, an expert scuba diver, and intelligent to the point of genius. He may be a police buff or a cop."

"You got all this from the morning paper?" Dahlgren asked.

"Well, no," Matheson said, and smiled. "When I joined the Bureau, my goal was to work my way up to the Investigative Support Unit and become a profiler. My dissertation was on organized killers."

"Organized?" Dahlgren asked. "Like in organized crime?"

"No," she said. "Multiple murderers are classified as either organized or unorganized. An unorganized sex killer, for example, might be an unemployed man of average to low intelligence who commits crimes of opportunity, leaves the crime scene sloppy, and even fails to deposit his semen."

"Then an organized killer is the opposite," Dahlgren said.

"Right. He thinks, he plans, he gets the job done, and he is harder to catch," she said. "Considering the amount of planning that was involved in the placement of the victims, what you have is a very organized killer."

"And he *plants* his seed?" Dahlgren asked.

"Not necessarily," Matheson said. "There is certainly a sexual component, but the sexual act doesn't seem to be the goal. Performing sexually in the environment these bodies were placed in would be . . ."

"Difficult," Dahlgren said.

"Difficult," Matheson said. "Also, there is something else."

"What?" Brown asked.

"I'm going on sketchy information here," Matheson said cautiously, "but I'd say there is a ritual of some kind involved. It may be something religious. But I've got a strange feeling in the pit of my stomach about it."

"A strange feeling?" Dahlgren asked.

"I follow my hunches," Matheson said. "Don't you?"

"I think we all do," Brown said.

"Let me be up front about this," Matheson said. "This is an area where the Bureau and I part company, but I feel most crimes leave a kind of psychic fingerprint. If you can tap into that, things become clearer."

Dahlgren rolled his eyes.

"Don't be so skeptical, Mr. Dahlgren," Matheson said. "The best profilers—Douglas and Ressler, for example—can rarely explain what they do. Oh, they talk about gathering as much data as they can, immersing themselves in the case, but when it comes to explaining how they make that critical leap from their mind to the mind of the killer, they can't. It's my belief that leap is as much psychic as it is scientific."

Dahlgren suppressed a chuckle.

"Laugh," Matheson said. "But scratch the surface of virtually every scientific advance, and you find this process at work—Kekule dreaming the structure of benzene as a snake eating its own tail, for example. Perhaps it's a part of the mind we don't yet understand, but that makes it no less remarkable."

"Next you'll be talking about quantum mechanics, spooky action at a distance, and remote viewing," Dahlgren said. "But when you're twenty minutes from the exit to a sump, and you only have gas for ten minutes, you're dead. Those are the cold equations, Agent Matheson."

Brown held up his hand.

"Why don't you just agree to disagree, okay?"

"So from this point," Matheson said, "you acknowledge that the Bureau is taking the lead. Agents don't waste time interviewing witnesses in nonfederal cases, Chief."

"Meaning you're the boss," Dahlgren said.

"We'll be dealing with you and nobody else?" Brown asked.

"For as long as I'm on the case, yes."

"Then I don't care if you commune with the elves and faeries," Brown said. "Welcome aboard, Agent Matheson."

"Thanks, I think," she said. "But what about you, Mr. Dahlgren? I think I had better have your support as well. I don't dive—can't even swim, as a matter of fact—and you're going to have to be our eyes and ears down there."

Dahlgren looked pensively over the subterranean lake.

"Just so you know," Dahlgren said slowly, "I don't take orders. That's why I'm a *private* investigator. And I'm only here until the money runs out."

"When's that?" Matheson asked.

"We're a small department," Brown said. "Maybe a week."

"And who are you letting pay for all of *this*?" Matheson asked.

"Loren McAfee," Brown said. "He owns the mine. He said he was going to get some heat and communication down here anyway."

"Where is he?"

"He's teaching high school," Brown said.

The telephone on the desk began to blink and then ring.

"Finally," Brown said. "I had my office line directed here. Excuse me." He punched the flashing button and picked up the receiver.

"This is the hot line," he said, smiling at Dahlgren. "Really?" He motioned for a sheet of paper, and Dahlgren found him a legal pad from the box of office supplies next to the desk. He started taking notes, then slowed as the call continued.

"Sir, could you hold for just a moment? I've got another call." He put the caller on hold. "We're dredging up all the kooks. This guy saw the drawings on a Tulsa station last night. Claims victim number three is his dead wife."

"And?" Matheson asked.

"His wife was reported missing in 1968."

Brown shook his head and resumed the conversation.

"Sir?" he asked. "Sorry for the delay. We appreciate your call, and we'll check it out just as soon—"

"Wait," Dahlgren said. "Have him describe her."

Brown covered the mouthpiece.

"We released the drawings," Brown protested. "And we gave a description of their age, weight, hair, and eye color."

Dahlgren was up from his chair and at the board, looking at the evidence photos he had taken.

"Ask him if she had any birthmarks."

"That woman has not been in the water for thirty-six years."

"Just ask," Dahlgren said.

Brown shrugged.

"Oh, Mr. Davis. There's one other thing I forgot. Did your wife—that's right, Regina—did she have any identifying marks, such as a scar, a birthmark, or a tattoo anywhere?" He turned to Dahlgren at the board. "A liver-colored birthmark the shape of Africa on her shoulder? Left or right?"

Dahlgren unpinned a close-up of victim three's back and placed it on the desk in front of Brown. Matheson rose from the chair for a better look. There was a smudge the shape of Africa on the right shoulder blade.

"You don't say," Brown said. "The right shoulder."

Brown glanced from Dahlgren to Matheson.

"Mr. Davis, I wonder if it would be too much trouble to ask you to come here to Bonne Terre and take a look at the body? We're trying for a positive identification. Yes sir, I know you're seventy-two and don't drive, but we could arrange transportation for you. Could we have a car pick you up tomorrow?"

Matheson had uncapped her pen from the inside of her jacket pocket, and she quickly and neatly wrote on a corner of Brown's legal pad: *dental & med records, family photos.* She paused, then added: *missing persons report.*

"Also, sir, there are some things we would like you to bring, if you could locate them."

"I hope you don't mind," William Bryce said as he left the elevator and joined the group drinking coffee from paper cups outside the unmarked basement room, "but I'd really like to see how this pans out."

"No problem," Dahlgren said. "Agent Matheson, have you met Wild Bill Bryce?"

"We've seen one another professionally once or twice," Matheson said, shaking Bryce's hand. "But this is the first time I've heard that nickname."

It surprised everyone to see Bryce blush.

"It was something they called me a long time ago," he said. "I suppose I'm not so wild anymore. I'm interested because I hear this Davis was a vet as well. Korea and 'Nam."

"I didn't know," Matheson said.

"He doesn't talk about it much," Dahlgren said.

"Who does?" Bryce asked with a smile.

"What did you do in-country?" Matheson asked.

"I was a tunnel rat," Byrce said. "I was the one they sent

157

down into the VC tunnels with a twelve-gauge pump shotgun, a government-issued plastic flashlight, and a cranium full of adrenaline."

Michael Schwartz arrived beneath the emergency entrance to Parkland Hospital with seventy-two-year-old Denny Davis in the front seat of his patrol car at eight o'clock the following night.

Dahlgren, Brown, Bryce, and Matheson had been waiting for more than two hours, but Davis had said he was hungry, so the young man had felt obligated to stop at a Cracker Barrel along the way and get the nice old guy a decent meal. They had been running on fast food ever since leaving Ardmore that morning, and their progress had been impeded by the frequent stops Davis had to make to urinate.

Finally the elevator chimed in the hospital basement and Schwartz allowed the old man to step off first. Davis wore tan slacks and a blue windbreaker over a white golf shirt, and he regarded each of the individuals that Schwartz introduced through a pair of thick, black-rimmed glasses.

"He brought this," Schwartz said, offering a manila envelope. Matheson took it and glanced inside. "Medical," she said. "Pictures. Dental X-rays."

"Where is she?" Davis asked.

"Sir, we're keeping the bodies in here," Brown said, louder than necessary.

"I'm old," Davis said. "Not deaf."

"Sorry," Brown said as he unlocked the door and found the light switch on the inside wall. Davis had started to remove his jacket, but Dahlgren suggested that it would be better if he kept it on.

"Why?" Davis asked.

"It's cold in here," Dahlgren explained.

The room was a maintenance storage room, and the aquaria were resting at waist level on wooden frames built from four-by-fours, all evenly spaced in the center of the room, and each with its own fluorescent light fixture. All were draped with blue hospital sheets.

"Which one?" Brown asked.

"This one, I think," Dahlgren said, and lifted a corner of the sheet, revealing a pile of bones. "No, sorry. That's number one."

Dahlgren moved to the next one and read the evidence label.

"Here she is," Dahlgren said.

"Bring him a chair," Matheson said.

"I can stand," Davis said.

Brown pulled the chain on the fluorescent light overhead, and as it hummed and glowed to life, Dahlgren took a breath and removed the sheet as reverently as possible.

"This is very strange," Davis said.

"We'll explain shortly," Matheson said. "Please, sir, take a look."

Number three was floating a few inches above the bottom of the tank, and turned slightly to one side, toward her visitors. She had been a particularly handsome woman in life, with firm breasts, a flat stomach, and gently rounded hips. Her areolas were the size of half-dollars and were the same color of purple as her lips under the fluorescents. Her mouth was slightly open, and her jaw slack, revealing a row of even white teeth. Her shoulder-length straight red hair covered her head.

"Mr. Davis," Brown asked, "is that your wife?"

"I can't see her face."

Matheson quickly handed Brown the manila envelope, took off her suit jacket, rolled up her sleeve, and stepped to the rear of the tank. She shot Dahlgren a *do you have a better idea?* look as she reached down and touched the dead woman on the right shoulder, just above a birthmark shaped like Africa. She pushed gently down, and as the body turned, the hair floated away from her face.

"Oh, God," Davis said.

159

Bryce was close enough and quick enough to catch the old man before he hit the floor.

"Get that chair," Bryce said, holding Davis beneath the arms. Schwartz found a chair in the corner and wheeled it over, and the trooper gently placed the old man into it.

Matheson knelt in front of Davis while rolling down her sleeve, mine water dripping down her forearm and pooling on the floor, watching his eyes.

"Should I get help?" Schwartz asked.

"He's conscious," Matheson said. "But yes, find a nurse."

Brown was holding an eight-by-ten family portrait in his hand, comparing the smiling face in the faded color photograph to that of the handsome but expressionless woman in the aquarium. He turned the photograph around to show the others.

It was the same woman.

Dahlgren thought she looked very sixties, like Dana Delaney in *China Beach*. He couldn't help but imagine the electronic *woop-woop-woop* from the Supremes intro.

"I don't understand," the old man said, his eyes fluttering.

"Sir, your wife's body has been artificially preserved," Matheson said. "We don't understand how."

"I was in Saigon," Davis said weakly. "Career Army. Supply. I was twelve years older than Regina, and my buddies said she'd just run off with a younger man, but I never thought so. I knew something terrible had happened. I never remarried, you know. I couldn't, not knowing if she was alive or dead."

"Now you know," Matheson said.

"She was murdered?"

"Sir, we think so," she said.

A nurse bustled into the room, followed by Schwartz.

"What's the problem?" the nurse asked. She was a large woman, and she didn't like to be told what to do by police officers half her age, or not knowing what was going on inside her own hospital.

"This gentleman passed out," Matheson said. "We'd like him checked."

"I can't do anything, he's not a . . ."

The nurse saw the body floating in the aquarium.

". . . patient," she said.

"Would you please just render some assistance?" Matheson had moved close to the woman, and was talking softly but forcefully within inches of her face. "This gentleman has had a profound shock by identifying the body of his beautiful and very dead wife, who has been missing for thirty-six years. Don't ask. Just find your fucking heart and help us."

The nurse knelt, looked into the old man's eyes, then grasped his wrist and felt for his pulse.

"How're you doing, sir?" she asked. "My name is Flo, and I'm going to take care of you for a bit. I think we need to take you down to the emergency department, where we can get your blood pressure and have the doctors take a look."

"That's my wife," Davis said. "Her name's Regina."

"That's what I heard," Flo said. "I'm sorry."

"What I'd really like is a cup of water," Davis said. "Can I have some water? And a little time alone? With Regina, I mean?"

"Of course," Flo said. "For just a moment. I'll stay with you, then we'll see the docs, okay?

Davis nodded.

"Everybody out," Matheson said.

She waited while the four men filed out of the room, then she flipped off the room lights, leaving Regina Davis illuminated by the fixture over her aquarium. Her seventy-two-year-old husband remained in the chair, with the nurse's arm around his shoulder.

Matheson gently closed the door.

"Now we know why the NCIC computer didn't turn up anything," she said softly. "It hadn't even been invented when these women disappeared."

* * *

Matheson glanced in disbelief at the blinking red and blue lights in her rearview mirror, then cursed beneath her breath. It was past midnight, she was tired, and she had just accelerated to cruising speed after ramping onto U.S. 67 on her way back to the Cape.

Dutifully, she slowed and pulled her dark blue Crown Vic to the shoulder.

The white Crown Vic pulled in behind her. She drummed her fingers on the steering wheel and watched in the rearview mirror as the officer took his time unbuckling his shoulder belt and gathering his things. Finally, he exited the car and slipped his baton into his ring holster. He slapped his ticket book against his thigh as he approached her door.

"Good morning," Rudy Buntz said. "Could I see your license and registration, please?"

"Federal officer," Matheson said, showing him her creds. "But you already know that."

Buntz reached for them, but she drew them away.

"You've seen my agent number," she said.

"Grace Matheson," Buntz said, carefully writing the name down in the ticket book. "I'm just wondering—is that miss or missus?"

"It's Special Agent Matheson," she said.

"The thing is, you were doing eighty-two miles per hour on a stretch of road that is posted sixty-five," he said, enjoying every syllable. "That's seventeen miles over the limit, and I'm going to have to cite you."

"I wasn't doing eighty-two," Matheson said. "Seventy, maybe."

"I can show you the readout on my radar unit, if you like."

"Don't give me that old saw," Matheson said. "I'm not some little chippy you've stopped in hopes of getting a payoff or a blow job. I'm a federal agent on official business. That super-

162

sedes your municipal code, and no judge in the country would even allow it in court, much less impose a fine."

"That's between you and the court," Buntz said. "Also, if you're running over the speed limit on gov'ment business, as you say, I suggest using the vehicle's emergency lights and siren."

"What's your problem, Officer?" Matheson asked. "You know this is ludicrous. Are you going to have me step out of the car? Are you going to search me? Are you going to arrest me for having a concealed weapon on my person?"

"No, ma'am," Buntz said. "If you would sign here. This is not an admission of guilt, just confirmation that you've received this summons and a promise to appear in court at the time and place stated on the back."

"I'm not signing."

"Then I could take you to jail right now," Buntz said. "Of course, we don't have a jail in Bonne Terre anymore, so I'd have to have you transported over to Farmington. I'm sure the judge would get you bonded out by one or two o'clock tomorrow afternoon."

He tore the ticket out of the book and handed it through the window. Matheson took it, slowly tore it into dime-sized pieces, and sprinkled it over her feet.

Buntz shook his head and leaned in her window.

"I don't like feds, and I bag me one whenever I can," he said. "And I don't understand why they let cunts like you join the federal fucking bureau of instigation. You should be home cooking and cleaning for some man, instead of being out here, wearing a suit, and pretending you are one."

Matheson forced herself to laugh, although she was empathizing with all the women Buntz had ever stopped on a deserted stretch of highway late at night. She was packing a 9mm pistol, and still she was scared.

"Officer Buntz, you have a choice," she said. "In five seconds I'm going to start my car and pull away and pretend, because I don't want the hassle of having your ass fired, this didn't happen."

She started the car and put it in gear.

"Oh, one other thing," she said. "I know your type, and you've succeeded in making me afraid. So if you ever stop me again, no matter what the reason, I will draw my piece and scatter your brains all over the road."

She punched the accelerator and the car shot forward, throwing chunks of rock and gravel, the rear end slewing until the tires bit into the asphalt of the highway with a chirp. Buntz shielded himself from the fusillade, which cracked the windshield of his patrol car and knocked out the driver's-side headlight.

Eighteen

Jolene Carter was bent at the waist, grasping her calves and pulling herself down, stretching before she ran, her blond hair brushing the ground. She was dressed in heavy gray sweats and wore a pair of headphones attached to a Discman at her waist. Her golden cross fell from beneath her sweatshirt and dangled at the end of its chain, sparkling in the crisp morning light.

Geiger's view of her, through the binoculars, was dusky and compressed. The jogging trail snaked behind her.

Finding her had been much simpler than Geiger had thought it would be. He had called the city and explained that he was a new resident and would like to know if there were any convenient trails in the southwest part of the city. There was the Springfield Conservation Nature Center, the helpful woman on the other end had suggested. It was run by the state, it opened at eight o'clock during the winter, and had trails of different lengths across its eighty wooded acres. And,

165

the woman had said, it was easy to find, just a half-mile from the intersection of U.S. Highways 60 and 65.

Jolene tucked the cross beneath the sweatshirt, then was off.

This morning, she was taking the shorter route, along the one-third-mile Fox Bluff trail. Geiger was walking down the longer trail that led to the photo blind on Lake Springfield, and he kept the Zeiss binoculars moving, never pausing too long on Jolene.

Then they were separated by woods.

Attendance was light at this season and hour, but the trail Jolene had chosen was too close to the center's administration building.

If she managed to scream, someone might hear.

It would not be this morning, Geiger knew, but it would be soon, and he would be ready. To anyone who might notice him on the photo blind trail, however, he was just another bird watcher, dressed in bulky clothing, his face hidden by a muffler, carrying binoculars and an amateur's SLR. But his backpack carried the necessary tools: the hypodermic kit, the duct tape, the orange kernmantel rope, and the custom dive knife with the black titanium blade and the red grips.

And since the end of the game was near, Geiger was carrying one other thing that he had never packed before, in a nylon holster with an extra clip, hidden by his loose clothing: a .380 Browning semiautomatic.

Jolene would be the last sacrifice, and Geiger was prepared to kill anyone who would try to stop it.

"We're looking for other victims, obviously, but we should take note of anything that looks unusual," McAfee said. This time Dahlgren and Matheson were listening as he briefed the dive team. "It's possible the killer may have dropped something behind: rope, clothes, a piece of gear that could be traced."

Dahlgren was already kitted up. Matheson looked out of

place in her Hoover blues. She was also cold, and although she had an overcoat, her arms were folded across her chest. Cal Bentham brought her a steaming cup of coffee, and she nodded her thanks.

"What do we do if we find something?" Norman asked.

"Don't touch it," Dahlgren said. "Call for help."

Claire Connelly had been listening with her arms crossed as well, but not because she was cold. "So," she said, and brushed her blond hair away from her green eyes. "Who's in charge?"

"I am," Matheson said. "At least up here. Chief Brown is responsible for security and logistics. But under the water, it's Dahlgren's jurisdiction. You follow his orders as you would mine."

"I wouldn't follow your orders," Claire said.

Matheson smiled.

"Claire," she said, "I know you're a good spelunker—"

"We prefer caver," Claire said. "I'm a *caver*, a cave diving instructor, an officer in the St. Louis grotto, and this team's safety diver. So it's my responsibility to explain to you the way this works, and apparently to remind Loren: When we dive, any member of the team can call it, for any reason, no questions asked."

"Claire," Loren said.

"Don't," she said. "Let's discuss this. I don't know what's going on with you, Loren, but you've obviously joined the girls in blue. You need to think about your team first."

Staci Johnson nodded.

"I hear you," Loren said. "And I probably needed that reminder. You're still the safety diver, Claire. You see something you don't like, call it. But where evidence is concerned, it's Dahlgren's ballgame."

"What's your problem?" Addison, the former Coast Guard diver, asked. "Nobody's asking you to do anything unsafe. This is just chain of command."

Potts nodded.

"Maybe I don't want him diving with me," Claire said defensively. "How long have you been out of cave diving, anyway? Ten years?"

"It's been nine years since San Augustín," Dahlgren said.

"Then why don't we get some members of the grotto to help us instead," she said. "They've offered."

"I'd rather keep the team small," Dahlgren said. "Adding more people would just increase the odds for an accident. Besides, how many body recoveries have you done, Claire? Ten?"

"Less."

"Five?"

"About," she said.

"I've worked more than two hundred body recoveries and crime scenes," Dahlgren said. "But, Claire, I need your help. Does anybody know the mine better than you?"

"No," Claire said.

"That may not be absolutely true," Norman said hesitantly. "No offense, Claire, but whoever did those girls must know the mine better than any of us. He might still be out there."

"Good point," Dahlgren said. "But you know how difficult cave diving is. Just imagine doing it in conjunction with murder. So I think you're likely to find his body at the bottom of one of these shafts."

"That's the scenario we're hoping for," Matheson said. "It would tie up loose ends and allow everybody to sleep better. But it still would be far less than the bastard deserves."

Claire nodded.

"And none of the victims that we've identified so far were abducted more recently than 1982," Dahlgren said.

"Which one was that?" Staci asked.

"The first one," Matheson said.

"Miss October," Staci said.

"Her name was Christine Wright," Matheson said. "Her

family called in after seeing your sketches on CNN. She was twenty-one and abducted from a suburb of Little Rock."

"So how many have been identified?" Potts asked.

"Four of the six," Matheson said. "The other two were from Carthage, Illinois, and Memphis. Their vitals are on the board in the big plastic bag behind us, if you're interested, but please don't discuss what you see there with anyone. If the bastard is still alive, we don't want to give him any help."

"Why are you all so sure it's a he?" Staci asked. "Couldn't a woman have done it?"

"Serial killers are virtually all white males," Matheson said, "and they usually strike within their own ethnic group. Name a sexual deviation, and it is overwhelmingly dominated by white males. Most ritualistic sex crimes are committed by white males. The odds are overwhelming that our killer is a guy."

"And white," Staci said.

"Hey, buddy," Potts told his black partner, slapping him on the back, "you're off the hook."

"Yeah, but you're not," Addison shot back.

Matheson ignored them.

"Dahlgren told me something interesting," she said. "Staci, did the way the bodies were grouped remind you of anything?"

"Yeah, paintings. From the Pre-Raphaelite Brotherhood."

"What is that?"

"A bunch of nineteenth-century artists who rebelled against the Royal Academy and started painting idealized scenes from mythology," she said. "They're best known for their portraits of brooding redheads. You've probably heard some of the stories about them—how Dante Rossetti married his favorite model and after her death dug her up to retrieve the poems he had thrown in the coffin with her, or how the girl who posed as the drowned Ophelia in a tub of cold water for Millais died of pneumonia. I've got some books that explain it, if you're interested."

"Thanks," Matheson said. "I'd like to see them."

There was a pause. McAfee looked at Claire Connelly questioningly. She nodded and uncrossed her arms.

"Any other questions?" McAfee asked. "No?"

"Just one other thing," Matheson said. "You're all civilians and free to leave. But given the circumstances, I'd prefer that you didn't. Would anybody like to be excused?"

Norman raised his hand.

"Take off," Matheson said.

"No, it's not that," Norman said, doing his best to keep a straight face. "I was just wondering—are you going to deputize us?"

Nineteen

Dahlgren tacked four-by-six photos of the victims they had found in the timekeeper's shack, the hospital, and in the ore cart on the east side of Mineral City. In black marker, beneath their expressionless faces, he had written: *#12, #13, #14.* In his hand he was holding a one-hour photo-processing envelope.

"Loren hasn't gotten you switched to a digital camera yet?" Matheson asked.

"I like film," Dahlgren said. "So do the courts."

"Thought you would shoot Nikon."

"David Doubilet inspired me to learn underwater photography," Dahlgren said. "He shot Canon, so I do too. I have a Nikonos as a backup. But Canons are for extreme sports, adventure, and wildlife photography. It's hard to beat the image size of the big Canon speedfinder in the underwater housing."

"You lost me," Matheson said. "All I heard was blah, blah, blah, housing."

Dahlgren smiled.

"You have an unusual sense of humor for a Hoover."

"I'm an unusual Hoover," she said.

She was seated at the desk, and before her was a yellow legal pad, a pencil, and the pile of art books Staci had loaned her. The sound was muted on the television behind her, but CNN had a live aerial shot of the blockhouse.

"I can see my Helio," Dahlgren said.

"What time is it?" Matheson asked as she sat down across from him. "No, what day is it?"

"Later than we think," Dahlgren said.

"Always is."

Dahlgren glanced at the Seiko.

"Ten-thirty."

Matheson took a sip of her own coffee.

"Where is everybody?"

"It's Sunday," Dahlgren said. "I suppose they went to church. Have you been here all night?"

"Apparently," she said.

"So we're alone down here," Dahlgren said.

"Don't worry," she said. "I won't attack you."

"I heard your lecture on sexual predators," Dahlgren said.

"I'm not worried," Matheson said.

"Trust me?"

Matheson shook her head, then pulled back her jacket to reveal the butt of her Sig-Sauer 228 in a waist holster.

"New agents are given Glocks these days," Mathson said. "But I prefer the Sig. The 9mm rounds are easier to control than the .40 or .45, and the gun fits my hand better. Also, most every other federal agency is still using the 9mm NATO round. To me, it just makes more sense. And I can put fourteen rounds in a three-inch circle at twenty-five yards."

She paused.

"And I don't like to say Glock," she said. "It's not a good

172

name for a gun. It's like the punch line of some sexist joke: and she was left holding her Glock in her hands."

"I don't like guns," Dahlgren said.

"Some family history there?"

"Nope," he said. "Just gave them up one day."

"Were you a collector? An enthusiast? An NRA member who raved about jackbooted thugs?"

"I was a hunter," he said.

She regarded Dahlgren thoughtfully over her coffee mug.

"What was the thing you mentioned a few days ago when Claire was challenging your credentials?"

"San Augustín? An accident."

One of the phones began to ring.

Matheson picked it up.

"Yeah, I know, Michael," she said after listening a moment. "I'm seeing it on television right now. Unless you think they're violating FAA regulations by flying too low, just ignore it. They can shoot whatever they want from a public vantage point. Yeah."

She scratched her head.

"Michael is a nice kid, but he needs to do his own thinking once in a blue moon," she said. "I just made some coffee. Want some?"

"Of course," Dahlgren said. "And a cigarette."

"*No fumar,*" Matheson said, filling one of the white mugs. "Oxygen and only God knows what else under pressure, remember? And you told me you quit."

"Doesn't mean I can't want one," Dahlgren said as he sprinkled salt into the mug.

"Is that good for you?"

"Family habit," Dahlgren said. "Old Navy habit, actually. My family has been Navy for generations. Ever hear of a Civil War admiral named Dahlgren, inventor of the Dahlgren Gun? Well, he was demonstrating his new gun in front of Lincoln's war cabinent, and it exploded, killing a bunch of them."

He moved to the desk, sat down, and rubbed his eyes.

"My father was a yeoman aboard the *Pennsylvania* at Pearl Harbor," he said. "The ship was in dry dock, and there wasn't a thing they could do while the Japs sank their sister ship, the *Arizona*. The *Pennsy* survived the war but was eventually sunk in one of the atomic bomb tests in the Pacific. She deserved a better fate."

"Any other Dahlgren sea tales?"

"Yeah," he said. "I have a brother who is eleven years older than I am, and he commanded a riverboat in Vietnam. He survived the war, but when they served rice at his wedding dinner, he said that was what the little yellow bastards ate and sent it back."

"Charming," Matheson said.

"We haven't spoken in three years," Dahlgren said. "But it's not his fault. I have as much trouble picking up the phone as he does. Just don't know what to say."

"You have prior service?"

"Nope," Dahlgren said. "I grew up in the seventies, became a dive bum, and—forgive the pun—fell into cave diving by accident. My best friend introduced me to cave diving when I was sixteen. My friend dropped out when somebody we knew died in a cave, but I was hooked."

"I don't understand the attraction," Matheson said. "Seems dangerous."

"Danger is part of the hook," Dahlgren said. "With the proper training, equipment, and experience, penetrating a cave becomes a technical problem instead of a test of courage. But caves, both wet and dry, are among the most unforgivable environments on earth. And then there's the element of sheer luck—and sometimes your luck runs out, even if you're the best."

"For example?"

"Your luck can run out in all sorts of ways," he said. "If

you're a dumbass, your luck runs out really quick. Open-water scuba divers, for example, who venture past the cavern zone—"

"What's that?"

"The area penetrated by sunlight, such as the mouth of a cave in an outdoor spring. Once you get beyond that, you're in the cave zone. Open-water divers are discouraged from taking lights with them, so they won't be tempted to explore beyond the natural light. If they do, they're likely to get lost in a silt-out because they didn't lay a line or have enough air left to find the exit. Or, if they did lay a line, they use floating ski rope instead of nylon and get hopelessly tangled up in it. They drown."

"But not cavers."

Dahlgren smiled.

"Even the top guns get into trouble," he said. "The world's best cave diver was generally acknowledged to be a Floridian named Sheck Exley. He had logged thousands of cave dives, had studied hundreds of cave accidents, and literally wrote the book on cave diving. He subtitled it a 'blueprint for survival,' and he gave us the ten commandments of staying alive."

"What are they?" Matheson asked.

"How is this important to the investigation?"

"I don't know, but I'm curious," she said, her pen poised over her legal pad.

"I'll summarize them," Dahlgren said. "Use a continuous guideline, save two-thirds of your air for the return trip, and always carry three lights per dive."

"That's only three."

"Avoid diving deeper than the recreational scuba limit of a hundred and thirty feet, use the safest possible scuba, build up your experience slowly. There are a couple of others that deal with practicing emergency situations outside the cave and avoiding stirring up silt."

"So what happened to Sheck?"

"He died trying to set a depth record of a thousand feet in a pit near San Augustín."

"So he broke his own rule about depth," Matheson said. "How is it possible to go to a thousand feet? That's deeper than ballistic subs, isn't it?"

"Sheck was a martial artist and, over the years, had trained his body to deal with the stresses involved in deep diving," Dahlgren said. "He could go three or four hundred feet on air—depths that would kill most of us. He was using mixed gas when he tried to set the depth record, and he made it to around nine hundred and twenty-five feet. At depths below six hundred feet, some weird physiological things start happening. With HPNS—high-pressure nervous syndrome—your eyes shrink, you hallucinate, your hands develop a tremor, and you can get insanely paranoid. You can convulse and die. This can be in combination with compression arthralgia, something the old Navy divers called 'no joint juice,' because your knees and elbows and wrists feel like they've rusted solid."

"My God," Matheson said. "That's horrible. Is that what happened to Sheck?"

"Maybe," Dahlgren said. "We'll never know for sure."

"Tell me about the bends," Matheson said. "How is it different than what you described?"

"It's very different," Dahlgren said. "It's caused by nitrogen bubbles that form in the bloodstream from staying down too long or coming up too fast. At depth, the nitrogen bubbles are microscopic. But nitrogen is an inert gas which tends to combine with itself in the bloodstream to form bigger bubbles when you come up, sort of like when you shake a bottle of pop and all those bubbles spew out the top. Except, when that happens to a diver, he takes a hit wherever the bubble happens to lodge—a joint, the back, the inner ear. Consequences can range from a mild rash to permanent disability to death."

"And rapture of the deep?"

"Also caused by nitrogen, but in a different way," Dahlgren said. "The deeper you go, the greater the partial pressures of the gases are in the mix you're breathing. Nitrogen, which makes up about eighty percent of the air we breathe, has a narcotic effect that is the equivalent of drinking a martini for every fifty feet of depth. At least, that's how they used to describe it."

"You get drunk," Matheson said.

"Divers can get so drunk on nitrogen that they see mermaids, ditch their tanks, or just forget to come up," Dahlgren said. "And just with alcohol, people have different tolerances to it. I'm usually not affected until a hundred and fifty or so, and then mildly. At two hundred, I'm sloppy drunk on nitrogen, so I have to breathe something with little or no nitrogen—trimix or heliox, usually. Those blends replace all or part of the nitrogen with helium. Makes you talk like Donald Duck."

"Have you been bent?"

"A couple times," Dahlgren said. "Mild cases, luckily. Lost the sensation in my hands, had a rash, felt like I had the flu, and my ears rang. I was caving both times, and it's hard to get Life-Flighted to a hyperbaric chamber when you're underground."

"So," Matheson said. "Sheck died near the same place you mentioned when Claire was questioning your credentials," Matheson said. "That town, what was the name? San Augustín. Rather coincidental."

"Not really," Dahlgren said. "San Augustín is cave-diving Everest. Located over a big limestone karst in south-central Mexico that is home to the Huautla cave system. Lots of strange stuff has happened there."

"What happened to you there?" she asked.

"Next question."

"Come on."

"It's none of your fucking business," Dahlgren said.

"Forget it," Matheson said. "I hated your guts when we first met. I was warming up to you, but now I don't remember why."

"You're breaking my heart," Dahlgren said. "So why don't you tell me your story? Why'd you lay all that talk on the chief and me about psychic fingerprints?"

"Wanted to be honest," Matheson said. "No surprises."

"How come you know so much about that oddball shit?"

"Just always interested," Matheson said. "Figure there was more in heaven and earth, you know? Subscribed to *Fortean Times* since I was fourteen, read every damn book written by John Keel, thought the *Night Stalker* was a documentary. Before I became a fed, I got a master's in mythology."

"How'd you wind up in Cape Girardeau?"

Matheson smiled.

"None of your fucking business."

"Fair enough," Dahlgren said. "Are you making any sense of Staci's theory about the PBR? No, that's not right. That's Pabst Blue Ribbon."

"The PRB—Pre-Raphaelite Brotherhood," Matheson said. "Those are the secret initials three artists began using on their paintings in the mid-1840s. Of the three, Dante Gabriel Rossetti was the most influential. There were eventually seven artists active in the group, if I'm interpreting this stuff correctly, but they influenced dozens of artists that came after, including Herbert Draper and John Waterhouse, who specialized in soulful and unsmiling redheaded women. They continue to influence artists, even today."

"Who was this Raphael?"

"A Renaissance painter who studied with Michelangelo and da Vinci," Matheson said. "The brothers were rebelling against what they felt was a dogmatization of art by the Royal Academy in London. The Academy held Raphael as the ideal to be emulated, down to the proportions of light and dark in a painting. The Academy essentially gave artists a license to paint, and if you didn't have its approval, you starved."

"So what drove these guys?"

"The movement is a little hard to pin down, because thematically they were all over the place—landscapes, illustrations, themes. Their logic was also more than a little convoluted; although many of their paintings are what you would call picture perfect, they said every scene should represent a real landscape or interior, not an idealized one, that only worthy subjects should be painted, figures should be grouped without regard to artistic arrangement, and—get this—that every figure should be inspired by a real model."

"And in our *tableaux mordants*, the figures *are* real models," Dahlgren said.

"The brotherhood painted a variety of subjects," Matheson said. "Arthurian legend, Shakespearean themes, Christian and classical mythology. They were heavily influenced by the Romantic movement, given to religious mysticism, and fascinated by the supernatural, the melancholy, and the mythic."

"Shakespeare and King Arthur?"

"These guys were English, so Arthur and Shakespeare were the cultural equivalents of the pantheon to the Greeks," Matheson said. "But they focused on the depressive aspects—the drowned Ophelia, for example, or the Lady of Shalott."

"Don't know that last one."

"In Arthurian legend, a woman doomed to the confines of her apartment, and viewing life only in a mirror that reflects the street below," she said. "But one day she spies Lancelot in his finery and she finally leaves the apartment, although she knows that it will cost her her life. She dies in a boat on the river to Camelot."

"Water and death," Dahlgren said. "Rinse, repeat."

"It could translate into sacrifice in a pathological mind," Matheson said. "But I can't be sure just how. The subject is ar-

179

cane, but paradoxically branches into many avenues in English art and literature. Ever read a book called *The White Goddess* by Robert Graves?"

"No," Dahlgren said.

"I did, back when I was mythological," Matheson said. "Graves argued that poetry originated in goddess worship. Our old buddy and PRB founder Dante Rossetti, by the way, was also a poet. That's the one Staci said dug up his wife to retrieve his poems."

"Is that true?"

"Yes," Matheson said. "After seven years, Rossetti exhumed the body of Lizzie Siddal, and her red hair had grown to fill the coffin. She was also the model that Staci said had sat for fellow artist John Millais in a tub of cold water, and died of pneumonia. But that part is prettier than the truth; Lizzie did get sick after modeling for *Ophelia*, but she did not die until years later, when she committed suicide by taking an overdose of laudanum. At the time, her husband was probably in the arms of his current mistress, Fanny Cornforth."

"Sounds like a great guy."

"Like most Victorians, he was confused," Matheson said. "He couldn't decide whether he wanted a whore or a Madonna. His life was a paradox of Christian virtue and that really old-time religion, sex-goddess worship. It makes sense. Graves said language and art came from worship of the ancient mother goddess, the fertility goddess, the goddess of the moon."

"That's odd," Dahlgren said. "To the Maya, the moon goddess Ixchel was also the goddess of fertility. I know, because I've dove the cenotes, the sacred wells. The island of Cozumel, ruled by Ixchel, was a pilgrimage site for Mayan women wishing to conceive."

"Not so odd," Matheson said. "Think about it. The moon goes through its phases and starts again in twenty-eight days.

What else has that period? And Ixchel has her equivalents in all ancient cultures. Spider Woman in North America, Ceres for the Romans, Demeter for the Greeks. And they're not just goddesses of agriculture and fertility—they're bloodthirsty bitches, demanders of human sacrifice."

"This fits into your ritual killer theory."

"Doesn't contradict it," Matheson said. "Ritual murder is a phrase the Bureau doesn't use often, but in a few cases it seems to fit. Unlike your average Henry Lee Lucas, the perp usually has some standing in the community."

"A professional?" Dahlgren said.

"Or a celebrity. A politician, perhaps," Matheson said. She was tapping the eraser of her Ticonderoga No. 2 pencil against her bottom lip. "A ritual killing wouldn't constitute a ritual unless it's performed in a place of worship. Doesn't the mine remind you of a cathedral?"

The phone rang.

Matheson punched the blinking light with the pencil eraser and shoved the receiver toward Dahlgren.

"Your turn," Matheson said.

Dahlgren took it.

"Mr. Dahlgren?" Michael Schwartz said while standing just outside the door to the blockhouse, speaking into a receiver that attached to a coil of cord that led inside. "Sorry to bother you, sir, but we have kind of a situation here. I can't reach the chief, and I need some direction."

A man in black was standing a few feet away from Schwartz, his hands clasped over a well-thumbed Bible. The expression behind his glasses was calm, and his mouth was neither a smile nor a frown.

"Well, we have a contingent of religious types that want to set up a tent here," Schwartz said. "To pray for the souls of the dead girls, I suppose. Yes, sir. I'll tell him."

Schwartz reached inside the blockhouse and replaced the phone in its wall cradle.

"Sir," he said, "somebody's coming up to talk to you."

"Coming up?" the preacher asked.

"Yes, sir," Schwartz said. "From the mine."

In a few minutes, Dahlgren emerged from the mule trail.

"Are you in charge?" the preacher asked. Behind him were thirty middle-class men and women, a few children, and the cars they came in. The adults seemed very serious, and most of them were holding Bibles.

"I am right now," Dahlgren said. "The owner of the property is at home and the chief of police is still in church. The federal agent leading the investigation is busy and asked me to talk to you on her behalf."

Dahlgren had no idea whether Brown was in church or not, but he thought it was a nice touch.

"What can I do for you?" Dahlgren asked.

The preacher cleared his throat.

"We're from the Revenant Harvest Church at Leadwood."

"Sorry, I'm not from around here. Where's that?"

"About five miles to the southwest," the preacher said. "We'd like your permission to set up a tent on the property and conduct services."

"A revival tent?"

"Well, we do use the tent for revivals," the preacher said. "But these services would be conducted for the souls of those eleven poor girls found in the mine."

"Fourteen," Dahlgren said softly. "We found three more yesterday."

The congregation gave a collective gasp.

"Terrible," the preacher said, and shook his head. "You see, Mr. . . ."

"Dahlgren."

"This may sound odd if you're not a religious man, Mr.

Dahlgren, but we're concerned about those girls. I know they are beyond human help now, but we think it would be a comfort if services could be conducted near the location where the girls were brought back into the light."

Cristo Rey, Dahlgren heard.

He turned away and looked over the bare trees to the November sky beyond.

The preacher paused.

"I'm sorry," he said. "Did I say something improper?"

"No," Dahlgren said, surprised to find that his throat was so tight he could barely get the words out. He wiped his eyes with the palm of his hand and felt foolish for having felt clever by saying the chief was at church.

"Are you sure you're okay?" the preacher asked, placing a hand on his shoulder.

"I'm fine."

The preacher nodded.

"We thought you would probably turn us down," the preacher said, "seeing as how much the news has been covering the case, and since the federal government became involved."

"This is private property," Dahlgren said.

"I understand," the preacher said. "Sorry to bother you."

"No," Dahlgren said. "What I mean is that this is private property, and I'm giving you permission on behalf of the owner, Loren McAfee. The feds can go . . . Well, they'll just have to deal with it."

"Praise God."

"A few rules," Dahlgren said. "Behave yourself. I don't know what your church practices, but no rattlesnakes or speaking in tongues, or anything that most folks would consider bizarre. I don't want to see it tonight on CNN."

"We're just here to pray," the preacher said. "Would that be all right for you to see on television?"

"Mind your manners," Dahlgren said. "No proselytizing,

and if anybody else shows up and wants to pray with you—no matter if they're Catholics, Jews, or Wiccans—you make them welcome."

"Everyone's welcome to pray with us," he said. "Even witches."

Dahlgren smiled.

"Stay clear of the blockhouse and our police officers," he said. "You have your own liability insurance for this sort of thing, like when you do revivals? Good. But if the agent in charge here or the landowner is uncomfortable with your presence, you'll have to leave. Agreed?"

"Yes, sir," the preacher said, and shook Dahlgren's hand.

By the time he released it, the congregation was already unpacking the white-and-green tent from the back of a battered van.

"Make sure they set up out of the way," Dahlgren told Schwartz as he entered the blockhouse.

"What'll I tell the chief?" Schwartz asked.

"Tell him I said it was good PR," Dahlgren said. "Besides, we need some help. We're oh-for-fourteen with the killer."

Twenty

It was Thursday, a week before Thanksgiving, and Jolene Carter didn't have class until her Poetry of the Bible seminar at eleven o'clock, so she decided to jog all the way down the photo trail to the lake and back. The moon, which was nearly full, sailed like a ghost in the early-morning sky. While Jars of Clay kept her company through her headphones, she remembered being in grade school and marveling that the moon could still be seen in the early morning.

The trail seemed unusually deserted, but she thought it was probably due to the weather. It had turned much colder in the past couple of days, and now in addition to her sweats she was wearing a fleece vest. Her breath came out of her nose and mouth like the steam from a locomotive, and she could feel the cold ground through the soles of her Nikes. It was probably time to hang up the running shoes, she thought, and start watching her exercise videos instead.

When she first saw the flower, she jogged past it.

It was red and yellow and on a tall green stem.

A few yards down the trail she stopped, panting, leaning forward and resting her hands on her knees. Then she wiped her nose with the back of her hand and walked back. She knelt down and inspected the flower.

She looked up when she heard footsteps. She saw a bird-watcher coming down the trail toward her, binoculars swinging from his neck, the pack over his shoulder.

Jolene nodded curtly, the bird-watcher nodded, and she returned her attention to the flower while the footsteps grew closer.

Cautiously, she touched a petal.

It was plastic.

Geiger passed a loop of the kernmantel over her head, knocking her headphones off in the process, and cinched it around her neck with his left hand while clamping his right hand over her mouth.

Jolene's eyes went wide with terror as her hands went instinctively to the rope around her neck, trying desperately to loosen it. She began struggling and kicking, but she was already off balance, and it was a simple matter for Geiger to flip her over on her stomach and put a knee in the middle of her back, still holding the rope clenched in his left hand.

He removed a syringe from his pack, pulled down her sweatpants, and injected the Rohypnol into the fatty tissue of her right cheek. Then he was dragging her off the path even before the drug started to take effect, her feet kicking and her heels digging into the ground.

When the fight had finally left her, he slung her over his shoulder and carried her down the hill, to where the Crown Vic was parked on a dirt road near the lake. He opened the trunk and placed Jolene carefully inside.

He inspected her neck.

Geiger was afraid that he might have used too much force on the rope, that he might have crushed her larynx or windpipe, but there was no damage other than a mild abrasion. He inspected the golden cross for a moment, then let it fall. He cut two lengths of kernmantel, bound Jolene's wrists and ankles with it, then stripped off six inches of duct tape from the roll and placed it over Jolene's mouth.

He unbuckled the Discman from her waist, removed the CD, and threw the player back in the trunk. He slammed the lid. As he drove away, he removed the muffler and inserted the CD into the stereo. He listened for a few minutes, then lowered the window and tossed the CD out once he was on the highway.

A podium bristling with microphones had been placed on a folding table in front of the blockhouse, and Matheson gripped the sides as she looked over the pack of journalists waiting for the morning briefing. Just beyond the journalists, the green-and-white-striped revival tent was bucking against the November wind, and it seemed to Matheson that more people were beneath it than had been there the day before.

"Today two more victims recovered from the abandoned St. Joan Lead Mine were identified," Matheson said, dispensing with any preliminaries. "They are Kristen Vogler, twenty-two, of Kansas City, Missouri, and Jo Caldwell, twenty-four, of Springdale, Arkansas. Their disappearances were reported in 1985 and 1973, respectively."

Matheson was not yet finished, but hands were already flying skyward.

"They were victims number seven and ten to be found by the divers," Matheson said. "The total number of victims stands where it was yesterday, at fourteen."

Hands remained in the air.

"Initial leads to the identities of Vogler and Caldwell came from family members, based on sketches of the women," she said. "Positive identification came in the form of dental records. Okay, you in the front row. You're new, aren't you? Tell me where you're from."

"*Rocky Mountain News.*"

"You're a long way from home."

"Victim number five, Brenda Carlisle, disappeared from Denver in 1975."

"I understand," Matheson said. "What's your question?"

"Some of the family members of the victims have joined the prayer service at the tent behind us," he asked, then flipped through his notes. "Brenda's uncle and a niece are here, as well as a gentleman from Oklahoma by the name of Davis. They told me they are going to stay until the bodies can be released from the morgue at Parkland Hospital."

"Is there a question there?"

"Two, actually," the reporter said. "Did you know about the family members gathering with this fundamentalist Leadwood congregation, and do you know when the bodies of the victims will be released to their families?"

Matheson cleared her throat.

"No, I did not know the families were here, but I understand the reason they are remaining," Matheson said. "And as to your second question, the answer is simply that nobody knows. It might be a few days, it might be longer, depending on how long it takes to wrap up this case."

"Why are you holding the bodies?" the reporter asked. "Isn't it customary to release the bodies to the families after they've been identified?"

"This is an unusual crime scene," Matheson said. "Customary just doesn't apply."

"So the rumors about the bodies melting when exposed to air are true?" Dana Casteel asked.

"I don't comment on rumors," Matheson said. "Like the others, these women were drowned," Matheson said. "This was confirmed by the diatom test, which detects microscopic particles in the victim's bones ordinarily found in water—"

"Were they drained of blood as well?"

"I can't comment."

"Why not?" Dana asked.

"It's part of the investigation, and, frankly, I don't know the answer for all of the victims."

"Then at least some were drained of blood, right?"

Matheson smiled.

"Dana, you're not thinking vampire, are you?"

The pack laughed.

"No," she said, blushing. "Are you?"

"At this early stage in the investigation, we are leaving no theory unchecked," Matheson said. "But I think I can safely rule out the undead. Unfortunately, nothing that comes from our imagination can rival the things that some among us have done to others of us."

Geiger guided the black Crown Vic along the eastbound lanes of Highway 60, passing heavy trucks with bleating exhausts and bellowing jake brakes, and Amish carriages with the triangular slow-moving vehicle signs and pulled by horses that seemed to do nothing but shit and piss with every step. He stopped for lunch at Willow Springs, at a mom-and-pop restaurant, where he had a surprisingly good turkey-and-Swiss sandwich and a cup of coffee, then pulled the Vic into a deserted car wash and, before washing away the mud from the dirt road near the jogging trail, opened the trunk and checked on Jolene.

She was beginning to stir.

He gave her another injection and slammed the trunk.

Geiger followed 60 east as it became narrow and more winding, and he often found himself trapped behind logging trucks before being presented with a section of road straight and long enough to pass. The terrain became increasingly rugged as he drove through the Mark Twain National Forest in Shannon and Carter Counties. He pulled off the highway near Van Buren to kill a few hours with some real bird-watching and nature photography along the Eleven Point River. He was running well ahead of schedule, and he needed the dead of night.

When the sun had finally set, he checked on Jolene again, considered giving her another injection, but decided against it. He picked up State Highway 34, meandering to the northeast, toward Piedmont, where he spent another hour over dinner at a disappointing Thai restaurant. Then it was a short jog from there to Highway 67, which wound its way more or less to the north, and by ten o'clock the cruise control on the Crown Vic was set just a few miles over the speed limit as it entered the city limits of Bonne Terre.

The white police car had been parked on the median, and a few seconds after Geiger passed it nosed its way onto the northbound lane, snapped on its headlights, and began to accelerate rapidly. When the car—another Crown Vic—paced Geiger a few lengths back and didn't pass, Geiger knew he was going to be pulled over. There was no reason for him to be stopped—he wasn't even doing five miles over the speed limit—but he knew it was going to happen.

The red and blue lights came on, and Geiger pulled the black Crown Vic onto the shoulder and killed the engine, just like a model citizen.

Then Geiger reached down and unsnapped the thumb strap holding the .380 Browning in its holster, then made sure his baggy fleece shirt was covering the butt of the gun. The shoulder harness was in the way, so he unbuckled the lap belt.

What was this yokel doing pulling him over?

The Crown Vic was clearly an official car, had a POLICE INTERCEPTOR badge on the trunk lid, and the black-and-white GS plate was clearly federal. Had he gotten a rookie who just didn't know any better?

He hoped the officer would run a twenty-eight on the tag number, because it would come back on a black Crown Vic registered to the FBI. Of course, it wouldn't be the same Crown Vic, but nobody was likely to compare VIN numbers in the middle of the night.

Geiger had made the license tag himself, from a photograph of a black Crown Vic taken on a tour of the FBI academy at Quantico the year before. He had blown up the license plate on his home computer, printed it out on card stock, sealed them with acrylic from a spray can, and fitted it over a thin metal "I Love Elvis" plate he had bought during his only visit to Graceland. Even when he was standing a few feet away, it looked like the real thing, because of the mock relief provided by the photograph.

But the officer didn't run the tag.

Instead, he opened the car door, slipped his baton into its keeper, picked up his ticket book, and strode forward.

Geiger was considering his options.

The officer hadn't radioed in a description, but there probably was a video camera recording the scene from a mount on the rearview mirror. Even if there wasn't, the officer may have jotted down the information before stepping out. Once he arrived at Geiger's door, he would have a good look at his face. And what if he asked to see Geiger's credentials? He didn't have fake identification to go with the tag, although now it seemed a good idea.

Should he kill him immediately?

No, Geiger decided. Find out what Barney Fife wants first.

He waited until the officer was nearly at the door before lowering the electric window.

"Good evening," Rudy Buntz said, slapping his ticket book against his thigh. "Sir, may I see your license and registration, please?"

Geiger smiled and pulled his wallet from his back pocket and showed him his Missouri driver's license tucked into a plastic window.

"Take it out, please," Buntz said. "And I need your registration."

"Federal car," Geiger stuttered.

"Mr. Geiger," Buntz said, glancing at the license, "did you know you were doing seventy-nine miles per hour? I clocked you just beneath the overpass. I can show you the readout on my radar unit, if you like."

"Doc," Geiger managed.

Buntz tucked his flashlight beneath his left arm while he began writing down Geiger's DL number on the municipal ticket form.

"I'm sorry," he said. "What?"

"Doc-tor," Geiger stammered. "I'm a doctor."

"Listen, bud," Buntz said. "I don't care if you're the fucking queen of England, I'm writing you a ticket for speeding. What are you, some kind of federal fucking bureau of instigation psychologist?"

Geiger smiled and sucked in his breath.

There was a thump as Jolene turned. She was almost awake and had noticed the car had stopped moving.

"What was that?"

Geiger shrugged.

Jolene called out. It was muffled by the duct tape, but still recognizable as a human cry.

In the next instant, Geiger knew the cop would draw his gun and order him to open up the trunk. So while Buntz was still looking at the rear of the car, his hands still holding a cheap chrome pen and the open ticket book, Geiger shot him.

The bark of the Browning was surprisingly loud, much louder than Geiger remembered when practicing on the police range. It was followed by the *tink-tink-tink* of the spent cartridge on the asphalt. He was holding the gun in both hands, just outside the open window, and a wisp of smoke drifted from the action.

Buntz had been knocked backward to the pavement, the flashlight, pen, and ticket book flying. He blinked and looked down with disbelief at the smoking hole in his blue uniform, just over his sternum. He couldn't speak, or even remember for a moment why he was on the pavement. Then, instinctively, he was reaching for his Glock.

The bastard's wearing a vest, Geiger thought.

Geiger sprang out of the car and stamped his foot down, and he heard the ulna crack as he pinned the cop's right hand to the road. He was distracted a moment by Jolene's screaming. Then he aimed at the bridge of the cop's nose and fired three times. He could hear the *thunk* of the slugs as they slammed into the asphalt beneath.

"The queen of England?" Geiger asked. "*That's* the best you could do? It might have been funny had you included a reference to the Crown Victoria, but that was probably beyond you. At the least, I expected a taunt about my stuttering—'cat got your tongue?' or 'spit it out, mister.'"

It was the first time he had killed with a gun, and as he noted the blood seeping onto the road from the back of his victim's head, he realized it wasn't nearly as antiseptic as he had feared it might be. He had seen plenty of gunshot victims on the slab in the morgue, of course, but to be holding a warm gun over a corpse was quite different.

Wasn't that a Beatles song?

He looked down the road in both directions.

There was a car coming from the north, but it was at least a mile away, and in the opposite lane.

Geiger replaced the Browning in its holster.

The motor of the white Crown Vic was idling, the lights still flashing. Geiger took a handkerchief from his back pocket, opened the car door, and looked over the interior. There were no notes on the seat, or a computer, or even a video camera mounted on the rearview mirror. It must be an impoverished department, Geiger decided.

The car in the opposite lane passed without slowing.

Geiger picked up the flashlight, ticket book, and driver's license from the ground. He would leave the casings and, of course, the slugs behind. They couldn't be traced, because there were no ballistics or firing pin marks on file for the gun, since it had never before been used in a crime; they would have to catch him with the gun to be able to make a match, and in that event it wouldn't matter.

But Geiger had the nagging feeling that he was missing something. Though he knew that every second he spent at the scene dramatically increased his odds of being caught, he forced himself to stop and think.

He knelt, looked at the nearly headless body of the police officer, then probed his pockets. In the left breast pocket he found a small Olympus microcassette recorder, still running. He'd nearly forgotten that a lot of cops used them for car stops, even in jurisdictions where it wasn't entirely clear whether the tactic was legal. He was glad he found it, and not just for the most compelling reason.

He hated the sound of his own stuttering voice.

Geiger threw the flashlight and the recorder and other objects into the backpack that lay open on the passenger's seat of his Crown Vic and slammed the door. He pulled away quickly but smoothly, with Jolene still screaming in the trunk. The spot would be crawling with law enforcement in ten or fifteen minutes, but by then he would be off Highway 67, rolling down a dark lane toward Big River.

Twenty-one

At daybreak, Clancy Brown stood near the covered corpse of Rudy Buntz, trying to imagine what had happened shortly after midnight on this short stretch of Highway 67 that bisected Bonne Terre.

"He wasn't even supposed to be out here," Brown said. "It's in the city limits, but I told him to leave Sixty-seven to the troopers unless there was an accident or some other emergency to respond to."

Matheson was standing far back, behind the white police car, debating on whether she should share her own experience regarding Officer Buntz. She decided that she should not, if only because one should not speak ill of the dead—and, perhaps, it would be difficult to explain why she had threatened to kill Buntz a couple of weeks before it actually happened.

"You know how long it's been since we've had a murder in Bonne Terre?" Brown asked.

Matheson shook her head.

"Eight years," he said. "Since before I came. A domestic

that got out of hand. And now? We've got the bodies of four-teen women twenty years dead and the body of one city officer who was shot less than eight hours ago."

"Think there's a connection?" Matheson asked.

"Yeah," Brown said. "My rotten luck."

Bryce came up behind Brown and touched him lightly on the shoulder. "Have you seen enough?" he asked.

"More than enough," Brown said.

"Sorry, but it's time to leave," Bryce said. "You too, Agent Matheson. We need to remove the body and finish working the scene. The patrol will handle it from here."

"I'm not even here—at least not officially," Matheson said. "Just a friend of Chief Brown. Clancy, let's say we go get some coffee."

Brown nodded, and they moved toward Matheson's car.

Jolene had heard the gunshots, and had lain in darkness in the trunk of the moving car, estimating her chances for survival. She concluded they were slim, and continued to pray. She was still praying when the trunk lid opened and a man pointed a flashlight in her face. She wasn't surprised when, a moment later, she saw the barrel of the gun. Then she felt something sting her thigh, and she soon lost consciousness.

The black Crown Vic was parked beside the ruins of an old mill on Big River, deep in the Pike Run Hills, on property that Geiger's family had owned since before he was born, and which he alone had owned since his parents and uncle had died. But the tax bills from the county courthouse in Farm-ington still came in Gustaf Jakobe's name. They had remained unchanged because Geiger had paid them regularly with money orders since his uncle's death more than two decades before. The gate a half-mile up the rocky road was securely locked, and the woods were so thick around the mill site that the car couldn't be seen, especially from the air.

The family acreage was in a loop of the Big River, enclosed on three sides by water. The land was so rugged that it would grow few things except rocks and White Mule moonshine, so it was never referred to as the family farm, but always as the home place.

On the other side of the river, to the north, was St. Francois State Park, three thousand acres of the ridges and hollows where Geiger had played as a boy. The area was where the first French settlers had gouged lead from the ground, where Civil War guerrilla Sam Hildebrand had brooded in a cave between bouts of vengeance, and where moonshiners had done a brisk business from since long before Prohibition to long after.

When Geiger was nine, his uncle Gus had shown him the big cave on the bluff overlooking Big River where Sam Hildebrand and his rifle Killdevil had taken refuge. After having three brothers killed by Union soldiers and sympathizers, he swore vengeance. One of his brothers had been killed and stuffed in a sinkhole, another had been taken from the lead mine at Bonne Terre and executed by a company of federals, and his thirteen-year-old brother, Henry, was shot to death while the family's cabin burned. For a decade, Sam Hildebrand raised hell in the Pike Hills, killing and stealing from the Yankees, and continuing the war long after Appomatox, despite a heavy price on his head.

His downfall started, Uncle Gus had said, when Hildebrand lost Killdevil in an ambush at Three Rivers. It was like King Arthur losing Excalibur. Then, in 1872, Hildebrand was killed in a drunken brawl while resisting arrest, and he managed to draw three hidden knives, each of which was taken away from him. He had a fourth knife, however, and when he plunged it into the constable's thigh, Sam Hildebrand was shot dead and his body returned to the St. Francois County Courthouse at Farmington, where it lay in state for three days, and during which family members refused to identify him to thwart the efforts of the constables to collect the reward.

Like the Hildebrands, Uncle Gus had explained, the Geigers were German, and had been in the Pike Run Hills for just as long as old Sam's family and were nearly as mean. Like the Hildebrands, the Geigers had been related to Pope Gregory and had been run out of Europe with the rise of Protestantism.

The Jakobes, his mother's people, were tough as well, but in a different way: Not only were they strong, they had a spare helping of brains as well as backbone, and they had adopted their name as radical leftists during the French revolution. Sometime in the past, given their improbable but frequent association with Catholic Germans, the spelling of the name was changed from a *c* to a *k*, although the pronunciation remained the same.

Uncle Gus never married and had no children, so he delighted in spending long summer afternoons with Jakob in the Pike Run Hills, teaching him to fish and hunt and to use a knife to clean his catch.

Uncle Gus was also frequently powered by the White Mule shine that he learned to cook during the Depression, because at $28 a gallon, it paid more than eight backbreaking hours in the mine. Consequently, he treated Jakob with the confidence deserving a much older protégé. And Jakob had never let him down.

There were secrets in the hills, Uncle Gus had drunkenly said.

On Jakob's tenth birthday, the week before his missionary parents were to pluck him away to another continent, Uncle Gus initiated him into the mystery of the Pike Run Hills.

It began with the 240-foot narrow-gauge railway tunnel that had been cut through a ridge of the St. Francois Mountains in the late 1800s, to allow the steam engines to transport the ore that was mined at Bonne Terre to the smelters at Herculaneum on the Mississippi. The tunnel attracted gougers through the turn of the century, but was eventually picked clean of whatever lead and zinc and tiff that could be found there, and most people forgot about it.

At the old mill located near Big River, Uncle Gus showed Jakob a passage that led to the railway tunnel and had been used as an escape route for clever entrepreneurs cooking shine near the mill. The passage was narrow and spooky and had originally been gouged out of the mountain by poor miners following a seam of lead and looking for the mother lode. Once inside the tunnel, it was more spacious—twenty-three feet to the ceiling, and sixteen feet from one side to the other. Near the middle of the tunnel was an entrance to a shaft that had been sunk from Homer Carter's store, on top of the mountain, again in hopes of wrenching wealth from the earth. Despite sloping two hundred feet beneath the floor of the tunnel, the shaft failed to bring up enough ore to pay for the picks and axes that had been used to dig it.

The shaft had, however, struck something unexpected and insurmountable: an underground river. The exploration had been abandoned and eventually forgotten, until Uncle Gus stumbled upon it as a boy during the Depression.

By candlelight, Gus had ventured down the sloping shaft. At the bottom he discovered no river. The pumps working full-time at the mines in Bonne Terre, four miles away, had reduced the underground stream to a trickling waterfall in a lozenge-shaped cavern the size of a cathedral.

At the very top of the cavern, above the layers of rose-colored dolomite, was a glittering pocket of quartz. Below it were the stair steps and ledges and cutbacks the underground river had eaten from the rock over the course of geologic ages, and during water levels that changed when the St. Francois Mountains were an atoll in the middle of the sea—four times before human memory, Gus said.

On the other side of the cavern was a canyonlike passage that led to the southwest, and eventually connected with an exploratory drift of the St. Joan mine. The miners, frightened by the amount of water they had found waiting for them in the subterranean lake, had erected there a set of iron doors that would be forced closed should a massive surge of water blast through.

It was possible, Gus had explained, to walk all the way underground from the old mill at their home in the Pike Run Hills to the St. Joan Lead Mine in Bonne Terre. Over the course of the summer, Gus had shown him how to do nearly that, stopping only when they came to the iron doors.

Later, after the mine closed and the pumps stopped, water again filled the cathedral cavern. After Jakob came back alone from the River of Doubt, he realized that he could make the trip again, if only he could get his hands on a Cousteau Aqua-Lung.

Twenty-two

Staci hummed as she worked. She was sitting cross-legged, working in grease pencil on a large tablet placed flat on the dock, with a half-dozen of Dahlgren's evidence photos spread around her.

Dahlgren was standing a few feet behind her, arms folded, staring at the map board. Inside the plastic tent, Matheson was talking in low tones into her cell phone.

Staci's humming slowly shaped itself into a poem.

"'Where Alph, the sacred river ran,'" she sang to her own tune, "'through caverns measureless to man.'"

"Coleridge," Dahlgren said.

Staci looked up and smiled.

"'And all should cry, beware, beware!'" she sang. "'His flashing eyes, his floating hair! Weave a circle around him thrice, and close your eyes with holy dread, for he on honey-dew hath fed, and drunk the milk of Paradise.'"

"Never heard that part of the poem," Dahlgren said.

"You didn't read far enough," she chided. "There are only

fifty-four lines. Strange, but I never thought I'd glimpse anything as beautiful, or as terrifying, in real life as that verse."

"You do a nice job with it."

"Thanks," Staci said. "Learned that by heart in high school. Wonder if I would be cave diving now if I hadn't? You know he was high when he wrote it?"

"No," Dahlgren said. "But I never studied poetry much."

"At least, that's the story. In a sleep brought on by 'two grains of opium' to relieve illness, the whole thing came to him," Staci said. "Two or three hundred lines. But when he woke, he set about writing down the poem, but was interrupted at the fifty-fourth line by a mysterious gentleman on business from the nearby town of Porlock. After being held up for more than an hour, when he returned to his work, he found that the rest of the poem had vanished from his memory."

"You seem to know a lot about it."

"I know a lot about the Romantics," Staci said. "Coleridge didn't publish the poem until twenty years had passed, and when he did, in 1816, he had abandoned poetry altogether. He published it with an apology, saying it was merely a 'psychological curiosity.' It became one of the best-known poems in the English language. Strangely enough, 1816 was also the year that Mary Shelley competed in a storytelling contest with her lover, Shelley, and Lord Byron. The result was *Frankenstein*."

"You're into this stuff."

"Beats reality," Staci said. "Have you noticed how many redheads there are among the victims?"

"No," Dahlgren said. "But now that you mention it, there are, let's see, ten of sixteen victims with red hair?"

"Eleven," Staci said. "That's what, in percentages?"

"About seventy percent."

"It's like going to a science-fiction convention," Staci said. "How many redheads are there in the general population?"

"Without looking it up, and including bottle jobs, I'd

guess twenty percent," Dahlgren said. "Thirty, tops. Could be coincidence."

"Yeah," Staci said. "But the thing is, the Pre-Raphaelite Brotherhood had a thing for redheads. They didn't paint all reds, but mostly—maybe three-quarters."

"Why reds?"

"It was considered rebellious back then," Staci said. "Another way to thumb their nose at convention. The Victorians considered red hair not particularly attractive. People with red hair were shunned, considered base and not to be trusted, too given to their animal natures. It was the color of Judas Iscariot's hair and beard."

"So, what do you think was going on with these guys?"

"The PRB!" Staci asked. "The same stuff that goes on with us today, only more extreme. What we are afraid to express, they painted. They didn't do men well, because men seemed to bore them, but they got the females right. Their girls are bored and haunted by sexual longing, while the women are waiting—for love, for marriage, for death."

Staci smiled.

"Old Millais defected to the Academy, but he still managed some shockers. The brooding faces of the girls in *Autumn Leaves*, for example, could have come from this year's teen angst movie. The Brothers' women are the faces that peer back at us from movie screens and the magazines today. I suspect it goes deeper than fashion—goddesses, seduction, power. The eternal. And, there's something else."

"What?"

"They knew how women long to be set free by death," she said. "That's why they obsessively painted Ophelia committing suicide by falling from the willow branch into the brook, when it was the Victorian fashion to omit all such unsettling references from performances of *Hamlet*. But the Brotherhood knew that sexually stifled women long for death, and water death is particularly satisfying. Drifting away in the subconscious. Like Virginia Woolf, who filled her pockets with stones and waded into a river."

"Are you sexually stifled?" Dahlgren asked.

"Of course," Staci said. "Men are bastards."

Dahlgren coughed.

"Aren't you supposed to turn your head when you do that?" she asked. "You know, I think I'll start painting *men*."

"Can't wait," Dahlgren said. "What do you think those two represent?"

Stacie picked up her drawing and held it at arm's length.

"Hard to say. They seem to be looking down, and one has dark hair with a red scarf across her thighs."

Staci chewed her lower lip.

"Waterhouse again," she said. *"Nymphs Find the Head of Orpheus."*

Matheson ended her conversation and walked out of the tent.

"That was the St. Louis SAC."

"No alphabet soup," Dahlgren said.

"My superior," she said. "Wants to pull me off and assign a team. I convinced him to hold off, at least for a week or two. But the case is getting so high-profile that it's making him skittish."

"We're almost done with the survey," Dahlgren said. "There are only three or four more buildings to check in Mineral City. None of the victims have been more recent than the late eighties, so maybe our guy is retired."

"Perhaps," Matheson said. "But these guys don't stop until they're put in prison, they can't get it up anymore, or they're dead."

Staci rolled her eyes.

"What do we have that ties these victims together?" Dahlgren asked.

"The time of year they were abducted, around Thanksgiving."

"Anything else?"

"Nada," Matheson said.

"There has to be," Dahlgren said.

"The paintings," Staci said. "It's the Brotherhood."

"But if so, why?" Matheson asked. "It doesn't provide us with motive."

"What have the pathologists found?"

"Not much," Matheson said. "They are not used to working on corpses in aquariums. It's been impossible to do a proper autopsy for fear of reducing the subjects to a puddle of goo."

"Then you need a better pathologist," Dahlgren said.

"Who?" Matheson said. "All the best ones are on the coasts."

"What about that guy in St. Louis?" Dahlgren asked. "The one who wrote the book."

McAfee stepped up onto the dock from the mule trail, still dressed in his schoolteacher clothes, carrying a bucket of shad. He went to Nemo's cage and swung open the door, then dumped the shad onto the deck.

"Who ordered the Playboy Channel?" he asked.

Nemo barked his appreciation.

"Nobody," Dahlgren said. "Not exactly. The cable guy said he did it for free. It didn't show up on the bill, did it?"

"I haven't got a bill yet," McAfee said. "But I came in this morning, before going to school, and caught Norman watching it in the plastic tent."

Staci made a face.

"He wasn't, you know?"

"Sorry," McAfee said. "I didn't see you sitting there."

"It's all right if he wants to whack off to sluts," Staci said. "He's my friend, not my boyfriend. It's disgusting, is all."

"He wasn't masturbating," McAfee said, and Dahlgren knew he was lying by the way he said it. "It's just not very professional, is all, having soft-core on the dock. I knew a diver in Florida who played pornography continuously in his trailer, no matter who was there. It was a little uncomfortable."

205

"The Playboy Channel?" Matheson asked.

"Talk to the cable guy," Dahlgren said.

"You bet I will," she said. "I don't want the SAC or the press coming down here for a tour and being greeted by a perfect digital picture of two blond bimbos washing a Jeep in their knickers."

"Good image," Dahlgren said.

Cal Bentham, at the support station on the opposite side of the dock, was motioning for their attention.

"Maybe he'd like it," Dahlgren said, rising from the dock where he'd been looking at Staci's sketches.

"I don't think he swings that way."

"Dahlgren," Cal called. "Claire needs you. She's on the VOX."

"For Pete's sake," McAfee muttered, following Dahlgren. "Did they find another victim?"

Cal was holding out the microphone.

"No, it's something else."

Matheson trailed behind.

Dahlgren took the microphone, leaned against the VOX console, and took a breath before keying it and asking, "Claire, what have you got?"

"We've got a diver." Claire's voice came from the speaker.

"Yes," Matheson said softly.

"Your voice is pretty clear, so you must not be deep," Dahlgren said. "Where are you?"

Cal was getting a map and spreading it on the console in front of Dahlgren.

"We're on a ledge just above the keyhole," she said. "The floor is two hundred feet here, but this ledge is about a hundred and ten."

Both Cal and McAfee pointed to the spot.

"Norman was floating on his back, goofing off, blowing smoke-ring bubbles, when he saw the lights from his helmet reflect in the faceplate."

"Who else is with her?" Dahlgren asked.

"Potts and Addison," Cal said.

Dahlgren keyed the mike.

"Have you touched him?"

"You're kidding, right?"

"Sorry," Dahlgren said. "Describe him."

"He's a skeleton in a wet suit wedged up between the ledge and the ceiling, like somebody jammed him there," Claire said.

"That's not uncommon," Dahlgren said. "When the dumb-asses—sorry, I mean the victims—realize they're going to die, they sometimes back themselves in nooks and crannies in the ceilings. Some psychological thing, maybe so their body won't float around, or so they have their back against something. Describe the gear."

"Say again?"

"Describe his scuba."

"Okay," Claire said. "He—or she or it—is wearing a black neoprene wet suit, three-quarter-inch, with the old yellow U.S. Divers logo on the breast. The wet suit is ripped, like he's been in some kind of knife fight."

"Again, not unusual," Dahlgren said. "That's where the stories of buddies knife fighting each other for air come from. Actually, it's from expansion as decomposition fills the body with gas, tearing the wet suit. In a few days, the gas escapes. Go on."

"He's strapped to a single steel 72, one of the old ones with a J-valve," Clair said. "Single-hose regulator, no octopus, and no SPG. Horsecollar BC. Wrist-mounted depth gauge. The skull is still attached to the body because it's jammed so tightly into the crevice, and it's wearing a big boxcar mask. He's only wearing one fin, and his feet are still attached because they're encased in panty house. The right hand is gone, but the other is still in the glove. Oh, and he's got a big manly shark-killing U.S. Divers knife in a scabbard strapped to his leg."

"Any lights?"

"No light," Claire said. "It was probably tethered to his missing hand. No backups."

"Good job," Dahlgren said. "Sounds like we've got a blast from the past."

"What do you want us to do with him?"

"Stand by," Dahlgren said, then turned to the others.

"Can somebody take a body bag down to them?"

"You can't do it?" Matheson asked.

Dahlgren shook his head. "Still on my surface interval from this morning's dive," he said. "Can't go back in the water for another hour. This guy's already a skeleton, so he won't melt, and I'd like to take a look at him as soon as possible."

"I'll do it," McAfee said.

Dahlgren keyed the mike.

"Claire, Loren is coming down with a bag. Sit tight."

"I'm sitting," she said, "but I'm not tight."

"Take pictures," Dahlgren told McAfee.

"I'll make some fresh coffee," Cal said. "The stuff in the pot has been there since I got here at first light."

"Don't know when I ate last," Matheson said. "Yesterday, I think."

"Vargo's on the hill is open again," McAfee suggested.

"I've whipped up a little stew, if you'd rather," Cal said. "It's been cooking all morning. Should be just right by now."

"Thanks," Matheson said. "That would be fine."

"I didn't know you could cook," Dahlgren said.

Cal smiled broadly.

"At the NEDU—"

"What's that?" Matheson asked.

"Navy Experimental Dive Unit," McAfee answered. "It's where they test all the new dive equipment for Navy, do medical experiments, gather data. Remember Sealab? Cal was one of the original divers, along with Scott Carpenter."

Matheson raised her eyebrows.

"During saturation trials, when we had people in the dry pods for weeks on end, we had to be there around the clock to monitor the life support," Cal said. "So I learned to cook. Warm meals helped."

After a few cups of strong coffee and a bowl of stew, Matheson betrayed her contentment with a sigh and placed her sensible black shoes on the desk.

"Have plans for Thanksgiving?" she asked Dahlgren.

Thirty minutes later, Cal and Dahlgren grasped the straps on either end of the body bag and hauled it onto the dock. McAfee climbed out of the water and began to shed his gear.

"Where are the others?" Matheson asked.

"Doing their deco stops," McAfee said. "I just went down and came back up and didn't exceed the no-deco limits. But Claire's team had already been down an hour when they discovered our mystery guest."

They placed the body bag on the edge of the dock and carefully unzipped it, letting the water drain down the wooden steps into the water.

The body was just as Claire had described it, except the skull had rolled around during the trip. It was now between the femurs.

"Okay, let's not touch the bones or the wet suit," Dahlgren said. "We're interested in the gear right now. Loren, can you get some shots of this as we disentangle the backpack and take the cylinder away? Good. Easy, now."

Dahlgren lifted the old gray cylinder out of the bag while Cal kept the second stage of the regulator and its hose from snagging. He laid the cylinder down on the dock. Then he went back inside the bag, unbuckled the depth gauge from the skeletal wrist, and held it out for McAfee to get a shot of it with the digital.

"No maximum-depth needle," McAfee said.

"Haven't seen one of these in thirty years," Dahlgren said,

then turned his attention to the shoulder of the cylinder, just below the valve.

"What's the SPG read?" McAfee asked.

"There is no pressure gauge," Cal said. "The tank's a J-valve. When you have to pull the handle, you're down to five hundred pounds. That's your gauge."

"The reserve has been pulled," Dahlgren said, noting the position of the rod attached to the tank valve. "I'll bet he sucked the tank dry and drowned. Got a rag?"

Cal took a red bandanna from his back pocket. Dahlgren took it and rubbed the shoulder of the tank, then turned it so the light overhead would cast some relief onto the numbers stamped there.

"Is it him?" Matheson asked.

"No," Dahlgren said.

"How can you be so sure?" Matheson asked. "You haven't been looking at him for five minutes. You said he ran out of air and drowned, and that is probably what would happen when our guy got careless."

"I'm sorry, it's not our killer," Dahlgren said.

"Then what's he doing down here?"

"Cave divers sneak into all sorts of places where they're not wanted, and they often go alone," Dahlgren said. "But look at these numbers stamped here in the steel. They mean July 1973, when his tank was last hydrostatted, which is pressure testing required every five years. He couldn't have gotten air fills later than 1978. Unfortunately, we have some victims from the eighties."

"Goddammit," Matheson swore. "Why can't this be easy?"

"Some respect, please," Cal said. "You didn't look at the rest of his tank. He scratched a message into it with the point of his dive knife."

Cal rubbed his palm over the farewell.

Carol, it said. *Love you always. Tell kids sorry. Lost.*

Matheson looked away.

"At least he was calm," Cal said.

"How can you tell?" Matheson asked. She was holding the white handkerchief from her suit pocket to her mouth.

"He knew he was going to die and took the time to doff his tank and scratch out good-bye," Cal said. "Then he put his tank back on, replaced his dive knife in its scabbard, and found a crevice to back into. He may have dicked up, but he was no coward, and he was determined to make a clean exit. And all of us have made mistakes that would have put us in that bag if our luck hadn't held."

Dahlgren stood.

"Loren, can you quietly contact the local scuba clubs and NSS grottoes and see if they know of anybody who went missing between 1973 and 1978?" Dahlgren asked. "I would rather not have a stranger tell Carol and the kids."

Jolene woke in darkness.

She was cold, shivering spasmodically, and her ears hurt. Somewhere there was the slosh and drip of water. With great effort, she formed a question through her chattering teeth.

"Am I dead?" she asked.

But even she didn't recognize the sound that came out of her mouth. Instead, it was a high-pitched squeal that did not resemble human speech. Then there was a click, and she was bathed in the harsh glow of a handheld light.

Jolene was nude except for the gold cross that hung around her neck. Instinctively, she hugged her knees to her chest, trying to hide as much of her body as possible.

"Try again," a voice came to her inside her head. "Bring the microphone down and speak clearly and slowly into it."

For the first time, she noticed she was wearing a small headphone apparatus. The earpiece was tucked into her ear canal, where it would transmit sound directly to her mastoid bone, without intervening air spaces. The boom mike was pointing away from her mouth.

She hesitated a moment, then adjusted the microphone. Very slowly, she asked:

"Am I dead?"

The heavily processed voice didn't sound like her own, and although it echoed harshly from unseen walls, it was intelligible.

"Of course not," the man said.

Ultraviolet lights buzzed to life, allowing her to see the confines of her prison. It was a domed chamber, and the walls fluoresced with otherworldly colors as the atoms in the calcite and other minerals were excited by the black light.

In the surreal glow, she could see a man sitting on top of a rock, his hand holding a remote for the lights. Behind him was a lake. Against a wall were some industrial-looking quart bottles that appeared to hold food and water. There were some blankets, and some machinery that Jolene didn't recognize. Some of the machinery had fans, nearly a yard in circumference, and their blades spun lazily.

Geiger took a blanket from the pile, but before he handed it over, he grasped her chin and clucked over the bruises from the kidnapping.

"A shame," he said. His processed voice came from inside her head again. He, too, was wearing a headset descrambler. "But they will heal, in time."

She slapped his hand away.

"Where am I?" Jolene asked into her microphone.

"The Moon Pool."

Geiger smiled.

"What I say next is important, so pay attention: Escape is impossible. You can't swim out, because we're four hundred feet down. Besides, the water's too cold. Even if you could make it to the surface, which you can't, you would die of decompression sickness."

Jolene looked at him, unbelieving.

"It's caused by the nitrogen in your bloodstream. The

bends, they call it. Well-named, too, because that's the rather painful position in which you die—doubled over."

Jolene said something unintelligible.

"Into the microphone, please."

"I don't understand."

"It is a little technical, isn't it?"

Jolene was confused.

"I don't understand how I got here," she said. "Who are you and how do you know my name? And why do we have to talk into microphones?"

"It's the density of the air," Geiger said. "Together with the amount of helium in the gas we're breathing. Our voices are processed electronically through these boxes so we can understand one another."

"And?" Jolene asked.

Geiger brushed the hair back from his forehead.

"My name is Jakob Geiger," he said. "I know your name because I heard you on the radio a short while ago and have been watching you since."

"You're a stalker?"

"That's not the word the authorities would use."

Jolene pulled the blanket tighter around her.

"You were injected with Rohypnol."

"The date-rape drug?"

"It's ten times as effective as Valium," Geiger said. "But not to worry, there was no rape involved. The drug was for sedation only, to keep you quiet during the—well, the abduction—and calm during the dive. Do your ears hurt?"

"Yes," she said. "And my sinuses."

"The most difficult part is equalizing the pressure in your ears as we go down. I tried to go slowly, but it's hard to do a Valsalva maneuver when you're unconscious."

"I have no idea what you're talking about," Jolene said. "How'd you get me down here?"

213

"In this," Geiger said, handing her an old Kirby Morgan commercial diving helmet. She turned it over in her hands, noticing the chipped yellow paint and the dozens of fine scratches in the faceplate. Next to where Geiger had picked up the helmet was a black dry suit.

"And an Aqua Zep."

"A what?"

"An underwater scooter," Geiger said. "You're lucky. If the pressure hadn't equalized in your ears and sinuses, you could have ruptured an eardrum. Very painful. I finally managed to get you to yawn by briefly reducing your oxygen level. Still, I imagined there would be some discomfort."

Jolene's head began to clear a bit.

"You're going to kill me," she said. "If you weren't, you wouldn't be telling me all this."

"Yes," Geiger said. "But not right away. We have some time before that, time to get to know each other. You really are quite remarkable, you know. Are you troubled?"

"Of course I'm troubled—I'm petrified, as a matter of fact. I would scream, but nobody would hear me."

"You *have* been listening."

Jolene held her head in her hands.

"What kind of monster are you?"

"I'm your monster, Jolene."

He motioned behind him.

"You need to eat, for your health," he said. "It's all there in those plastic bottles. Sorry, but no hot meals here. The risk posed by fire is too great."

"I would rather choke than eat your food."

"Suit yourself."

"What about water?" she asked.

"It's all around you," Geiger said. "Don't worry, it's quite safe. But when it is time to relieve yourself, there are some plastic bags in the supplies. I suggest you use them, because you don't want to be defecating into your water supply."

"I'm cold."

"Not life-threatening if you use the blankets. You'd die in a matter of hours in water this cold, but air is not so thermally efficient."

Geiger began to kit up, then paused. He motioned at a row of flowers beneath a bank of lights.

"It is quite wonderful that we have flowers in bloom. These are a species of narcissus known as Angel's Tears. Their natural growing season is midwinter, so they thrive here. Do you like them?"

Jolene shook her head.

Geiger glanced at his wrist computer.

"There will be plenty of time for small talk later," he said. "I must be leaving if I'm going to keep to my decompression schedule. But don't worry—I'll return every few days, to check on your welfare, to recharge the chemical scrubbers, and bring more food. The lights are on a cycle—to save energy, one hour in every eight."

Geiger paused, then fingered Jolene's necklace.

"This is the source of your strength?"

"Yes," she said. "My father gave it to me."

"Where is he now?"

"He died," she said. "Stomach cancer."

"You believe he is waiting for you? In heaven?"

Jolene nodded, then glanced away as tears began to spill down her cheeks.

"I believe I will see my parents, as well," Geiger said. "But in a much different place, an older place. You will see it soon enough. Farewell."

She dropped her head in her hands and began to sob. The sound that filled the chamber was an unearthly keen.

Twenty-three

In the basement morgue at the University of Missouri School of Medicine at St. Louis, Geiger was up to his elbows in an obese elderly woman. He was humming "The Impossible Dream." The song was muffled, however, because he was singing behind a plastic face guard.

His assistant, Smith, was standing across the slab and was taking the bits of tissue Geiger handed across, carefully labeling and placing them in tubes for analysis.

Both were absorbed in their work and did not notice Grace Matheson standing near the double doors to the morgue, the Subtern case file and a copy of Geiger's book beneath her arm.

"Doctor?" she asked.

No response.

She stepped closer.

"Doctors?" she asked, more forcefully.

Geiger gave a start, then flipped up his face guard.

"Sorry," Matheson said. "I tried knocking, but you were singing so loudly—"

"N-n-not a problem," Geiger said.

There was an uncomfortable pause.

Geiger smiled reassuringly.

"Didn't you know Dr. Geiger stutters?" Smith asked.

"No," she said.

Geiger shrugged.

"He felt it wasn't relevant for the book," Smith said, "and I must agree. His personal story is only the introduction. The book is really about advances in forensic science."

"Of course," Matheson said, then glanced at their bloody gloves. "You'll forgive me if we don't shake hands."

Geiger attempted to pronounce a word that sounded like psychology, then gave up and glanced at his assistant.

"Dr. Geiger's stutter is psychogenic," Smith said.

"It originated in some emotional trauma?"

"Quite right," Smith said. "It goes away when he sings."

Matheson nodded.

"I assume you're a cop," Smith said. "I'm sorry, but you should have made an appointment. I can't imagine how you got down here."

"This may have something to do with it," Matheson said, and showed them her credentials. "I'm in charge of the Bonne Terre case. I had business at the Bureau's field office downtown, and thought I'd swing by here as well."

Geiger's eyes flashed at this.

"I spoke with Dr. Smith and attempted to make an appointment," Matheson said. "But I wasn't having much luck."

"I remember talking to you," Smith said. "I said Dr. Geiger could see you sometime next month."

"That won't do," Matheson said. "We need help now."

Geiger looked at Matheson, then looked at Smith.

"All right," Smith said. "Go on."

"Our local pathologists are in over their heads, if you'll forgive the pun," Matheson said. "Actually, I don't know what pathologist would be comfortable with this, considering that we have the bodies of sixteen victims floating in one-hundred-and-eighty-gallon aquariums."

"Why?" Smith asked.

"They melt in air," Matheson said. "Dr. Geiger, you are the best pathologist in between the coasts, maybe the best forensic pathologist in the country. We are at a dead end in this case. We desperately need your help."

"What is it that you'd like Dr. Geiger to do?" Smith asked.

"I want Dr. Geiger to come to Bonne Terre and examine these victims at our makeshift morgue," Matheson said. "The Bureau would be terribly grateful for your help. Also, if you're thinking about writing a sequel to your book, I thought it would make an interesting case—once it is closed, of course."

Geiger smiled and inclined his head toward Matheson.

"It would be Dr. Geiger's pleasure," Smith said.

"Tomorrow?" Matheson asked.

"It's Thanksgiving," Smith said.

"Still," Matheson said.

Smith looked at Geiger.

"Next week?"

"Shall I send a Bureau car for you?" Matheson asked.

"Not necessary," Smith said. "I'll drive Dr. Geiger. How far is Bonne Terre? I'm not familiar with that section of the country."

"An hour, tops," Matheson said.

Smith nodded.

"And the book?" Geiger asked, stuttering.

"Could you sign it?" Matheson said.

Jolene fumbled with the blanket in the darkness, folding it into quarters, then determined which corner was the center. Holding the corner tightly, she shook the blanket free, then used her teeth to rip a hole in the center. After a few minutes of chewing she had a hole big enough to work her fingers into, then used her hands to widen the hole. Finally, it was big enough to fit over her head, and she wore the blanket like a poncho.

Her head was pounding, her sinuses were blocked, and the back of her throat was irritated. In addition to her other woes, Jolene noted, she was working on a sinus infection.

Then the lights came on, and she made another mark on the wall with a rock. There were five of them now. At eight hours each, nearly two days had passed.

She inspected the plastic bottles of food.

Finally, she uncapped one, shook out some food sticks, and read the labels. She kept the peanut-butter and cherry ones, but shoved the apricot-flavored ones back into the bottle.

"Lord," she said in a voice that was unintelligible, even to herself, but Jolene continued because she reckoned God would understand. "I thank you for this—well, this peanut-butter stick—because I've got to keep up my strength in order to get out of here. Alive, I mean. With your help. Amen."

She chewed slowly, looking at the marks on the wall and reckoning the days. Her eyes got misty, then she forced herself to regain control.

"Great," she said. "Today's Thanksgiving."

Vargo's was a three-story brick-and-limestone-facade landmark on top of the hill overlooking the tailings pile. A big porch with white awnings and an iron railing faced south. A red neon sign high on the east wall, facing U.S. 67, said "VAR-GO's." Below that, in glowing blue neon, was "Restaurant and Lounge."

Dahlgren and Matheson faced each other across a high-backed red vinyl booth against a window, and through the frost-covered glass they could see snowflakes falling from the leaden sky. A skein of snow had coated Benham Street, and already cars were beginning to spin their tires as they climbed the hill toward downtown.

"Nobody around here knows how to drive in snow,"

Dahlgren said. "I'm going to call Bruno and have him bring my Jeep out and take the Helio back. Looks like I'm going to need four-wheel drive, and it's not good for the aircraft to be out in weather like this."

"Bruno?"

"My mechanic," Dahlgren said. "Actually, my friend. We've been together a long time. He keeps the Helio flying, repairs my dive equipment, maintains the compressor and cascade system, services the Jeep, and tells me when I'm in over my head."

"Are you?"

"Guess I'll know when he gets here," Dahlgren said.

"How are you going to fly your plane out in the middle of the circus down there?" Matheson asked, referring to the revival tents and satellite trucks and all the rest that had sprung up around the mine entrance.

"Use the Jeep to tow it far enough away so I can get a clear five hundred feet," Dahlgren said. Then his tone changed. "Look, I'm glad you suggested this."

"I thought it was a good idea, considering."

"That neither of us have anything better to do?"

"Something like that," Matheson said. "Under the circumstances, with the holiday and everything, don't you think I could call you Richard?"

"Just don't call me—"

"Dick, I know. You can call me Grace."

Dahlgren nodded cautiously.

"My SAC wants a major case meeting," Matheson said.

"When?" Dahlgren asked.

"Next Tuesday," Matheson said. "With the mayor and council, representatives from the highway patrol, and the governor's office."

"Good luck," Dahlgren said.

"I need you there."

220

"I'm not getting paid," Dahlgren complained. "Brown said he was out of money. I don't even know what I'm still doing here."

"Sure you do," Matheson said. "It's the right thing."

The waitress came, and they both had to glance at the menus they had neglected since sitting down. The waitress looked to Dahlgren to be about seventeen.

"We have a holiday special," she said, chewing a wad of gum. "Turkey and dressing, of course. Mashed potatoes, cranberry sauce. Pecan pie for desert."

"Okay," Matheson said. "That's appropriate. I'll have that."

"Make that two," Dahlgren said.

"What's your name?" Matheson asked.

"Angie," she said, popping her gum.

"Angie, would it be possible to get some merlot with dinner?"

She made a face.

"What's that?"

"Wine," Dahlgren said.

"I know we have beer, and some liquor, but I don't know what kind of wine we have."

"Okay, how about a B-and-B?" Matheson asked.

"A DMV?" the waitress asked.

"Mexican beer?" Dahlgren asked.

"Corona."

"Bottled here," Dahlgren said. "Okay, let's keep it simple. Bring me a long-necked Bud. How about you, Grace?"

"Any kind of wine."

"I'll check," the waitress said. "Do you want a stein with your beer?"

"Explain," Dahlgren said.

"Well, it's a tradition to drink your beer from a German stein here, then to keep it in back of the bar until you come back. That is one of the last Falstaff bars still in use, and I guess it's like a million years old."

"It's beautiful," Matheson said. "I looked at it when we came in. So those dozens of wonderful beer steins belong to people here in town?"

"They used to," Angie said. "This is where most folks raised around here got their first taste of beer. My dad tells me that most of the boys the steins belong to never came back."

"Never came back from where?" Matheson asked.

"Vietnam," Angie said.

"Angie," Dahlgren said. "I don't deserve one."

"A lot of the guys still get them," she said. "Iraq, you know. I thought maybe you were . . . military. You have that look."

"Angie," Matheson said, "this is Richard Dahlgren, and he is in charge of the divers who are bringing the murder victims up from the mine."

Angie's eyes got wide.

"You're Dahlgren?" she asked. "I've been reading about you every day in the local papers. My God, it must be so scary down there. And you're the lady FBI agent I saw on television. Um, what's your name?"

"Matheson."

"No, that wasn't it."

"Yes, it is," she said. "Look, I think Richard deserves a stein, don't you? You keep it here for him, and when all of this is over and we catch this bastard that was killing these women, he can come back here and claim it."

When Angie left to turn in the order, Dahlgren shook his head disapprovingly at Matheson.

"I wish you hadn't done that," he said. "I'm no hero."

"Heroes are ordinary people in extra-ordinary circumstances," she said. "That's you, my friend. All of the divers should have their own steins as well. You guys are the ones going down in the mines. It gives me the creeps just to think about it."

"It's not that bad."

"Yeah, right."

"Maybe I could show you."

"I'd have to be really drunk."

In a few moments, Angie returned with a tray. She placed a glass of merlot and an elaborately colored German stein with a flip-top lid on the table. She filled the stein with Budweiser.

"This is on the house," she said. "My father insisted when I told him who you were. He said he'll put your name on the bottom and it will go up on the bar, together with all the rest."

"Be gracious," Matheson whispered.

"Thanks," Dahlgren said.

Angie beamed.

"Um, do you know how to do a corkscrew?" she asked. "I've never opened a bottle of wine before, and I'm afraid of messing it up."

"Let me see it," Dahlgren said. He spiraled the screw through the wax top and into the cork, then pulled. The cork came out with a satisfying pop.

"That was neat," Angie said. "You guys sit tight. Your meals will be out in a shake."

Dahlgren filled Matheson's glass.

"I think we're the only customers here," Matheson said.

"No," Dahlgren said. "There are a few around back. We're just the only ones out front."

Matheson held the glass aloft.

"Happy Thanksgiving," she said.

Dahlgren repeated the phrase as he touched the stein to her glass.

"I think it's time we came clean with one another," Matheson said as she put down her glass. "I'll tell you what I'm doing in Cape Girardeau if you tell me what happened in that cave—what do you call it?"

"*Cueva del hueso.*"

"That's it," she said. "What does it mean?"

"The cave of the bone," Dahlgren said. "Or the cave of the stone. *Hueso* means both, depending on the context." He took a long drink of beer, then placed the stein on the table-top. "Okay, I'm game. But you go first, just to make sure you're going to come clean, as you phrased it."

Matheson held out her hand, and they shook. He held her hand for a bit too long afterward. She withdrew her hand quickly, took a breath, and began.

"I'm what is known in the agency as a four-bagger," she said.

"I assume that's not a good thing."

"It's just one mistake from the door," she said. "A four-bagger means you've been subject to censure, probation, suspension, and relocation."

"What did you do?" Dahlgren asked.

"One night, after I came home late from a stakeout in San Francisco, my live-in shit of a boyfriend knocked one of my front teeth out," Matheson said, taking another drink of wine. "So I took my service piece and fired four rounds between his legs."

"Kill him?"

"Didn't even touch him."

"Did you miss?"

"If I'd been aiming to hit him, he'd be dead by now. And I'd be in prison," Matheson said. "No, I just wanted to scare him. In the academy, you have to put eighty percent of your rounds in the kill zone, the torso, to qualify. My average was ninety-seven percent."

"Did it scare him?"

"For a while," Matheson said. "But when I moved out a week later, he called my supervisor and filed a formal complaint. I had dug the slugs out of the floor by the time the Bureau investigated, but it still looked bad. And I told the truth."

"No sympathy for battered women?"

"I'm not a woman," Matheson said. "I'm an agent."

"Got it."

"So that's why, along with what it considers my whacko ideas about violent crimes and psychic imprints, the Bureau sent me to the Cape," Matheson said. "I thought I was finished until this case came along. If we can close it, I'll have something that resembles a career back. It won't be as significant as if we're dealing with an active serial killer, but still, it has garnered a lot of media attention."

"What was the attraction?"

"From the media?"

"No, to what's-his-face."

"Randy?" Matheson asked. "He was somebody I thought I could save, I suppose. That's the usual formula for an unhappy, middle-aged female, isn't it?"

"You've got a few years before middle age."

"Not that many," she said into her wineglass. "Your turn."

Dahlgren took another sip of beer.

"I was the leader of an expedition that was attempting to connect *cueva del hueso* with the Huautla system. We failed. At two hundred and seventy-six feet, my dive partner and I made a series of mistakes which resulted in having only enough gas for one us to make it out alive. End of story."

"What was his name?

"Taylor. And *she* was my friend."

"Girlfriend?" she asked. "Lover?"

"Lover," Dahlgren said.

"How did you decide which one of you would survive?"

"It was a unilateral decision," Dahlgren said. "She killed herself by breathing pure oxygen. She was gone before I could save her."

"No wonder you're fucked up," Matheson said.

"Tell me what you really think."

"So you got out."

"Barely."

"There's more to the story," Matheson said.

"I haven't told anyone."

"Then it's time," she said.

Dahlgren took another gulp of beer, then looked out the window at the accumulating snowfall.

"Tell me about Taylor," Matheson urged.

Hearing Matheson speak her name seemed odd to Dahlgren.

"After Taylor breathed the O_2 and died," he said, "I was in a state of confusion. I had lost the line again, things were silted out because of our thrashing, and I was ready to give up. It was like I was in a Christmas globe with orange snowflakes that had the hell shaken out of it. I didn't know up from down. It seemed to me that my exhaust bubbles were racing to the floor instead of the ceiling. Then something happened."

"What kind of something?"

"It started as a shimmering at the edge of my vision, and I figured it would morph into the famous tunnel of light and I would die as well," he said. "Only, I didn't, and the glow got brighter, and I became aware of a green shape moving through the water, beyond the silt."

"What was it?"

"I couldn't tell at first," Dahlgren said. "I thought it was one of the other Hell Divers come looking for us, although the light was the wrong color, but it didn't make sense for anything else to be in the water."

Matheson nodded, then waited uncomfortably as the waitress approached the table.

"Another round?" she asked.

"Yes, please," Matheson said.

"You wouldn't happen to have a cigarette, would you?" Dahlgren asked. "I'm dying for a smoke."

"Sure," Angie said brightly. "Just bought a fresh pack—"

"He doesn't need it," Matheson said. "He's older than you are, and he should be wiser. Give us about ten minutes before you come back with that round, okay?"

Angie blinked. Dahlgren knew she was thinking, *bitch*.

"And dear?" Matheson asked. "Just bring the bottle of wine."

"No problemo," she said, and turned briskly.

"Never fails," Matheson said. "Continue, please."

"I swam toward the light, of course," Dahlgren said. "But I would just about reach it, then it would recede, and I was getting angry. Why would the other divers swim away from me? Couldn't they see I was towing Taylor's body?"

Dahlgren took another drink.

"Then the green light stood still long enough for me to reach it," he said.

"What was it?"

Dahlgren rubbed his jaw.

"It was a green goddess," he said. "Perhaps one of the Mazatec elementals, but certainly a goddess. Tall and slim with flowing black hair and jade-green skin. She glowed from the inside, like some kind of bioluminescent organism, and she was smiling beatifically. She was beckoning to me."

"What did you think?"

"I thought I was dead," Dahlgren said. "Or unconscious, having some kind of dream while I drowned. I decided to keep following her. I figured that if I was dead anyway, it didn't matter. I might as well follow. I was expecting a light at the end of the tunnel, dead relatives, my grandmother, maybe Jesus or the Easter Bunny, but never a meso-American earth spirit."

"So you followed."

"The water cleared," Dahlgren said. "I don't know how long I swam after her, but it must have been several minutes. Eventually she stopped again, and when I caught up to her she was hovering over the guideline."

"And the way out of the cave?"

"Yeah," Dahlgren said. "That's the way it worked. But before I hauled ass down the line, I looked back over my shoulder. She smiled and said, 'When you see me next, you won't swim out.'"

"What do you think that means?"

"It's obvious, don't you think?" Dahlgren asked. "It means I'm going to die in a cave. At least, if you believe in that sort

227

of thing, and assuming it wasn't a hallucination produced by my grief- and nitrogen-addled brain."

"You're not sure it was real."

"Who knows?" Dahlgren asked. "I've heard the same effect can be produced with small doses of ketamine."

"No, that's an out-of-body experience," Matheson said. "I don't think they can summon green goddesses at will in the laboratory just yet."

Dahlgren shrugged.

"Have you talked much about Taylor?"

"No," he said. "I had a few words with her ex-husband, who came to claim the body in San Augustín on behalf of her family in Austin. He told me I'd killed her. And you know what? I think he's right."

Dahlgren motioned for Angie to bring another round.

"Is that why you hate yourself so much?"

"Maybe," Dahlgren said.

"And this would explain your reckless and even suicidal behavior in retrieving videotapes from the trunks of submerged patrol cars during thunderstorms?"

"Theoretically," Dahlgren said.

"Taylor was an adult," Matheson said.

"She trusted me."

"It was her choice."

Dahlgren felt like a bolt of electricity had been shot through him. *Just choices.* He hadn't told anyone what Taylor had scrawled on her slate before she grabbed the oxygen regulator. *My choice.* And he had wiped the slate clean before rising from the sump with her body, not wanting to explain to strangers the nature of their private conversations.

"What's wrong?" Matheson asked. "You look like somebody just swam over your grave."

"Funny," Dahlgren said. "And inappropriate."

"I just want you to know that I don't think the green goddess was predicting your death," Matheson said. "It doesn't

228

work that way. This psychic stuff is much too obtuse for that. Like with remote viewing. They can see the damnedest stuff, and come up with incredibly detailed but partial data, but it doesn't make sense until after the fact."

Angie came with the drinks, and with their dinners.

"Thanks," Dahlgren said.

"Sure you don't want that cigarette?" Angie said, glancing defiantly at Matheson.

"That's okay," he said. "I really am trying to stop."

Matheson picked up her fork, then paused.

"If such things were possible," she said, "I think Taylor would want me to say something on her behalf."

Dahlgren looked skeptical.

"How could you possibly know what Taylor would say?"

"Easy," Matheson said. "Because it's the same thing I would say to somebody I gave up my life for: Don't waste the gift. Start living."

Later, after they had paid the check and Dahlgren had left Angie a ten-dollar tip, they paused on the restaurant's big concrete porch. Matheson slipped her arm around the small of Dahlgren's back.

"What's it like to dive?" she asked.

"It's fun," Dahlgren said. "At least at first. Eventually, it takes someplace like Mineral City to remind you how fun it was."

"I was thinking of taking a course," she said.

"Why?" Dahlgren said. "It sounds uncharacteristic for you."

"I can't say I relish the idea of having my head underwater," Matheson said. "But I think I may be missing something in this case by not trying it. Maybe I could go someplace warm and take one of those short courses."

"A resort course?" Dahlgren scoffed. "You could try it here, if you like. McAfee has plenty of instructors on his team. Hell, my instructor cert is probably still good."

"It's winter," she said.

"Same temp in the mine year-round," Dahlgren said. "The water is just as cold. Besides, I'd like to see you in neoprene. We could send your picture into *Ocean Planet* magazine."

"Why?"

They were so close now that their clouded breath mingled.

"They run pictures of scuba babes on the back pages," Dahlgren said. "Some of them are even, you know, naked. And I've been harboring this fantasy of me and you getting wet."

They kissed.

"That was sweet," Matheson said.

Dahlgren looked troubled.

"What's wrong?"

"I don't know."

"Is it me?" Matheson asked.

"No," Dahlgren said. "It's me."

"It's not like kissing your sister, is it?"

"I don't have a sister," Dahlgren said. "And no, it's not like that. It just doesn't feel right, somehow. After talking about Taylor, I mean."

"By the way, you pronounce 'naked' funny," Matheson said. "*Nekkid.* You sound like some cowboy."

"I am some cowboy," Dahlgren said.

"Are you telling me you haven't had sex since Taylor died?"

"Of course I've had sex," Dahlgren said.

"Okay," Matheson said. "The last time, the most recent time. How old was she?"

"I don't know," Dahlgren said. "I didn't ask."

"Forties?"

"No."

"Thirties?"

"Maybe."

"A little under thirty?"

"Probably. You think I'm a pig?"

"No," Matheson said. "What color was her hair? No, let me tell you. It was blond, wasn't it? And was she athletic? But vulnerable somehow?"

"She was an EMT," Dahlgren said.

"You're not going to find Taylor," Matheson said. "She's dead, remember?"

"That's not what I'm doing," Dahlgren said.

"Okay, the time before last. Age?"

"I get the point," Dahlgren said, and he had the odd sensation of seeing himself from the outside. Did his life run according to a set of rules he was barely conscious of? "Let's move on. Can we?"

"The question," Matheson said, "is can you? Because if you can't, you're going to be very lonely very soon. Taylor will be twenty-five forever, and you—and the rest of the human race—will just keep getting older. Think this will keep working when you're on the other side of fifty, and waitresses tell you what a cute daughter you have?"

"Cut it out."

"Is it emotional or just sexual?" Matheson asked. "I could wear a wig, I guess, but there's not much I can do about my age."

"Now you're being cruel."

Matheson paused.

"You're right," she said. "My feelings are hurt. I never was any good at this dating thing anyway. If you don't want a fuck buddy, how about a drinking buddy?"

"You're my friend, Grace."

"Friends," she said. "It can be such an ugly word. Do me a favor, okay? When you start hitting on Staci, would you make sure I'm not around? In a certain light, her hair looks almost blond. Won't take too much convincing for her to do a bottle job. Nail her now, and she'll grow into the role. That way you'll get a few more years out of her. Bonus points: She dives. Don't argue, just promise."

Dahlgren blushed. He hadn't thought about Staci that way before, but now he realized she did look a little like Taylor, and it excited him. And dammit, there was something about a woman's body just shy of thirty. He was suddenly angry at Matheson, because she was right, and because he could never look at Staci again without thinking about fucking her.

Matheson started to speak again but stopped herself.

"That's why Randy hit me."

"There's no excuse for that."

"The problem is I can't keep my mouth shut. I have to blurt out the truth, no matter how much it hurts, and particularly when people don't believe me," she said. "Call me Cassandra."

Matheson smiled sadly.

"And I know you would never hit me," she said. "Seems I can only have the men who do. Now, think we can find a liquor store open in this town on Thanksgiving night?"

"Probably not," Dahlgren said. "But Loren keeps a few bottles at the house, for company."

"Good," Matheson said. "I feel like getting absolutely hammered."

The battered white Wrangler with the black soft top clawed its way slowly up the snow-covered road that led to the top of the remediation site. The tattered tire cover had the same skull-and-dive-knife HELL DIVERS logo as on the nose of Dahlgren's plane. As the Jeep neared the bunkhouse, Michael Schwartz waved it to a stop.

The big man behind the wheel struggled with the zipper, attempting to get the driver's window down, then finally gave up and just opened the door.

"Looking for Dahlgren," he said. "This is his Jeep. I'm here to drop this off and fly the Helio back."

"You mean the airplane?"

"The same."

"I don't think there's room to take off here," Michael said.

232

"People have set up all of these tents and stuff, and you'd have to have all the newspeople move their cars."

Bruno looked through the frosted windshield.

"It'll make it, easy," Bruno said. "But I'm going to yoke the tail wheel to the Jeep and drag it over yonder, where I can take a good run at it."

"Think that's a good idea?"

"It's a worse idea to let an aircraft sit out in weather like this," Bruno said. "Don't worry about me. I've been putting airplanes in tight places and flying them out long before you were even a gleam in your mother's eye. Now, where's Dahlgren?"

Dahlgren was wrapped in a sleeping bag with his legs curled up, asleep on the top of the big desk inside the plastic tent on the dock.

"Passed out again," Bruno said as he slapped Dahlgren's mummified feet.

"What?"

Dahlgren rose on an elbow.

"Passed out, I said. Man, you smell like a brewery."

"I was asleep," Dahlgren said, swinging his feet to the floor and letting the bag fall from his shoulders, revealing the tops of a set of well-worn black polypropylene underwear. "Man, it's cold in here. That's why I'm up on the desk. The deck is too damn cold."

"You don't have a bed around here?"

"Not close," Dahlgren said.

"And you need a bath."

"Yeah, I guess."

Cal brought them coffee, and while Dahlgren sat cross-legged on the desk and tried to get his eyes to focus, Bruno offered his thanks and found a crate to sit on. He was afraid he might break the office chair Dahlgren offered.

"How's the Jeep?"

233

"Engine ran good, but the synchros are starting to howl."

"Can I get it home?"

"Probably," Bruno said. "If it gets too bad, just leave it in fourth gear and double-clutch the hell out of it."

"What's it going to cost to fix?"

"A grand to rebuild the tranny," Bruno said. "Maybe a little more to do it right, maybe a little less if you can find an AX-5 from the junkyard."

"Terrific," Dahlgren said.

"Why don't you get a decent car?" Bruno asked. "That Jeep has a hundred and thirty thousand miles on it, but looks like it has three hundred thousand. The four-banger doesn't have the power to pull that hat off your head, the soft top leaks, and it's so noisy on the highway that my ears are still ringing."

"I love that Jeep," Dahlgren said. "It has character."

"It's a mess," Bruno said. "It's something a high-school kid with a bad case of the blue balls would drive, and wonder why he's not getting laid. What about a new Wrangler? An adult Jeep? You know—six-cylinder, hard top, air-conditioning. You could actually hear the stereo on the highway."

"Air-conditioning?" Dahlgren said with a sneer. "Do I look like somebody's grandfather?"

"No, but you act like somebody's grandkid," Bruno said.

Dahlgren waved him off.

"So how's it going?" Bruno asked.

"Not well," Dahlgren said. "We still have no clue who did this." In five minutes, Dahlgren had given him the high points of the investigation, including the link to the Pre-Raphaelites and the patterns in the abductions.

"So this guy grabs girls around Thanksgiving?" Bruno asked.

Dahlgren nodded.

"Think he's gotten this year's prize?"

Dahlgren looked up from his coffee.

"We don't think he's still operating," Dahlgren said. "None

234

of the girls we've found so far have even been from the nineties, and we're about three-quarters finished with the search of Mineral City."

Bruno scratched his beard and looked at the board behind Dahlgren.

"Yeah, but."

"But what?"

"There's more to the mine than just Mineral City, right? Deeper parts, I mean."

"Sure," Dahlgren said, sliding down from the desk. He winced when his bare feet hit the cold wood of the dock. "It has three separate levels, the drifts go for miles in every direction, and some of the ore dumps and so forth are four hundred feet deep. But that's way deeper than our boy would go."

"Why?" Bruno asked. "Haven't you noticed something about the years the girls were found, and at what depths?"

Dahlgren hadn't thought about it before. The girls weren't found in chronological order, so the depths had seemed random to him. But when Dahlgren looked at the years of the abductions, he found that the depths were increasing as the dates got later.

"He began at a hundred feet in 1967," Bruno said. "By 1983, he's doubled that depth. The guy is using his experience and advances in diving technology to go deeper every couple of years. The reason you haven't found any bodies from the nineties is that Mineral City is too shallow for him. By now, he's got to be pushing four hundred feet."

Dahlgren cursed.

"He'd be too old by now to do this."

"Let's see," Bruno said. "You're what, thirty-six?"

"Thirty-seven," Dahlgren said. "Thanks for remembering my birthday this year. The party was a blast."

"Quit whining. Do you think you're still going to be diving in your fifties? No, wait before you answer. That's less than twelve years away. I've got underwear older than that. Think of all the divers you know who are still as good in their fifties as they ever were when they were younger. They may even be better, because they're smarter and more experienced."

"There's no evidence," Dahlgren said. "No recent bodies."

"You haven't looked," Bruno said.

"Bruno," Dahlgren said, "they ran out of money to pay me two weeks ago. I was hoping to wrap this thing up this week. If I stay much longer than that on this case, I'll go bankrupt. No more Jeeps, period. And I'll lose the Helio."

"They're just things," Bruno said. "They can be replaced. But you can't replace people. What if this mother is still in business? He could keep killing for years."

Dahlgren rubbed his eyes.

"Dammit, Bruno. When the Jeep and the Helio go up for auction, I hope you remember this conversation."

"They won't auction the Jeep," Bruno said. "They'll just give it a Christian burial. See you later. I've got a preflight to do. Want to make a bet on how much water you've got in your fuel from all this snow?"

An hour later, Dahlgren watched the Helio skate down the slope toward St. Joseph's Cemetery at the eastern edge of the remediation area. Bruno throttled out and the turbocharger began to scream, and the aircraft lifted off the ground like a hawk leaving a fence post. Bruno banked, the sun glinting from the canted wings, and then he set a course due west.

Dahlgren waved, and Bruno dipped a wing.

Then Dahlgren stepped into the blockhouse and took the phone from the wall hook and thumbed in Matheson's number.

"Hey," Dahlgren said. "It's me. How the hell are you? That good, huh? Me too. Listen, I think we should send a team deeper, check out some of the drifts away from Mineral City."

Dahlgren listened for a moment.

"Yeah, I know what I said about the limits of open-circuit scuba, even with mixed gas," Dahlgren said. "But that was the eighties."

Twenty-four

"Why can't we hear them anymore?" Matheson asked.

"The VOX is line-of-sight," Dahlgren said. "They've entered a drift and the signal can't go through rock. Even if it could, they're so deep now we couldn't understand them. The gas molecules—"

"Just say it's science," Matheson said, "and spare me the explanation. I don't know how my car works, but it gets me here every morning, doesn't it?"

Cal laughed.

"Pilots and divers just have to think differently," Dahlgren said, finally, then settled back in the chair to watch the red LED numbers on the console count up the bottom time of McAfee and his team.

There was a slosh and the sound of dripping of water as Nemo breached the dock and galumphed toward the group around the console. He couldn't run, because sea lions have their hinge joints encased in their bodes, but by pointing his rear feet forward and pushing off his pelvic bone, he could "run" with a undulating movement peculiar to seals and other pinnipeds.

Matheson froze as he approached, not wanting to offer any encouragement.

"Loren really has to do something," she said.

"What, you don't like animals?" Dahlgren asked.

Nemo turned his head and looked at her with dark liquid eyes and a face full of whiskers. He had a glob of something in his mouth.

"Animals make me uncomfortable," Matheson said. "But that's beside the point. Loren is violating federal law by keeping him here," she said. "It doesn't matter if he found Nemo stranded in monofilament in a kelp bed, the Marine Mammal Protection Act says you can't keep a seal for a pet. He has to go back to the wild."

"But he would die," Dahlgren said.

"Loren has a permit," Cal said, "from the National Oceanic and Atmospheric Administration. It allows him to keep Nemo for research purposes."

"What kind of research?" Matheson asked.

"Sea lions are diving mammals," Cal said. "So are we."

"They just do it better," Dahlgren said.

"And Nemo will never be able to go back to the sea," Cal said.

"Why not?" she asked.

"He's acquired what marine biologists call 'aberrant' behavior," Cal said. "He's attracted to humans. He's an adolescent and playful now, but when he's grown, he'll weigh five or six hundred pounds. It would be like releasing a bear into the wild that craves human company and is used to being fed by them—it doesn't make for pleasant encounters."

"What will happen to him?" Matheson asked.

"Depends," Cal said. "He'll stay here for at least another year or so. But mammals tend to get vicious when they reach maturity."

"I'll say," Grace said.

"Loren will deal with it when the time comes," Cal said. "I'm sure a zoo or an aquatic park will take him."

"And if nobody wants him?"

"Loren will have to put him down," Cal said. Then he winked at Matheson and said, in a barely audible voice, "Or say he did and slip him back into the sea somewhere in the third world where the locals will feed him."

Matheson nodded. Then she asked:

"Why don't seals get the bends?"

"Because they don't breathe compressed air," Dahlgren said.

"Sea lion blood has about five times as much hemoglobin as human blood," Cal said. "That's the stuff that carries oxygen, so that's why they're able to swim so deep for so long—several hundred feet, and for up to twenty minutes. Loren is trying to figure out a way to apply that to humans."

"Can you imagine doing a twenty-minute free dive to six hundred feet?" Dahlgren asked as he rubbed Nemo's head. "No equipment and no decompression. I'm jealous."

Dahlgren waved a hand in front of his face.

"Good Lord, what has Loren been feeding you?"

"He hasn't fed him today," Cal said.

"I thought Loren said there were no fish in here."

"There aren't," Cal said. "Sometimes he puts some fish in the water for Nemo to chase. But not today."

"Well, he's got something in his mouth," Dahlgren said. "I'm not about to attempt to take it away from him, because he outweighs me. No, wait. It's not fish. Something in a paper wrapper."

Nemo threw his head back happily and let the gob slide down his throat.

"Nothing like that, just goldfish or minnows," Cal said. "Whatever he can buy cheap at the bait store. Nemo probably got into the trash."

The speaker on the console interrupted with a squawk that sounded only vaguely human. The red bottom time numbers had just passed forty-two minutes.

"What did he say?" Matheson asked.

"Not sure," Cal said as he as he grabbed the computer mouse and adjusted a couple of the faders on the descrambler's graphic interface on the monitor sunk into the console. "Loren, say again."

More gibberish.

"How deep are they?" Dahlgren asked.

"They're coming up from three-twenty station," Cal said. "They have to be above three hundred for us even to get them." He turned and adjusted the descrambler again, and McAfee's voice began to resemble human speech.

"—on a trapeze."

"What the hell is he talking about?" Matheson asked.

"Trapezes are the walkways near the ceilings of the drifts," Cal said. "It's the only way the miners could reach some of the ore. Say again, Loren."

"We found a body sitting on a trap just inside the drift off three-twenty station," he said. "Nude, like the others. And another redhead."

"Okay," Matheson said. "We've got a body at more than three hundred feet. That doesn't necessarily mean our killer has been active in the last few years, does it? Richard, you told me that what's-his-name—Sheckley?—had trained himself to dive to three or four hundred feet on air? So it's possible our guy did the same thing."

"Sheck Exley," Dahlgren said. "That's unlikely. And this is the first drift we've examined. There could be bodies in all of the tunnels."

"Or none," Matheson said.

They were sitting in the plastic tent, waiting while McAfee loaded the Compact Flash card into the reader of his laptop

241

computer. McAfee's hair was still wet, and he was shivering despite the fleece jacket he wore.

"Okay, here she is," McAfee said as he clicked open the folder, revealing a group of thumbnails. "This is a good one." He clicked again, and the laptop displayed a full-screen-sized photograph of a redheaded woman wearing only a blue silk scarf around her neck, seated on the rough trapeze board.

"Can we get Staci in here and start doing a sketch?" Matheson asked. "I'd like to try to identify this woman so we know what we're dealing with."

Dahlgren peered at the screen.

"Richard, what's wrong?" Matheson asked.

"Go to one of the close-ups," Dahlgren said.

"Of what?" McAfee asked.

"Her face."

McAfee clicked through several images, and when he came to one in which her face nearly filled the screen, Dahlgren asked him to stop.

She had freckles stretching across the bridge of her nose.

"We don't need Staci to identify this one," he said.

Dahlgren parted the plastic and asked Cal to bring his seabag from the locker where it was stowed. Then he threw the bag on the floor, unzipped it, and began rummaging through the clothes, magazines, and other crap he had thrown into it before leaving the airport.

"Seems like I packed last year, not last month," Dahlgren said. "Okay, here it is."

He took a manila folder out of the bag, opened it, and removed an eight-by-ten color photograph.

"That's her," McAfee said.

"It certainly looks like her," Matheson agreed. "Where'd you get this?"

"A woman by the name of Starla Dwyer gave me this the day I left for this job," Dahlgren said. "Her husband is on death row just down the road from us, scheduled for execution sometime soon."

"For her murder?" McAfee asked.

"Then he's our killer," Matheson said, taking the photograph and holding it next to the laptop screen.

"No, no, no," Dahlgren said while frantically leafing through the file, looking for more information. "This poor bastard is thirty-something. He wasn't even born when our guy started killing. When do they do executions in Missouri?"

Matheson was already picking up the phone.

"There was one scheduled for last night," McAfee said. "They were talking about it on the news. Prisons are an industry in this part of the state, and executions are events."

"When do they do them?" Matheson asked as she dialed the St. Louis field office.

"Ten o'clock at night, usually," McAfee said. "But they can hold indefinitely beyond the appointed time if the Supreme Court might hear an appeal or if the governor is considering a stay."

Dahlgren looked at his Seiko. It was one o'clock in the afternoon.

"Does anybody know for sure if there was an execution last night?" Matheson asked. "Isn't there a copy of a daily newspaper someplace down here?"

"No, just last week's local paper," McAfee said.

"Dammit," Matheson said. "Turn on the television. Find a local news channel. What's the inmate's name?"

"Dwyer," Dahlgren said. "Duane Dwyer."

"We'll have to make a positive identification somehow," Matheson said as she dialed the St. Louis office. "But it sure as hell looks like the same woman. What was her name?"

"Jennifer Lynn," Dahlgren said.

"This is Agent Matheson," she said briskly. "I need to speak to the SAC right away. No, I won't hold. I don't care if he's still in a lunch meeting. Yes, I'm not acting very professionally right now, and I don't care if he's taking a fucking dump while reading the *Post-Dispatch* sports section, I've got to talk to him."

Matheson waited.

To Dahlgren: "This guy have priors?"

"Drugs," Dahlgren said, looking at Dwyer's rap sheet. "Nothing violent."

"Then why'd he get the death penalty?"

"His taste in women," Dahlgren said. "Jennifer Lynn was his probation officer. Under Missouri law, that punches your ticket."

Matheson held up her hand.

When she spoke again it was in a diffident tone, but still urgent, and when she was finished she kept the line open, letting the receiver rest on her shoulder.

"There *was* a needle job today," she said. "He's not sure who it was. He's checking."

"What's a needle job?" Dahlgren asked.

"Lethal injection," she said.

McAfee started jumping channels on the television, but all he could find were commercials and soap operas. Dahlgren stared alternately at the photograph of Jennifer Lynn in life, and the image on the computer screen of Jennifer Lynn in death.

"Do either of you pray?" Matheson asked.

McAfee closed his eyes.

"I'm here," Matheson said into the receiver. "Yes, sir, I understand. Right away. Thank you, sir."

Matheson hung up.

"Well?" McAfee asked.

"They executed a sex murderer named Allison," Matheson said.

"Thank God," McAfee said.

"Dwyer is scheduled to die next week," she said. "Not

244

enough time for DNA results, but we can probably do dental or medical while she's in the aquarium. Maybe I can get that pathologist from St. Louis to help us. He's supposed to be here on Monday."

"That major case meeting scheduled for Tuesday?" Dahlgren said. "Let's make it tonight."

"I'll make the calls," she said.

Matheson chewed on a thumbnail while Dahlgren put his forehead down on the desk.

"I thought we had good news," McAfee said. "But neither of you looks happy."

"When did Jennifer Lynn disappear?" Matheson asked.

"Nineteen ninety-seven," he said, his voice muffled because his head was still on the desk.

"So as of five years ago, our killer was still operating," Matheson said. "And odds are that if he was still in business in 1997, he's still in business now."

"And he's never abducted a victim later than Thanksgiving," Dahlgren added.

"Holy shit," McAfee said. "It's the day after."

"That's right," Matheson said. "He's already grabbed this year's girl."

Twenty-five

Darkness.

Jolene was sitting cross-legged, wrapped in blankets, and she pressed her hands against her ears so that she wouldn't hear the distorted sound of her own voice.

"*Padre nuestro que estas en los cielos,*" she recited. "*Santificado sea tu nombre. Venga tu reino . . . Y no nos metas en entacion, mas libranos del ma; porque tuyo es el reino, y el poder, y la Gloria, por todos los siglos. Amen.*"

She waited a few moments, then began again:

"*Padre nuestro—*"

There was a click and the lights cycled on. Jolene blinked against the glare, then picked up a rock and made another mark on the wall of the chamber. Then she stood, stretched, and walked over to the pile of food. She unscrewed the cap of a quart Nalgene bottle crammed with food sticks and shook one out.

She unwrapped it and took a bite.

"Ugh," she said. "Apricot."

She tossed the rest of the stick into the water.

"Lord, forgive me," she said as she picked through the other flavors and found a peanut butter. "But what I really want is a cheeseburger and a Coke with ice."

The Bonne Terre Memorial Library had closed at five P.M., but at ten o'clock lights still burned in the meeting room. The long table normally used for council meetings was strewn with maps, legal pads, evidence photographs, and empty Styrofoam coffee cups.

The federal prosecutor from St. Louis removed his glasses, placed them on the legal pad in front of him, and rubbed the bridge of his nose. His name was J. Andreason, he had gray hair and a salt-and-pepper beard, and his red striped tie and conservative blue suit were photo-op perfect. Andreason had been a classmate of the current attorney general of the United States, who also happened to be a native of the Show Me State, and he seemed to share his old school chum's near-humorless demeanor.

"Agent Matheson," he said. "We've heard a great deal tonight from you and your colleagues, and all of it was heavily qualified. But it is late and time for plain talk. What are we dealing with?"

Matheson looked uncomfortably from Brown on her left to Dahlgren on her right. Before she could speak, her superior came to her defense.

"You're asking the impossible," the SAC from St. Louis, an affable man in his early fifties, said in Matheson's defense. "There just isn't enough evidence to draw a conclusion."

The prosecutor held up his hand.

"Donald, please," Andreason said. "Let the agent speak for herself. Sometimes we must make calls based on our best judgment and experience, and that's what I'm asking for now. Take your best swing, madam, because it's the only one you'll get."

Matheson nodded.

"Sir, I believe we have an active serial killer who has been abducting and then drowning women for nearly four decades," Matheson said. "There is a strong possibility that this year's victim has already been taken. I don't know for certain whether he kills the women immediately or holds them captive, but my gut tells me he holds them for days or even weeks, and then kills them at a ritually significant time."

"At last," Andreason said. "Go on."

"There is some physical evidence from the victims to support this theory, because their tissue exhibits signs of having become saturated with nitrogen," Matheson said. "That can only happen with the inspiration of compressed gas at depth over a considerable length of time."

Dahlgren nodded that she got it right.

"When?" Andreason asked. "When does he kill them?"

"My best guess?" Matheson asked. "Either the full moon or the solstice. Both are ritually significant."

"June twenty-first?"

"No, sir, the winter solstice. December twenty-first."

"Why?"

"It's the longest night of the year," Matheson said. "For ancient peoples, the dawn after the solstice marked the beginning of the return of the sun and seasons, the guarantee of another year. Myths about heroes or heroines being incarcerated in the underworld became allegories for this seasonal renewal."

"Do you have a best guess as to which myth?"

"Yes, sir, I do," Matheson said. "Our killer is reenacting the abduction of Persephone."

"Amplify."

"In Greek mythology, Persephone was gathering flowers when she was abducted by Hades, the lord of the underworld, to be his bride," Matheson said. "Persephone's mother, Demeter, was so distraught that she neglected her duties as the goddess of agriculture, and the earth became barren. Demeter left

Olympus and searched the world for her lost daughter, until she was finally told by Helios what happened."

Matheson glanced uncomfortably at Dahlgren.

"Demeter hid out in the guise of an old woman in the village of Eleusis," Matheson said, "where she nursed the king's young son. The story gets a little scattered here, but the consensus is that Demeter attempted to immortalize the son in fire but was stopped at the last moment, when she revealed her true identity."

"Immortalize?" Andreason asked. "You mean sacrifice."

"Yes," Matheson said. "In return for sparing the son, Demeter— or Zeus, depending on how you interpret the story—demanded that rites honoring her and her daughter be conducted every year at Eleusis. That's the origin of the Eleusian Mysteries, the most famous religious observance in the Greco-Roman world."

"I don't get it."

"Sir, we're dealing here with a religious system, which has its own peculiar logic," Matheson said. She added gently: "It would be like trying to explain to somebody who had never heard of Christianity how God can be the Father, the Son, and the Holy Ghost, all wrapped into one."

Andreason suppressed a smile.

"Point taken, agent," he said. "But just what were these Mysteries?"

"Nobody knows," Matheson said. "The Eleusian Mysteries are at once the most famous and the most secret religious rites of the classical world. Experts disagree on what they were. Some feel hallucinogens were involved, while others believe human sacrifice was at the core. Obviously, that's what the Subtern is doing. Most of the earliest religions incorporated human sacrifice. Even modern religious systems have a vestige of it—in communion, for example, the faithful believe they are literally eating the body and blood of Christ."

"Back to the Mysteries."

"Yes, sir," Matheson said. "They centered on the abduction of Persephone and celebrated the eventual reconciliation of Hades and Demeter—"

"They reconciled?"

"Zeus was tired of seeing the earth bare, and he ordered them to make up," Matheson said. "Since you can't defy Zeus, they came to an agreement that Persephone would spend a third of the year in the underworld with Hades but return to her mother for the rest," Matheson said.

"So those are the winter months?"

"Persephone is released in the spring, when the flowers bloom," Matheson said.

"And the Mysteries?"

"Initiates were taken underground," Matheson said. "According to some sources, they may have conversed with dead relatives or even Persephone herself. This was aided by drinking a potion that contained a drug, possibly ergot or a variety of psychedelic mushroom."

"What's ergot?"

"It's a fungus that grows on wheat and other cereal crops," Matheson said. "Also called rust."

"Now you're telling me more than I need to know."

"Sorry, sir."

"Back to the date," Andreason said. "What's our deadline?"

"This year, both the full moon and the solstice are on the same night," Matheson said. "I would bet my career on December twenty-first."

"You just did," the prosecutor said.

Andreason replaced his glasses.

"It was my belief that someone with more experience and a better service record should be put in charge of this investigation," he said. "This has been high profile from the start, and it will only get worse. SAC Lockwood, however, went to bat for you. He said that if you hadn't made the connection between the last victim and this inmate on death row, the state of Missouri would be executing an innocent man next week."

"Mr. Dahlgren made the connection," Matheson said.

"It was luck," Dahlgren protested.

"In our game, luck counts," Andreason said. "Now, we have three weeks in which to catch this bastard and free this year's Persephone, if Agent Matheson is correct. How do you propose we do that, Mr. Dahlgren?"

"I'm not a cop," he said. "I'm just a body-recovery and diving expert. It's not my job to rescue living people from overhead environments."

"It is now," the prosecutor said.

"That's not what I'm paid for," he said. "In fact, I'm not being paid at all."

"No?"

"Not since the chief's money ran out," Dahlgren said.

"That's true," Brown said. "My department is broke. He stayed because we needed him."

"We'll make arrangements," Andreason said. "Your service has been exemplary, even if your attitude has not. Our gratitude will be well-expressed. We'll talk details later."

"You bet," Dahlgren said.

"What do you need?" the prosecutor asked.

"A lot," Dahlgren said. "We have about a quarter of Mineral City left to search, but McAfee and his team can handle that. Our real problem is that we have a mine with nearly dozens of miles of flooded shafts and drifts, and it would take divers several years to search them all."

"Where would this year's victim be kept?"

"Some kind of underwater habitat or an airbell," Dahlgren said. "Finding that is our first priority. I'm sure we'll find more victims as we go along, because all of the years haven't been accounted for, and I don't think our guy is the type to skip any."

"We can get you more divers."

251

"More divers won't help," Dahlgren said. "The places we have to search are so deep that just figuring the decompression profiles for the several teams in the water at once would be a nightmare," Dahlgren said. "Also, there are technical issues. This isn't a job for open-circuit scuba. Rebreathers are absolutely necessary, and McAfee only has thirteen prototypes of the Bio-Lume."

"Navy SEALS use rebreathers, don't they?" the prosecutor asked. "Why can't you use those?"

"That's the old Mark 16," Dahlgren said. "It's great for stealthily putting a SEAL on a hostile shore from a Zodiac or shallow submarine, but not so great for long periods at depth. The Navy's been looking for a replacement for years, and none have made it through sea trials. We need to be able to adjust the oxygen partial pressure on the fly, and McAfee's rig is the only one I trust."

"You lost me there, but never mind," the prosecutor said. "So, what's the alternative?"

Dahlgren took a deep breath.

"A submersible," he said.

"A submarine?"

"More like a two-person research sub," Dahlgren said. "The shafts and drifts are big enough to accommodate a small one, and there is no current in the mine, so precise control is possible, even in confined spaces. Also, a submersible is at one atmosphere—surface pressure—so there's no risk of decompression sickness."

"So you want a submarine."

"Yes."

The prosecutor drummed his fingers on the table.

"Where do we find one?"

"The Navy has rescue and research vehicles, but they're too big," Dahlgren said. "We couldn't even get *Alvin* in the mine. Well, we could probably get her in, but not back out. But there are smaller submersibles, made for shallower water, like Harbor Branch's *Clelia*."

"How big is it?" Matheson asked.

"It's twenty-two feet long, but the beam is less than eight feet, and it's certified to a thousand feet salt water," Dahlgren said. "There are even smaller submersibles out there."

"How do we get it in the mine?" Brown asked, incredulous.

"Just take my word for it," Dahlgren said.

"These are used by research organizations?" Andreason asked.

"Or oil companies," Dahlgren said. "One salvage company I can think of. We're probably talking not more than a half-dozen in the Northern Hemisphere."

"Cost?"

"Hard to estimate," Dahlgren said. "But including the pilot and support necessary, a quarter of a million bucks a week would be a conservative guess."

Brown coughed.

Matheson looked worried.

"Do not let that estimate rattle you," Andreason said. "Do you know how much the investigations into the Zodiac killings cost? The Son of Sam? How about Eric Rudolph? We are lucky, in a way, that we have a clearly defined arena in which to wage this fight."

The prosecutor wrote a name and a number on a sheet of legal pad, tore it off, and shoved it across to Dahlgren.

"Call this number first thing and give my assistant the contact information for those six possibilities," he said. "It may take the resources of the Justice Department to do it, but I think I can say with some confidence that we will find you a submarine."

Andreason threw his legal pad into his briefcase.

"Last things," he said. "Agent Matheson, I don't want to see your theory about the killer's motive splashed across the six-o'clock news anytime soon."

"Understood," she said.

"Also, I would like to ask SAC Lockwood to assign whatever other agents and support personnel he deems necessary," he said. "But they will answer to you, so use them well. If you get into trouble, I expect you to ask for help."

"Absolutely," Matheson said.

Andreason stood.

"Anything else, sir?" she asked, rising with the others.

"Yes," the prosecutor said. "What was that name you came up with for this guy?"

"The Subtern," Matheson said.

"That's official from now on," Andreason said. "The Subtern Killer. Give *that* to the press. Better to spin it that way than let them come up with something to scare hell out of these good folks in the Bible Belt, like the Son of Satan."

Matheson nodded, but was thinking *Son of Satan* wasn't bad.

"And one other thing, Agent."

"Sir?"

"Catch this bastard."

William Bryce was waiting outside the library, sitting on the cold limestone steps beneath the portico, drinking a cup of coffee from a thermos lid and smoking a cigarette. He quickly threw the cigarette into the snow when he heard the front door open behind him.

Andreason and Lockwood brushed by him on their way to the SAC's car, but Matheson and Dahlgren lingered while Brown locked the library door.

"Trooper," Matheson said. "I didn't know you smoked."

"I don't," Bryce said. "At least, not when I'm on the job, not since they don't let us smoke in the cars anymore. But I'm off duty now."

"Got another?" Dahlgren asked.

Bryce reached for the pack in his pocket.

"Good try," Matheson said. "Don't give it to him."

Dahlgren smacked his forehead with the palm of his hand.

"Ignore him," she said. "He's been nico-clean for over a month now. It would be a shame to ruin it."

"She's got a point," Bryce said.

"Fuck this," Dahlgren said. "Christ, I've got to get some sleep." His boots left prints on the sidewalk as he strode off toward his Jeep.

"Hey, wait," Brown said. "I rode with you, remember?"

"I'll give you a lift," Matheson offered.

"That's all right," Brown said. "I've got to go back to the mine to pick up the Explorer, and it's not far from Loren's house. Dahlgren can take me. You've got over an hour to drive before you hit the sack."

Matheson nodded, even though she knew she'd sleep at the Super 8 that night. She knew Bryce must have been waiting to talk to her, because he hadn't moved while the others left.

"Move over," she said as she buttoned her overcoat and sat down on the steps next to Bryce. "Wow, that's cold."

"Quite a shock, isn't it?"

"Give me one of those cancer sticks," Matheson said as she watched the tires of Dahlgren's Jeep churn up snow and mud as he backed out of the parking space. After a few moments of grinding, the synchros finally spun down low enough for him to shove it into gear, and the Jeep lurched off into the night.

Bryce took two cigarettes from the pack, gave her one, and lit both of them with an old Zippo lighter with the First Cav emblem on it.

"Didn't know you smoked, either."

"Not since high school," Matheson said. "But I figured you had something important to talk about, and I needed some business to do with my hands. What's up?"

"We have a problem," Bryce said.

He took a long drag on his cigarette, then pulled a microcassette from the pocket of his nylon jacket. He held it in the palm of his right hand, as if trying to gauge the weight.

"Why didn't you tell me you threatened to kill Buntz?"

"Didn't think anybody would ever know," Matheson said. "So he taped it, huh?"

"Every word," Bryce said.

"Anybody else heard it?"

"Nope," he said.

"So that's your problem," she said.

"That's right," Bryce said. "The captain assigned me to search his house, and I find this stash of tapes. A shoe box full. Car stops, mostly women or other people he doesn't like. Apparently, he got off reliving them. A fair amount were sexual encounters, after a good deal of intimidation."

"Were they all women?" Matheson asked.

"All the sex acts involved women, yes," Bryce said. "These tapes aren't labeled, so I had to listen to them in order to catalog them. You know, unknown female subject pulled over for driving left of center, coerced into what sounds like fellatio, that sort of thing."

"I understand."

"I'm thinking, *Great, these folks are all suspects, at least there's plenty of motive.* And then I get to this one tape, and it's you, and you're threatening to splatter his brains all over the road if he ever stops you again," Bryce said.

"So, what do you do?"

"That's the thing," Bryce said. "I'm a by-the-book kind of guy. Always have been. But if I follow the book on this one, you're going to lose your job. The hell of it is that I think you did the right thing. You were a woman alone with an armed sexual predator on a lonely stretch of road late at night."

"I wasn't a woman," Matheson said. "I was an agent."

"And that's why you'd lose your job, considering your past." Bryce held up his hand. "I know about the target practice with your boyfriend."

"Man, word really gets around."

"It's rural Missouri," Bryce said. "We're bored."

"So what are you going to do?"

"I've thought about it for a long time," Bryce said. "I'm not sure I understand what is inside you. There seems to be something odd there, something that's eating at you from the inside out, and that scares me. But I also think you have the best chance of catching this creep in the mine."

"Do you trust me?"

"I don't have a choice," Bryce said. "But yes, I think so. And trust is an important commodity where I came from. It's also a reciprocal thing. Do you understand that?"

"Yes," Matheson said. "Your job is on the line, too."

"So I'm going to ask you one question," Bryce said. "And I'll bet you know what it is. Did you kill Buntz?"

Matheson had just been holding the cigarette in her right hand, but now she brought it to her lips and took a real drag. The tip glowed brightly, then she exhaled a column of smoke.

"No," she said. "But if he had stopped me again on the road under those circumstances, I would have. Somebody just beat me to it."

Bryce handed her the tape.

"We didn't have this conversation," he said. "And I miscounted when I inventoried the shoe box. There were only twenty-three tapes, not twenty-four."

Matheson nodded.

"I owe you one," she said.

"Watch my back, partner," Bryce said. He replaced the cup on the top of the thermos. "And do me a favor, okay? Destroy that damn tape, and don't threaten to kill anybody else. It damages your credibility. If you think your life is truly in danger, just cap the bastard."

"Wild Bill?" Matheson asked.

"Yeah?"

"I have a problem of my own."

"What's that?"

"It's a proximity thing," she said. "What are the odds of a

police officer being shot to death within a half-mile of the
scene of the worst serial killings in Missouri history?"

"Slim," Bryce said.

"There has to be a connection," she said.

"Buntz wasn't the killer," Bryce said. "He didn't have the
balls or the brains. And he never dived, as far as I know."

"Not Buntz," Matheson said. "The Subtern."

"The what?"

"The killer. Buntz pulled him over at the wrong time, and
got wasted for it. Is there any kind of help you can give me?
What kind of ballistics do you have?"

"Buntz was killed by three rounds from an older Belgium
Browning .380 auto," Bryce said. "We know that from the
slugs and the casings. He took another hit in the vest, probably the first one, which knocked him down. We could match
the slugs and casings if we had the gun."

"Any hits on NCIC?"

"Zip."

Matheson paused.

"What about the recorder?" she asked. "It had to be in his
shirt pocket."

"If he had it on him that night," Bryce said. "It was gone
before we found him. Wasn't in his apartment, either. And
Buntz didn't log these car stops, because he was expecting to
shake people down."

"Then that's the tape to look for," she said.

"Let's get out of here," Bryce said. "I'm freezing."

Twenty-six

In the plastic tent on the dock floating in the St. Joan Lead Mine, Matheson sat on the edge of the desk and regarded the foot-high stack of missing-persons reports next to her. They had been faxed and e-mailed from police departments from every state between the Appalachians and the Rockies.

"I hadn't realized there would be so many of them," she said.

Claire Connelly parted the plastic, walked over to the coffeepot, and filled her spun-aluminum Starbucks mug with coffee brewed from a $1.49, thirteen-ounce brick of Great Value "one hundred percent pure Arabica" from Wal-Mart.

She took a sip, holding the mug with both hands, beneath her nose, and regarded Matheson and in turn the woman who was helping her, a perky blond agent named Melissa.

"Do you guys need any help?" Claire asked, but the question was directed to Melissa.

"Thanks, we have it covered," Matheson said.

Claire shrugged but continued standing.

"If you need anything," Claire said in her lowest voice, "all you have to do is ask."

"Thanks," Matheson said, annoyed. "We'll remember that."

Claire, however, was rewarded with a broad smile from Melissa.

A fresh-faced twenty-something agent named Mark entered the tent with another armful of missing-persons reports.

"Where would you like these, ma'am?"

"On top of the others," Matheson said.

The phone, which was at the edge of the desk away from Matheson, began to ring.

Claire stared at it.

"Gee, could you?" Matheson asked.

At the edge of the dock next to the electrical and communications umbilicals, near where the old mule trail entered, Dahlgren was sitting backwards in a chair watching Cal service one of a half-dozen rebreathers lined up on the workbench.

"Ever hear of an outfit named Halliday Salvors?"

Cal had the guts of one of the Bio-Lume rebreathers spread out before him. He was repacking the scrubber canister with Sofnolime, and then would recharge the spherical oxygen and diluent bottles.

"A long time ago," Cal said. "Run by a guy by the name of Doc Halliday. No relation to the gunfighter, I think. He was a Marine medic in the Pacific theater who turned treasure hunter in the seventies, as I recall. He still alive?"

"Apparently," Dahlgren said. "They're sailing their mine-sweeper-turned-salvage-vessel up the Mississippi to Sainte Genevieve, where they're going to off-load their submersible onto a Union Pacific railcar and bring it here."

"You're kidding," Cal said.

"My new friend, the attorney general of the United States, has made this possible," Dahlgren said. "All it took was money. A half-million dollars a week, complete with pilot."

Cal laughed.

"Loren could build us one for that."

"Yeah, but he couldn't do it by next week," Dahlgren said. "We've got a choice between fast and expensive, or cheap and slow. We need fast. They're charging us double because they had to pull their ship off a salvage job on the gulf side of the Florida coast. But nobody else would even consider letting us put one down in a mine."

"How big's the sub?"

"Fourteen feet long," Dahlgren said. "Seven-foot beam. Forty-eight-inch-diameter pressure hull. Rated for twelve hundred feet."

"Manipulator arm?"

"Sure," Dahlgren said. "And some type of laser mapping system and some other things I'd never heard of."

"What's it weigh?"

"Nine tons."

Cal whistled.

"And they call it *Water Baby*."

Dripping water from his orange wet suit, Norman walked over to the workbench, carrying a rebreather by one of its harness straps. The helmet was tucked beneath his arm.

"Hey, Dahlgren," Claire called from the doorway to the plastic office. "Phone call. Somebody claiming to be the submersible operations coordinator on some ship called the *Argo* wants to know, in his words, 'exactly how the hell you're going to get his precious sub down into a fucking mine.'"

"Gotta run," Dahlgren said, then hurried toward the office.

"This the one that's been acting up?" Cal asked.

"Yeah, the cap color went to red after thirty minutes in the water," Norman said. "I did a systems check, but the computers didn't find anything wrong."

"Which number is that?"

"Seven," Norman said.

"Heck, I recharged the scrubber just yesterday," Cal said. "There can't be anything wrong with it."

"I don't know," Norman said. "I started getting a headache as soon as it glowed hypercapnic. It could have just been psychosomatic, but I bailed out anyway."

"Better to be safe," Cal said. "This rig has never been quite right anyway. Loren should just retire it."

"Maybe the microbe dudes in the CO_2 sensor have a sense of humor," Norman suggested.

"Something about it has a sense of humor," Cal said, snapping the scrubber canister into place. "Let me get this locked down and I'll swap you."

"Where do you want me to put this one?"

"Put some tape across the mouthpiece and put it at the end of the bench," Cal said. "I'm kind of backed up here, recharging scrubbers and refilling diluent bottles. I'll get to it when I can."

"Gotcha," Norman said.

He placed the rebreather on the deck and was reaching for the red warning tape when he noticed Staci stepping onto the dock from the mule trail.

"Hey, Staci!" Norman called.

"I'm busy," she said.

"Wait up. I've got a new joke for you," Norman said.

Staci groaned.

"You know why the skeleton was afraid to cross the road?"

"Because he didn't have the guts," Staci said.

Dahlgren parted the plastic and took the phone from Claire's hand, as Claire was already heading for the door.

"Dahlgren," he said, then began listening intently.

"Where do we start?" Melissa asked. She was sitting attentively toward the front of her seat, just as Matheson had figured she did at Quantico.

"What was your class?" Matheson asked.

"02-16," Melissa said, meaning class number 16 of the year 2002 at the FBI Training Academy at Quantico.

"How about you?" she asked Mark.

"00-7," he said. "Isn't that wicked?"

"Very wicked," Matheson said.

Matheson thought they made a cute couple. Melissa and Mark. They belonged on some reality television show, Matheson told herself, not a major murder investigation.

"Okay, boys and girls, we're going to triage these things," Matheson said.

The younger agents uncapped their pens and waited anxiously to take careful notes on their narrow pads.

"Here is our criteria," she said. "First, women who were reported missing—no, make that last seen—in the week before Thanksgiving. Sort into one pile. Then sort that pile for women between the ages of twenty and thirty. When you have that pile, then sort by hair color, and give priority to the redheads. Then we'll contact our agents in the nearest field offices and have them do 301s for each and every one."

"What about also weighting our priority list toward towns that have interstates?" Mark asked. "I've glanced at the victim list on the board, and it seems to be that most of the abductions took place near Eisenhower highways."

"Good idea," Matheson said.

"We should also start a database," Melissa said.

"Can you do that?" Matheson asked.

"Sure," she said. "They taught us how to use Excel and Access at the Academy. It's really easy. We could have one database for known victims, another for the missing-persons subjects, and cross-match them for hits."

"Terrific," Matheson said. "Do it. But with the abduction list, start with the victims at the top of the priority list and work your way down."

"Of course," Melissa said. "Um, can I ask you a question?"

"Certainly."

"What's your class, ma'am?"

Matheson cleared her throat.

"86-13."

"You don't look that old," Mark blurted out. From the horrified look on Melissa's face, he knew it was a mistake. "Begging your pardon, ma'am. That was intended to be a compliment. Should I shoot myself here, or just throw myself into the water at the edge of the dock?"

"Forget it," Matheson said. "Everybody makes mistakes. Frankly, I thought you were a couple of airheads when we first met, but now I know better. Nobody's getting voted off my island."

"Oh, *Survivor*," Mark said.

"We love that show," Melissa gushed.

Dahlgren was still holding the receiver to his ear, listening. Finally, he spoke.

"Just get the damn thing here, okay?" he said. "Our engineer has already worked out the details of getting *Water Baby* in the mine. You can talk to him."

Dahlgren slammed the phone down.

"Does Loren really have a plan?" Matheson asked.

"Not yet," Dahlgren said. "But he will."

Matheson unlocked the door to the room in the basement of Parkland Hospital, flipped on the lights, and used her hip to nudge open the door.

"We are very grateful that you've agreed to take a look, Dr. Geiger," Matheson said. "Of course, we're interested in what kind of preservative the killer used, and in whatever details you could tell us, but first we'd like you to attempt a positive identification on our latest victim, Jennifer Lynn."

Geiger stood motionless in the doorway, staring in awe at the twenty-one bodies floating in aquariums. The aquariums and their bases took up nearly every available foot of floor space in the former maintenance room.

"It's quite shocking the first time you see it, isn't it?" Matheson asked. "If we find any more victims, I don't know where we're going to put them." She paused, then corrected herself: "*When* we find more victims."

Geiger nodded and stepped into the room.

He started to walk toward an aquarium in a far corner but checked himself.

"Which one is Lynn?" he asked.

"The one in the corner," Matheson said. "Her medical and dental records are stacked on the chair beside her. Since it's impossible to get an X-ray while they're floating in the water, our pathologists have been doing a visual examination of their mouths to see if the fillings and dentition match."

Geiger nodded.

"Have you analyzed the water in the tanks?"

Matheson nodded.

"It's just water from the mine," she said. "Not a hazard. Whatever is in their bodies that reacts with air apparently stays in their bodies while they are immersed. Our pathologists said you could drink it and it wouldn't hurt you."

"I'd like to see their reports," Geiger said.

"They're in the chair, along with the other records."

"Where's your assistant?"

"I came alone," he said. "Gave Dr. Smith the day off."

Matheson paused uncertainly.

"Something you wish to say, Agent?"

"Yes," she said. "Dr. Geiger, I noticed that you have lost your stutter."

"It comes and it goes," he said with a shrug. "I'm sure it will be back all too soon."

"Well, I'll leave you to it," Matheson said and smiled.

"Shut the door, please," Geiger said. "And lock it. I don't want to be disturbed."

"Of course. I'll be just outside."

For the next half hour, Geiger walked from aquarium to

aquarium, peering into the faces of the women he had killed over the years. He finished his reflection in front of Jennifer Lynn. He did not look at any of the documents that were piled for him on the chair.

Matheson was waiting for him in the hallway, leaning against a wall on one foot.

"Any luck?"

"That's her," Geiger said through his stutter.

"Thank you," Matheson said. "Can I have your report by tomorrow? Time is running out for an old friend of hers on death row."

As Geiger nodded, Matheson's cell phone began to vibrate.

"Excuse me," she said, and turned away as she answered the phone. "Melissa, what have you got?" She listened for a moment, then said, "Yeah, but she's a blonde, right? Repeat that last, please. . . . A plastic flower?"

Twenty-seven

The snow covering the photo trail at the Springfield Nature Conservation Center had turned to mush and was seeping into Matheson's black pumps. She was holding a plastic flower in an evidence bag, and flanking her were a local detective and his partner, both of whom were wearing heavy coats and boots.

"Not much to see since the snow," the investigator said. He was an overweight and tired-looking man by the name of Rhodes who liked his friends to call him Rocky. He was in his early fifties, had long sideburns and a growing bald spot, and looked as if he had been dressed that morning by the costumer for *Boogie Nights*.

"What exactly are you looking for, Agent?" the partner, a small and immaculately dressed man named Burge, asked.

"Show me where this plastic flower was found."

"Up here, where the marker is," the investigator said, huffing while he marched up the trail, then pointing to where an orange flag on a wire was stuck in the ground.

Matheson knelt and placed her hand on the earth.

"Tell me again what you know," she said.

Rhodes opened his notebook.

"Report filed at oh eight hundred hours on Monday, November twenty-second, by Reporting Party Connie Carter. RP said her niece, Jolene Carter, white Caucasian aged twenty-three, had not checked in with her since the previous Thursday," Rhodes said.

"Go on."

"A black-and-white was dispatched to subject's apartment. It was empty, with mail and newspapers piled up, but with no signs of a struggle. A BOLO was issued for the subject's car, a yellow Volkswagen bug, which was found in the parking lot behind us."

"That's when we figured this was something more than some kid who's taken an unexpected vacation," Burge said nervously. "Kids don't abandon their cars."

Matheson stood and walked a few yards.

"Was the car processed?"

"Yeah, but we got nothing," Burge said.

"What about her apartment?"

"Nothing there, either," he said. "Just her prints."

Matheson shook her head.

"Who found this flower?"

"One of the park rangers," Rhodes said. "They thought it was odd. They also said Jolene regularly jogged here but switched trails from day to day."

On her hands and knees, Matheson continued searching. Her overcoat and dark blue skirt were quickly becoming caked in mud, and her panty hose already were beyond repair. The two local investigators stood by uncomfortably, not sure whether they should get down on their hands and knees as well.

"Agent, would you like us to help?" Burge asked.

"We can get some uniforms out here to do that," Rhodes offered.

"Step back, both of you," Matheson suddenly snapped.

She pulled a plastic glove from her pocket and slipped it over her right hand, then retrieved a set of headphones from the muck.

Rhodes shrugged.

"Could be from anybody," he said. "People lose stuff all the time."

"Bag them anyway," Matheson said.

She continued to search on her hands and knees while the investigator and his partner stood. When she rose, a plastic syringe was held gingerly between her gloved fingers.

"Have a lot of junkies here who jog?"

In the parking lot of the nature center, Dana Casteel was getting ready for a live stand-up. The Color Three truck was parked with its boom extended and the microwave snout pointing toward the station in town, where the noon news had begun ten minutes before.

The jogging trails were in the background, but Matheson and the local detectives had long since vanished from sight. Rocky Rhodes was one of Dana's regular sources of unattributed information, and since he had separated from his wife a month earlier he had seemed especially interested in helping her. He had tipped her off that the FBI was in town on urgent business, and although the reason hadn't been stated, scuttlebutt said it was connected with the Subtern Killer.

"What do you think they're doing back there?" Dave asked from behind the camera tripod.

"Looking for evidence," Dana said.

"Doh," Dave did in his best Homer Simpson voice.

"I don't know exactly what they're looking for," Dana said.

"You mean Rocky didn't whisper the reason to you during a little pillow talk?"

"In his dreams," Dana said. "But when he told me the feds were coming, I filed an FOIA request for all the missing-persons reports filed at the police and sheriff's departments within the last two weeks."

"Why?"

"You hadn't noticed?" Dana asked smugly. "All of the girls who've been found in the mine were abducted around Thanksgiving. I figured if the feds were in town on the Sub-tern case, it had to do with an abduction, and if it was urgent business like Rocky said, it had to be a recent abduction."

"What'd you come up with?"

"Nothing," Dana said. "They have seventy-two hours to respond to an open records request, and even then there are so many loopholes in the state law they can tie up the records forever if they want, either by saying the information is privileged under one of the exemptions to the Sunshine Law, or by claiming an outrageous cost for retrieving the data."

"So how'd you know the feds would come here?" Dave asked. "Rocky tell you?"

"Nope," Dana said. "I got lucky. I remembered I had seen these in the convenience stores all over the college district."

From her purse, she took a photocopy that had Jolene Carter's smiling color picture in the center. Beneath was a description of Jolene, a phone number, and the question, "Have you seen this young woman?"

"Red hair," Dave said.

"I called the number and got her aunt," Dana said. "She was hysterical with worry. I told her we could reach a lot more people than her photocopies could. She said Jolene's car had been towed from here after sitting unattended for three days."

"Here they come," Dave said.

"Is the station ready for us?"

"Hang on," Dave said, listening on his headset. "Yeah,

they're set. They'll be coming out of commercial in thirty seconds. Okay?"

Dana nodded. Over her shoulder, she could see Matheson and the two local detectives atop a rise on one of the trails, about a hundred yards away.

"Go in tight," Dana said. "Then do a slow zoom-out. I'll start talking as soon as the tally comes on."

Dave put his eye to the viewfinder and framed the shot.

The wind was blowing from the north, pushing Dana's hair over her eyes. She brushed it back, wet her lips, and recited mindlessly, "All good boys deserve favor. The quick brown fox jumped over the lazy dog. The only boy who could ever please me—"

Dave nodded, indicating he had the audio level.

"Ten seconds," he said.

Dave held three fingers beneath the lens, then two, then one, then pointed at Dana.

"This is Dana Casteel with another Color Three exclusive," she said into the microphone. "The Federal Bureau of Investigation arrived here about an hour ago, and although officials aren't discussing their reason for focusing on this remote nature trail, this is the same spot where a twenty-three-year-old Bible college student by the name of Jolene Carter was last seen a week before Thanksgiving."

Jolene took a breath and brushed hair from her face.

"According to an aunt, Jolene is in her final year at Ozark Bible College in Springfield, and is the host of a popular Christian radio program called *Lifeline*," Dana said. "Authorities have refused comment on whether Jolene's disappearance is connected with the gruesome Subtern killings at the other end of the Show Me State."

Here Dana bobbed her head and allowed a knowing smile.

"But the FBI's lead investigator on the Subtern case, Grace Matheson, is discernible behind me, in the company of local investigators. Also, Jolene's aunt, Connie Carter, said two young FBI agents called at her home late last night to inquire about Jolene's disappearance. Among the things the agents asked, Mrs. Carter said, was whether Jolene had known the recently identified Subtern victim from 1997, Jennifer Lynn. The agents also asked if Jolene knew any avid scuba divers or had ever visited Bonne Terre, Missouri." Dana had taught herself to pronounce it like a local, Missour-*ah*. "The answers to all of those questions, the aunt said, were negative. And on a final note, Connie Carter told Color Three News this morning that she was certain her niece was still alive. When asked how she knew, the aunt replied, 'Because God wills it.' Back to the studio."

Dana retained her smile until the tally light died.

"Well," Dave said as he looked up from the viewfinder. "If that doesn't whip these Bible-thumpers around here into a frenzy, nothing will."

At the St. Joan mine, the blockhouse had been cordoned off with yellow DO NOT CROSS tape. The crowd was pressed up against the tape, and as Dahlgren approached it on his way to the door, reporters hurled questions while family members held photographs of young women above their heads and asked if they'd seen their daughters.

Just as Dahlgren ducked beneath the tape, a grim-looking man in a white suit shook a white-bound Bible and then lunged toward him.

"Are you saved?" the man in white shouted. "Have you accepted Jesus as your personal Lord and savior? I assure you that Jolene Carter has."

He met Michael Schwartz just inside the doorway.

"Who the hell is Jolene Carter?" Dahlgren asked.

"Kidnapped last week in Springfield."

"Illinois?"

"Missouri," Schwartz said. "Haven't you talked to Agent

272

Matheson yet? There's a stack of messages waiting for you below."

Dahlgren had slept late at McAfee's house, and when he finally woke he avoided the news channels and had watched the end of *The Poseidon Adventure* on a lesser cable channel. He had seen it probably a hundred times in his life, but he was always fascinated by the scene in which Gene Hackman hangs from the wheel of a steam valve and argues with God, and he was always mildly surprised when, after closing the valve to allow the others to escape, Hackman drops into the flaming water below. As a kid he was so obsessed with the movie (and frankly, with Carol Lynley, before she was irrevocably replaced in his pubescent affections by Jenny Agutter) that he had gotten a dog-eared copy of the original novel by Paul Gallico and kept reading it until he finally understood it. Dahlgren now kept the paperback, along with a few other underwater adventures, including *Twenty Thousand Leagues Under the Sea*, on a metal shelf in his office next to his technical manuals.

Dahlgren was still thinking alternately about Lynley in her orange sweater and Agutter in the diaphanous green number from *Logan's Run* when he parted the plastic to the office and sat down at the desk, picked up the message with Matheson's cell number on it, and picked up the phone. Before he dialed, however, the thought struck him—prompted by his association of Matheson with the conversation they'd had at Vargo's on Thanksgiving night—that both Lynley and Agutter were athletic yet vulnerable blondes, and again he felt the odd sensation of viewing his life from the outside.

He dialed the number, then put it on speakerphone when McAfee walked in.

"Where the hell have you been?" Matheson asked.

"Didn't know I had to okay it with you before I slept in," Dahlgren said. "Besides, I stayed up late while McAfee devised a plan to squeeze the submersible into the mine. Things are a circus here. And where the hell are you?"

"Springfield," Matheson said. "They've been reporting on television that we're investigating the disappearance of a local girl as this year's victim."

"Are you?"

"Yes," Matheson said.

"How sure are you?"

"I'm not sure yet," she said, "but I'm leaning in that direction. Red hair, snatched before Thanksgiving, a syringe with a trace of Rohypnol left behind. Also, something odd: a plastic flower."

"What does that have to do with it?"

"The myth, remember? Persephone was gathering flowers."

"Right," Dahlgren said dubiously.

"So what has our boy genius worked out for the submersible?"

"I'm here," McAfee said.

"Sorry," Matheson said.

"Never mind," McAfee said. "Dahlgren should have told you. Essentially, we have two options. We can take it down the mule trail, but the problem there is not its size, but its weight. It will fit easily enough down the trail, but it weighs nine tons. It's not like hauling the aquariums out in Staci's old truck. We'd have to use a cable system and one hell of a winch, and I don't know how we'd get it into the water without sinking the dock."

"The other option?" Matheson asked.

"Knock the cap off Shaft Number One and lower it directly down into the water from two hundred feet. There's no head frame left, so we could place whatever we needed directly over the shaft. Again, we'd need a cable system, but we could use a crane on the back of a truck. And we wouldn't be threading the cable at a difficult angle down a winding trail. The shaft is really much safer."

"Is the shaft big enough for the sub?"

"It might be a tight fit," McAfee said. "But according to the most recent plans I have for the mine, they were running two ore skips and a cage for the miners in the shaft when they closed in 1962. The skips were six feet square, and so was the cage. That makes the size of the shaft at least six by eighteen."

"I thought Dahlgren said the sub was, what, seven across?"

"Well, they had to have some extra room around the skips, at least a foot," McAfee said. "And Dahlgren says there are some things they can take off the sub to make it a little narrower. But that's why I said it might be a tight fit."

"Risks?"

"The cable is the major risk with each," McAfee said. "If it breaks on the mule trail, it could cut people in two. If it breaks over the shaft, that's less likely, but it might damage the sub as it came down on top of it. And if it sinks, it would go all the way to the bottom of the sump. At four hundred feet, recovery would be expensive."

"What about ground subsidence?"

"The shaft had a lot of ore hauled through it in a hundred years," McAfee said. "I think it's still pretty stable. The unknown is how much concrete they've capped it with. My guess is that it's just a yard or two and some rebar. We can probably have it cleared in a few hours, with the right crew."

"The crew will be the closest National Guard engineering battalion that isn't in Iraq," Matheson said.

"Works for me," McAfee said.

"Dahlgren. You concur?"

"Loren's right. I thought the mule trail was the best option, but the shaft is a cleaner entry and exit point. Get the Guard started as quick as possible, because the submersible will be here tomorrow."

"Today," McAfee corrected. "Who do you call for the National Guard, anyway?"

"The governor."

"Ask her for some crowd control while you're at it,"

Dahlgren said. "They're selling barbecued-chicken sandwiches and hot chocolate up above. Next thing you know, they'll be hawking fucking T-shirts with this girl's picture on them."

"We'll just clear the area," Matheson said.

"I'd rather you not do that," McAfee said softly.

"Why not?" Matheson asked.

"This is drawing a lot of church folk," McAfee said. "People in this part of the country take their religion seriously, and ever since the television started reporting this morning that Jolene Carter is a Bible college student, they've been coming in droves. It's become sort of a Burning Man Festival for fundamentalists."

"Interesting," Matheson said. "I would have thought you wouldn't want to run the insurance risk of having so many accidents waiting to happen on your property. I'd think you'd want these kooks driven off."

McAfee sighed.

"We've carried twenty-three bodies out of my property," McAfee said. "They canceled my insurance last month. And I know these kooks, as you call them. They're not the type to sue."

"Why are you so sure?" she asked.

"My dad is a fundamentalist preacher in Tennessee."

"What denomination?" Matheson asked.

"Pentecostal," McAfee said.

"Holy Rollers," Dahlgren said.

McAfee shot him a wicked look.

"Church of God," McAfee said, "with Signs Following."

"Snake handlers," Matheson said with clinical interest.

"He takes up serpents," McAfee said. "If you have a problem with that, let me know now. I don't share all of his beliefs, but I respect his choices."

"No problem," Matheson said. "As long as he leaves the snakes at home. It's illegal, you know. Oh, and there's one other thing. Do either of you know a botanist, or perhaps even a mycologist, within driving distance of Bonne Terre I could consult?"

"I don't even know what a mycologist is," Dahlgren said.

"A botanist who studies fungi," McAfee said.

"You mean like mushrooms?" Dahlgren asked.

"That's it," he said.

"Groovy," Dahlgren said.

Twenty-eight

The chamber rang with an explosion that sounded like a hammer hitting a giant anvil, followed by a couple of big splashes. Water trickled beneath the plastic walls into the office, soaking Dahlgren's cowboy boots.

"What the hell?"

Dahlgren dashed outside and met Cal standing on the dock, looking up, his ears stuffed with cotton. Staci was kneeling on the dock, also holding her ears.

"Out," Cal said, and he didn't have to tell Staci twice. "Get Norman and take him with you." She got to her feet, took Norman by the hand, and they ran toward the safety of the mule trail.

"Here," Cal said, offering Dahlgren a wad of cotton. "I had an aspirin bottle on my workbench."

"Great," Dahlgren said, breaking the wad into two pieces and twisting it into his ears. "We'll need the aspirin later. What the hell are they doing?"

"The National Guard deemed the concrete and rebar too

thick to jackhammer through quickly," Cal said. "So they're using ordnance. They apparently sent word down to clear the dock, but Michael got here a little late."

There was another explosion that Dahlgren felt reverberate in his solar plexus, followed by a chunk of concrete the size of a compact car falling into the water and leaving a tremendous geyser of water in its wake, and a wave that washed over the dock that was big enough to cover their ankles.

"I'll make sure the equipment is secure," Cal said. "We don't want any cylinders or rebreathers washed over the side. Then I'll cover the electronics and computers with a tarp or whatever else I can find. You run up there and cut the power to the umbilicals."

Dahlgren nodded.

"Do it quick," Cal called. "If they sink this dock, I don't want to be on it when that industrial three-phase hits the water."

After Dahlgren cut the power to the dock by pulling the level on the big panel in the blockhouse, he ran outside and climbed the hill to where he could see a group of soldiers scurrying down into a hole, preparing to set another charge.

"Who's in command?" Dahlgren asked.

"Step back, sir," a soldier in desert camo with two stripes on his sleeve said. "This is a secure area, and authorized personnel only are allowed. We've got fire in the hole."

"I know," Dahlgren said. "I was in the fucking hole."

"No use for profanity, sir."

"You boys local?"

"Farmington," the corporal said. "We're Company A of the 1140th Engineering Battalion."

"A *combat* engineering battalion," Dahlgren said.

"Absolutely," the corporal said. "Especially things in the middle of sand piles. Now, step back."

"Corporal, I'm authorized to be here," Dahlgren said. "I'm in charge of everything below, and you boys are raining chunks of concrete the size of Hyundais into the water not a hundred yards from where we're working. So I need to talk to your company commander or whoever else is in charge up here."

"Captain Schoville is in command," the corporal said, pointing to an officer with his arms crossed, leaning against a khaki-colored Humvee, talking to a captain and a master sergeant.

"Lieutenant Schoville," Dahlgren said as he strode over. "Belay the fucking ordnance. You're going to kill somebody below."

"There's nobody below," Schofield said, coming erect. "And I'm Captain Schoville, and you'd better watch your filthy mouth."

"Two bars in the Navy make a lieutenant," Dahlgren said. "And you're looking at somebody who was down there, with three other members of the dive team. I'm responsible for them."

"Sir? Should I knock him on his can?" the sergeant asked.

"We're on the same side," Dahlgren said impatiently. "And because I'm a civilian, I don't have to watch my filthy mouth. You set off another charge and you're likely to sink the dock we use for the staging area. That would make our agent-in-charge extremely unhappy. That, in turn, would make her new friend the governor very unhappy."

Schoville smoothed his mustache.

"Didn't know civilians were down there," he said. "We were just trying to expedite opening that shaft with a little C-4. I was told there was some haste."

"There is," Dahlgren said. "But let's not kill anybody in the process."

Schoville nodded.

"We've breached the concrete and rebar," he said. "It was thicker than we'd been told. But I think we can clear the rest with pneumatic tools. There will still be some debris falling, so keep your people clear."

"How much longer?"

"The work will go slower without blasting," Schoville said. "It might be an hour, it might be tomorrow morning. We'll give you the all clear."

"Here's my cell number," Dahlgren said, giving him a card. "Call me the moment you're through."

"This submersible we're waiting on," Schoville said. "Are we going to have to put straps under it, or will there be a hard point to attach a cable?"

"There's a lift-line attachment on the deck behind the sail," Dahlgren said. "It's a balance point, and the vessel will rotate easily in a three-sixty around it. But you can't put straps around the sub or you'll crush the fiberglass shell and the equipment pods. You also have to be careful around the thrusters and the rudders. The strongest part of the sub is the pressure sphere, which is only four feet in diameter. The rest is just bolt-ons. How are you going to lower it into the mine?"

"That's the easy part," Schoville said.

Dahlgren met Staci coming out of the blockhouse.

"What in the world is going on?" she asked, shielding her eyes from the sun. She was wearing blue jeans and a fleece pullover, and clutched her sketch pad and drawing pencils beneath one arm.

It was one of those days in late fall that defied the season. Although the ground had been covered with snow just a few days before, the mercurial midwestern weather had decided instead to bless eastern Missouri with a sunny day with temperatures in the fifties. In the cold winter light, Dahlgren decided, her hair did look more blond than red.

"Ever hear of Floyd Collins?" Dahlgren asked.

"The guy trapped in the cave in Kentucky in the twenties."

"Supposed to be the world's greatest cave explorer, and he was alone, with one light, no helmet, inadequate clothing, didn't tell anybody where he was going," Dahlgren said. "He gets trapped when a rock falls on his foot. The rescue effort turns into a circus that lasts nearly three weeks, and the nation listens breathlessly as a radio reporter named Skeets Miller gives a blow-by-blow of Floyd's final days."

"So you think this girl, Jolene Carter, is our twenty-first-century equivalent?"

"Theoretically," Dahlgren said.

As the weather had warmed, more people were drawn to the barren expanse around the blockhouse that marked the entrance to the St. Joan Lead Mine. Now a half-dozen revival tents dotted the mine wastes, and men in white shirts and ties and women in long dresses and their hair in tight buns strolled lazily between them, their faces turned toward the sun. In addition to the trailer selling barbecued-chicken sandwiches, two others were setting up, offering hamburgers and hot dogs and funnel cakes. From an unseen PA system, the sound of an old-time gospel string band sang of seeing the light and flying away.

"I can't believe they're selling food," Dahlgren said.

"Seems practical to me," Staci said. "Even Bible-thumpers have to eat. Actually, I find it kind of comforting, all of these people turning out in support of somebody they've never heard of. How in the world did they organize so quickly? I know it was on television, but these folks seemed to have acted with one mind."

"Good question," Dahlgren asked.

As one of the serious white-shirted men walked by, Dahlgren held out his hand and said, "Excuse me. How did all of you know to come here?"

The man stopped, but was obviously suspicious of Dahlgren in his cowboy boots, blue jeans, and peasant shirt. Still, he gave a straightforward answer.

"The churches have a telephone contact list," he said evenly. "The list was activated this morning, but of course there was an incident earlier. It was decided that the closer we are to Miss Carter, the more our prayers might be of comfort to her."

Staci nodded.

"But don't prayers count wherever they're said?" Dahlgren asked. "How do you know these are of more comfort?"

"We don't," the man said. "But that doesn't mean we shouldn't try. If it were you trapped down in the mine, friend, wouldn't you want your brothers and sisters praying for you?"

"No, I'd want them searching for me," Dahlgren said.

The man blinked at the sunlight, considering his next reply.

"You two are among the divers, aren't you?" he asked. "I saw you on television. Our prayers are with you as well."

"Thank you," Staci said, and touched the man's sleeve. Suddenly, she was self-conscious that she wasn't in the water, looking. "We're been ordered out of the mine while the National Guard punches a hole for us to get some equipment in."

"Praise God," the man said. "That sounds like progress."

"You mentioned an incident earlier," Dahlgren said. "Do you mind telling me what it was?"

"Richard," Staci said, pulling on his arm. "He's told us enough. Leave him be."

"I'm not trying to upset him," Dahlgren said. "I'm interested. What was the incident?"

"I wasn't a witness to it," the man said. "So anything I say would be secondhand. Perhaps you'd best talk to Reverend Miller from Leadwood. You can find him over at the Revenant Harvest tent, the green-and-white-striped one."

"I know him," Dahlgren said. "Thanks."

The man held out his hand, and Dahlgren shook it awkwardly.

As they walked through the crowd toward the Leadwood tent, Staci clutched Dahlgren's left arm with her free hand.

"You shouldn't be so hard on these people," she said.

Max McCoy

"I'm just curious," he said.

He found Miller sitting in a wooden folding chair in the back of the tent, an open Bible across his knees.

"Reverend?"

Miller removed his reading glasses and looked up.

"You're the man who gave us permission," he said.

"Yes, Richard Dahlgren."

They shook.

"This is Staci Johnson, one of our divers."

"Miss Johnson," Miller said politely.

"Please, don't get up."

"Has the time come for you to tell us to move, Mr. Dahlgren? You see, I remember our agreement."

"That's not why I'm here," Dahlgren said. "I met one of your, well, fellow believers a few minutes ago, and he said something unusual had happened. When I asked him to explain, he suggested that I come talk to you."

Miller smiled, holding his reading glasses and his Bible carefully atop his knees. The Bible was open to Luke, and Dahlgren caught a glimpse of a verse in red beneath Miller's thumb: *Behold, I give unto you the power to tread on serpents and scorpions, and over the power of the enemy; and nothing by any means shall hurt you.*

"Care to pull up a chair?"

Dahlgren grabbed a couple of the folding chairs. Staci sat down, and Dahlgren straddled his, leaning his forearms on the back of the chair.

"I'm not sure how much you know about our traditions," Miller said. "In general, you can say we are a branch of the Church of Gods with Signs Following."

"Pentecostals," Dahlgren said.

"Our tradition goes back to January 1, 1901, at Topeka, Kansas, when Charles F. Parham succeeded in recovering one of the nine original spiritual gifts—speaking in tongues."

"*Glossalia*," Staci said.

284

"I know about Parham," Dahlgren said.

"Then you know he introduced this gift at a revival in Houston to a colored gentleman named Seymour, who brought it to the Azusa Street Mission in Los Angeles, where hundreds received it," Miller said. "It eventually spread throughout the world. And although Parham's recovery of the gift of tongues was more than a century ago, the blessings continue. Have you not heard of the Toronto blessing?"

"No," Dahlgren said impatiently. "I want to know about here and now."

"We're getting to that," Miller said warmly. "Now, in 1995, what has come to be known as the Fourth Blessing occurred at a church in Toronto. It was spontaneous, divinely inspired laughter—holy laughter. Then, a couple of years later, something else began to happen. Tongues of fire began to appear above congregations."

"Holy fire," Dahlgren said.

"Just as the Bible says it did above the heads of the apostles when the Holy Ghost descended upon them during Pentecost," Miller said. "It is a curious blue flame that burns without heat but is awesome to behold."

"And it happened here?"

Miller paused.

"It has happened every night during the seven-o'clock service for the last three days," Miller said. "When this happens, believers begin to make telephone calls, and the faithful rush in from across the country, hoping to get a glimpse for themselves."

"But this isn't Pentecost," Staci said. "That's in the spring, isn't it?"

"The seventh Sunday after Easter," Miller said. "But for some mysterious reason, God has decided to provide a sign here, at this time."

"Why?" Dahlgren asked.

Staci realized he was suddenly angry.

"Unfortunately," Miller said, "we are not privy to His reasons, just His will."

"And you think it was His will that a few dozen girls died in this pit behind me so you could have a carnival?" Dahlgren asked. "I've been getting this crap all of my life. You know, I grew up in Baxter Springs, where old Frank Parham moved his church after going bust in Topeka. He was long gone by the time I arrived on the scene, but the place where his worldwide head-quarters were was still there, just a few blocks from where I lived. It was an old brewery on the side of a hill. And his son dug these stupid holes in the ground all over that hillside, looking for the Ten Commandments. Do you think he ever found them?"

Staci tugged on Dahlgren's arm.

"I apologize," she said.

"Don't apologize for me," Dahlgren said.

"Why are you so angry?" Staci asked. Then, to Miller: "He's just skeptical."

"A Doubting Thomas, eh?" Miller said. "Won't be satisfied until you thrust your hand into the wound in her side?"

"What did you say?" Dahlgren asked.

"The wound in Christ's side," Miller said. "The disciple Thomas did not believe until—"

"Yes, I know the story. But you said *her* side."

Staci nodded her agreement.

"I'm sorry," Miller said. "I must be more tired than I thought. I didn't mean to upset you, especially after the kind-ness you extended on that day we met."

Dahlgren stood.

"I'm sorry you don't believe," Miller said gently.

"That's not the problem," Dahlgren said. "I do believe, and I don't want to. Blame it on my childhood, because I can't help myself. And that puts me in the position of believing in an all-powerful God that slays the innocent, and I will not bow my neck to such a bloodthirsty sonuvabitch."

Staci removed her hand from Dahlgren's arm so quickly that it was as if she feared a burn.

Miller carefully donned his reading glasses. Keeping his

eyes on the page, he said: "Son, I don't know what has caused you so much pain. But if you think I'm shocked by what you've said, or that I'm about to chide you for being angry, I'm not. You're not the first."

Then Miller looked up.

"Jacob wrestled the whole of one long night with God in the wilderness," he said. "At daybreak, the match ended in a draw, and Jacob was given a new name: Israel—contender with God. So my advice to you is this: Don't stop fighting until you see the dawn."

Angie was working, and brought Dahlgren his stein of beer without having to be asked. When Staci asked for a beer as well, Angie placed her hands on her hips and said unapologetically, "I'll need to see some ID."

"Jesus," Staci muttered as she dutifully dug her Missouri driver's license out of her jeans pocket. "Satisfied?"

"Okay," Angie said.

"Stick around, kid," Dahlgren said. "You'll long for the days when they carded you."

"Don't lecture me about the good old days, gramps," Staci said. "And what was all that with the preacher back there? Do you always go around trying to piss people off?"

"I don't have to try," he said.

After they had eaten their sandwiches and drained the last of their beer, Staci had cooled somewhat. She rubbed her forefinger around the wet rim of her empty glass and asked, "What's the story with you and Matheson?"

"No story," Dahlgren said.

"Yeah," Staci said. "Right. Everybody knows she wants your bones."

"Pardon?"

"It's the way she stands next to you," Staci said. "Always a little too close. Pointing her knees at you when she sits. Talking low."

"You're seeing something I'm not," Dahlgren lied.

"She too old for you?"

"What is she, forty? That's not bad."

"She'd qualify for an antique license if she were a car," Staci said with the cruelty of youth. "What are you?"

"Thirty-six," Dahlgren said.

"Liar," Staci said. "You're thirty-seven."

"Yeah, I had a birthday. How did you know?"

Staci giggled.

"Loren doesn't lock the file cabinet where he keeps everybody's C-cards and releases," she said. "I was curious, so I looked at your folder. You've got quite an impressive certification record."

"Your logbook is the only thing that's really important," Dahlgren said. "The rest of it is just bullshit. Just because you passed some class doesn't mean you're a cave diver—not until you've gotten enough dives under your belt to have the living shit scared out of you. It's like riding a motorcycle. Do it every day for six months, and then you're ready to start learning."

Dahlgren motioned for another beer.

"Want another?"

"Shouldn't," Staci said. "We may be diving soon."

"Not this afternoon," Dahlgren said. "They have to get that hole drilled, and then the submersible's supposed to be here. This is strictly surface interval. But you're right, we shouldn't show up with beer on our breath."

"I've got some gum," Staci said. She began searching the pockets of her jeans.

"Why were you curious?" Dahlgren asked.

"I wanted to see if you were too old for me," Staci said as she handed him a warm stick of Big Red.

"Am I?" Dahlgren asked, unwrapping the gum.

"Fifteen years," she said. "What do you think?"

"Definitely," Dahlgren said as he folded the gum into his mouth.

288

Staci cocked her head.

"I'm not so sure."

"I'm sure," Dahlgren said, but even as he said it he wanted nothing more than to push his hands up beneath her fleece top and cup her small unbridled breasts.

"I know that look," Staci said as she popped the gum into her mouth. "You're not sure of a damn thing, are you?"

Matheson knocked on the door at the end of the hall on the second floor of the science building at Washington University in St. Louis. When there was no answer in ten seconds, she tried the door, and it swung open.

"Dr. Ross?" she called.

The cramped office was overflowing with plants and books. Every available flat surface held either a pot or a reference book, the window was packed with ferns, and vines crept down from the acoustical tile ceiling.

"Who's there?" a voice called from a room farther in.

"Dr. Ross, it's Agent Matheson," she said. "I called earlier today from Springfield. I appreciate you seeing me on such short notice."

A long-haired man in his late twenties seemed to materialize in the room, peering at her through a pair of old-fashioned wire-rim glasses.

"No problem," he said. "I have no life."

"I'm sure that's not true," Matheson said politely.

"No, it's absolutely true," he said. "And by the way, I'm not a doctor, just an instructor, another wage slave in the white-collar ghetto. Is one of my friends in trouble again?"

"No, it's not like that."

"You wouldn't tell me anyway."

"Probably not," Matheson agreed. "Look, Mr. Ross—"

"Call me Terry."

"Do you think we could sit down?"

He motioned toward the hall, and they sat side by side in a

pair of uncomfortable plastic chairs ordinarily used by students awaiting advisement. Matheson took off her overcoat, placed it in over the back of her seat for a little cushion against the industrial-grade plastic, and crossed her legs. She had changed her clothes since crawling along the jogging trail in Springfield, but now noticed she had missed wiping away a smudge of dirt on the inside of her left calf.

She noticed that Ross had noticed it, too.

"Look, Mr. Ross," Matheson said. "I'm here to ask for some background that may help catch the Subtern Killer. You wouldn't mind sharing information for a cause like that, would you?"

"You mean the one who's been hiding the girls in the mine."

"Right."

"I'm a mycologist," Ross protested. "Fungi don't grow in mines, so I'm afraid I won't be able to help you."

"It's not what's in the mine that I need your help with," Matheson said. "It's what's in the killer's mind."

"Clever play on words. Continue."

"This must be confidential," she said. "No leaks."

"Who would I tell?" he asked. "I have no life."

"Right. Okay, I need a crash course in the use of psychedelic mushrooms," she said. "A variety of mushroom known as *Amanita muscaria* was found in the stomachs of the girls. I think it may have something to do with the killer reenacting the abduction of Persephone."

"Oh, right. The Greek myth and all," he said. "Perhaps you're familiar with the entheogen theory of religion? Entheogen means the god within. It's applied to a class of naturally occurring psychoactive drugs, such as ergot and some mushrooms."

"Yes, I know. Where's it found?"

"In temperate zones all over the world," Ross said. "It figures in the mythologies of many cultures. The Wassons believed it may have been the soma in the Rig Veda, for example. The theory goes that this magic-mushroom mind expansion was the basis for the earliest religions and spurred the rise of agriculture, which in turn gave birth to civilization."

"This is a well-known theory?"

"I wouldn't call it well-known, but it certainly isn't a secret," Ross said. "The Wassons were amateur mycologists who began their work in the 1950s. But just a decade or so ago, McKenna pushed the theory even further by suggesting that mushrooms and other fungi are a sentient life-form that sparked the evolution of human consciousness."

"I appreciate your help, Mr. Ross."

"Terry. Call me Terry," he said. "I can give you a couple of books on the subject, if you like. *Persephone's Quest* and *The Archaic Revival* are the most relevant."

"That's very kind of you," Matheson said. "I have to ask, what are you friends in trouble for?"

"Growing mushrooms, of course," he said. "And I ain't talking shiitakes. But none of them are the killer. They're enlightened, Grace, not homicidal. May I call you Grace?"

"No."

"Got it."

"What's it like?"

"Beg your pardon?"

"Taking the mushrooms," Matheson said.

"I've just heard stories," Ross said.

"I'm not setting you up," Matheson said. "I'm dead serious here. I need to understand the experience, for the sake of the investigation. It's something I call immersion research. It takes a lot of time to do right, but I don't have a lot of time left in this case. I need a leg up."

Ross tried to keep from glancing at the mud stain on her inner calf. He crossed his legs, took a breath, and looked away.

"It's a place beyond time and space," he said. "A place where telepathy and precognition work. There are entities there—real, not imagined. But it's hard to explain. It sounds like nonsense to talk about it. It's just something you have to experience to understand."

"It's not something a federal agent does," Matheson said.

"Oh, I wouldn't recommend it for casual use," Ross said. "It makes most people sick at first. You're puking your guts out, and if you aren't with people you can trust to take care of you, it can be a truly bad experience."

"Sounds charming," Matheson said.

The sun had risen to a hand above the horizon when Dahlgren drove up the hill toward the shaft. Frost was on the ground and there wasn't much activity yet at the tent city below, so he'd had little trouble driving past the blockhouse and the National Guardsmen, who by now recognized the battered white Jeep and the sound of its dying transmission.

The *Water Baby* was on a flatbed trailer that had been backed to within a few yards of the shaft, which the engineering battalion had opened and then surrounded with a pad of steel and concrete to keep the walls from sloughing into the dark rectangle. A thirty-foot crane on treads had been placed on the opposite side of the shaft, and Dahlgren could see the silhouette of the operator waiting in the cab. A dozen other soldiers were waiting as well, frozen in activity, looking toward the submersible.

With its insectlike manipulator arm and crash bars, its acrylic observation dome, and contrasting yellow and black trim, the sub looked like a cartoon robot from a Saturday-morning kids' show. The hatch was open and a man was peering out.

McAfee was watching with his arms crossed.

"What's wrong?" Dahlgren asked.

"The pilot won't get out of the sub," McAfee said. "We tried to explain to him that it's unsafe, that if the cable breaks or something unforeseen happens his life will be at risk, but he simply will not leave."

"Jesus Christ," Dahlgren said. "Did you talk to him?"

"Of course," McAfee said. "He said *Water Baby* is his responsibility. It was personally entrusted to him by its designer, Dr. Sam Halliday. He won't budge."

"Let me talk to him," Dahlgren said.

McAfee smiled.

"Be my guest."

"What's his name?"

"Rael Janot," McAfee said.

"Rael, huh? Okay."

As Dahlgren walked over to the flatbed, the pilot slumped lower and began to close the hatch behind him.

"Let's talk," Dahlgren said, holding his palms up. "Okay?"

The hatch stopped.

Dahlgren pulled his jeans up over his knees and squatted down in the gravel, his head down, but maintaining eye contact.

"I can understand taking your responsibilities seriously," Dahlgren said. "I wish more people would. Nobody seems to care about anything. It's refreshing to meet somebody with integrity."

The hatch swung open.

"Good," Dahlgren said.

The man nodded, pulled himself up, and sat on the lip of the hatch, his legs still in the sub.

"Now that we have an understanding," Dahlgren continued, "let me assure you that you don't want to ride this sub two hundred feet down that shaft. It's too dangerous. And right now, you're holding up the investigation. We only got a little daylight left, and it would be nice to get the *Water Baby* into the mine before it's gone."

"*Wat-air Bay-bee*," the pilot said, slapping the hatch.

"Right," Dahlgren said, and stood. "Now get down from there."

"*Non, cela ne m'interesse pas,*" the man shouted. "*Laissez-moi tranquille!*"

Then he closed and dogged the hatch.

"He doesn't speak English."

"Not a word," McAfee said.

"What did he just say?"

"That's he's not interested in anything a smelly American like you has to say," McAfee said, and laughed. "And to leave him the hell alone."

"You couldn't have told me?"

"I've been talking to him for half an hour," McAfee said. "I thought maybe you'd have a better chance with your command of body language."

"I'll show you body language," Dahlgren said, but restrained himself from flipping McAfee the bird. "Now what? Where's the submersible-operations guy?"

"Below, studying the shaft from the bottom and figuring out what the chance is of snagging on what structure is remaining," McAfee said. "I talked to him a few minutes ago. He thinks it's close, but that we can drop *Water Baby* through."

"Who the hell names a submersible *Water Baby?*" Dahlgren asked. "Sounds like a children's book."

"It is," McAfee said. "*Water Babies* is a very twisted children's book about a dirty boy who finds a sleeping girl that is so clean that he is ashamed of himself."

"How do you know about this?" Dahlgren asked.

"I know stuff," McAfee said, then shrugged. "The boy, Tom, throws himself into a brook, where he falls into a deep sleep. When he wakes, he finds himself transformed into a tiny water *thing*, naked, with gills. It was written by a Victorian cleric named Kingsley who had just a few sexual hang-ups."

"Didn't they all?" Matheson said, coming up behind them.

"Oh, *Alice* and all that," McAfee said. "Hey, speaking of Alice, did you find your magic-mushroom expert?"

"Yes," Matheson said without elaboration. "What's going on? Nobody's working."

McAfee briefed her.

"Dammit," Matheson said. "We don't have time for this."

"Glad you're here," Captain Schoville told Matheson as he walked toward her, followed by the lieutenant and the sergeant from before. "I'm about to order my men to wrestle that crazy sonuvabitch out of that cabin so we can accomplish our objective."

"That would be what public relations professionals call negative publicity," Matheson said. "We're in Missouri, not Baghdad. Despite the fundamentalism, there are a few differences. Besides, it's not our submersible or our pilot. We're just renting."

"You're the boss," the captain said.

"If he wants to ride it down, shouldn't it be his call?" Dahlgren asked.

"That's insane," the major said.

"Of course," Matheson said. "But what's the worst that could happen if we left him in the sub and lowered it down the hole?"

"A catastrophic failure might kill him," McAfee said.

"Give me odds."

"Slim," the major said. "One in twenty against."

"He's French?" she asked.

"Yes."

"Do it," Matheson said.

Twenty-nine

As the keel of the *Water Baby* kissed the surface of the water, Dahlgren sighed with relief. Beside him were the ex–military buddies, Addison and Potts, and they were already kitted up.

"She's ours now," Dahlgren said. "Potts, Addison. Get in the water and free that line."

They dropped into the water.

Standing to one side was Cal Bentham, drinking coffee from a mug with a faded Sealab logo. He was watching with a curious detachment, and Dahlgren wondered what memory he was reliving. When he realized Dahlgren was looking at him, he shifted uncomfortably.

"Where's Claire and her team?" Dahlgren asked.

Cal looked at his watch.

"On their way through the keyhole by now."

"Get on the VOX and advise them the submersible is in the water," Dahlgren said. "Have them surface on the shallow side of the dock, just to be safe."

Cal nodded, then tossed the rest of his coffee into the water and went to the communication console. McAfee was already there, fiddling with the rack-mounted Orcatron underwater telephone he had installed the day before. He picked up the microphone and attempted to summon the submersible.

"*Water Baby*," McAfee said into the handset. "*Ecoutez.*"

Although the subphone was a single-sideband, suppressed carrier system like the VOX system used by the divers, it operated on the lower frequency normally used to communicate with the *Argo*, the submersible's mother ship, or Navy vessels. The submersible also had an all-channel VHF radio for surface communications, but it would be of little use in the mine.

"*Bonjour.*"

"Welcome to the Good Earth," McAfee said in French. "It is December fourteenth, the time is sixteen thirty-eight Zulu, and the temperature is always seventeen degrees. It's wet here, but it never rains. We thought you might like to start with an orientation tour of Mineral City first. You can begin your descent as soon as our divers have released the cable and completed their visual check. In the meantime, is there anything you require?"

McAfee listened for a moment.

"But of course. Red or white?"

At the opposite side of the cavern, Geiger floated motionless in the water, neutrally buoyant, breathing silently from his Prism rebreather, only his eyes and the top of his head out of the water.

He had removed his mask so that a chance reflection from the lens would not give him away. He had watched the painfully slow lowering of the *Water Baby* from the shaft above, and the column of light that now carved a rectangle of azure water from the subterranean lake was an affront. A flight of dust and dead leaves descended the pillar of sunlight, swirling lazily, and finally polluted the crystal water.

Geiger had been confident there would be time to complete

this last cycle, despite the efforts of the FBI and the team of divers. But now, as he watched the lights of the *Water Baby* glowing a hundred yards away and the divers scrambling over her deck, anxiety swelled within him. This machine would go farther, deeper, and longer than divers.

Air hissed from the saddle flotation tanks as water covered the deck of the submersible. By the time the sail was under, the lateral thrusters were spinning the *Water Baby* on its axis, and a brace of 650-watt Birns & Sawyer underwater lights were sweeping through the water.

As the beam neared Geiger, he ducked beneath a rocky overhang. When it had passed, he swam out again and watched as the underwater floods began to illuminate Mineral City. The *Water Baby* shrank in size, then disappeared altogether as it dropped over the wall toward the sunken city.

Claire Connelly paused at the keyhole, her hand lightly touching the guideline, allowing Norman and Staci to catch up. Norman was trying to tell another one of his bad jokes, but his speech was still so distorted that Staci wasn't getting it.

"Come on," Claire said, pointed to her dive computer, and beckoned them forward.

This was a part of the mine that she and McAfee had visited a year earlier but had not been explored since. There was a room the size of a basketball court beyond the keyhole, an ore dump that led to the main shaft, and a locomotive at 270 feet. Staci was disappointed in the locomotive when she finally saw it. Instead of the prairie steam engine she imagined, the locomotive was the low-slung electric type common in mines during the middle of the twentieth century.

Claire had thought the room with the locomotive might have been an appealing backdrop for one of the killer's tableaux, and that she and McAfee might have missed something the year before. But the morning's search had turned up nothing.

"All caves look alike in the dark," Norman said as he squeezed through the keyhole. "Get it? All caves look alike . . . Hey, who has the red dry suit?"

"What?" Claire asked. The only intelligible part of Norman's transmission was *red dry suit?*, and Claire struggled to see over the top of Staci's rebreather.

Norman had come nearly mask-to-mask with Geiger on the other side of the keyhole, as Geiger was making his exit from the main chamber after surveilling the submersible.

Startled, Norman stared at the figure in red.

Geiger reached out, spun Norman around, and wrapped his legs around his waist. Norman struggled, but he couldn't reach behind far enough to get a grip on Geiger. They became inverted in the water and began to sink, but Geiger had calmly drawn his red-handled dive knife from the scabbard strapped to his leg.

Claire glimpsed just enough to realize that Norman was inverted, with somebody on his back, and she pulled Staci out of the way and wiggled through the keyhole while telling Staci to go deeper and hide.

Claire swam frantically, but by the time she reached them, Geiger had already sliced through the collar of Norman's suit and into his carotid. Blood was pumping out, blooming in the water like black ink, and since he was inverted, water was pouring into his helmet. Norman transmitted a gurgling sound until the water reached the VOX unit and shorted it out. Keeping the knife in his right hand, Geiger released Norman, then reached around and found his power inflator with his left and depressed the button for a few seconds. Norman's body rose upward, trailing a dark plume of blood.

Then he turned to face Claire.

He motioned for her to approach.

She turned and swam away from the keyhole, hoping Staci would stay put inside.

Geiger gave chase, kicking vigorously, his arms held at his

sides to offer less resistance to the water. Claire killed the lights on her helmet and her wrist, hoping to be engulfed by the darkness, but stayed close to the wall of the cavern, rising slowly as she went. The visibility was so great, however, that she could not elude her pursuer's light. And because she was younger, she managed to keep ten yards between them—until she attempted to speak.

"Help" was the first word that she could manage between breaths. "Help me."

She was above two hundred feet now, and Cal had her on the VOX.

"What's wrong?" she heard Cal ask. "Where are you?"

"Northeast wall," she panted. "Norman's dead. I'm next. Send help."

She dared a glance behind her and saw that the man in the red dry suit was only a few feet behind her. What frightened her most was not the knife he held by his side but the intense concentration she saw in the blue eyes behind the mask.

Claire had never swum so hard for so long in a rebreather rig, and adding to her panic was that the cap color on her carbon dioxide monitor was winking from blue to red. Her rig was still delivering oxygen at a partial pressure of 1.6 ATA, and the digital depth readout in her mask was flashing red with a down arrow, indicating she was ascending too quickly.

Claire knew that carbon dioxide building (in this case caused by trying to talk instead of breathe), coupled with a deep dive and hard exercise, was an invitation for CNS toxicity. But she was being chased by a fast-swimming man with a big knife, and it wasn't impractical for her to pause and manually lower her oxygen set point.

Claire knew she was in even worse trouble when her ears began to ring, her fingertips tingled, and her vision narrowed. This slowed her enough so that Geiger latched on to the blade of her right fin. As he yanked it away from her foot, crippling her ability to swim, Claire began to seizure.

She floated with her back arched, her arms and legs jerking, and her head back. Geiger paused, watching the display, trying to decide whether he should proceed with stabbing her, or whether she would die on her own. But he finally decided that since she was wearing a helmet, there was little danger of her drowning, and that she would probably recover from the oxygen toxicity.

He swam toward her, reaching for her harness with his left hand while rising the knife in his right. Suddenly, cold water smacked his face like a fist, and he was blind.

Staci had come up behind, jerked his mask off, and swum away with it looped over her right arm. Then she grabbed Claire's hand and pulled her through the water as fast as she could in the opposite direction, toward a breakdown pile she knew was at the base of the wall. After she settled behind it, she switched off all of her lights and held Claire's twitching body close to her.

Geiger found how difficult it was to hold a foot-long knife in one hand, retrieve a backup mask from a pouch clipped to a backpack harness, put the mask on and make sure it had a good seal, and them clear it by forcing air through his nose to displace the water. By the time he had completed the task well enough that he could see again, although there was still half an inch of water sloshing in the bottom of the mask, there was no indication of where the unexpected third diver had hidden with the other. He shone his wrist-mounted light over the walls and floor, but there wasn't even a bit of murk to suggest a passage.

Geiger knew it was time to leave. The other divers would come looking for their friends soon enough, even if they hadn't managed to contact the surface.

Geiger replaced his knife in its scabbard. As he swam away, he swept some of his hair from the side of the mask, where it was causing the seal to leak, and then blew the rest of the water out of it.

* * *

Dahlgren was the first to reach Staci, followed by Potts and Addison riding the deck of the *Water Baby*. Staci had already lowered Claire's O_2 set point, and although she had come out of the seizure, she was incoherent. They placed her in the basket below the acrylic hemisphere and took her to the surface, observing the deco stops indicated by her computer.

"Are you okay?" Dahlgren asked once they were on the dock.

"I'm in one piece," Staci said. She still had Geiger's mask looped over her arm. "Where's Norman?"

Dahlgren looked away.

"Tell me," Staci said.

"He shot to the surface about the time we got the distress call from Claire," he said. "He didn't have a chance. He's dead, Staci."

"How?"

"His throat was cut," Dahlgren said. "And his lungs were blown."

Tears welled in Staci's eyes, but she did not sob.

"Is he still in the water?"

"Cal retrieved him while we went after you and Claire," Dahlgren said. "He's in a bag in the compressor shed, waiting for the coroner."

"I suppose you want this," Staci said, holding out Geiger's mask.

"Where'd you get that?"

"It's *his*," Staci said. "I was so worried that I forgot about it until just now."

She explained how she snatched it from the killer's head, buying enough time to hide herself and Claire behind the breakdown.

Dahlgren took a pen from his shirt pocket and lifted the mask from Staci's hand by the strap. It was too late to tell her not to handle it, but there still might be a fingerprint left, perhaps on the inside of the lens.

It was a low-volume, goggle-style black rubber mask with a red plastic frame, one of thousands sold during the seventies and eighties. At first, Dahlgren thought there was still some water in the mask, because there were lines across the bottoms of each side of the goggle lens. When he looked closer, he realized the mask was dry and that the lines were where a pair of bifocal lenses had been fitted to the mask.

As Dahlgren bagged the mask, a pair of EMTs loaded Claire onto a gurney, then four National Guardsmen picked her up and hustled her up the mule trail. More Guardsmen stood on the dock, looking over the water, M-16s cradled in their arms.

"The sonuvabitch was in the cavern with us," Staci said. "How could you let that happen?"

Thirty

Jolene Carter was on her knees in the darkness.

"Then the mariners were afraid, and every man cried unto his god," she said imperfectly. She had been fighting the cold by reciting all of the verses she knew, and she had long since exhausted all of the New Testament verses she knew by heart. Now she was trying to recall something from the Old Testament. The first few chapters of Genesis had occupied her well until she got bogged down in all those begats. Then bits of Jonah had begun to come.

"They cast forth their wares into the sea," Jolene continued. She had torn away some fabric from the blanket, which she had wadded into balls and stuffed into her ears, so she could clasp her hands in front of her without being forced to listen to the sound of her own inhumanly distorted voice.

"But Jonah was gone down inside the ship, and was asleep, and the shipmaster came to him and said, sleeper arise, and call upon thy God so we will perish not."

Jolene paused while she thought of what happened next. A

shiver raced down her spine, and her jaw spasmed for a moment before she regained control.

"They cast Jonah into the sea, and the sea stopped her raging, and Jonah was in the belly of the fish. And Jonah said, out of the belly of hell I cried, and Thou heardest my voice . . ."

She faltered.

"And Thou heardest my voice," she repeated through chattering teeth.

But she was too tired and cold to think of what came after. She drew the blankets around her and lay down, hoping for sleep to take her. When she couldn't, she crawled to the stack of Nalgene bottles and, by shaking them, found one containing food sticks. She unscrewed the top and pulled out a stick, tore off the wrapper, and tried it.

"Apricot," she said, and threw the stick into the water.

"Diving operations are canceled," Dahlgren said, speaking in a low tone and leaning anxiously across the desk toward Matheson. "The exception is the submersible."

"You're letting him get away with it?" Matheson asked.

"I'm not letting this fucker do anything," Dahlgren said. "I'm just trying to keep the rest of our people alive. It's too dangerous to put them back in the water. I think the *Water Baby* is safe, but who knows what this guy is capable of?"

"This is the first time we've seen him," Matheson said. "We know where he is. I think we should throw everything into the water we have."

"You said I was in charge below the surface," Dahlgren said. "You said it was my call. Well, I'm calling it. It's too dangerous. And by the way, Grace, they're people, not things to be thrown into the water."

"You know I didn't mean it that way," Matheson said without much vigor. "We're running out of time. If I'm right, we have less than a week."

"They found a print inside the mask," Dahlgren said.

"No hits in the database," Matheson said. "If he's a professional, or has some standing, chances are he's had a privileged upbringing and never been fingerprinted. And we have the same problem with that old Browning used to kill Buntz. We have the slugs and could match them if we just knew where to look."

"You're convinced it's related?"

"I don't believe in chance," Matheson said, "just meaningful coincidences. What do you think our odds are of coming up with anything on the lens inserts?"

"I made some calls," Dahlgren said. "The mask company is out of business, but there are still a half-dozen firms making lens inserts for masks. Unfortunately, this one didn't put their name on the product, so I'm stuck. What about hair or scalp or something else genetic in the mask?"

"There probably is some genetic material there, and lab is looking, but even if they find something it takes at least a couple of weeks to get the results back, and the odds of having the killer's DNA on file are slim. Game over."

Dahlgren reflexively glanced at his watch. In the digital window, the date had begun blinking.

"Shit," he said.

"What's wrong?"

"My watch battery is nearly dead."

Matheson put her face in her hands.

"There's something I'm not connecting with," she said, looking up at Dahlgren. "I have this feeling gnawing at my gut that I know the answer that will stop this, but I can't hear it because of all this noise in my head."

Matheson's cell phone chirped.

"And on top of everything, I'm jealous that you're concerned about Staci's safety and not mine," she said, letting the phone ring. "Sometimes I'm just a stupid girl. No, don't say anything. You'd just lie."

She finally answered her cell. Her face turned grave, and she turned away from Dahlgren as she listened.

"Yes, sir," she finally said, then switched off.

Just as Matheson was about to speak, McAfee parted the plastic and strode into the office. His face was red, and when he spoke his voice quavered.

"It's over," he said. "Get your own divers."

"No more divers," Dahlgren said. "Nothing in the water except the submersible. How's Claire?"

"She'll make it," he said, then pressed his lips tightly together. Dahlgren knew he was thinking, *no thanks to you.* "They expect she'll be released tomorrow."

"She didn't take a hit?"

"No symptoms," McAfee said. "Just the oxtox."

"Good," Dahlgren said, but it seemed inadequate.

"They've scheduled Norman's funeral for ten o'clock the day after tomorrow," McAfee said. "The Sparks Funeral Home, in town."

"We'll be there," Matheson said.

"His folks want to bury him in his wet suit," McAfee said. "But it has these holes in it. So Cal is out there patching it up. Norman and his stupid jokes."

McAfee began to cry.

As he wiped the tears from his cheeks, he said: "I'm not going to allow any of my team in the mine until this guy is caught," he said. "I can't order Cal out, because he has to help me provide support for the submersible. I don't think he'd go anyway. But I wouldn't be down here if I wasn't needed."

"The dock is secure," Matheson said. "We have an around-the-clock security presence. The killer couldn't get through those soldiers."

"I feel better already."

McAfee left.

"I suppose I deserved that," she said.

307

"The phone call," Dahlgren said. "News?"

"Yeah," Matheson said. "That was the SAC. I'm being summoned to his office tomorrow in St. Louis. I think he's going to relieve me."

Jolene woke.

Something was moving in the darkness at the edge of the water. She sat up, pulling the blanket tight around her, then the lights came on and Geiger was standing over her, holding the remote, water dripping from his dry suit. He slipped the rebreather from his back and then motioned for her to take up the descrambler.

She shook her head and backed away.

He pointed at his watch and shook his head.

It's not time yet, he mouthed.

She switched the unit on and picked up the headset.

"Then what are you doing here?" Jolene asked.

"Passing through," Geiger said. He seemed winded, as if he had just engaged in some vigorous activity.

"What day is it?" she asked.

"It is always the same day here," Geiger said. "But your hour has not yet come."

"I'm cold," she said.

"Of course you are," Geiger said. "But it won't kill you, not if you use enough protection. People who are freezing to death cease to shiver. Mind your blankets. Make sure you eat and stay hydrated."

"How much longer?"

He paused. Geiger had never had a sacrifice ask him how much longer she had, and he had never expected one to ask in such a controlled manner.

"A few days," he said.

"Two?" Jolene asked.

"More," Geiger said.

"Three?"

"Yes," Geiger said. "Why do you ask?"

"I want to know how much longer I'll be cold," Jolene said, and as she said it she imagined herself on the sun-washed Texas beach she had once visited with her aunt. "And I'm lonely, too. Almost lonely enough to be glad to see even you."

"Very good," Geiger said. "Calm enough to summon wit."

"Enjoy yourself now," Jolene said. "The abyss awaits."

"You have no idea what awaits," Geiger said. "But you will, when I return. Sorry that I can't stay and chat theology, but the laws of physics demand that I fly."

Dahlgren was sitting cross-legged on the dock. Within arm's reach in front of him, placed with obvious care, was a filter cigarette and a disposable lighter.

Behind him, a phone was ringing in the plastic office.

Cal muttered, got up from his station at the communications console, and answered the phone. He popped back out in a moment, cradling the receiver.

"It's the *Daily Mail* of London," he said. "They want to know the latest on the Subtern. What should I tell them?"

"Tell them to clear the line," Matheson said as she stepped onto the dock. She was carrying a cardboard box beneath her arm.

"Good enough," Cal said.

Matheson walked over to Dahlgren.

"Who gave you that cigarette?" she asked, standing over him.

"The submersible pilot," he said.

Matheson knelt. She picked up the cigarette and flung it into the water, then pocketed the lighter.

"Lucky I was here to save you from yourself," she said. "Besides, there's oxygen on the dock. No smoking, remember?"

"Did you come back here just to torture me?"

"It's an added bonus," she said.

She held out the package.

"This was sent to me by a friend I made at the Academy,

back in the Jurassic," Matheson said. "She's now a spook with the—well, with some federal agency. I called her last week with a technical question. She had this sent by courier."

Dahlgren opened the box.

"What the hell was the question?"

He withdrew a pistol unlike anything he had seen before. It had four barrels, an exaggerated trigger guard, and a four-shot clip that loaded from behind.

"I asked her for advice on the best small arm for combat swimmers," Matheson said. "And this is what she sent me. It's a 4.5-millimeter SPP underwater pistol."

Cal couldn't help but eavesdrop, and he whistled as he and McAfee walked over.

"You familiar with this?" Dahlgren asked.

"Yes," Cal said. "Before I left the experimental dive unit, and after the wall fell, the Russians let us examine some of these things. There's an assault-rifle version as well."

"It works underwater, right?" Matheson asked.

"And on land," Cal said. "We don't know everything, because the Russians would only let us test it in the bay and not in the ocean simulation tank. But it fires steel darts that supercavitate underwater."

"What?" Matheson asked.

"Supercavitation," McAfee said. "An air bubble forms around the projectile, which eliminates drag and gives potentially unlimited velocity. These darts will slice right through a steel plate—or a diver, for that matter."

"This is science fiction, right?" Dahlgren asked.

"Hell no," Cal said. "The Russians are experts at this type of thing. They even have a torpedo called the *Squall* which supercavitates. No need for a warhead, because the torpedo itself just punches a hole right through an enemy sub. That's probably what the *Kursk* was testing when it sank."

"Effective range?" Matheson asked.

"Your guess is as good as mine," Cal said. "But if you're close enough to point it at something, you're probably close enough to kill it. Just remember to cock it before each shot, because this version isn't double-action."

There was an awkward pause.

"Why don't we let these kids play," Cal said, and walked back to the console. McAfee followed.

"I don't know, Grace," Dahlgren said. "Guns are more your style."

"Apparently, you just point and shoot," Matheson said. "I wish we had enough rounds to test it, but we only have the one clip."

"You're not listening," Dahlgren said. "Do you really think this is necessary?"

"What are you going to do when you meet this monster down below?" Matheson asked. "Politely ask him to give up?"

"There's no time left for any diving," Dahlgren said, reflexively glancing at his watch. The Seiko was frantically flashing "Dec. 19." He still hadn't had time to get the battery replaced.

"We don't know what there's time for, Dick."

"Don't call me Dick."

"Then stop acting like one," she said, scooping up the gun.

Ross's apartment was much like his cubicle at the university in St. Louis: overflowing with books and plants and pervaded by a strong earthy smell.

The floor of the living room was painted wood, and Matheson and Ross sat on a braided rug, facing each other. The room light was extinguished, but candles glowed in the empty spaces between the vines and leaves. On the CD player was some light New Age music.

"This is weird, you being a fed and all," Ross said.

"Consider it research," Matheson said, a little too lightly.

Ross laughed a little too loudly.

"Are the candles necessary?"

"Sets the mood," Ross said. "But I can turn the room lights on, if you like."

"That's okay," Matheson said. "But I would prefer some different music. The Doors seem appropriate, but perhaps too suggestive. Actually, no music at all would be good."

He crawled over and killed the stereo.

"No problem, Agent Matheson."

"You can call me Grace," she said. "Don't get any ideas—this is strictly business. But if you're going to hold my hair while I puke into your toilet, I think it's a little silly to continue to be so formal."

"Okay, Grace," Ross said, trying her name in his mouth. "Now, are you going to tell me what you're really doing here? Most people come looking for an answer, a glimpse of something beyond themselves, a sign that God or something really is out there, a miracle. It might help if I knew."

He held out a plastic bag of dried mushrooms.

"Terry," she said, "I'm looking for the structure of benzene."

"I don't get it."

"Trying to kick-start the subconscious," she said. "I don't have time to wait for nature. Or I doubt that I'm talented enough for it to happen naturally. Maybe I'm just looking for a miracle."

"That's a tough one," he said.

"You knew the job was dangerous when you took it," she said.

He laughed, again too hard.

"This isn't peyote?" she asked.

"No, A. muscaria," he said. "Just like you asked for. And by the way, they're not cheap. I don't exactly live on a full professor's salary."

"There's money in my wallet," Matheson said, taking a pinch of the mushrooms and imagining filling out an expense report for mushrooms, comma, magic. "I'll pay you what it cost, and give you something for your trouble. Isn't that how it works?"

She put the pinch in her mouth and made a face. It tasted like she was eating dirt.

"You've got to take more than that," Ross said.

"Christ, you didn't tell me they were going to taste so bad," Matheson said, but scooped more from the plastic bag and shoved them into her mouth.

"Grace," Ross said suddenly. "You're not wearing your piece, are you?"

Thirty-one

Matheson felt as if somebody had punched her in the solar plexus as she suddenly purged the contents of her stomach onto the braided rug.

"Don't worry," Ross said. "I'll clean it up."

Matheson leaned back, wiped her mouth with the back of her hand, and looked at him accusingly.

"You said I might vomit," she said. "You didn't mention that I wouldn't be able to make it to the can and then feel like I was fucking dying."

"Most people don't get this sick," he said as he got up to fetch paper towels and spray cleaner from the kitchen. She doubled over again, but this time she brought up nothing but a trickle.

"You can't tell anybody about this," she said.

"About the mushrooms?" he asked, wiping the floor with a wad of paper towels.

"About me puking," she said. "And if you tell anybody

314

about the organics, I will just have to cap your ass. Oh God, now I'm afraid I'm not going to die."

She crawled up onto the couch, shoving some books off the cushions onto the floor, and stretched out.

"I'm seeing . . . patterns."

"Describe them."

"Spirals," she said. "Swirls. The things that you see over cartoon characters when they get anvils dropped on their little heads."

"Birdies?"

"No, not birds."

"Just kidding," he said. "The patterns are normal."

"It's making me sicker," Matheson said.

"You're over that now," Ross said. "Don't fight it. Sometimes it helps to look at a comic or a magazine or something. I used to get really into R. Crumb when I first started using psychedelics, but then I switched to *The Sandman* and I had this really terrifying experience. Grace? Can you hear me?"

Matheson nodded.

"Grace, what do you see?"

"Water," she said. "Rocks."

Grace could hear Ross asking more questions, but his voice grew more and more faint, and finally disappeared. She was dropping through the earth, through layers of rock and stone and voids filled with water, to a point a billion and a half years ancient, a third the age of the earth.

Suddenly, she was thrust up through the crust of the earth and found herself on the highest granite peak of a huge volcanic island commanding a blue-green algae reef. In addition to slowly transforming the rock beneath, the chlorophyll-rich algae was helping prepare the atmosphere by turning nitrogen into compounds that would be useful to life during the Cambrian Explosion. She knew with alarming clarity that she was on top of a 12,000-foot peak that would become Taum Sauk

Mountain, in Iron County about thirty miles southwest of Bonne Terre, and, a portion of her consciousness whispered to her, the highest point in the state of Missouri.

This is my reading, she thought as she watched 800 million years of erosion and four seas reduce the smoking mountain range that would have rivaled the Cascades to a cold granite roof topping the contemporary Ozarks, the oldest mountains in the interior of the United States. The St. Francois Mountains, as they would be named in the penultimate moment of geologic time, had become foothills, and Taum Sauk was reduced to less than 2,000 feet. The spaces between the granite ribs of the ancient peaks had become filled with the dolomite, limestone, and sandstone, and the lead and zinc and the other ores that men would gouge from the earth.

So my trip is a geology lesson, Matheson thought in the corner of her mind that remained coldly skeptical, but even before she had finished the thought another part of her mind said, *This is where the blue-green algae and the changed atmosphere and the Cambrian Explosion eventually lead,* and she found herself standing in shallow water that stung her ankles, in a cave lit by torches. Row upon row of calcite-encrusted skulls glistened in the firelight, and as Matheson stepped forward, she realized she was treading on human mandibles.

Matheson shuddered.

In the water knelt Jolene Carter, nude, but coated in something that looked like blue mud. Even her hair was stiff with it. Her arms were crossed against her breasts, but her eyes were staring unblinking at the red figure in front of her. It was a shaman, smeared in red, with a flint-knapped blade in his right hand and a bowl of something in his left.

I didn't read this.

"Jolene?" Matheson asked, stepping forward, her feet smarting on the sharp bones, and reaching for her Sig. She was surprised that the gun wasn't in its holster. "Jolene Carter?"

Jolene looked at her and smiled.

"Come with me," Matheson said, holding out her hand.

Jolene held a forefinger to her lips.

Matheson became aware of other figures in the water, just at the edge of the torchlight, their eyes and teeth glistening. They were women, nude and also smeared in blue, and she recognized some of their faces from the pictures on the board at the St. Joan mine. There must have been forty of them, Matheson estimated, arranged in a semicircle in the water.

Matheson drew her black AA Maglite and shone the beam from the krypton bulb over the faces of the women. Jennifer Lynn held her palm up in a greeting, but her face was expressionless and her eyes had no pupils, only whites.

"Okay," Matheson said, loudly. "This is scaring me."

"Watch," Jolene said softly.

Jolene's face and breasts were smeared with the shaman's red handprints. Standing beside her in the water was a boy of probably ten years, staring in mute horror.

"Jolene," Matheson said, her voice reverberating from the walls of the chamber with authority. "Take my hand. Let's go."

Jolene turned, taking her eyes from the shaman, and looked at Matheson with a beatific smile.

"Remember," Jolene said. "Whatever they do, it is done merely to our bodies. Not our souls."

The boy beside her nodded. The boy was also nude, she noticed for the first time, and had an erection.

"And you must forgive them," Jolene said. "For they know not what they do. We are all in God's hands now."

The shaman had worked his way around behind Jolene, and he drew the Paleolithic knife across her throat, blood welling in the line the blade had traced, then spilling down her breasts.

"No!" Matheson screamed, and leapt forward, stumbling on the jawbones, and grasped the red arm that held the knife. The shaman did not struggle, but instead turned and looked at her with an expression of resignation.

He allowed the flint knife to drop into the water.

Jolene slumped backward into the water, floating faceup, her red hair pillowing around her head. Matheson pushed past the shaman and scooped up Jolene in her arms, holding her close as the life seeped from her, in a perfect imitation of the *Pietà*.

The boy stared for a moment with wide eyes that conveyed a mixture of grief and terror, and his mouth opened, but no sound came out for what seemed a very long time. When it did, it was a gut-wrenching stuttering wail.

"M-M-M-M-M-Mother!" the boy screamed.

In the apartment, Matheson's eyes flew open in recognition. She was reclining on Ross's couch. Clearheaded, she swung her feet to the floor.

"Geiger," she said.

Ross was half asleep.

"What d'ja say?" he mumbled.

Daylight was streaming in through the window.

"Dammit," Matheson said. "What time is it?"

Ross looked at his watch.

"A few minutes after eight."

"I've got to run," she said. "Where are my gun and my credentials?"

"In the freezer," Ross said sleepily. "Above the ice trays. And thanks for last night."

Matheson froze.

"We didn't . . ."

"Naw," he said. "But I gotcha, didn't I?"

Matheson stuck her badge and wallet in her jacket, then placed her freezing-cold Sig in the holster at her waist.

"Where the hell's my cell phone?" she asked.

"I dunno. You didn't have one."

"Then I need to use your phone."

"Can't afford one," Ross said. "But there's a pay phone at the Seven-Eleven at the end of the block."

Matheson paused in the bathroom and cursed as she saw the vomit stains on her clothes, the red-rimmed eyes, the hair that looked as if it had been styled by aborigines. And she didn't even want to think about her breath.

Fortunately, she carried an extra set of clothes in the trunk of her blue Crown Vic. She had probably left the cell phone on the console as well.

"Do you have a shower?"

"Yeah," he said. "Cold water only. They turned off my gas."

"I'm off to find a motel," she said. "Thanks for getting me through this. And mum's the word."

Walking a little unsteadily to her Vic parked at the curb outside Ross's apartment, she found her car keys in her jacket pocket, unlocked the door, and dialed Dahlgren's cell number.

"I know you're asleep," she said. "But shut up and listen. I need you to find Chief Brown and Wild Bill Bryce and tell them to meet me at seven o'clock in the morning at the FBI field office in St. Louis. No, I can't explain why, and no, you can't come. I'm still in charge, at least until they relieve me this afternoon. I've got more calls to make, so just do this for me. Richard?"

She punched the end button, then gathered her breath for a moment. What was she going to tell the SAC? How was she going to match Geiger with what she already knew? They had a print from the inside of the lens of the mask that Staci had managed to grapple from the head of the killer. Then what? That wasn't enough to successfully plead for a warrant to force Geiger's fingerprints. But then she remembered the envelope with Geiger's report on Jennifer Lynn, which was still in its envelope in a file drawer of the desk in the St. Joan mine.

She dialed the telephone on the dock.

Melissa answered on the second ring.

"Good girl," Matheson said. "Do you remember in the Academy they taught us to lift a latent print with ninhydrin?"

* * *

319

Something had emerged from the water and was moving in the darkness. Had the days gone by so quickly? she wondered. The last thing she remembered was praying that God would allow her to find a way to escape, and she was vaguely ashamed of herself. She had prayed to be spared rather than praying for salvation and the strength to meet her end. Wasn't she ready to face her Creator? No, she admitted to herself guiltily. Not yet. She would fight when the time came. But had she literally slept the rest of her life away?

When the lights did not come on after a few moments, however, she knew it was something other than her killer.

Jolene could hear claws scrabbling over the stone, and the sound frightened her so that she had to put her fist in her mouth to keep from screaming. When the Nalgene bottles began to clatter over, she could not suppress a small cry, but it was enough to draw the attention of whatever was in the darkness.

Jolene backed against the chamber wall as the creature came closer. Her heart thumped out a fast backbeat in her chest as she heard it sniffing, felt its whiskers, smelled the fishy breath.

"That's awful," Jolene said.

The creature pushed its nose into Jolene's hand, seeking affection.

"What are you?" Jolene asked, rubbing the sleek head.

There were animal grunts of joy.

By the time the lights clicked on half an hour later, Jolene knew it was some kind of seal, and she was hugging it as one would the family dog.

She turned his collar around so she could read the tag with the NOAA permit number and contact information. "I don't think you're Loren McAfee," Jolene said. "What's your name?"

She was sure Nemo would tell her, if only he could.

Then she looked over at the Nalgene bottles scattered across the floor.

"The food sticks," she said with realization. "You *like* apricot."

Thirty-two

In the back of a Ford panel van parked near the corner of Morgan and North First Street, Grace Matheson stripped down to her bra and slipped a Kevlar vest over her head.

"Yes, dammit," she said, feeling seven pairs of male eyes on her as she buttoned a periwinkle blouse over the vest. "It's Victoria's Secret. Get over it."

"Any other exits?" the tactical squad leader asked.

He was in his mid-thirties, with short-cropped brown hair, and he was chewing a piece of Bazooka bubble gum. He was also wearing a vest over his black fatigues, and on the back of the vest was printed in bold yellow letters: FBI.

"The super said the freight elevator is the only way in, and that the fire escape in the alley is the only way out," Matheson said.

She was attempting to put her navy-blue jacket on over the vest, but the vest was too bulky in the shoulders. Finally, she wadded the jacket into a ball and threw it into the front seat of the van.

"You have the paper?" the leader asked.

"In my pocket."

Matheson handed him the slightly crumpled arrest warrant, and he examined it by the light of his flashlight. "Fingerprint match, huh?" Then he turned to a folder and withdrew enlarged copies of Geiger's driver's license photo and handed it to the other five members of the squad.

"It's not a very good likeness," Matheson said. "Give me your jacket, Mark."

The younger agent wriggled out of his jacket, and Matheson slipped it on over the vest, then rolled the cuffs up a couple of turns.

"But it's him?"

"Yes," Matheson said.

"Ordinarily, we'd like to have a little better briefing," the squad leader said with just a little sulk in his voice. "Are you sure we need this much firepower for one guy?"

"He's only killed thirty or forty individuals, including a police officer and a member of our team at the mine," Matheson said. "What do you think?"

"This guy will shit his pants when he sees us, is what I think," he said.

"And remember—"

"Take him alive if we can," the squad leader said, handing the warrant back.

"Okay, oh six forty-seven. Let's get into position and wait for Agent Matheson's signal. Are you sure you want to do this yourself, ma'am?"

"Absolutely," she said. "He'll open the door if he just sees me. If he gets a look at the rest of you, we'll have a standoff."

"He's not going to think it's odd that you're knocking on his front door at seven in the morning in a man's jacket and, if he looks close, a bulletproof vest?"

"He'll be curious," she said. "And he doesn't see me as a threat. Thinks he's a lot smarter than I am."

The squad leader blew a bubble and let it pop, then peeled it off his chin. He stuffed the gum back in his mouth and asked, "Is he?"

"Yes," Matheson said.

"Here," Melissa said, taking off her scarf. "Your vest is still showing."

Matheson knotted the scarf, then fluffed it.

"Better," Melissa said.

Matheson grasped the handle and swung open one of the rear doors. It was still dark, although dawn was beginning to smudge the eastern sky. The tactical team came quickly out of the van, assault rifles and helmets in their hands.

Mark and Melissa started to crawl out the back, but Matheson stopped them.

"You guys sit this one out, okay?"

"Oh six forty-eight," the squad leader said. "In a few minutes, this area is going to be bustling with week-before-Christmas business. We either do this now or we wait until after midnight."

"Now," Matheson said. "I want somebody under that fire escape if he makes a run for it."

"He won't run," the squad leader said. "He's a serial killer, right? They have this thing about authority. They just go limp."

"Ritual killer," Matheson said. "Different animal."

"Radios on Tac three," the squad leader said. "Once again, Agent. Two of us will be on the roof, two outside the freight elevator, one on the fire escape, and one on the bottom. I'll be right beside you, Agent. Any questions?"

Matheson checked to make sure she could reach her Sig easily in its holster beneath Mark's jacket, felt for the two extra twenty-round clips, then asked, "Ever shot anybody?"

"Not personally," the squad leader said.

Matheson sighed.

"I have," she said.

* * *

Matheson pressed the buzzer for one full second, then released it. She tried not to glance at the squad leader, crouched down against the wall on the latch side of the door, in goggles and helmet, cradling a Heckler & Koch MP-5 assault rifle.

After thirty seconds had passed, she pressed the buzzer again and held it this time for two seconds. Then they could hear the sound of feet padding across the floor and, after a moment:

"Yes?"

"Doctor, this is Special Agent Matheson," she said.

"It's not even seven o'clock," came the scratchy reply from the speaker beside the door. "Not one to make appointments. How'd you get in?"

"The super," Matheson said, pleased that she didn't have to lie.

"How'd you know I was here?"

"Sir?" Matheson asked. "I'm not sure—"

"Wait."

There was the sound of scraping chains and locks being turned, and as the battered door swung angrily open, Matheson pulled the Sig from its holster in the small of her back and held it in a combat grip in front of her.

"Damn," Frank Smith said. He was wearing Geiger's red robe over a pair of silk boxer shorts.

"Down," the squad leader said, training the muzzle of the H & K on him. "Get down. Spread your legs and hands."

"It's not him," Matheson said. "I should have known. He didn't stutter."

"Are you alone?" the squad leader asked.

"No," Smith said.

The leader swept past them into the apartment, followed by the tactical agents who had been hiding in the freight elevator.

"Where is he?" Matheson asked as she knelt beside him.

She pointed her gun to the ceiling, keeping it in a two-handed grip. "Where's Geiger?"

"Geiger?" Smith said.

Matheson smelled ammonia and moved back to avoid a growing puddle of urine.

"Yes, Geiger," Matheson shouted.

There was a woman's scream from inside the apartment.

"Dr. Geiger always takes vacation this week," Smith said. "I've house-sat for him for the last eight years. It's a nice apartment, you know."

"Where is Geiger right now?"

"He says he goes back home in memory of his family."

"Where's home?"

"Bonne Terre," Smith said.

"Dammit," Matheson said.

"You didn't know? You said you'd read his book."

"I lied," Matheson said. "I didn't read the fucking book, I just wanted his help. Who's inside?"

Smith swallowed hard.

"The dean's wife."

From the handheld radio in her pocket, she could hear the squad leader giving the all clear. He told the others they could leave their positions.

Through the open door, Matheson could see inside the apartment far enough to count three framed Pre-Raphaelite prints: Waterhouse's *Consulting the Oracle*, Draper's *The Young Martyr*, and Millais's *Ophelia*.

"You don't think Dr. Geiger is . . . ," Smith asked, then his eyes widened.

"You and whatever her name is will have to dress and come down to the federal building with us," Matheson said. "This apartment will have to be swept for evidence. Come on, get up."

The freight elevator rumbled to a stop.

She had switched her Sig to her left hand and had her right under Smith's arm to help him up, as she saw the elevator door swing open and Geiger step out. He was looking absently down at the keys in his right hand, separating his front-door keys from the rest, and then he glanced up and met Matheson's stare.

"Don't move, Dr. Geiger," Matheson said, pointing her gun in his direction.

"You can't shoot me," Geiger said.

"Don't bet on it."

"If I'm dead, you'll never save Jolene," he said, and saw the narrowing of Matheson's eyes. "That's right, she's still alive—but if you kill me, nobody will ever find her, and she dies alone in the darkness."

Geiger crouched and drew the Browning from its ankle holster as Matheson pushed Smith into the apartment with her right hand and fired the Sig with her left.

The sound of gunfire was so loud that it didn't seem like a sound at all to Matheson, but felt like needles jabbing into both ears. In a moment, the entry was filled with smoke and plaster dust, and the woman in the back room began screaming again.

Matheson had fired three rounds with her off hand, just pointing the gun in Geiger's direction, before managing to hunker behind the door frame and switch the gun to her right. By this time Geiger had backed into the freight elevator and hit the down button, firing as he went, and as the door swung down, but just before the elevator began to move, Matheson managed to get off one well-aimed shot.

The Sig barked and blood exploded from Geiger's right thigh and left a splatter pattern on the elevator wall behind. Then the elevator jerked and was on its way back down, and by the time the squad leader came through the door behind the muzzle of his H & K, it was over.

"Are you hit?" he said.

"No," Matheson said, her hands shaking. "But he is. Leg."

"Any way to stop that elevator?"

"Not that I know of," Matheson said.

"Fire escape," he told the others, and they ran for the back window. "I'll try to get the others on the radio and have them waiting," he told Matheson. "Stay here with the screamer and keep her in back. Don't let her see that."

"See wh—!" Matheson started to ask, but the squad leader was already gone, following the others toward the fire escape. Then she looked inside the apartment and saw Smith crumpled on the floor in the red robe in what seemed a lake of blood. He had taken one of Geiger's rounds beneath his left arm, at an angle that would take the .380 hollowpoint mushrooming through his heart.

"Shit," Matheson said.

Jolene and the California sea lion sat side by side, with Jolene feeding him another apricot food stick.

"Where'd you come from?" she asked, wiping her runny nose on the edge of her blanket poncho. "Who do you belong to? Oh, how I wish you could talk."

Jolene reached up and unclasped the chain that held the golden cross around her neck. She held it tightly in the palm of her left hand as she unbuckled Nemo's collar, then let the chain fall and threaded the collar through it. Then she wrapped the chain around it several times before she rebuckled it.

"Take this back to the world," she said.

Nemo nudged her hand for more pets.

"Go," she said.

The sea lion did not, of course.

Jolene stood.

"Go," she said again, louder.

Nemo backed away.

"I don't want you anymore. Get! Scat! Out of here!"

Even through her makeshift earplugs, Jolene could not stand the distorted racket she was making.

Nemo grunted his dissatisfaction, then galumphed to the edge of the water. He looked longingly back. She waved her arms menacingly, and he dove in.

Jolene sat down and was very still for a few moments.

Then the lights clicked off.

As he approached the no-wake zone, Geiger throttled back and the growl of the twin Mercury outboards settled to a purr. Then the wake overtook him, and the old CrisCraft Excalibur waddled for a moment in the surge, then found her edge.

With the morning sun behind him, the shadow of Geiger's boat preceded him into the port of Sainte Genevieve. Behind, the Mississippi was burnished copper, the sun a molten orange disk, and the sky was the color of gunmetal.

It began to snow.

Geiger's leg throbbed.

Matheson's slug had passed through the muscle of his outside thigh without hitting bone or artery, but it had taken a lot of tissue with it. Geiger had managed to staunch most of the bleeding by packing in and applying a tight dressing, but he could still feel a warm trickle running down his leg and pooling in his right shoe.

He cursed himself for going back to the apartment.

He had spent the day before in Memphis, touring the replica of the Parthenon, attempting to commune with the old gods. The experience had left him empty; the mood had been spoiled, perhaps, by the throngs in their NASCAR baseball caps. In a moment of sentimentality, he had decided to come back to the apartment to retrieve the original of the photograph that had been published on the back of his book, the one of him as a boy with his mother and father, on the banks of the River of Doubt. He had always planned to have that photograph buried with him, and it seemed appropriate now that he keep it on his person.

Of course, it had nearly cost him the game.

The shot that had killed Smith was unintentional. Geiger was surprised by how difficult it was to aim the Browning during the brief firefight, and he found himself pointing at the gun in Matheson's hand instead of her torso. One of the shots he'd fired while she switched hands had hit Smith, but he wasn't really sorry he had killed his assistant. Smith was a fool, a sycophant, and incapable of continuing the grand work.

And he had been wearing Geiger's robe.

The escape was easy enough. He had gotten off the freight elevator on the floor below, climbed the fire escape to the roof, and crossed over onto the next building before the tactical squad had time to return to their positions. Then he had made his way down to the street, where the black Crown Vic was waiting, and as he drove away he saw the black panel van at the corner that the agents must have arrived in. Two rather youngish agents in conservative suits were waiting outside the van, their arms folded, and they stared as he passed within a few feet of them as he rounded the corner, his face hidden by the Vic's tinted windows.

Now, as Geiger made his way to his private slip, he let the CrisCraft idle for a moment as he passed a curious-looking vessel docked at the river port.

It was a wooden-hulled World War II minesweeper that had been converted to a salvage ship. Although the lines of the *Argo* were reminiscent of her more famous cousin, the *Calypso*, this vessel was built for treasure hunting, not research, and she wasn't nearly as pretty or well-maintained as the *Calypso*; rust stains dripped from her scuppers. As he passed beneath the stern of the ship, he could read her home port:

NEW ORLEANS. A couple of big orange magnetometer "fish" were stowed on each side of her stern, and the big A-frame on her fantail, which normally carried the *Water Baby*, was empty.

Thirty-three

Leaning on the top of the communications console, Dahlgren glanced at his Seiko for the thousandth time since he'd arrived in Bonne Terre. No date was displayed in the digital window, and the second hand was frozen.

The watch had finally died.

Brown was standing next to him, his ever-present Styrofoam cup of coffee in his hand. When he sat it on the top of the console, McAfee frowned.

"Do you mind?" he asked. "If that gets spilled on the electronics, it won't be beneficial."

"Sorry," Brown said, removing the cup.

"Any contact with the submersible?" Dahlgren asked.

"Not for about thirty minutes," McAfee said. "I had Rael on the subphone as he descended the main shaft, but I lost him when he entered an ore dump just above the sump at four hundred feet. There's some drifts down there we've never explored."

"It must be tight down there," Dahlgren said.

"It's room and pillar, just like on the upper levels," McAfee said. "Plenty of room in the stopes, unless he goes into one of the older exploratory drifts."

"Any word from Matheson yet?" Brown asked.

Dahlgren shook his head.

Brown could see the Universal Coordinated Time on the communications console: 14:48.

"Coming up on nine o'clock," the chief said. "They should have served the warrant by now."

Dahlgren's cell phone rang.

"Grace," he said. Then: "Are you all right? Good. Do you think he's able to travel? What next?"

"What?" Brown said.

Dahlgren held up a finger.

"She's on her way," she said. "So Mark and Melissa saw a black Crown Vic? Well, it doesn't have to be registered in his name, or registered at all. People do it all the time. Well, the people I know do. . . . He's got nowhere else to run, Grace. He has to come here."

"Damn," Brown said, understanding the meaning.

"But, Grace, I don't think an APB and roadblocks are good enough. Sure, his apartment is only an hour from here, but do you really think he would continue driving, knowing every cop in Missouri was looking for him? This guy's more comfortable in the water. He'd come by boat."

He looked at McAfee.

"Where's the closest river port?" Dahlgren asked.

"For what, commercial traffic?" McAfee asked. "Sainte Genevieve."

"No, the closest to accommodate a small boat," Dahlgren said, then listened to Matheson for a moment. "And with a hospital nearby."

"That would be Crystal City," McAfee said. "It's just a little closer as the crow flies than Sainte Gen, but the roads are bet-

332

ter—you can take Highway 67 all the way. And there's a hospital on an island in the river."

"How far in river miles is it from St. Louis?"

"Twenty-five or thirty," McAfee said. "A fast boat could make it in well under an hour."

Dahlgren relayed the information.

"Yes, right away."

"Chief, Matheson is just leaving St. Louis, so she wants you to contact the highway patrol dispatcher and see if there's anybody close to Crystal City," he said. "Drop in on the hospital to inquire about gunshot victims, and then ask at the biggest marinas if anybody arrived in a hurry. Also, she wants Sainte Genevieve checked out as well. She says it would be faster for you to request it than for her to go through the field office in St. Louis."

"I'm on it," he said.

"And, Chief," Dahlgren said. "Matheson says if they make Geiger, avoid contact if possible. Wait until the feds can back them up, or they might have a bloody mess on their hands."

Holding a Remington 870 pump shotgun loaded with double-ought buck, Wild Bill Bryce stood on the dock looking over a twenty-year-old CrisCraft with twin Mercury outboards that were still hot to the touch. The boat had bloody footprints all over its bottom.

The marina owner had told Bryce that the slip had belonged for years to Gustaf Jakobe, but that the slip was empty most of the year, except in the winter, when the Excalibur was often docked there.

When Bryce had poked around the boat long enough to satisfy himself that nobody was hiding in it, he returned to the marina office and told them to keep everyone away from the boat until the FBI came to secure it. Then he walked back up the long floating walkway from the marina to the parking lot, where he had left his patrol cruiser idling to keep the windows free of frost.

He got in, replaced the Remington pump muzzle-up in its dash mount, and picked up the mike.

A voice behind him said, "Don't."

In the rearview mirror, he saw the muzzle of an old Browning semiautomatic pistol pointed at him through the cage that separated the front from the back.

Bryce replaced the mike in its cradle.

Geiger lowered the gun.

"I'll unload the magazine through the back of the seat into your kidneys if you don't cooperate," Geiger said.

"Okay, friend," Bryce said.

"Drive," Geiger said. Funny, but he noticed he never stuttered when he had a gun or a knife in his hand. "Keep your hands where I can see them. And when we come to the trash barrel at the exit, I want you to take your side arm by two fingers, wrap it in that newspaper on the seat, and toss it out the window like you're disposing of some trash."

The roadblock on K Highway was just east of the gates of the Eastern Reception Diagnostic and Correctional Center, a recent addition to the Missouri prison system that had become Bonne Terre's largest employer since the lead mines closed in the 1960s. Bryce slowed the cruiser while Geiger squeezed himself onto the rear floorboard. The sheriff's deputy in the yellow slicker with snow on the shoulders waved him through, barely glancing at the trooper as he tugged the front of his hat. Bryce touched the brim of his in return.

"Dispatch is going to want to know what I've been doing for the last half hour," Bryce said. "If I tell them I'm in Bonne Terre instead of Sainte Gen, they're going to be curious to know why."

"Take a right on Highway Sixty-seven," Geiger said. "Just

after we cross the bridge over Big River, I want you to slow down and turn east on a dirt road."

"You're the boss," Bryce said.

Just before the bridge the patrol cruiser pulled off onto the snow-covered lane, proceeded two miles, then stopped in front of the locked gate.

"Now what?" Bryce asked.

"Drive through it," Geiger said.

"Okay," he said. "But I have to take a run at it."

Bryce shifted into reverse and put his arm on the back of the front seat while he backed the patrol car forty yards up the lane. Then he stopped, put the transmission in drive, then eased down on the pedal, letting the rear wheels find a grip on the snow-covered dirt. Once the patrol car was moving, he just kept pressing the accelerator forward. They were doing forty miles an hour before Geiger recognized Bryce's intention.

"Hey" was all Geiger got out before Bryce whipped the wheel at the last moment, missing the gate but striking an oak tree that stood to one side.

Bryce had his shoulder harness on and his airbag inflated, but Geiger wasn't strapped in. He was thrown face-first into the metal grid that separated the seats.

The cruiser climbed the trunk of the tree, slid off and slammed hard onto the driver's side into the snow, then rolled over onto its top, tangled in the fence.

Bryce was dazed from the impact of the airbag. He was bleeding from the corner of his mouth, where his teeth had punctured the inside of his lip, and the side of his face that had been toward the bag was already beginning to swell. But in a moment he remembered the killer with the Browning in the backseat, and was climbing toward the passenger's door. He got the latch open, but the sheet metal was in a bind and the door wouldn't budge by hand, so he spun around and used his legs to kick it open. Once he had wiggled through, he reached back inside and grabbed the barrel of the pump shotgun.

A shot rang out from the backseat. Deflected by the security grid, the slug punched a spiderwebbed hole in the windshield. There was another shot, and the passenger's window exploded, showering rectangular bits of glass over Bryce as he rolled off the patrol car to the ground, still clutching the shotgun. He started to make a dash for the safety of the trees, but his legs became tangled in the fence and he fell. He lost one of his shoes as he freed himself. He fired one quick blast behind as he ran, and the buckshot blew open the trunk lid and shattered the passenger taillights.

As he slid behind a tree, a round from the .380 kicked up snow at his elbow. He jammed his back flat against the ground, and he could feel the knotty tree roots beneath him. Panting, he clutched the Remington to his chest. Then he pumped the slide, chambering a fresh round. Then he turned and dared a glance over the barrel of the shotgun.

He fired again.

Gasoline began to pour from a half-dozen holes where the second round had punctured the fuel tank, melting the snow around the back of the car. From the engine compartment, sparks were sprinkling down from where the insulation over a battery cable had been severed against a radiator support.

In a few moments, the puddle of gasoline had spread far enough forward to be ignited from the sparks. With a sharp *kawthump*, the patrol car was immersed in flame.

Bryce hoped the bastard hadn't made it out. His handheld radio was in the interior of the patrol car, so it would be a long walk with one shoe to the highway.

"The roadblocks turned up nothing," Matheson said, resting her elbows on the desk. "Zip in Crystal City. And we're still waiting to hear from Sainte Genevieve. Bryce still hasn't reported."

"It's a river port," Dahlgren said. "More places to look."

"You shot the bastard in the leg?" Brown asked.

"I didn't want to kill him," she said, "just stop him. I know I hit him, because his blood was splashed all over the elevator. Too bad I didn't break his fucking femur."

The telephone rang.

"Somebody answer it," she said. "I can't stand the suspense."

Brown grasped the receiver.

"Hello," he said. Then: "Where?" And after a minute of listening: "I'll tell her. Thanks."

"Good news, I hope," Dahlgren said.

"Your suspect kidnapped Bryce at a marina in Sainte Gen," Brown said.

"My God, is he—"

"Wild Bill is alive," Brown said. "He wrecked the car and escaped, although he had a rather cold walk to the highway."

"Where?" Matheson asked.

"In the Pike Run Hills along Big River, near the St. Francois State Park," Brown said.

"Show me," she said, spreading a county map on the table.

"Here," Brown said, indicating the spot with his index finger. "The highway patrol is throwing everything they've got into that loop in the river."

"We need to get some federal agents there as well," she said.

"The patrol said St. Louis already had ATF and Bureau tactical teams on their way, as well as some canine units."

"I need to be there," Matheson said, standing up.

"Grace," the chief said. "Maybe you'd better stay here."

"Why?"

"Look at the scale on the map," Brown said. "The spot where Bryce last saw this bastard is only four miles away. Geiger didn't burn up in the car. If he's hiding out in the Pike Run Hills, the dogs will find him. If not, he's already in the mine."

The *Water Baby* proceeded slowly, moving about an inch per second down the passage, its forward lights illuminating the passage like a train going through a tunnel. The digital depth gauge on the instrument panel read 130 meters, while the altimeter—which measured the distance from the keel to the bottom—fluctuated between 1 and 1.25.

Rael Janot had an unlit cigarette dangling from his mouth as he pushed the submersible down the drift using joysticks that controlled the propeller and the vertical, lateral, and horizontal thrusters on the exterior of the craft. Occasionally, he would have to hug the bottom of the drift so as to duck beneath the skeletal trapezes that hung from the ceiling.

Eventually, he came to a skip pocket, one of the sloping passages where ore was dropped down toward the bottom of one level to the next, and finally to be loaded on skips to be taken up the main shaft to the surface. Rael didn't like the narrowness of the drift he was exploring, and since the skip pocket was twice as big, he decided to follow it upward.

The submersible ascended slowly, and after thirty meters entered a stope, or a room supported by pillars, the size of a commercial aircraft hangar. He checked his charts. The submersible had an onboard tracking system, but without a support ship, GPS, or underwater transponders as reference points, the computer system was useless in the mine.

Instead, Rael had been forced to track his position on grid paper the size of a tablecloth that had the outlines and depths of the known shafts and drifts sketched in by McAfee. He was now far beyond any known areas.

With more room to maneuver, Rael took the submersible around the perimeter of the stope. He found six more girls, each in individual tableaus, on one side of the room. Each was redheaded and nude. He keyed the headset and attempted to contact the dock, but of course there was too much rock in between.

After carefully taking video of each of the girls, he pushed the submersible forward and found another drift at the opposite side. It was narrower than the other drifts, but not so narrow as to prevent exploration.

He nudged the *Water Baby* inside this new passage.

Thirty-four

Snow swirled from the sky.

It dusted the Christmas tree, complete with winking lights and a star on top, that had been erected in the center of the tent city next to the St. Joan mine. Cries of "hallelujah" mingled with New Age chanting. Vendors hawked hot dogs and popcorn and cotton candy, along with T-shirts emblazoned with Jolene's picture.

Atop the hill where the submersible had been lowered into the shaft, Dana Casteel was doing a final broadcast for Color Three in Springfield. Next week, she would go to work for a Fox affiliate in Los Angeles.

"Sunset on December twenty-first," she said solemnly.

In the glare of the video lights, she began to walk, mike in hand. In the background was the tent city. The winter sun, framed in the nude branches of the trees, was about to slip below the horizon. "It's now five o'clock, and the beginning of the longest night of the year. The prayers of an anxious nation are with kidnapped Bible college student Jolene Carter, held somewhere in the labyrinth beneath my feet."

She stopped walking.

"But hope is running out," she said.

She continued walking.

"The manhunt for suspected serial murderer Jakob Geiger has stalled. Sources say that Geiger, who may have murdered as many as forty young women, is the only one who can tell investigators where Jolene Carter is hidden. Geiger escaped from authorities early today after a shoot-out at his posh St. Louis apartment, then escaped from a Missouri Highway Patrol officer in the heavily wooded Pike Run Hills, just a few miles north of us. Since that time, he has managed to elude the most intensive manhunt ever in southeastern Missourah."

She had walked far enough now that Clancy Brown was in the frame, waiting with his hands crossed in front of him.

"With us is the chief of police of tiny Bonne Terre, Missourah," Dana said. "Chief Brown, can you describe the situation in the old St. Joan Lead Mine below us?"

"We're still working the case," he said. "The investigators, led by FBI special agent Grace Matheson, are busy pursuing what leads they have. The submersible is searching the mine drifts. We're doing everything we can do."

"But at this late hour, isn't hope lagging?" she asked.

"No," Brown said. "That's why they call it hope."

The submersible hovered a few feet from the bottom of the passage, motionless. In the glare of the forward lights was a pair of iron doors, mossy with rust, partially open.

Rael had powered down the lights to conserve energy, and was sitting in the dark, the unlit cigarette dangling from his lip, watching the blinking lights on the console around him, trying to decide what to do.

What were the doors for?

He could probably squeeze the *Water Baby* through, but it

would be a tight fit. What he was really worried about was what was on the other side. Only enough light spilled through the doors to illuminate part of the passage, and what he couldn't see worried him. It was possible that he would be able to get past the doors only to become trapped in a hopelessly narrow passage, or entangled in some unseen mine debris.

He had already traveled more than two kilometers underwater, about a third of the submersible's range. If trapped, there was enough life support on board in the form of electrical potential, oxygen scrubbers, and food and water to last one person ten days. But without contact with the dock, he could not be sure they would find him even in that amount of time.

Rael powered up the aft lights, nudged the screw and thrusters, and began the tedious process of backing out of the drift.

The digital clock on the communications console read 00:20 Zulu.

"It's tomorrow in London," Dahlgren said.

"Well, it's still today here," Matheson said.

"What's the word from up north?"

"A couple of hundred agents and National Guardsmen are tearing apart the rocks and the trees, but not even the dogs have turned up a trace of Geiger," Matheson said. "The dark is going to bring that to a standstill, because you just can't search at night. If we had just had a little luck, if it had just stopped snowing, we could have followed his footprints."

"How's Bryce?"

"Wild Bill is beat up, has a case of frostbite on one set of toes, and is chagrined at having let the bastard escape, but he'll survive. Any word from the submersible?"

"Loren told me there hasn't been any contact in a couple of hours," Dahlgren said. "How much time do we have left, Grace? Midnight?"

"No," Matheson said. "An hour before dawn."

"How'd you figure that out?"

"It's the solstice," she said. "You can look it up in just about any almanac or on the Web. It occurs at different times each year, because our calendar doesn't precisely match the orbit of the earth around the sun. This year, the solstice is at 6:42 A.M., an hour and two minutes before dawn."

There was splashing from the edge of the dock, and the soldiers aimed their weapons at the dark form emerging from the water.

Matheson had drawn her Sig as well.

"Stand down," Dahlgren said, and the soldiers lowered their M-16s. "It's Nemo." Cal and McAfee came running over from the communications console.

The sea lion was attempting to reach Dahlgren and the others on the dock, but was barely able to crawl. Dahlgren knelt beside the crying sea lion and started to touch him, but McAfee placed a hand on his shoulder.

"Don't," McAfee said. "He could bite."

"What's wrong with him?" Matheson asked.

"I don't know," McAfee said.

"He's in pain, that's for sure," Dahlgren said.

The sea lion looked up with its dark glassy eyes, then shuddered and doubled over.

"Let him bite me," Dahlgren said, and placed his hand on the sea lion's head. Nemo growled, then allowed it.

"What's around his collar?" Matheson asked.

"Some kind of chain," Dahlgren said as he unbuckled the collar. He handed it to Matheson, who unwound it and held the golden cross in her hand.

"It's Jolene's," she said. "It's the one she's wearing in the picture her aunt sent."

"Then I know what's wrong with Nemo," Dahlgren said. "He's bent."

"How?" Matheson said. "I thought you said seals couldn't—"

"He's been breathing compressed air," McAfee said.

"The same compressed air that Jolene Carter has," Dahlgren said.

"Cal, try like hell to contact that submersible on the hydrophone," McAfee said. "We've got to tell him the girl is still alive down there somewhere."

Cal nodded and went back to the console.

Dahlgren was already coming out of his boots and jeans.

"Let me do it," McAfee said. "It's my sea lion."

"You can't," Dahlgren said. "Nobody else here speaks French."

"What are you doing?" Matheson asked.

"I'm kitting up," Dahlgren said. "I'm taking Nemo back down to recompress him, or else he'll die. He may die anyway. But I don't have time to talk about it."

McAfee was already getting Dahlgren's gear from the locker.

"Grace, grab me one of those rebreathers," Dahlgren said.

"Which?"

"Any one," he said. "Hurry."

Matheson ran over and picked up the first rebreather she saw, the one with the number seven on the side, and carried it to Dahlgren.

Dahlgren was down to his boxers, then he was nude.

Matheson turned, then ran to the office.

"Put the collar back on him, would you? I need something to hang on to."

As Dahlgren shoved his way into the black neoprene, he cursed the tightness of the garment, and McAfee helped him smooth the arms and legs and then closed the zippers. He had the rebreather and helmet on in another moment, nudging and dragging Nemo to the edge of the dock. As he held out his feet, one at a time, McAfee slipped the straps of his fins over his heels and was about to drop into the water and pull Nemo with him when Matheson rushed out of the office and shoved the Russian underwater pistol into the thigh pocket of his suit.

"No," Dahlgren said.

"The bastard may be under there waiting," she said.

"Take it," McAfee agreed. "You may have to put Nemo down, and you don't want to do it with your dive knife."

Dahlgren slid into the water, then pulled Nemo after him while the others pushed.

"This is Cal. Can you hear me?"

Dahlgren purged the air from the BC, grasped Nemo, and the dock receded from view. As the numbers in the heads-down display increased much more slowly than expected, Dahlgren realized that this rig was set to metric.

"Yeah, I've got you," Dahlgren said. "Give me your best guess on deco for a sea lion."

"Think he's saturated?"

"Maybe."

"Take him down to a hundred feet and see if there's any response."

As he passed the shallow platform, Dahlgren worked his jaw to clear his ears.

At thirty-five meters, Nemo was still hunched in pain.

"He's still bent," Dahlgren said. "I'm going deeper."

"We'll switch the floods on in Mineral City for you," Cal said.

Dahlgren had to kick to swim over to the edge of the wall, and while Nemo hadn't resisted free fall with Dahlgren, the sea lion did not like to be tugged. While Dahlgren pulled on his collar, Nemo twisted, causing Dahlgren to corkscrew with him, then nipped him on the hand, tearing the neoprene and drawing blood.

Then they were over, and falling again.

"I think he's coming around," Dahlgren said.

"Yeah?"

"He just bit me."

"Bad?"

"Would have been without gloves."

At two hundred feet, just before touching down in the middle of Mineral City, Nemo was suddenly flexible again. He began to swim deeper, taking Dahlgren with him.

"Okay, gang," Dahlgren said. "What now? Nemo's unbent, but he wants to go deeper."

"Come up," McAfee said. "Let him go."

"Yeah, but."

"But what?" McAfee said. "I'm calling it. Come up."

The sea lion had tugged Dahlgren into the shaft, and they were sinking rapidly.

"No," Dahlgren said.

"Richard, can you hear me?"

"Yes."

"Richard?"

They couldn't hear him, but the dock's signal was strong enough to bounce down the sides of the shaft.

"Where is he?" he could hear Matheson ask.

"Dammit, I don't know," McAfee said, and there was the bang of a fist on the console. "I had him at seventy meters, but now his signal's blocked."

"He went deeper," Matheson said.

"Yeah, probably down the shaft," McAfee said. "He should have let Nemo go. Does he really think the life of one sea lion is worth risking his own?"

"No," Matheson said slowly. "He thinks the life of one twenty-three-year-old girl is."

Then the dock's signal faded.

At a hundred meters, the sea lion was still heading down the shaft, with Dahlgren free-falling behind. The numbers in the heads-down display remained green, so Dahlgren continued. The lights on his helmet and at his wrist cut through the blackness to reveal only yard after yard of chiseled rock, punctuated occasionally by a drift or an ore dump.

Nemo seemed to be headed all the way to the bottom of the shaft, but before they reached the sump the sea lion turned sharply and swam up a slanting ore chute.

Dahlgren hovered outside the entrance to the chute.

In the shaft, he knew where he was. He could find his way back to safety simply by following the shaft straight up. But the chute presented a lethal trap. There were no guidelines to follow into the chute. And Dahlgren was alone, without so much as a jump reel. He had already been down for twenty minutes, and at a hundred and twenty meters, he was accumulating a heavy decompression penalty.

To top things off, he had a headache.

But then he remembered Jolene. What if she were trapped inside an air bell just inside the chute? How could he forgive himself if only a few yards of rock separated them?

But how would he get her out if he found her? Her blood would be saturated with nitrogen after this much time at depth. Even if he could bring her up, the inert gas in her bloodstream would tear her apart. She would certainly die.

A quick look couldn't hurt, he decided. He would keep the mouth of the chute within range of his lights, and turn back before he became disoriented.

Dahlgren swam into the chute.

By the time he noticed the capnic color indicator winking from blue to red, his head hurt so badly that he had a difficult time recalling exactly what it meant. His vision had narrowed so that he felt as if he were looking in the wrong end of a telescope. In a corner of his mind, he knew he had become suddenly and dramatically stupid, and he knew that it was because his rig had gone hypercapnic for some reason. His body was retaining too much carbon dioxide, which upset the delicate blood–gas balance and caused what McAfee would call an "atypical intolerance" to the oxygen partial pressure the rig was delivering. To keep from succumbing to oxygen toxicity, he needed to manually reduce the oxygen set point, but the mental fog had so engulfed him that he didn't care.

A few moments after his face began twitching, he convulsed.

His body jerked and writhed, but he did not drown because there was no regulator to spit out. Instead, the rig kept delivering gas to his helmet at an oxygen partial pressure that under normal circumstances would be appropriate. Finally, his body calmed. As he drifted motionless in the void, his lights touching nothing, she came to him.

She was as beautiful as he had remembered, with flowing black hair and luminous green skin, and a smile that radiated comfort. Dahlgren was surprised that Taylor was not with her. He had expected to see her as she had been, blond and capable yet vulnerable, waiting for him at the end of a tunnel or, perhaps, on the other side of a pool of silver water. She would have been eager to report on what she had experienced since they had parted, what the customs and folklore of this new place were, to brief him on what he could expect on this final plunge into the unknown. He was sad she wasn't there.

Dahlgren asked where Taylor was.

Flown was the reply. *Long ago.*

The goddess beckoned him forward, as she had done so many years before beneath a different stone. Dahlgren followed, reluctant, protesting that he would rather wait for Taylor, but the goddess shook her head. How deep were they? The numbers in the heads-down display made no sense.

Dahlgren kicked forward.

There was nothing in his vision except the goddess, and it seemed as if he were chasing her through empty space. A ribbon of something black was oozing from a tear in the back of his right glove, but when he brought his hand close to the helmet lights, the ribbon turned to crimson.

Come, the goddess commanded.

Dahlgren lazily followed the apparition, sensing that it really did not matter, that it was just something created by chemicals released by his dying brain. Where was Taylor's body? he wondered. He had had her by the collar of her wet suit just a moment earlier. *Two can't make it,* she had said. *But one can.* One. Just One. Life enough for One. Taylor had also written something on her wrist slate. What was it? Something they had talked about many times, but Dahlgren could not remember what.

The goddess stopped and pointed upward.

The line? Where's the guideline?

Good-bye, the goddess told him. *You won't see me again.*

Dahlgren laughed.

Somebody was babbling in French inside his helmet.

The goddess faded, leaving only darkness behind.

Dahlgren shook his head and kicked in the direction the goddess had indicated, and he wasn't surprised to find that he was leaving the clean-cut sides of the mine for a natural cave passage.

"*Mon Dieu,*" the voice in his head pleaded. "*S'il vous plaît, non.*"

Dahlgren came to floating beneath a silver pool.

His head still ached, his hand hurt, and he was cold, but his mind was clearing. The cap color on the rig had gone back to blue, the oxygen set point was 1.3, and the depth readout was at 127 meters. That couldn't be right, he thought, because McAfee had told him the deepest part of the mine, the sump at the bottom of Number One Shaft, was four hundred feet, or about one hundred twenty meters, the deepest any lead had been found at Bonne Terre.

But Dahlgren knew he was floating beneath an air bell, and

that there was a light source above. It had to be *the* air bell. He switched off his helmet and wrist lights and ascended slowly, and the closer he came to the surface, the bigger he realized the pool was. He slowly swam over to the side, where the stone made a natural set of steps leading upward, and he slowly raised his head until his eyes were above the surface of the water.

Jolene Carter knelt blindfolded on the floor of the chamber, her wrists bound with leather in front of her, and she was shivering and wearing nothing but a scrap of white silk over her shoulders.

A figure that Dahlgren recognized as Geiger from the photographs stood over her in his red dry suit. He was holding a wooden bowl in his hands, and around him were some of the things he intended to use later: scalpels, tubing, a hand-operated bilge pump normally used by kayakers, five quart bottles of a clear fluid with a bluish tinge.

Geiger was offering the wooden bowl.

Jolene was clearly refusing to drink.

Dahlgren could not hear their conversation, but he could see their lips moving. Then he raised his head a little higher from the water, and their voices came to him as weird chirps and squeals, and he knew they were breathing heliox. How in the world did the bastard manage that? Then Dahlgren saw the cylinders and the scrubbers behind them, the big fans on the scrubbers turning slowly. They were both wearing descramblers.

Dahlgren found the VOX channel selector on the wrist-mounted keypad and scrolled through the frequencies until he found their voices.

"This is essential," Geiger said. "You must drink."

Geiger was standing a little unsteadily, favoring his right leg, and he was growing impatient. It was apparent that they had struggled, because the undersides of Jolene's forearms were marked with defensive abrasions, there was a deep bruise

349

on her thigh, and Geiger's face was deeply scratched. It had ended, Dahlgren realized, only when Geiger had placed the blade of a knife to her throat, because blood dribbled from a diagonal line beneath her jaw.

Geiger pressed the bowl to her lips.

"I forgive you," Jolene said.

She sipped.

"All of it," he urged. "You must drink all of it, and then tell me what you see."

Now what? Dahlgren asked himself as he removed his fins.

First, pop a fluorescent dye pack to mark the location. He took one from his harness pouch, opened it, and let it fall into the water below.

Second, "Stop it," he said, striding out of the water.

Geiger looked genuinely shocked.

"Who's there?" Jolene asked.

"You're too late," Geiger said.

Dahlgren tugged the glove from his right hand by clenching the fingers between his teeth and pulling. Then he unsheathed the dive knife from the holster on the rebreather's left harness strap, revealing a four-inch blade with a blunt tip.

Geiger laughed.

With his left hand, he drew his red-handled knife with the nine-inch blade from the plastic scabbard on his thigh.

Dahlgren dropped his knife.

"Wise move," Geiger said.

Then Dahlgren brought the underwater pistol out of his thigh pocket and pointed it at Geiger. But the cold had gotten to him; he had been in the water too long for just a wet suit, and his teeth were chattering and the barrel of the gun quivered.

Geiger smiled.

Dahlgren cocked the hammer.

"You're not going to shoot me," he said.

Jolene knocked the bowl from Geiger's right hand.

"Shoot him," she screamed.

Geiger slapped her with the back of his right hand, knocking her backward.

"He can't fire a gun in here," Geiger said. "We're at—"

Dahlgren pulled the trigger.

The steel dart lashed out, missed Geiger, but sliced into one of the battery packs, glanced off the chamber wall, ricocheted off the domed ceiling, and struck the water behind Dahlgren.

The battery pack was shorted, and the lights began to strobe.

"Impressive," Geiger said. "Loud, but impressive."

Jolene had her hands clasped over her ears.

"Drop the knife," Dahlgren said.

"You can hear me," Geiger said. "Oh yes, a VOX unit."

"Drop it."

Geiger lowered the knife.

"Who are you?" Geiger asked. "Wait, don't tell me. I've seen your face on the news. You're Dahlgren, aren't you? Yes, that's your name. I know your story, Mr. Dahlgren. What a shame about your girlfriend in that cave in Mexico. What was her name? Taylor something. Taylor Christian?"

"Chastain," Dahlgren said.

"Of course," Geiger said. "That misadventure certainly got a lot of press, didn't it?"

"Shut up," Dahlgren said.

"Touch a nerve, did we?"

Geiger was standing very still, but the barrel of Dahlgren's gun was quivering.

"Drop the knife," Dahlgren said.

"*Kill* him," Jolene said. "What are you waiting for? Do you think this is a fucking movie? You have to have a *conversation* first, maybe ask if he's feeling lucky? For Christ's sake, just shoot the motherfucker."

"Really, there's no need for profanity," Geiger said.

351

Holding the pistol in both hands, Dahlgren took three steps forward to make sure he wouldn't miss this time.

The knife hung limply from Geiger's fingers.

"You're not feeling well, are you?" Geiger asked. "A central nervous system problem? Oxygen toxicity, perhaps? At this depth, a touch of HPNS wouldn't be out of the question. And, of course, you're freezing to death. Really, you should have thought to bring a dry suit."

The lights flickered, then went off.

Dahlgren braced himself for an assault, but there was none.

"She belongs to me," Geiger said.

Because the voice was coming from his earpiece, he had no sense of where Geiger was.

But Geiger had located Jolene.

When the lights winked on again, he was holding Jolene in front of him, his left hand clasped over her mouth, his right hand holding the knife to the side of her neck.

Her eyes were wide with fear.

Dahlgren cocked the gun.

"Let her go," he said.

"If I do, how are you going to get her to the surface without killing her?" Geiger asked. "Her blood is saturated with nitrogen. It would take days to decompress her."

"Let me worry about that," Dahlgren said.

"Worry?" Geiger said.

He lowered the knife from Jolene's throat and shrugged.

"She's already dead," Geiger said.

He plunged the knife into her side, then tossed her like a doll into the water. Geiger held his palms upward, the bloody knife dangling from his right hand.

"It is done," he said.

Dahlgren fired, but missed again. The steel dart whizzed around the interior of the chamber, sparking from the walls, reducing its velocity, then thudded to a stop in Geiger's chest. Geiger looked down, incredulous at the steel shaft poking from his sternum, then slumped to the floor.

Dropping the gun, Dahlgren dove into the water.

Jolene was sinking quickly beside a column of fluorescent green dye, and Dahlgren kicked hard with his feet to catch her. Then he scooped her up, inflated the BC, and rose back to the surface of the air bell.

She sputtered and coughed and grasped her bleeding side.

Then she noticed Geiger's body.

"Is he dead?" she wheezed.

But she had lost the descrambler and Dahlgren couldn't understand her question. Jolene was fighting for breath, her face was turning blue, and there was an odd crackling noise coming from her wound. Dahlgren placed his hand over the wound in her side in an attempt to staunch the flow of blood, then she collapsed against him.

"Please, God," Dahlgren said, and it came out as more an argument than a prayer. "Help me. And if you won't help me, then help this girl. What has she done to deserve this? At least Taylor knew the risks. What did this girl know?"

The water, stained green from the dye pack, began to glow.

"What now?" Dahlgren asked.

The emerald water boiled.

The *Water Baby* surfaced, flooding the chamber with light.

"*Ou est-ce?*" Rael Janot asked.

Dahlgren saw the amazed pilot staring up into the chamber from the acrylic observation dome, just beneath the water.

"Help me," Dahlgren said, hugging the injured girl. "She's hurt. She's bleeding."

"*Elle saigne?*"

"Yes," Dahlgren said, struggling to recall his junior-high-school French. "*Tres mal?*"

Dahlgren kept his palm pressed against the wound in Jolene's side as Rael Janot cracked a valve and equalized the pressure inside the submersible as quickly as he dared. Through the observation dome, he saw Janot pinching his nose and clearing his ears repeatedly as he took the equivalent of a four-hundred-foot plunge in just a few minutes. Finally, the hatch inside the sail swung open and Janot pulled himself out of the twenty-four-inch opening. He was shaking his head and tugging at one of his ears as he climbed down the hull and slid into the water. He was holding the submersible's first-aid kit high above his head.

"Great," Dahlgren said, then ditched his rebreather.

Janot opened the kit and handed Dahlgren several large gauze pads. Dahlgren pressed them against the stab wound, then taped the dressings in place. It didn't stop the flow of blood, but it slowed it.

Dahlgren nodded.

They waded into the water with Jolene between them, then Janot motioned with a nod of his head for Dahlgren to get aboard first.

Dahlgren clambered up the work basket and utility bar that held the sub's manipulator arm, then positioned himself inside the sail, over the hatch, as Janot followed, holding Jolene against him.

Once Janot had made it up into the sail with Jolene, Dahlgren lowered himself down into the submersible through the open hatch. Then he reached up, grasped Jolene by the thighs, and eased her down as Janot grasped her arms.

The submersible began to jostle, as if Janot were moving around on top, and Jolene suddenly dropped into Dahlgren's arms, followed by a splatter of blood.

"Easy," Dahlgren said, lowering Jolene to the cramped deck.

Then, through the dome, he saw the red leg of a dry suit atop the utility bar, followed by a loop of Janot's intestines. The rest of his body followed, and his throat had been slashed so deeply that his head was barely attached.

Dahlgren swung the hatch shut just as Geiger was reaching for it, then quickly dogged it. He slid past Jolene into the pilot's seat, grabbed the joystick, and pushed it down. The thrusters responded, banging the submersible against the edge of the chamber, damaging the manipulator arm.

"Shit," Dahlgren said.

He took a breath and looked over the controls, then found a control marked BALLAST that resembled the throttle of an aircraft. He pushed it forward slightly, and he could hear water being blown out of the saddle tanks by compressed air, and the sub rose higher in the water. Then he pulled the control back, and the submersible sank like a stone.

When he had the submersible at neutral buoyancy, he carried Jolene to the passenger seat and strapped her in. Then he nudged the joystick and turned the submersible slowly on its axis.

"Okay, which way?" he said to himself as the lights illuminated the craggy walls of the canyonlike passage. Should he follow the passage to the right or left? *Think,* he told himself. On the console, he saw the sub's compass moving through the degrees as the sub rotated. He knew that he had gone to the northeast after chasing Nemo into the ore chute, so when the compass read SW, he pushed the stick gently forward.

He guided the submersible through the twisting passage, clumsily scraping walls and dislodging boulders. He squeezed the craft into the old drift that led to the mine. He shattered part of the fiberglass fender rail on the port side as he passed the iron doors, then in a few hundred yards of narrow drift entered a large pillared room. From here, he told himself, he had to find the drift or the chute on the other side and just follow it down. Hadn't McAfee said that everything eventually led back at a downward angle to the main shaft?

Then he saw Geiger's hand on top of the utility bar.

Geiger was pulling himself to the front of the submersible. He was wearing the helmet and rebreather that Dahlgren had ditched, and in one hand he held the underwater pistol. The steel dart was still sticking from the center of his chest, and he must have been close to freezing to death, but behind the faceplate Geiger was grinning.

"Sonuvabitch," Dahlgren said.

He reached for the smaller joystick that said ARM and attempted to use the manipulator arm to brush Geiger off, but the arm wouldn't move. It had been disabled at Dahlgren's first attempt to pilot the sub out of the Moon Pool.

Dahlgren saw the ore chute on the other side of the room and pushed the joystick forward. The submersible began to pick up speed.

Geiger climbed down the acrylic dome and planted his feet in the work basket, his deflated dry suit wrinkling and flapping around his limbs. The submersible had nearly reached the mouth of the ore dump when, struggling against the water pressing around him, Geiger managed to cock the underwater pistol and press the muzzle against the acrylic.

Dahlgren jerked the joystick hard to starboard, ramming the submersible into the wall just inside the chute at a velocity of four and a half knots.

Dahlgren was thrown forward against the dome, which was protected from the impact only by the work basket and utility bars. Warning lights began blinking all over the console: leaks in the battery pods, propeller shaft, and machinery section, and a hydrogen gas warning.

Half the sub's exterior lights exploded with impact, sparks flew as the starboard thrusters were crushed, and gas began streaming from the oxygen tanks on that side.

Geiger flew backward, the pistol wrenched from his hand.

The pistol twirled in the water, then came down hard on its firing pin against the dome, its muzzle pointing forward. There were a flash and a thud, and in a fraction of a second the supercavitating dart had punched a perfect half-inch hole into the faceplate. Blood wreathed Geiger's head. The dart had struck him below the left cheekbone, exited the back of his head, and buried itself into the rock behind.

Geiger's body receded into the darkness as the submersible

tumbled down the chute. Jolene was strapped into her seat, and her head swung limply as the *Water Baby* rolled, but Dahlgren found himself slamming around the cabin.

Finally, the submersible stabilized at a forty-five-degree-angle level but continued to slide down the steep chute. Dahlgren fought his way back to the pilot seat. He tried the joystick, but the submersible spun crazily with only half of its thrusters still operating. Then he tried the ballast control and blew air out of the tanks to slow their fall.

When the submersible finally exited the chute, along with an avalanche of rock and muck that it had dislodged, it was descending at only a foot or so per minute. The ballast control, however, was no longer working. The compressed air gauges read zero, and Dahlgren knew there must have been a leak caused by the crash.

The *Water Baby* drifted slowly down the main shaft and eventually came to rest, upright, at the bottom of the sump. The cloud of muck that resulted from the touch-down reduced visibility to zero.

The remaining exterior lights died.

It was suddenly very quiet, and Dahlgren thought the absence of sound was worse than the cacophony that had preceded it. Then he heard the soft hiss of the flowmeter as it began adding pure oxygen to the cabin.

Dahlgren's right eye began twitching.

He shut down the flowmeter, then checked the digital O_2 readout on the computer monitor: 15 percent. But that would be calculated for one atmosphere, wouldn't it? Dahlgren rubbed his temple, then looked at the depth readout on the console: present depth beneath the keel was 120 M / 394 F. The interior of the cabin, however, had been pressured at nearly their maximum depth of 127 M / 417 F.

Using 400 feet as a nice round number, Dahlgren tried to calculate in his mind how many atmospheres of pressure they

357

were under. One atmosphere for every 33 feet, he told himself, then add 1.0 for the surface pressure. That worked out to about 13. Thirteen times greater than the surface.

Then, to figure the partial pressure of the oxygen, you multiply the percentage by the atmospheres absolute and round it off. Thirteen times 15—that had to be closing in on 2 ATA.

"Crap," Dahlgren croaked.

Oxygen partial pressures of greater than 2 ATA could be tolerated only for a few minutes without risking death. With her chest wound, Jolene was in particular danger.

He sat on the deck, trying not to move, waiting for him and Jolene to breathe down the oxygen to a safer level. When he was still conscious after twenty minutes, and the O_2 readout was 13 percent, he dared some activity: He tried the subphone, but it was dead. He tried to guess how long their life support would last. Under normal circumstances, he knew that two people could last in the cabin for several days, maybe a week. But the electrical system was dying, the scrubbers probably wouldn't work at this pressure, and they had no contact with the surface.

Then he opened the three-ring binder containing the submersible's manual and, in the dim glow of the cabin light, began flipping pages. Finally, he found the section he was looking for, under Section 6, emergency procedures, paragraph 3: Drop Ballast.

With the one-inch wrench he found beneath the pilot's seat, where the manual said it would be stowed, Dahlgren turned the head of the bolt that came up through the bottom of the pressure hull and into the cabin. It had been difficult to get started, but after thirty or forty revolutions, Dahlgren was convinced nothing was happening. Then the five hundred pounds of cast iron beneath the submersible dropped free. The *Water Baby* fought against the suction of the bottom for a moment, then began to rise.

Now comes the interesting part, Dahlgren thought sleepily as the submersible drifted up the shaft and he listened to the vessel creak and groan. *At what depth do we explode from the interior pressurization?*

Thirty-five

Matheson sat at the command console, chin in her hands, staring at the UCT clock: 03:57. McAfee was at the sub-phone, trying to contact the submersible for the second time in the last five minutes.

He listened carefully to the headset, then shook his head.

"Christ," Matheson said. "You think he's dead?"

"I don't know," McAfee said.

Matheson looked over at the sea lion, which had returned to the dock an hour after Dahlgren had taken him down. Nemo looked away, and Matheson imagined there was guilt in his eyes.

Cal, who was standing behind Matheson, put a hand on her shoulder. He was about to say something when the water in the middle of the cavern, over the main shaft, began to boil.

The *Water Baby* breached the surface like a whale, then bobbed like a cork on the surface, listing twenty degrees to port, sparks still dripping from the damaged starboard side.

"My God," Matheson said, reaching out for Cal's arm. "What's happened?"

McAfee tried the subphone again.

"The VHF," Cal said.

McAfee picked up the handheld from the top of the console.

"*Water Baby*, do you copy?" he asked.

After a moment, a high-pitched squawk responded.

"Helium," Cal said.

"In the sub?" McAfee asked.

"Somehow, yes," Cal said. "Can you feed the VHF through the descrambler?"

McAfee thought for a moment.

"Yeah," he said, then rummaged beneath the console for a patch cord. Finding the one he was looking for, he fed the earphone signal into the descrambler input, then adjusted the processed signal until the speech could be understood.

"—copy on the dock?"

McAfee keyed the mike three times.

"Why don't you talk?"

"It doesn't work the other way," McAfee said.

"I'll take that for a yes. Don't open our hatch. Repeat, do not open hatch. Pressurized at four hundred feet. This is Dahlgren, with Jolene Carter. In need of medical attention. Stabbed. Collapsed lung, I think. Oh, Geiger's dead. So is Janot. Geiger gutted him like a fish."

"Get them out," Matheson said impatiently.

"We can't," McAfee said. "It would kill them."

"He sounds drunk."

"He probably is," Cal said. "God knows what kind of mix he's breathing."

"Do they have enough oxygen?"

"That isn't the problem now," Cal said. "The problem is having too much oxygen."

"I can't believe the sub is holding together," McAfee said.

361

"So how the hell do we get them out?" Matheson asked.

"I don't know," McAfee said. "I guess we could somehow bleed down the pressure slowly, if we knew which fitting to crack and if we could get to it."

Cal shook his head.

"But the girl would be at saturation level," McAfee continued. "It'll take days to decompress her. We don't know what kind of gas the submersible has left, or even whether it will hold together. Right now, it's just a bomb waiting to explode. What we need is a recompression chamber, but there aren't any big enough to put an entire submersible in."

"There's at least one," Cal said.

Dahlgren woke just as the CH-54 Skycrane was lifting off from above the shaft. It had squatted, insectlike, over the hole the National Guard had blown in the top of the shaft, and had winched the *Water Baby* tight up against its thorax. After the damaged submersible had been strapped in place, a cordon of soldiers had held the television crews and the inhabitants of the tent city back while the helicopter took flight.

The sun had just risen over the horizon, bathing the snow-covered ground and the tent city and the upturned faces in warm orange light. Through the acrylic dome, Dahlgren saw Bonne Terre stretching beneath him to the west, and the woods and fields and mountains beyond. Then the helicopter swung around, and it seemed to Dahlgren as if they were flying into the sun, with the Missouri landscape rolling forever below.

Thirty-six

Jack Conrad sat alone at the end of the conference table in
room 205, waiting and thinking. An hour before, he'd been
flying a civilian security patrol in his Cessna 172 over Tyndall
Air Base when his beeper went off. When he called the duty
officer, he had heard an unbelievable story about a submersible with an interior pressure of four hundred feet that
was on its way by Skycrane to the parking lot outside the Experimental Dive Unit's Ocean Simulation Facility.

The CO wanted a save, the duty officer had said.

And as the NEDU's scientific director, that save—or, alter-
natively, the spectacular ball-busting failure for all involved—
was up to Conrad.

But as he sat in the conference room, waiting for the briefing at eleven hundred, Conrad pondered all of the things that
could go wrong, and he could think of nothing that could go
right. It was a scenario that promised failure.

The Skycrane would have to refuel at least a couple of
times before reaching Panama City, and if it managed to reach

the NEDU without crashing or otherwise creating an embarrassing moment, then it was up to Conrad to get the sub into the OSF and decompress its occupants as rapidly as possible.

Luckily, it was Christmas week and there was no testing going on at the OSF, so the pod was empty. But there would be personnel to call in to operate the ocean pod, at least seven for each eight-hour watch, which meant a staff of twenty-one, not counting medical and science staff.

There would be bitching.

And he had never heard of the submersible *Water Baby*. His people were trying to track down her designer, Sam Halliday, to get some plans. Conrad didn't understand why the sub hadn't just exploded by now. And if the interior of the sub had really been pressurized at four hundred feet during some kind of accident, then the occupants should be dead, with blood drying beneath their ruptured ears.

Conrad was certain they would find corpses after they got the sub into the OSF and pressed it down. Perhaps the others, he thought, could distance themselves in some way from the stench of failure. Then, when his career was over, perhaps he could pursue the new research he'd been thinking about doing for some time: to conduct interviews with divers who reported unusual experiences during near-fatal events.

A man in his early sixties, wearing jeans and tennis shoes, switched on the light to the conference room and allowed a woman in a blue business suit to enter first. Each wore two visitor badges, one for the naval base and another for the NEDU. For a moment, he didn't recognize the man. Then Conrad stood and held out his hand.

"Calvin, how are you?"

"Doc," Cal said, "I've seen better holidays."

Cal introduced her to Matheson.

"How'd you get mixed up in this?"

"Too much time on my hands after I retired."

"How'd you get here so quickly?" Conrad asked.

"Bureau jet," Matheson said.

"This is the guy who tried to bend me for all those years," Cal said. "He nearly succeeded a couple of times."

The woman nodded. Her eyes were red, and she looked tired.

Others began to drift into the room: the NEDU diving officer, the scientist in charge of decompression algorithm modeling, the executive officer.

Then came Lieutenant Lorca, a bright-eyed Hispanic medical officer fresh out of dive school. Wearing a freshly pressed uniform, he entered the room a little too tentatively and was nearly bowled over by Lieutenant Roosevelt, another junior medical dive officer. Roosevelt was wearing sweats, looked like a prizefighter, and talked like the corpsman from Jersey that he was before going to medical school.

"Sorry, Lorca," Roosevelt said. "Didn't seeya there."

Then Commander Nathaniel Raphael Semmes entered the room.

Semmes was in his mid-forties, seemed in perfect health, and had a military bearing that seemed to Matheson to be somehow *angular*. Rafe Semmes had been in charge of the dive and salvage teams that had recovered the bodies from the interior of the bombed USS *Cole* and kept it from sinking, so Matheson knew he was willing to gamble on an acceptable risk; had the ship sunk, it would have severed the umbilicals and taken his divers with it. Also, Cal had told her, he was a descendant of the captain of the legendary Confederate raider *Alabama*. Matheson recognized the irony, considering Dahlgren's family tree.

Semmes took a seat at the head of the table, leaned back slightly, and looked around the room, his eyes scanning each face. He gave a nod to Cal, then looked expectantly at Matheson.

"FBI?" Semmes asked.

"Yes," Matheson said.

Semmes nodded.

"Here it is," Semmes said with more than a hint of southern accent. "Our boss, the Director of Ocean Engineering at Naval Seas Systems Command in Washington, has directed me to render assistance to the occupants of a crippled submersible, ETA fourteen hundred hours. I understand this is related to the Missouri FBI case you've seen on the news, but please restrict your questions to those that have a direct bearing on solving our problem. Agent?"

"Thanks," Matheson said.

"Number of occupants?" Lorca asked.

"Two," Matheson said. "A thirty-eight-year-old male and a twenty-three-year-old female. The girl has a stab wound to her side."

"What about the condition of the sub?" Roosevelt broke in. Matheson looked at Cal.

"It's damaged, but there's some electrical power left, enough to keep the cabin warm en route," Cal said. "Scrubbers are nonoperative, and the interior is pressurized to 13.1 atmospheres."

"They're dead," Roosevelt said.

"No, they're breathing some type of heliox mixture," Cal said. "Don't know the exact mix, but they're still alive, so the oxygen partial pressure has to be less than 1.6."

"Conscious?"

"Semiconscious," Cal said.

"Damn," Roosevelt said. "How'd the girl get a stab wound? No, never mind. What else can you tell us about their health?"

"The male is a cave diver and was in good health before the incident," Cal said. "He has been at four hundred feet since about eight o'clock last night. We think the girl is saturated and probably suffering from exposure as well. Her wound has been dressed, but she's lost blood, and she's been in the water as well."

"After the stab wound?" Lorca asked.

"Terrific," Roosevelt mumbled.

"Sorry we couldn't bring you healthier problems," Matheson said.

"Don't mind the lieutenant here," Semmes said. "Like all Yankees, he drinks unsweetened tea and is lacking in manners. Agent, I promise you we will do what is best."

Then he turned to Conrad. "Jack, your thoughts?"

"We don't know much about the submersible," he said. "My primary concern is getting this dirty sub in the OSF and pressing it down without injuring any of our people. We don't know the likelihood of a failure of the pressure hull or even a fitting, and until we get the sub down, the results could be catastrophic."

"Assuming a safe recompression," Semmes prompted. "Can we decompress the occupants?"

"Perhaps," Conrad said. "If they haven't suffocated or frozen to death during the flight."

"How long to bring them up?"

"With accelerated decompression? Ballpark, three days."

Then the commander turned to the junior medical officers.

"Gentlemen," he said, "your superiors are unavailable. Captain Summerstone is with the SEALs on Coronado Island in San Diego, and Commander Lane is on a submarine somewhere in the Caribbean. I must, therefore, rely on the likes of you."

"Thank you, sir," Lieutenant Lorca said.

Roosevelt knew it wasn't a compliment.

"Can we save the girl?" Semmes asked.

Lorca said "yes" while Roosevelt said "no."

"First," Semmes said. "Tell me why we can't."

"Sir," Roosevelt said. "Surgery has never been performed at anything approaching four hundred feet. Under ordinary circumstances, a patient with a collapsed lung would be put on a ventilator and given general anesthesia. But general at this depth is out of the question, and no ventilator I know of will operate in air that thick."

"Your turn, Lieutenant Lorca."

"He's right, sir, but I think there are ways around these problems," Lorca said. "If the girl has a collapsed lung from a side wound, and assuming no other organs are involved, the repair procedure is fairly simple. We can get her into one of the upper pods, bag her by hand, then tube her and reinflate the lung. Then we give her a massive dose of antibiotics and hope for the best."

"Anesthesia?" Roosevelt asked.

"We could use a local."

"Not good enough," Roosevelt said. "This girl needs to be knocked out. Semiconscious won't do."

"Then we lock her out in Delta or Bravo and narc her out on the nitrogen in air," Lorca said. "At thirteen atmospheres, that's a pretty good general."

"And you're going to operate narced as well?"

"It could be done," Lorca said.

"But it couldn't be called surgery," Roosevelt said. He stretched, flexed his biceps, and turned his neck until it popped. Matheson was staring at how large his hands were. "But you could use the BIBS mask."

"Right," Lorca said. "We could be breathing heliox while we operated, and she would be narced on air."

Both were quiet.

A sailor slipped into the room and handed Semmes a note. He read it, then put it aside.

"What's a BIBS mask?" Matheson asked.

"An emergency breathing apparatus," Conrad said.

"What's Delta and Bravo?"

"The Ocean Simulation Facility is a three-story complex," Conrad said. "There's a fifty-five-thousand-gallon wet chamber on the bottom and five interconnected dry chambers on top, Alpha through Echo, that can be entered and exited from outside. One of the outer chambers, and the center chamber, would be used as airlocks."

Semmes cleared his throat.

"Jack," he said, "I've got a message from that Halliday character who designed the sub. Says it could withstand a certain amount of interior pressurization, but is unsure about thirteen atmospheres. There's a number for you to call for data on probability failure."

Semmes turned back to the medical officers and crossed his arms.

"So you're suggesting that I let you both climb inside the OSF and do meatball surgery?" he asked. "No, experimental surgery. Something that's never been tried before?"

"Not me, sir," Roosevelt said. "I've just completed my turn as a subject in one of Dr. Conrad's heat stress and DCI studies in the manned testing pool. I can't dive. Lorca would have to perform the surgery, with me helping from outside."

Roosevelt looked questioningly at Lorca.

Lorca nodded.

"Sir," Roosevelt said. "I think it is possible."

"Possible encompasses a great deal of water," Semmes said. "Give me better coordinates. What is the chance that you and your friend won't kill this girl?"

"Fair," Roosevelt said.

"And her chance of survival with decompression alone?"

"She's hypothermic, has a collapsed lung, and has been in the water," Lorca said. "Complications will kill her before we can get her out of the OSF."

Two hours later, the Skycrane landed in the parking lot during a gentle winter rain that was whipped into a hurricane by the helicopter's rotors. After the *Water Baby* had been placed in a cradle and rolled into the wet chamber, the warrant officer in charge of diving operations attempted to peer into the clouded acrylic observation dome.

"What can you see?" Conrad asked from the deck.

"Nothing," the warrant officer said. "Too much sweat. Anything on the VHF?"

"Not a word," Conrad said.

Then the warrant officer scrambled out, and the big dome-shaped door was swung into place and locked. The operators in the control room on the second floor began increasing the pressure in the wet pod—and above, in the dry chamber, where the diving officer and a couple of sailors with blankets waited.

When the OSF had reached 420 feet salt water on heliox, the warrant went down the ladder, through the trunk that separated the wet and dry chambers, and dropped the few feet onto the deck of the submersible. He took a hammer from his belt and rapped on the hatch of the submersible.

There was no response.

"Let's hope this doesn't splatter my nuts against the wall," he muttered into his headset as he knelt down, faced away, and turned the wheel to undog to the hatch. But when he tried to open it, the hatch still felt as solid as if it were locked.

"Thank God we weren't too shallow," he said. "Up, just a touch."

The hatch whistled briefly.

The warrant swung it open and dropped down into the submersible, muttering and cussing under his breath. In a moment he was handing up Jolene Carter, bloody and unconscious, and the sailors wrapped her in a blanket and handed her up. She was barely breathing, and when she did, there was a peculiar rattling sound.

"There's another one down here."

"Alive?" Conrad asked.

"Yeah, but he don't know where he is," the warrant said. "Dumb bastard just asked me for a smoke."

Lorca took a breath from the BIBS mask, held it, then used the laryngoscope to peer down Jolene's throat and attempt to spread her vocal cords with a Miller blade. If he couldn't get the endotrachial tube past her larynx by the time he was out of breath, it was time to start over, because she would certainly be out of breath by then.

"So far, so good," Lorca said as he exhaled.

He withdrew the pilot hose and the female corpsman attached an AMBU bag and began squeezing. Lorca slipped the BIBS mask back over his head and replaced the headset.

"We can't use O_2, so let's try for twenty breaths a minute," Lorca said. He glanced over at the DinaMap machine pulse-ox readout, which registered the saturation of hemoglobin as determined by the infrared probe clipped to the tip of Jolene's finger. It was 91 percent. Low, but acceptable. Her blood pressure was stable, her pulse was steady, but her cardiac trace was becoming erratic.

"What's wrong with her trace?" Roosevelt asked. He was on the medical deck on the third floor, peering at the DinaMap machine through a television monitor.

"Ventricular irritability," Lorca said.

"Hit her with some lydocaine."

"Hit her with anything and it's liable to kill her."

"If you don't, she might go into arrest while you've got a tube in her chest," Roosevelt said.

"Okay," Lorca said. "Four-mcg drip."

Jolene lay on the cot in Bravo chamber, a rolled towel beneath her back, her eyes sunken. The corpsman turned, mixed an IV bag, and started the drip into the heparin lock already on top of Jolene's wrist.

Lorca put his stethoscope next to the knife wound and listened.

"Any sucking?"

"No," Lorca said. "But it sounds weird."

"Air density," Roosevelt said. "Just tube her."

Lorca took the pencil-sized needle from the chest kit, began to insert it between the fifth and sixth ribs, then paused.

"What's wrong?"

"My hands are shaking," Lorca said.

"Relax," Roosevelt said. "Even you can't screw this up, unless you wait too long."

Lorca closed his eyes.

"You're waiting too long."

"Give me a minute."

"Take off your mask."

"What?"

"The heliox is making you jittery," Roosevelt said. "Take a gulp of nitrogen to calm your nerves. Instant courage."

Lorca hesitated.

"Just do it."

He removed the mask and filled his lungs.

Lorca slipped the tube between Jolene's ribs. He pulled the needle out and attached the flexible hose to the catheter. Rose-colored fluid began to drain from Jolene's chest cavity into the vacuum jar on the floor.

"Don't you hate being right?" Lorca asked.

"Get used to it," Roosevelt said. "We're a team now, buddy."

"Crap," Dahlgren said, struggling to an elbow on a cot inside Delta chamber. He looked at the flat white interior, the steel floor, the exposed head, and the aluminum sink. "I must be dead, because I'm inside a fucking submarine."

"No, you're not," said the corpsman at his side.

He glanced over at the young woman. Her camo sleeves were rolled up to her elbows, revealing well-muscled forearms, and her straight blond hair was cut short.

"Which?" Dahlgren asked. "Not dead or not inside a submarine?"

The corpsman explained where Dahlgren was.

"Get out," he said. Then: "Where's Jolene?"

A few minutes after 4 P.M. on Christmas Eve, Jack Conrad swung open the hatch to Alpha chamber. Dahlgren waited as Jolene was carried out on a stretcher, then he stepped over the steel lip onto the platform. Jolene gave Dahlgren a wave as she was carried down the steps toward an ambulance waiting below, and Dahlgren waved back.

"She's been through hell," Dahlgren said.

"You have no sense of irony, do you?" Matheson asked.

Before Dahlgren could answer, Cal came up and slapped him on the back. Then Jack Conrad held out his hand, and Dahlgren grabbed it.

"You don't know how glad I am that you're walking out of there," Conrad said, "instead of, well, you know."

"Being carried out feet-first?" Dahlgren asked.

"Something like that," Conrad said. "Let me ask you something. I'm doing some research on divers who have had unusual experiences during near-fatal encounters."

"You mean out-of-body experiences?" Matheson asked, her interest piqued.

"That, and other things," Conrad said. "Just curiosity on my part. But did anything like that happen to you? Any tunnels or dead relatives or anything unusual?"

Dahlgren stared at him.

"Sorry," he said. "Nothing like that, Doc."

Conrad nodded.

"You know what I want?" Dahlgren asked.

"A shower?" Matheson asked.

"Besides that."

"A cigarette?" Matheson asked wearily.

"Hell, no," Dahlgren said. "I want to see the sky."

"Strong enough to walk?" Cal asked.

Dahlgren nodded.

"Come on," Cal said. "I'll show you a great view."

After a flight of stairs, a hallway, and a few turns, Cal opened a door onto a metal walk. It was a clear afternoon. A minesweeper, the USS *Robin*, was at anchor. Frigate birds wheeled overhead.

Dahlgren filled his lungs.

373

"I'd forgotten the taste of clean air."

"That's the Coast Guard station across the bay," Cal said. "Over there, that's Alligator Bayou. And, of course, the Navy has its minesweeper school here."

Matheson stepped onto the walk.

"Give us a sec, would you?" she asked.

"I'll call Loren," Cal said. "Tell him you're okay."

The door swung shut.

"I talked to Jolene earlier," Matheson said. "You know, through the headset. She told me that she wanted you to have this."

She dangled the golden cross.

"I'll be damned," Dahlgren said, taking it.

"Probably," Matheson said. "But right now, you're a bona fide hero. The press is camped out at the guard station at the base entrance, waiting to get a glimpse of you. Why don't you consider giving an interview?"

"Don't feel much like it," Dahlgren said.

"Why not?" Matheson asked. "You could make *Outside* magazine again. Charm the camos right off that blond corpsman who took care of you."

"I'd rather not think about Norman or Janot or all those girls for a while," he said. "Let me clean up. Then let's grab Cal and maybe that Doc Conrad fellow and find some seafood. I'm starving. Lobster's in season."

Matheson nodded.

"Okay," she said. "But I wish you hadn't lied to Conrad."

"Lied?" Dahlgren asked. "About what?"

Matheson sighed as she reached for the door latch.

"The spooky stuff," she said.

"The goddess?" Dahlgren asked. "That was all inside my head."

"Maybe," Matheson said, then swung open the door and held it with her hip. "But you didn't swim out, did you?"

BODY PARTS
VICKI STIEFEL

They call it the Grief Shop. It's the Office of the Chief Medical Examiner for Massachusetts, and Tally Whyte is the director of its Grief Assistance Program. She lives with death every day, counseling families of homicide victims. But now death is striking close to home. In fact, the next death Tally deals with may be her own.

Boston is in the grip of a serial killer known as the Harvester, due to his fondness for keeping bloody souvenirs of his victims. But many of those victims are people that Tally knew, through her work or as friends. Tally realizes there's a connection, a link that only she can find. But she'd better find it fast. The Harvester is getting closer.

- -

Dorchester Publishing Co., Inc.
P.O. Box 6640   5317-9
Wayne, PA 19087-8640 $6.99 US/$8.99 CAN

Please add $2.50 for shipping and handling for the first book and $.75 for each additional book. NY and PA residents, add appropriate sales tax. No cash, stamps, or CODs. Canadian orders require $2.00 for shipping and handling and must be paid in U.S. dollars. Prices and availability subject to change. **Payment must accompany all orders.**

Name: _____

Address: _____

City: _____ State: _____ Zip: _____

E-mail: _____

I have enclosed $_____ in payment for the checked book(s).

For more information on these books, check out our website at www.dorchesterpub.com.
_____ *Please send me a free catalog.*

THE
CRIMINALIST
WILLIAM RELLING JR.

Detective Rachel Siegel is a twelve-year veteran of the San Patricio Sheriff's Department. But she's never seen anything like the handiwork of the Pied Piper, the vicious serial killer who's been terrifying that part of California for months. Because she's the best at what she does, it's now her job to catch this maniac—but she has very personal reasons, too, for wanting him stopped

Kenneth Bennett works for the Department of Neuropsychiatry at St. Louis's Washington University. There's something special about the Pied Piper case that draws Bennett almost against his will to the west coast. He has no choice but to help Siegel in her frantic search—even if it gets both of them killed in the process.

Dorchester Publishing Co., Inc.
P.O. Box 6640
5278-4
Wayne, PA 19087-8640
$6.99 US/$8.99 CAN

Please add $2.50 for shipping and handling for the first book and $.75 for each additional book. NY and PA residents, add appropriate sales tax. No cash, stamps, or CODs. Canadian orders require $2.00 for shipping and handling and must be paid in U.S. dollars. Prices and availability subject to change. **Payment must accompany all orders.**

Name: _____

Address: _____

City: _____ State: _____ Zip: _____

E-mail: _____

I have enclosed $_____ in payment for the checked book(s).

For more information on these books, check out our website at www.dorchesterpub.com.
____ *Please send me a free catalog.*